A TALE OF A TURNKEY

THE PILLAR OF EYES

THE PILLAR OF EYES

LIAM BOWDITCH

N
Crass Rock
Gusterton
Mountpane
River Pane
Lake Gillün
Lumpton Fell
Widden Fields
Castle Peak
The Eastern Steppe
Willow's Pass
Guntrick Castle
Ridick Bight
Eastern Caves
Fort Gaze
Fithering's Bay
Ridikus Island
Ridikus Harbour
Fort Ridik
Rushing's Hall
Eastern Sway
Bidle's Edge
Court Marsh
Deepmont
Byhollow
Summer's Reach
Green Hollow River
Dinethdale
Fort Blithe
Little Brace
Murraytown
River Soop
Dül Pass
Flat Stone Bay
Chase Isles
Fort Tippin
North-Eastern Graelind

A big thank you to Spiffing Covers.

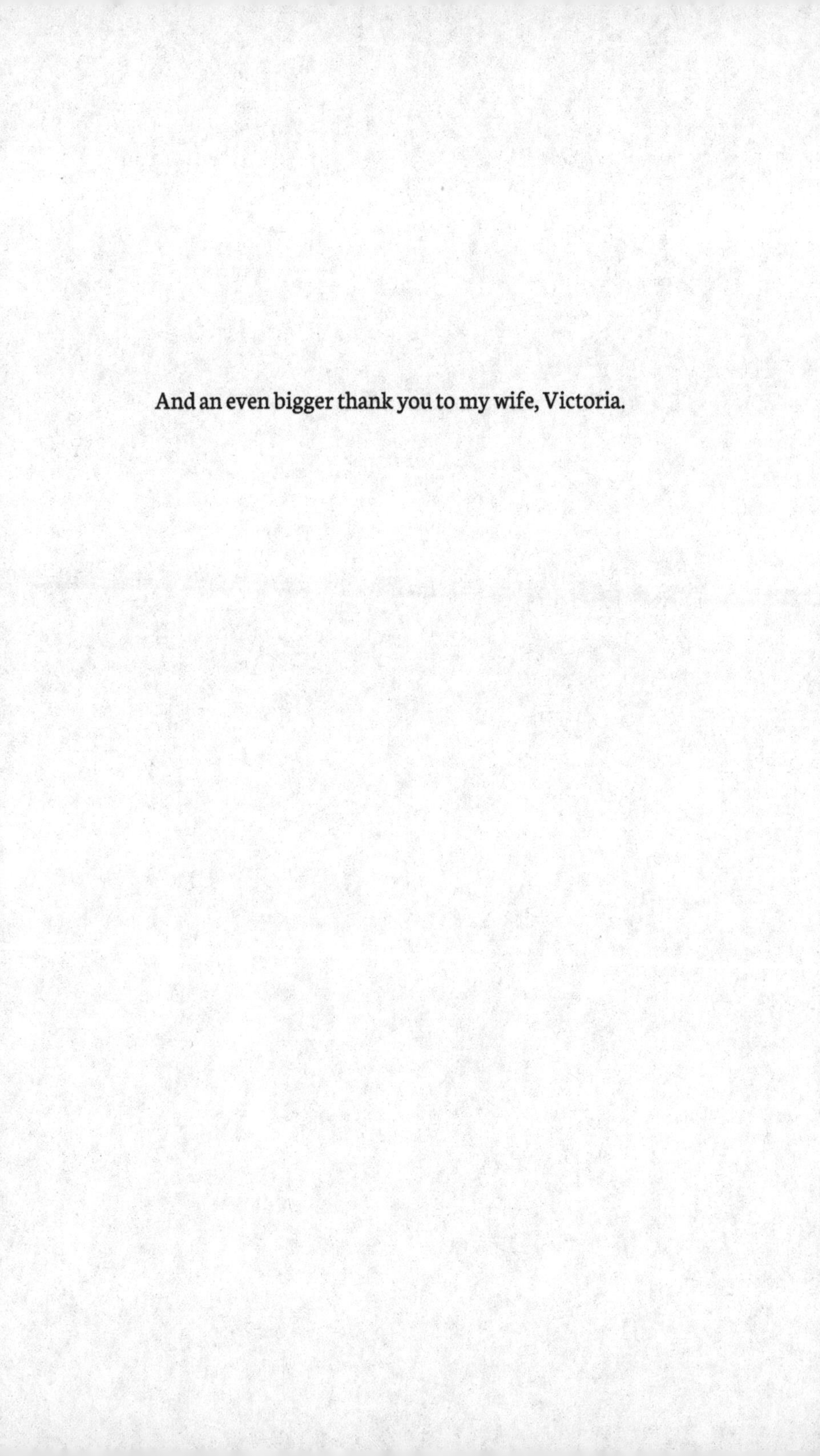

And an even bigger thank you to my wife, Victoria.

Chapter 1
The *Baliant*

The country of Graelind; a wonderful and prosperous island nation, scattered with coastal forts, riverside towns and cities of stone. A country of merchants, farmers and fisherman, a country where the fields were rich in crops and where the summer endured in decorative colours found upon every fell and in every thicket. An island from which many ships came and went, transporting goods to nearby nations to trade the local produce in return for foreign fruits, silks and delicacies. And as one could imagine, when ships full of expensive goods make for the sea, there will always be callous opportunists stalking the horizon.

The coasts of Graelind were protected by many naval vessels, manned by officers of the law and their crew; a defiant class of honourable men that reaped great pleasure from the capture and punishment of pirates.

Pirates; the accused, the feared, these rotten souls had a dread about them and in numbers they came forth with power. Towns burned in their wake and the seas trembled as their ships littered the map – it was the defiance of the Graelind navy that kept these beasts at bay.

One of those naval vessels in particular, went by the name of the *Baliant*. On board this great ship were fourteen high-ranking officers, each clothed in the finest attire. From buckled leather boots, to a long, slate-grey coat, golden on the cuff and collar, finished exquisitely with silver buttons down both sides.

They brandished swords that were each identical and engraved alike, that hung from white bandoliers, embellished with the symbol of a starling.

A crew of one hundred strong, each as loyal as the last, working their hands numb and their backs twisted for days and weeks at a time.

The captain of this vessel was Wallace Galaway; a superbly smart man with a brown moustache that spiralled up at the sides, flawlessly joining a thick, round beard of the same shade. His hat sat atop his head on a slight tilt, with a peacock feather that stuck proudly from the golden band that wrapped around its crown. He was the most respected leader and was credited for the capture of many of the country's most evil men. For three decades, his lurking presence on the water had tormented his foes.

The officers had a profound respect for one another and every last one of them were regarded as equals, yet the ship's turnkey was held above all but the captain. His name was Edward Clavell; a tall, strong man with a clean-shaven face that beamed red around his cheeks. He was the keeper of keys, to the cells in the very pits of the ship, and to his authority would the others abide.

In deep winter, the nights brought a fierce cold to the seas, yet the *Baliant* sailed on mightily. She was strong, rugged, built by the greatest ship makers in the world and had earned the nickname – The Golden Lady.

Brightly coloured with bold reds and yellows down both sides and boasting huge white sails that reached far into the sky; equipped with the power of sixty guns, she was an alluring yet formidable lady of the water.

Every evening, when the edge of the earth lost the sun, the crew would sit down together and eat, smoke their tobacco pipes and tell old stories and tales. Tales of battle and mischief. Yes, some were true, but most were revised to suit the exuberant imaginations the Graelinders were known for.

It was the tenth cold night of January and the crew were sat for supper as usual, pressed in tightly around tables, becoming more and more restless with each second. The cook on board was called Raven, and from what little supplies he had, he was always able to make the best of them. From cockles to crab found near the shores, to eggs from the chickens they kept on deck. Not exactly meals of grandeur, but it was just enough to drive off those rumbling sensations in one's stomach.

Feeding them all was no easy task, and Raven would often find himself in the middle of a frenzy, where hungry crewmen with far less manners than the officers would wreak havoc and cause disorder, all for a few less-than-perfect eggs.

The night's supper was in full flow when talk turned towards the sighting of an unfriendly looking vessel that was spotted that very morning by a startled fisherman who'd given word of its path west. An average size brigantine to the frightened man's account; with unmistakable markings strewn across its sails, the markings of the rotten.

Not all were in favour of a pursuit, for this was to be their last night before home, of what had been four, long weeks at sea. But their orders remained the same, to track down and engage, whether the sightings held any truth in them or not.

What was once a rather pleasant supper, now had all the rumblings of an argument. An inevitable friction quickly bubbled within the cabin; one of the disgruntled crewmen stood angrily to his feet, still clasping his bowl.

"We've worked our fingers to the bone and froze on this ship for four weeks!" he cried; his eyes puffy like two bruised peaches.

Another man leapt up, spilling pottage across the table.

"Yeah, it's easy for the captain," he snarled. "Tucked up in his hammock, enjoying his damn dreams. I've had to sleep next to *this* foul thing, snoring and gargling!"

The under-fire crewman jumped to his feet, pointing his finger in rage before screaming back an insult. A fight unfolded and both men were restrained.

Officer Edward Clavell gave a sharp call from the officers table.

"I will have order in this room immediately!" he snapped, with a harsh stroke of conviction. "Listen, men," he began again. "Captain's orders are *final* on this ship, let me hear one more of you chime in! Just one more run, and maybe, one more fight. Then you can all rest, but until the job is done, I will have *order!* Don't make me inform the captain about your petty squabbling."

For just a second, you could hear a pin drop as the crewmen gradually began to regain their decorum. Captain Galaway had already retired to his quarters, and Officer Clavell had heard quite enough of the bickering for one night, with the deck above seeming like the retreat he needed.

On a calm evening and with a keen ear, the birds of the night could be heard skimming the waves and the distant sounds of their predatorial dive as they speared into the dark water, were distinct. The nights brought the crewmen solace. Many of them would take out their lanterns and sit under the stars to rest.

Edward Clavell often walked the deck himself, sometimes for hours, and was never bothered. It was his own escape and his need for such would at times cause a vexation to present itself. The ship could feel claustrophobic and that was more than Edward could bear even in the best of his moods. He would describe the deep darknesses of the *Baliant* as voids suitable for caged beasts alone. If he wasn't sleeping or eating, he was pacing, staring at the vastness beyond, the endless canvas upon which many chapters of his life were written.

He stepped onto the deck, pulled his winter coat around his shoulders and tucked a faded, white neckerchief into his collar. He mustn't have been outside for more than a minute before the light from Captain Galaway's cabin caught his eye.

Still rearranging himself, he stepped up to the door, giving it a gentle knock whilst pushing it open with his boot.

"A word please, Captain?" he asked.

"Yes of course, my lad, come in," said Galaway, waving Edward inside. "A little peace from that unruly lot, ey?"

The captain began to gather up a few items that had found themselves flung across the chairs and he did so with his pipe tucked firmly between his teeth, taking the occasional toot.

"Please, sit!" he said, from the corner of this mouth. "What is it, Officer?"

"On this occasion, I feel the men's squabbling is almost justified, Captain," said Edward, who found he could reason with the crew a little better than the captain could.

Galaway was in the middle of another toot.

"Nonsense!" he coughed. "We have a duty, as you well know, Edward, and that is to protect these coasts. If our lives are lost whilst we do, then so be it."

"The men are more than willing to give their lives for their country, there's no question," explained Edward. "But the promise of home has found their hearts."

"I wouldn't question their loyalty, Edward, nor would I let a chance slip by of such magnitude. Imagine another Graelind ship burnt to ashes, after *we* let the enemy sail unchallenged!"

Before Edward could respond, Captain Galaway had already given him a rather austere look to which words couldn't have added any more necessary emphasis.

The turnkey, quickly remembering his rank, just nodded in agreement.

"Of course, Captain," he said, pausing for a few seconds. "I often wonder, Wallace, what it is the men do when they get home, just out of curiosity? I don't know half of them as well as I should."

"Many of them have nothing to go home to, Edward," said Galaway. "And through the years I've found those types can often make the best sailors; there's nothing keeping them on land, you see. What will you do?"

"I don't imagine moving from my armchair," said Edward, laughing. "I'll leave you in peace, Captain; see you at first light."

Leaving the cabin, Edward Clavell placed a clasped fist against his chest as a gesture of allegiance, practised by all the Kingsman of Graelind; a gesture that Galaway promptly returned. "Goodnight, my lad," he said, smiling.

In the short while that Edward had been speaking with Captain Galaway, the crewmen had begun to leave the ship's dining quarters, most of them having turned in for bed. The officers each had their own private cabin and hammock. However, the crew not being so lucky, all slept in rooms of twelve or sixteen, in beds bunked four high. Comfort walked hand in hand with rank and the crewmen settled their heads not three feet from one another and on mats as hard as wood. The stench was foul and there was very little light but for the odd candle flame burning in the darkness.

The *Baliant* lay on the water in solitude, and on this night, very much alike to any other, the men slept deeply and rocked to the motion of each shallow wave that bumped up against her hull.

A morning which brought with it a pink skyline and the usual rooster call. The crew scrambled the deck to set the masts as Captain Galaway assumed his position at the helm, duly joined by all his officers on the quarterdeck.

The *Baliant* swiftly cut through the waves, the miles soon disappearing behind them. Edward Clavell was standing by his captain, turning up his collar, watching his breath turn to steam as it left his lips.

"There will be blood spilt today, Captain, I can feel it," he said, scanning the horizon.

"Just the blood of our enemies," replied Galaway, tapping the officer on the shoulder. "The sooner we rid the seas of these scumeths, the better. Then, you won't ever need to leave that armchair of yours, my lad."

Holding the ship steady in the wind and his nerves even steadier in his hand, Galaway gripped the wheel tight, barking orders to whom all followed. He was stood proudly above all his men, watching as the wind shuddered the feather in his cap.

The day passed by, and the pink hue of the morning had long disappeared, welcoming the evening's haze as it began to settle in the sky around them. Another day of hardship from a disgruntled yet steadfast crew.

The *Baliant* was quickly making haste towards the northwestern pinnacle of Graelind, where their eyes would soon be delivered the sight of the distant shadow they were looking for.

Patiently they waited, until the call from the crewman above triggered a squint in the captain's eyes. The exact brigantine described to them came into vision, lit up with lanterns that shone like golden beacons in the evening sky.

"Man the guns!" ordered Galaway.

They crept behind, silently stalking, as ripple after ripple between the two ships disappeared beneath the *Baliant*'s hull ... when eventually, they became parallel with the enemy vessel.

Far up into the stars, they saw what they had feared, as a pirate flag quivered in the wind as clear as the moon. Her name was familiar: the *Venturous*!

Immediately the crew bounded for the steel levers which lowered dozens of stepped wooden bridges, whilst the rest readied their blades, pistols and muskets. The ladders fell into place and were held steady by sharp, iron spikes that gripped the enemy ship's outer beams.

A long pause, then *bang*, as a gunfight erupted like a deathly roar of drums – the *Baliant* was under attack.

The captain pulled two pistols from his bandolier and gave quick orders to discharge their broadsides upon the enemy.

"FIRE!" he screamed, as more and more pirates jumped into sight, firing weapons, screaming and throwing all kinds of foul objects.

The barrage of gunfire was fearsome and deafening, but as it ceased for a second, the crew of the *Baliant* sprung once again from their cover, unloading their muskets with no sense of mercy. The pirate crew swung themselves from the masts only to be shot down; as their limp, bullet-ridden bodies fell to the water beneath, splashing into the blackness of the eastern sea.

The broadside cannons boomed, and their sheer, devastating power ripped apart the outnumbered and outmatched pirate vessel, leaving her splintered beyond repair.

The pirates stood little chance as the *Baliant* rose to a quick victory where none were left alive ... or so it seemed.

Once the fight had come to an end, the smell of conflict still lay thick in the air, the smoke from the cannons glistening in the moonlight far above, stinging the nose. Bodies lay scattered on the deck and a sharp silence now engulfed the night.

"Listen up! Salvage anything valuable," said Galaway, stuffing gunpowder down the barrel of his pistols. "Take the weapons and ammunition, be sure to check for *anyone* who still has breath in their lungs!"

Nothing of any great value was found this night, save a few personal items left behind amongst the dead. Edward Clavell commanded he entered their captain's cabin alone.

It was a dark, frigid cabin, with a pungent smell of rotting wood and tobacco. He began to search, always on the lookout for anything of worth, or even the odd trinket. Having scoured the room, he spotted a chest in the corner under some old books and maps and began to walk over to it, curiously squinting, nudging away chairs and old boxes that blocked his path.

With the floorboards creaking under his boots, he put the books and maps to one side and brushed off all the dust from the box's lid. Inside this mysterious box was a sword handle with no blade, a looking glass, more maps of unknown lands, an old pipe not worth a coin and an abundance of fresh tobacco in old tins, which of course explained that dreadful smell.

Yet under the tins something caught his eye; a parchment scroll encased in a pure silver jacket.

This had his attention, for the craftsmanship was exquisite and deliberate. Edward quickly pulled the looking glass close to his face to examine the details of its exterior, only for his knowledge of such graved markings to fall short.

Before he had chance to read the words within, he was interrupted by the sound of heavy boot steps growing increasingly louder behind him. Edward quickly nestled his finding into his breast pocket.

"Officer Clavell," said Officer Hackett. "We need to move. Captain's orders to torch the ship. Wouldn't want you getting trapped down here now, would we?"

Edward began to leave the pirate captain's cabin, waving the tobacco tins as he passed Hackett on the stairs.

Once all the crew had gathered themselves and had begun to make their strides back across the bridges, there came a bellowing cry from the brig below.

"So, it appears we've searched this ship with our eyes closed gentlemen!" said Galaway, demanding that the lower parts of the ship were reinvestigated.

With muskets in hand, they followed their ears, and to their surprise, they found a man in a cell, chained to the bars with his hands hoisted toward the sky. The captain barged his way through the crowd of aiming muskets. "Who are you, prisoner in the darkness?" he asked, his eyes narrowing.

The man said nothing in return.

"Remove his bonds," said Galaway. "Now! Hurry!"

Covered in bruises, congealed blood and sores from the iron shackles that clasped his wrists, the prisoner could barely stand. It was all too clear that he'd suffered in these bonds for days, maybe even weeks, and was now nothing but a broken shell, beaten and sore.

"Officer Clavell, see this man to a cell, at once," said Galaway. "He might well be of some use to us in the morning. Now ... burn this rotting pile of timber to the seabed!"

Officer Hackett was the most medically proficient on board and attended to the yet nameless man with the necessary care and courtesy; for the captain believed that perhaps his time in chains could well lead to the information of other seafaring mischiefs.

They placed warm sheets, blankets and pillows on the floor of a cell and laid the beaten man on top, which was far more than any prisoner on *this* ship had ever been fortunate enough to enjoy before. Perhaps this time Captain Galaway had had a change of heart. Pirates were simply lower than rats, yet something felt a little different about this particular character.

The crew returned; the *Venturous* was torched, lighting up the starry sky; the ship now nothing but a flaming pyre in the vast black sea.

They all gathered on the deck and watched as the wind gently carried the warmth of the flames towards them. In silence, they looked on in victory.

"Captain, may we speak ... alone?" asked Edward.

"Of course, my lad," replied Galaway, ushering the two of them to a more private part of the deck.

"I found something ... on the ship," said Edward, reaching into his coat.

"What is it, Officer?" asked Galaway.

Edward paused for a long while, unable to find his words. The captain's face grew increasingly interested in what he had to say, maybe even suspicious.

"Just some tobacco, Captain, for your pipe," said Edward, handing him the tins. "Most of the crew know I don't smoke the stuff – thought I'd sneak you the tins before one of the lads had me for them."

Galaway smiled heartily. "Cheers to that, my lad," he gleamed, staring at the burning ship; the orange tendrils leaping around the deck. "It feels every bit like January, doesn't it? I'm going to head inside, take these boots off. Perhaps I'll smoke a pipe full."

The dark night once again brought with it the smell of fresh crab and the noise of crackling eggs; and tonight, of all nights, the crew deserved a decent meal to fill their bellies and warm their souls.

That evening seemed different; it was more joyous, merrier. During supper, the captain stood to formally thank his men for their spirit in battle and their resolve in all else.

"I have a few words!" he called, raising his glass. "Each and every last one of you have fought tirelessly for our nation. But remember, our fight will never be over, yet we will *always* be here to defend it. Let us rejoice in our victory, and let us hope that all the threats to our lands die as easily as those *bastards* did tonight!"

The crew erupted into celebration, beginning to bang on the tables and chant, *"Graelind, Graelind, Graelind."*

Edward enjoyed the jubilation and couldn't help but smile as the men around him relished in another victory. They had lost no one on this night; there was no better reason to celebrate.

The moon was now hidden behind silver streaks of cloud so only lanterns lit the *Baliant*. After a few drinks, the crew wobbled to their cabins, set down their coats and unbuckled their boots. While most of the crew lay in the 'comfort' of their beds, thinking of home and family, Edward Clavell was still sitting alone at the supper table. He was finishing the last drops of his glass, when suddenly he remembered the scroll he'd found. After checking over both shoulders, he opened its silver case and rolled out the parchment within. It read,

> *No mercy for the living,*
> *darkness I will breed,*
> *torment for the greedy,*
> *an army I will lead.*
> *I am the one Black Diamond,*
> *from the song that you all sing,*
> *and I will tell you where to find me,*
> *in a crown only fit for a King.*

"The Black Diamond?" he whispered to himself, placing it back into his coat pocket. Edward had only ever heard tales about such a gem and was always curious. But, having sunk at least four glasses of whiskey – from the effects of which his mind now tingled a little – he decided to set aside the matter until morning.

Placing his glass on the table he returned to the deck, to take in one last breath of the sea air before bed.

Chapter 2

The Prisoner in the Darkness

It was unusually quiet the next morning with not a single unpleasant sound in the air. As the first golden beams of sunlight crept over the horizon, the rooster gave its early call.

Raven was back in the kitchen rustling together some eggs for the crew's morning fare. Captain Galaway was out early as usual, standing by the ship's wheel, his eyes thoroughly engaged on his compass, ready to begin navigating their journey home.

Their course would take them south: past the Eastern caves, around the island of Ridikus, between the Chase Isles and up the Green Hollow River, right into the heart of the country's capital - Summer's Reach.

Edward's habit of pacing the ship travelled from night to morning and he did so with the jail keys tucked firmly inside his coat. The turnkey would normally have more than just a single prisoner in his lock-up but the rest of the pirate filth - or 'rotten souls' as they were commonly referred to - were lost to the sea. The cells of the brig remained bare, but for one.

Edward left the deck through a hatch in the floor, at the far front of the ship, just below the forecastle. Shutting the way behind him he stepped carefully down the wooden stairs, onto a narrow corridor many metres below. This led straight to an iron door which was opened with a huge wheel key in the centre and could only be locked from the outside - with one way in and one way out.

With a solid push the door swung open. Edward lifted his lantern out in front of him until the walls of the brig caught light. He moved forward into the dark room as his steps became strides, until he reached the man in the cell. The brightness of the lantern caused a painful squint in the man's eyes - he turned his face away to adjust. Edward raised the light to better his own vision, revealing an expression of dread across a broken and torn profile.

"What is your name?" he asked, inquisitively.

"It's ... Peter," replied the man quietly. He could barely gasp a word. "Peter Beaumont."

"I'm Edward ... Edward Clavell."

"Tell me why I'm here?" asked Peter. "Why didn't you see me shot and burned like the rest of them?"

"Because something told my captain you needn't meet your end in such a way, pirate," said Edward. "So, tell me why that crew of filth had you chained by your arms, leaving you beaten half to death?"

"The captain thought me a thief!" snapped Peter. "And I'm no pirate, more of an adventurer, certainly not a thief! I'm the one who's been robbed!"

Edward had a strange feeling in his stomach, the glimmer of malice in Peter's eyes worried him and his often-exemplary judge of character seemed to be eluding him.

"And what is it they stole?" asked Edward, moving closer.

"A scroll encased in a pure silver jacket," said Peter, regaining his balance as he stepped up from the cell floor.

Edward looked puzzled, hovering his hand over his pocket before pulling it away quickly.

"Yet I fear it is now lost to the sea along with the men that took it from me," said Peter sadly.

"Tell me, Peter, how a mere trinket is of such worth to you," said Edward nonchalantly.

Peter's face curled in anger as he realised how much he hated it being called a 'mere trinket'.

"There is more to it than meets the eye, if you must know," he growled. "Inside that silver casing there's a riddle which speaks of a diamond, and in the wrong hands, I truly dread to think. It would bring only ruin to this world."

Peter clasped his body in pain, falling down onto one knee, coughing and wheezing.

"What sort of diamond?" asked Edward, his eyes squinting.

"One of unthinkable power," said Peter, through the pain.

Edward measured Peter's words. "You must rest," he said, desperate to leave so he could make sense of all this. "I'll see to it you're delivered something warm to drink, right away."

He walked off, confused but deeply intrigued. Just as he was about to leave, Peter said, in a fearless whisper, "Edward Clavell. Upon my release I will make certain that I have what is mine returned – even if I have to take it from your pocket myself."

Edward stopped by the door. "How did you know?"

"Observation. I saw you sneaking a look at it," said Peter. "Right after your ... gratuitous act of kindness."

Edward looked at the scabby old pillow Peter held in his hand.

"Thanks, by the way," said Peter, sarcastically. "It's made a real difference to the feel of the place."

Edward removed the scroll from his pocket, caring little for the pirate's coarse words. "I doubt you'll be needing this where *you're* going," he said, closing the door behind him.

It was midday, the easterly winds had returned as expected and the *Baliant* was at full speed, brushing past the waves as if they were mere ripples.

Wallace Galaway had been the captain of this ship for many years and after countless successful voyages he'd become highly respected to say the least. For the whole of his life, the *Baliant* was all he'd ever really known; starting out as a short, snotty-nosed youth, working down by the harbour for a few coins, eventually fulfilling his dream of becoming a crewman. Galaway's story was not too dissimilar to that of his nephew's, James Percy. A charismatic young crewman whose duty it was to keep on the lookout for any trouble – the crow's nest his humble post, a vantage point not just for sea and horizon so it seemed.

James Percy gazed down at a rather odd sight. The deck of the *Baliant* absent of Officer Clavell. Maybe it was just his youthful nature and mischievous imagination that allowed his next move to unfold but he was quickly down to the deck.

"Have you seen Officer Clavell?" he asked another crewman, who was busy scrubbing the ship.

"With Galaway, I'd imagine," replied the crewman. "Came up from the brig acting all strange, though."

"How so?" asked James Percy.

"Maybe you should ask him yourself, rather than standing in the way of my bucket!"

"Very well, I will," said James Percy, straightening his trousers. "Oh, an' Inky, you've missed a spot!"

James Percy kicked the mop bucket clear across the deck.

Ray Inkleman, the poor lad whose bucket got the kick, was James Percy's best friend. They had grown up together back in the city and not a day ever passed without one of them playing a prank of some sort.

"Bastard!" shouted Inky, setting off on a chase.

"Percy! Inkleman!" snapped Galaway, shaking his head in frustration. Two fully grown men have never stopped in their tracks so fast.

James Percy made for the back of the ship, still giggling to himself, noticing that his uncle was alone on the quarterdeck. He crept his gaze around a corner, where Edward Clavell was rather secretively examining an object he seemed particularly interested in.

James shifted back before the officer snapped his head for a look. He just knew Edward had found something; you'll do well not to learn the intricacies of a man's character, watching all day from up in the crow's nest.

The next day an excitement brewed, as the entrance to the Green Hollow River approached. Onward they sailed through the cloudy morning, chased along the muddy riverbanks by excited children from the small towns of Byhollow and Dinethdale.

A once tight waterway began to blossom into a huge lake with the harbour of Summer's Reach on its southern bank.

Built from the water's edge were several landing stages, that stretched far out into the lake's deeper waters – a ship the size of the *Baliant* could easily run aground by chancing the rocky bed of the shallows.

They dropped anchor just before noon as expected; the noise of the bustling square could be heard from afar as the clouds parted to reveal a pearly glow that speared onto the city streets.

With joy filling their hearts, the crew left the ship and set down their feet on solid ground for the first time in weeks. With swords in sheaths, muskets hanging over their backs and their chest full of belongings in one hand – they raced for home.

Handing the cell keys to the docksman who'd come aboard, Edward stepped down the roped ladders, landing soundly on the harbour deck before shouting, "Take the prisoner to the Plummet, see he isn't harmed."

With a long and deep breath of air he hurried through the streets with only one thing on his mind ... or maybe two.

Wallace Galaway was always the last to leave; the captain's home truly was at sea, never quite himself unless he had a hold of the *Baliant's* wheel. But as the thought of his beloved wife and family crossed his mind, he began to smile as he gazed back upon the vast assemblage of timber and iron that had been his home for the majority of his life.

He made his way through the crowded streets, once again able to admire the elegant beauty of the city for the first time in what seemed to him like years.

Summer's Reach truly was the most stunning of places, set beneath a sharp line of steep fells to the west and thick forest to the south. The harbour itself was looked upon by the city's palace; the King's stronghold, built of glistening, white stone with turrets on all four of its corners. The city square ran the entire length of the palace's eastern wall and out beyond, as far as one's eye could see. There were wonderful markets selling fruits, wines, breads and biscuits down by the riverbank. Fishmongers set out their displays along the harbour and countless taverns could be found on almost every corner. Never was there a more homely place in the whole of Graelind.

With each home as restful as the last, the people cared little about anything that wasn't joyous and only about the things that brought happiness and peace into their lives: family, warm food, the odd song and of course ... something fine to drink. In a way, the people of Graelind were *famous* for their love of all things fermented, but in truth it just kept better than water.

Back at the harbour, the docksman followed their orders and escorted the man in question to the Plummet - the capital's most secure prison - where many pirates and mercenaries were held for crimes of the most dreadful kind.

Peter's face was covered as they ushered him quickly into a beaten old wagon. The docksman took little heed of Edward's words, ensuring Peter took a few good punches to the stomach any time he opened his mouth. He spent that night in a cell even more bleak than the *Baliant's*, for the decision on his future and freedom hung tantalisingly in the balance. Inescapably so, if Peter was found to be of a pirate kind, he would endure only the quick end at the gallows he deserved.

One by one, the crew arrived home to their families, with *this* night being one to remember; although, much of it was spent in manners identical to any other 'first night home'. Many of the crewmen would just sit amongst their family and look on, happily. Some would dance, chant and drink, some would long for the touch of grass. Some would head off into the hills to breathe the air free of any sea-smell. Edward was a man who liked to sit, think, read books and stare at his fireplace. Tonight, his thoughts had turned towards Peter, his mind still struggling to understand why he'd been told of such a treasure, by a man who knew a clue to its whereabouts was tucked away inside his pocket.

Bang! Bang! Bang! came a heavy knock on each of the officers' doors. It was a message from the palace – an invitation – to come forth and engage in a sort of welcome home meeting.

The commander of the Kingsguard and the King's Justice was Lord Augustus Harrington, a ruthless man who answered only to the King of Graelind and his word was the law.

It was relatively normal for such meetings to take place after voyages, yet this time Lord Harrington had been particularly cruel to call upon his subordinates not a half hour after the rooster call. To say the least, there were some thick heads and foul breath on that day.

The officers arrived at the palace, smartening their parade uniforms, stroking their ruffled, misplaced hair the morning's quick get-up was responsible for.

Only the fourteen officers of the *Baliant*, Captain Wallace Galaway and Lord Harrington attended, all seated around a huge table, each with a small token of reward laid out in front of them. Normally, this would be a brimming bag of silver spinnels and today was no different.

Augustus Harrington had an odd look about him that could never have been forgotten. His stature made the average man look short but the long, grey sideburns that reached down to his chin were his most distinctly strange feature. He was an officer himself – back in the day – also serving in the Graelind army for many years, making him no stranger to life on the front line.

"Officers," he said, pacing behind each man with his hands clasped behind his back. "It's truly a pleasure to welcome you home safe."

Sitting down in his chair, he picked up a large bottle of whiskey, beginning to peel the neat, golden wax from around its cork. He poured each man a glass to celebrate another successful voyage, sliding them across the table one by one, watching as the mere smell of it brought a tingle to the officers' stomachs.

"So, what do we know?" asked Harrington, licking his lips and wincing, as the strong burn slipped down his throat. "I hear you've brought me a prisoner! Anyone I've heard of; is the bastard known to the city?"

"He was far too beaten when we found him, my lord," said Galaway. "He had little to say."

"Does the swine have a name?" said Harrington.

"Peter," said Edward, shuffling forward in his chair. "He claims to be some sort of adventurer. I spoke a few words with him yesterday, he's a very peculiar character to say the least."

"What business does an adventurer have on board a stinking pirate ship?" said Harrington, shaking his head. "Not to mention being shackled to one. Sounds like we've another rotten soul in our midst."

The rest of the crew had their eyes fixed on Officer Clavell, for it had now come to light that he was the only one to have spoken to the pirate. Edward seemed to stutter as he searched his mind for the words that would calm Harrington's nerve.

"Just an unfortunate case of wrong place at the wrong time I believe, my lord," is what Edward came up with.

Harrington scoffed. "I'm afraid that in such times that doesn't seem like a plausible explanation, Officer Clavell. Anyway, now, let's be done with this, I've places to be. Do we trial this man?"

Edward's choice to keep his hand firmly by his side had no discernible effect on the vote's outcome, as every other officer including the captain, raised theirs in favour.

"That will be all then, officers," said Harrington, pointing to the door. They all began to leave the table, one after another entering the hallway outside, where Galaway quickly caught up with Edward.

"I really don't think it's wise what you're doing," said Galaway, whispering. "Keeping information from Harrington is dangerous, Edward, and you know it! I know you've spoken to this bloody prisoner and you've been acting awfully strange since. Remember, secrets can be a heavy burden, don't let your mind be muddled by false hope."

"I'm sorry, Captain, but I've no idea what you're talking about," said Edward, innocently.

"I know you better than any one of my children, Edward," said

Galaway. "Don't think that I haven't seen you sneaking around with that silver trinket."

Edward fixed his lips to speak.

"Go home to your armchair," said Galaway, crossly.

Edward left the palace, feeling a thick knot of nerves ravel up inside his stomach. He felt stupid, because for a little while he'd considered pursuing what he'd found. "You're an idiot, Edward," he said to himself, stepping out into the market.

He began to sift through his memory, consciously trying to remember what he already knew about the Black Diamond. He turned that thought over and over in his mind, before stepping inside his front door.

Summer's Reach was split into three districts: Bardrain's Square, within which you would find the King's palace, the markets and the city's harbour. The Old Carry, a series of grandiose villas upon the hillside, reserved for only those who had the coin to reside in such a delectable corner of the city. And finally, there was Harkness; a huge stretch of houses and taverns that run for miles along the banks of the river. The part of the city where most of the people lived. The part of the city where Edward lived with his wife Charlotte.

Charlotte knocked on the window, it was time for dinner, and as the smell of roasting beef escaped from the open crack in the door, Edward dusted off his hands and came inside.

Although Raven's skills in the kitchen were to be admired, nothing quite compared to the hearty food in this home. Edward truly appreciated whatever it was Charlotte put before him. He wasn't much of a cook himself, capable of frying sliced bacon and perhaps a few eggs, but that was about it. Charlotte had often grimaced watching Edward try and tackle the kitchen, stopping him in his tracks with a soft hand to the arm, saying, "I think it's best I did it, don't you?"

Once supper had passed, all the plates and cups had been cleared away, and a few carefully chosen logs were thrown upon the fire. Edward found himself sprawled in his chair, nursing his full belly. Charlotte came back from the kitchen holding a steaming pot of honey tea. Edward couldn't stop smiling at her. She was the most beautiful person he'd ever seen, just sitting there: with her brown hair flowing down her shoulders, resting on her chest beside the ruby necklace she'd worn for years. Edward sunk deeper into his chair and relaxed, as the warmth echoed around the room and the glimmering light of the flames danced upon the walls, until the embers finally slept.

Chapter 3

Truth, Tales and Secrets

Edward woke from his armchair to the unwelcome sound of voices coming from the kitchen. He sprung up from his seat, wondering who he might have the 'pleasure' of meeting at such an hour in the morning. But as he entered, he came across only an empty room, with no explanation to the voices at all.

He stepped outside where only the branches blowing in the wind made any sound. Even the birds in the trees had barely begun to make melody so early, yet he was sure he'd heard someone speak his name.

It was some time before Edward realised he must have been dreaming and shaking his head of the matter, he made the most of being in the garden by taking some water from the well for his morning wash.

Back inside, he sat the bucket on the kitchen table, pulled the shirt from his back and splashed his face with the almost freezing water which confirmed his consciousness.

Reaching out for a towel, Edward dried around his face and shoulders, then fetched himself a fresh shirt. When he'd filled the kettle and set it down on the stove, his ears picked up a strange noise of crackling, like something burning, coming from the living room.

Creeping slowly along the hallway, he then peaked round the corner to find it was Charlotte replenishing the logs that had burned out through the night.

"Good morning, my love," she said with a smile. "It seems you've brought the winter home with you; although home is a much warmer place when you're here."

She stood up and moved closer, resting her head against his chest. "I hope that someday my return will be a lasting one," said Edward. "I've lost far too much time away from home. It's a long way from a promise, for now, but I see a different journey in my future. One that will see me home to stay."

The kettle on the stove began to whistle as Edward pressed his lips gently against Charlotte's forehead. She smiled; her dark hair like curls of silk ribbon, her iridescent grey-brown eyes shone back at him with a twinkle.

"The perfect medicine for a cold day," he said, walking into the kitchen. "Take a seat, I'll fetch it over."

Edward brought over a tray, laying it down on the table beside the fireplace. On it, a hot teapot, two cups and a stack of biscuits.

"Charlotte, darling, did I hear you speaking with someone this morning?" he asked, pulling a spoon from his shirt pocket.

"No?" said Charlotte, confused. "I'd barely been awake five minutes before you walked in."

"Oh? I was sure there were voices in the kitchen," said Edward curiously. "Perhaps just my imagination."

Looking over suspiciously, Charlotte could see Edward's attention wasn't entirely directed towards his tea and biscuits, scarcely perched on his armchair, almost without a blink in his eye.

"You've looked awfully anxious since your return, my love," she said. "I fear that less of you comes home each time. Now, you wouldn't be keeping anything from me, would you?"

"Of course not, darling," replied Edward, gazing into the fire, stirring his pot of tea. "But I will have to leave early this morning, I have an errand to run."

"Very well," said Charlotte. "But I suggest whatever errand you have to run ends swiftly before dusk. We have company this evening."

After a while, Charlotte cleared the table of the half-finished cups, watching curiously as Edward left the room in a hurry - she wondered what had gotten into him.

"You're leaving without breakfast, my love?" she asked loudly, as the front door slammed into its casing.

The frost on the windows was thick. The sun could hardly pierce the dense cloud, yet just like any other morning the streets of Summer's Reach filled up with faces. Market stalls were restocked, fishing boats untied from the harbour as rushes of cold wind flooded the crisp smell of nature down the alleys.

Edward pushed his way through the crowds that gathered around the market stalls, coming to a stop by the river where an old wooden barge lay bobbing in the water. He hopped in and sat down, before the bargeman paddled them off to the other side in exchange for a silver spinnel.

He stepped out, tipped his cap in thanks and set off up into the farmlands, leaving the city behind him.

He came to a narrow creek that drained from the lakes in the hills. Stretching from one side to the other was an old bridge that led over to a great height of cobbled steps, up and onto a vast vineyard.

A little out of breath, he stumbled into the vines that entangled each trellis, for the cold of winter had certainly halted any growth, leaving a field once teaming with purple clusters of grapes naked in its winter dormancy.

Edward steered his way through, navigating from memory alone, slipping out through the other side, brushing a few twigs off his jacket sleeves. These old shortcuts had often got him out of trouble back in his younger days, for these fields offered a faster route into the city from all the surrounding villages, enabling quick escapes from the consequences of his adolescent mischief.

The edge of the vineyard then fell off down an embankment and at the very bottom it became level with a muddy road, with almost spire-like trees down both sides, as far as the eye could see. He walked the long and twisted track, and at the end – perhaps around a mile further – stood a little village called Deepmont, where Edward had lived as a child.

Most of the people never left these parts and stayed on the farms working the cattle just like their fathers. Deepmont was a land full of particularly private folk, and in truth, the only times you would see such people in the capital was when they drove their wagons into the markets to sell off their stock. So, as one could imagine, when a villager leaves home in pursuit of adventure, it doesn't go without a nosey whisper or two.

Deepmont sat high on the edge of a shallow vale, looking down onto the town of Court Marsh and the forest that encircled it. For Edward, this was a familiar sight to say the least, although it had been many years since he had set foot on lands so full of memory.

Finally, his feet left the muddy road, joining a pathway which followed a line of cottages around to a neat row of stables behind them.

There were two horses in the stables, of shire breed; one of them had brown hair with spots of brilliant white, whilst the other was as dark as the night beyond the moon. Edward walked up to them, rubbed the spotted one on the back as it stretched to munch the hay balled up on the ground.

The familiar smell tingled memories and lingered long in his nostrils. Edward had a fondness for such animals; they were more graceful than the chickens he was used to hearing, rattling around in their cages aboard the *Baliant*. Edward often found it strange how some animals were so fondly taken care of yet others not so much.

No further than fifty yards down the path, there sat a single house by a beck, with a waterwheel nestled to its side. The face of the building was almost entirely covered in green ivy that stretched around its entire perimeter – the house looked protected, somehow.

Walking the path to the front door, Edward took the final steps carefully before knocking.

After a few moments the door crept open and there stood an elderly lady with a walking cane grasped in her hand.

"I'm awfully sorry to bother you, my lady," said Edward, politely lifting off his cap. "I'm looking for Roland Fane."

The lady looked deep into his eyes and without a word she shut the door sharply, a draft of air swishing as it slammed.

Rather astounded by this discourtesy, Edward made one more attempt, only this time, no face appeared at all. Taking a few steps backwards, he turned away and headed out from the garden, closing the gate behind him. But before he could gain full stride a voice came calling. "How many years has it been, Edward?"

"Many more than I intended, my old friend," replied Edward, recognising the voice and turning back towards the door.

And there stood an old man named Roland Fane.

"Well we can't have you standing out here in the bloody cold, come inside!" said Roland.

The warmth of the house brought a pink blush to Edward's cheeks as Roland ushered him towards a seat by the window overlooking the beck.

"Can I offer you some tea, Edward? We'd boiled a pot not long before you knocked."

"Yes, please!" said Edward, smiling.

Roland was the oldest man in Deepmont as a matter of fact; he was eighty years 'young' as he often liked to say.

"I can only apologise," he said, walking gingerly from the kitchen. "My wife's memory isn't quite the same as it used to be and I'm afraid your face has slipped her mind."

"No harm, sir," said Edward. "It has been so many years I barely recognised her myself."

"So, tell me, Edward," said Roland. "What brings you here, this day?"

"Well, there's plenty of time to think out at sea," said Edward, taking a warm cup from the old man's hand. "I realised it was high time I came to see how you were keeping."

"Well, aside from the terrible pain in my hands, feet and back, I'm doing just fine," laughed Roland. "I'll be eighty-one in the spring."

"It's wonderful to see you looking so spry," said Edward. "Come to think of it, I haven't seen my old friend William since I left Deepmont for the capital. I do hope he's keeping well too?"

"Aye. You and me both, my boy," said Roland. "We haven't seen our son in thirty years. Set off to find work and ... never came back."

Edward felt a sadness creep in. "Shame. Well, I do hope our paths will cross again, sometime," he said, his body deflating.

"Me too."

"Can I ask your advice?" said Edward, changing the subject. "Maybe I'm just being foolish but I've discovered something. It has regrettably awoken a side of me I thought I'd buried a long time ago. Apparently not deep enough."

Edward dragged his chair closer. "Would you tell me what you know about the Black Diamond? You used to sing a song about it when myself and William were children."

"Nothing but an old fantasy, lad," said Roland, as quick as a cat, although seeming to grimace to himself as he sipped on his tea. "Nothing more. I do remember the song though, well ... most of the first verse at least. Let's see."

Roland began to sing very low and soft.

> *Burning, oh mercy, I'm yearning,*
> *in tides that are turning,*
> *will you bring me the world?*
> *My sorrow, as I long for tomorrow,*
> *your power I'll borrow,*
> *will you bring me the world?*
> *In secret, you lie hidden in shadow,*

out of reach of the winds blow,
Will you bring me the world?
A diamond, with strength beyond measure,
a power to treasure,
in the deep of the world!

"Like I said, just an old fantasy."

"Then can you explain this?" said Edward, taking out the scroll, reaching to proffer it towards the old man.

Roland looked a little perplexed; he unhooked his glasses from his shirt and slid them on. "What is it?" he asked, taking hold. "Looks like pure silver?"

"It is," said Edward. "Although it's the words written on the parchment that have *my* attention."

Roland unravelled it and read the words to himself. He looked at Edward and shrugged his shoulders. "Looks like someone is trying to have themselves a little fun; although elaborately, I'll admit. Nothing more, my boy."

"Take a closer look at the letters on the exterior," said Edward. "They're not of our language, but of the Karlün. Yet the letters when translated match those on the parchment exactly. Seems a little *too* elaborate, wouldn't you say?"

This triggered a reaction in Roland. *Nothing but an old fantasy, ey?* thought Edward. "Are you sure there's nothing more to it?" he pressed him again.

The old man had been cornered and not to his liking. He grunted to himself before giving in; sitting forward in his chair he took a deep breath, his weary eyes squinting. "Oh, very well." Roland let out a burst of air, collecting himself. "Power ... beyond ... measure!" he whispered; his eyes now alight. "Yet any man who touches it shall be bound to its grip forever."

Roland stood from his chair, clasping his beard. "The old tales speak of a man named Benjamin Blackwood," he continued earnestly. "Who many years ago sailed to Graelind with only a single black diamond as his cargo. But what was so very strange about this man were his eyes; they were pearly white, absent of any colour. He wandered the lands in search of work and lodgings, but he was turned away from every tavern, mill and smithy in the east. One day, his despair was so great he fled to the caves beneath the earth and it is there he stayed."

"And what became of the man?" asked Edward.

"No one truly knows, Edward," said Roland, shaking his head. "Yet, there's something unnatural living in those caves, so I doubt he survived for long."

"What do you mean?"

"Listen, Edward," said Roland, backtracking. "It's for the best you throw that scroll away. Trust me. That diamond is … evil!"

"So, you're saying there's something living down there, in the caves?" asked Edward, taking no heed of what the man was saying.

Roland found Edward's pressing rather uncouth, but the officer's persistence sparked more of the tale. "A very old kind, yes. Some sort of tribe," said Roland reluctantly. "One might say they are now possessed or bound to that wretched jewel - one or the other."

Edward's expression fell to the floor and the curiosity turned to dread, his heart twisting like rope. "How do you know all this?" he asked.

"I've seen it for myself," said Roland sharply. "Take my word for it; forsaken things like this must not be meddled with, ever! That diamond destroys all, causing only pain and suffering. I'm afraid Benjamin Blackwood was caught in the same eternal noose as those creatures. Yes, I say creatures, but they were once humans, ya know, or at least that's what they looked like to my eyes, and they were far keener in those days. Dear me, I remember the eyes; you'll never forget the eyes."

"I have the feeling you know a little more about this tale than you are willing to part with, my old friend?"

"I think I have told you quite enough," said the old man.

"I've just got one last question, if you don't mind, sir?" said Edward, biting his lip in the anticipation of seeing Roland's temper. "You speak of a power beyond measure, yet those poor … people, creatures … only endure its misery?"

"That's because the true way to wield that diamond is yet to be discovered," said Roland.

Edward watched as the wry smile on Roland's face quickly changed into a scowl as harsh as stone; he then realised that perhaps he had asked one too many questions.

"Like I said earlier, I'm just being foolish," said Edward. "Sea'll make ya go mad, as they say."

"Edward, listen! I am only telling you these things because I trust you not to act upon them. *Don't* be foolish! I've seen the horror. Don't go looking, do you promise me?"

Edward felt his throat tighten up for he was about to lie through his teeth.

"You're right," he said, submissively. "Best putting this whole thing behind me. There's much more for us to talk about, I'm sure."

"Indeed there is, lad," said Roland. "Tell me, did you ever marry that bonny lass from down the road?"

And on that note, Edward slunk into his chair and the talk of old times began. Before he knew it, he'd been sat there all day. Roland had been kind enough to make lunch and even Lady Fane had found a memory of Edward that had made her smile.

Time seemed to have flown by, confirmed by the short hand of Edward's watch that had just crept over the number four.

"You've been too kind, my old friend, but I must be off," said Edward, leaving his seat. "I'll visit again soon."

Edward made for the front door, held open by the old man. His frailties more apparent as Edward towered over him.

"Take care, Roland. Same to you, my lady."

Edward fixed his cap and left, turning back to see Roland waving from the doorway. "Come back soon, lad!" he called, with his hand cupped by his cheek. "And remember what I said!"

As Edward's steps took him back up the muddy lane, across the empty vineyard and over the stream, he began to wonder. His mind was thinking clearer now, yet his heart was ever more rapacious. The side of himself that he feared the most was showing its ugly grin and was now beginning to altogether reveal itself. That side of him was vengeance.

As an officer you are taught from the very beginning to never let your actions be ruled by vengeance. Yet Edward had seen more than a man's share of death and after all these years he'd simply just had enough of it. And now, having seen the scroll and the ink upon it, and having heard the words of a man he trusted speak of it - the Black Diamond had his undivided attention. If the stories were true, peace in Graelind could be closer than ever and that fluttered Edward's heart like nothing he'd ever felt. And then, of course, there was the small matter of the pirate locked away in the Plummet - could *he* help Edward find it?

Back in Summer's Reach, the dark of the evening had closed in. James Percy was down by the harbour tying up his battered old fishing wherry, gathering his day's catch in what daylight there was left. Now the night had fallen, the market lit up like a mirror to the starry sky, with lanterns hanging from each stall and outside every tavern. The sound of music brought many groups of dancing performers and magicians down through the streets. The city was now alive with joy and loud in song.

James had only that second thrown a small prize of snapper over his back when he caught a glimpse of Edward walking a path into Bardrain's Square. He decided to catch up.

"Edward!" he called, running up behind him. "What time can we expect you at the party tonight, sir?"

"The party?" asked Edward, seemingly confused.

"Don't let me hear you've forgotten?"

"Ah! Yes of course, how mindless of me," realised Edward. "The party."

"My Uncle Wallace is expecting us all to be there and we certainly wouldn't want to disappoint," said James excitedly.

"I'll be there, James, you can be sure of that. I could well be a little late, mind. Charlotte has made dinner and I might yet miss it at this rate. I'll see you this evening."

They both parted ways with Edward gaining an extra jump in his step to make it home in time. James, on the other hand, sneaked behind the stalls and popped up behind a fishmonger, ready to sell off his catch for a couple of silver spinnels.

As the market grew quiet, the taverns filled up from wall to wall. And so, the party began.

Chapter 4
The Drum & Fiddle

Galaway certainly knew how to host a good party, with each minute alive with anticipation as more and more faces rolled through the door of the Drum & Fiddle - the best tavern in Harkness. One by one the officers arrived, joined by their wives and friends, with cheerful greetings all around.

The landlord Mr Piggs, was beaming red in his face, clambering around the cellar hoping with every part of him that the ale he had stored would last the night. Barrel after barrel he brought up: ales from Court Marsh, wines from Deepmont, bottled rum from overseas and whiskey from Summer's Reach.

In Graelind, it wasn't truly a party without the chance to win a few silver spinnels, so the chessboards were set atop tables and the dice followed. Galaway had already begun to indulge in the luxuries, banging the table and calling around the room for a worthy player, always the first to challenge anyone who was willing to place a bet.

The roar of the fire beamed throughout, warm and content and every table was full, all sitting under little windows that each held a small lantern on its sill. In the corner by the door, a mountain of coats and jackets stood balanced, the guests continuing to chance its strength with each garment they laid upon it.

James Percy arrived with his younger brother Johnathon, who only turned up to these sorts of things to persuade his uncle to let him follow in his brother's footsteps as a sailor. But, he was yet to be eighteen years old.

Pulling his jacket from around his shoulders, James gave the room a quick glance, where four rows away sat his Uncle Wallace, raising his glass in acknowledgement of their arrival. However, James' gaze slipped past him, for he had seen a beauty his heart could barely endure. Sitting by the fire was a girl, with eyes of the clearest blue and hair golden like honey, almost flame like. A face he had never seen before, but one he was not likely to ever forget.

Gathering himself, he made his way over to the bar, gesturing to Mr Piggs who by now had lost all hope of there being enough for the evening's drinking.

"A pint of ale if you will, sir," he asked.

"Certainly," replied Piggs, sliding him a mug. "And for the young master?"

"He's fond of the rum," said James, shaking his head.

Galaway left his seat at the table and walked over to his nephews with a smirk that spread wide across his face.

"Something amusing you, uncle?" asked James.

"A shot whistling past your ear in battle bothers you little, yet you dare not speak to a woman?" replied Galaway, giggling.

"I've only just arrived and did I make it *that* obvious?" said James, a little sheepish.

"Well, if I hadn't seen you *walk* in, I might have thought you'd been *dragged* in, frozen stiff from the cold, with the way you were staring," said Galaway.

"Maybe after a few more ales I'll have the courage," said James, nervously laughing.

Galaway rubbed James' cheek with affection. "My dear nephew. Take every chance you are given, despite the fear of the consequence; the clock won't wait," he said, smiling.

At that moment, Johnathon leaned his head into the conversation. "Yet on the other hand, uncle, courage comes naturally to me, as you'll see when you make me a sailor on your ship. I intend to start as a crewman just like my brother," he said, sipping his rum, before his cheeky smile changed to a wince.

Galaway laughed. "It's the rum, foul stuff, but if it gives you a fearless spirit then we will take three of them, Mr Piggs."

His uncle's words were enough for James to muster the nerve to introduce himself to the girl, but not without a hint of hesitation.

Quickly emptying his glass, he passed it to Galaway, with a wince that curled much further than Johnathon's had.

Walking over towards her, trying to talk himself out of it the whole way, he arrived rather apprehensively. He realised it was now too late to turn back, having already made his cumbersome presence abundantly clear.

"May I sit with you, my lady?" he asked in a soft voice.

"Yes, of course," she replied, a little curious.

Sliding out a chair, he positioned it carefully beside her. Then, beginning to take his seat, the questionable craftsmanship betrayed him as the legs buckled with a crash underneath his weight. Every corner of the tavern erupted with laughter, as cheers echoed around the room. Galaway couldn't bear to look, hardly able to hold back his own emotion. He took a drink of his rum, shaking his head in disbelief as James lay flat on his back, embarrassed, reaching for anything to help pull himself from the floor.

"At the very least we have more firewood," chuckled James nervously, as he regained his stance.

"It doesn't appear you have luck on your side, on this night," she laughed.

"Or on many nights if the truth be told. I'm clumsy at the best of times," he said, brushing away the dust and splintered wood from his trousers.

"So, do you have a name, or have you bumped your head and forgotten?" the lady asked.

"James Percy, and yours, my lady?"

"Adeline Dawson."

"Would you dance with me, if it's not too much to ask, Miss Dawson?"

"What you lack in grace you certainly make up for in charm, Mr Percy. I'd be happy to."

He reached out his hand, pressing his palm against hers, as they both moved to the only empty space in the room, big enough for two. By this time his uncle had thrown down a wager for a game of dice with a disposed participant. This came as a relief to James, for it was one less pair of eyes watching him - a dancer he most certainly was not.

The music flowed through the Drum & Fiddle like water trickling down a stream, gaining energy by the minute. James blushed in concentration, trying not to stand on Adeline's feet.

In the midst of all the merrymaking, the creak of the front door couldn't be heard but the burst of winter air that rushed through as it flung open could most definitely be felt. Edward arrived as promised and a cold gust that shook the tavern to its bones followed him, leaving a few unsettled guests.

Joining the others at the tables, he settled himself down for the evening, enjoying the ale and the music, almost as if he had nothing on his mind at all. This of course wasn't true and had been an obvious tell to the likes of Charlotte and Galaway for days.

Hours went by, the supplies gradually beginning to deplete. Empty bottles rolled along the floor, the barrels now ringing hollow. Evening turned into night then night into morning, and with only a few guests remaining the mood took a subtle turn into tranquillity as the tavern slowly emptied. Edward was yet to leave and sat beside the fire pondering, before turning his head to find Galaway stretched across a bench, snoring like a wounded wild hog.

Sweeping the floor, an exhausted Piggs slipped the last drops of a bottle into his cup. "On me," he said tiresomely, to which Edward lifted it in thanks.

Then, from out of the corner of Edward's eye, he caught an unusual looking figure in the window, with a face like a shadow that was partially covered by a hood down to the brow. Its chilling pearly eyes stared through the glass with fierce intent, quickly unnerving him.

Edward was fixed to his seat and before he had time to think, the figure had disappeared. The room fell into near silence and only the sound of its footsteps creeping outside could be heard as it reappeared in every window it passed.

Concerned and very dubious, Edward walked cautiously over to the door, sharply yanking it open - but nothing could be seen. He stepped out onto the decking, hoping to capture a glimpse of this mysterious being but the darkness engulfed his vision almost entirely and Edward's hopes of seeing clearly were dashed, for the moon was now hidden behind the thick, blackening clouds that seemed to smother the city.

Slowly leaving the light behind, he scanned the area of thick trees for any sign of movement. In the dark, only the enchanting glisten of the stars was visible. Just as quick as it came, the being had vanished.

Edward was stood there, utterly amazed as he tried to understand what in the world could possess eyes so hurtful; and also, why it had made a connection with *him*.

Suddenly, he heard the soft sound of twigs breaking under foot coming from the hedge. Hurrying back inside, he reached for his jacket, which by now was in a small pile on the floor. With one last check on Galaway, he snatched up a lantern from the wall and headed straight for the forest.

The forest was filled with pines that stood high above him, densely packed in together. Edward followed his instinct and set off into the wooded unknown. His ears were pricked, his eyes peeled as he scrambled past each long trunk.

Inside the forest, nothing could be recognised of the outside world, in a way isolated from all else; even falling rain could scarcely rest amongst the roots.

Having walked only a few hundred yards, he came to a vast clearing, where the trees gave way to a wide expanse. At its centre, there was a water well made of stone that had sunk into the wet soil around it.

Lumbering through the dirt, Edward noticed fresh and clear footprints he then followed to the well. Lying next to it was a bucket and some old, frayed rope. The mechanism above had become covered in rust and was unusable. Edward peered over the brink, down into the emptiness, again finding nothing. However, as he gazed with more intent, he discovered what looked like a tunnel at the very bottom. Gathering what was left of the rope, he tied it to his lantern and began to lower the light down as far as it would reach, revealing a strange entrance to a passageway.

In that moment, a realisation came over him; surely the being had fled this way but following it would be unwise without greater reason to.

Thinking better of it, Edward pulled up the rope and left. This was the end to a very long day and he was slightly swaying from the whiskey. Charlotte would surely be worried about his late return and he doubted she'd be best pleased about him skulking around the woods in the pitch dark of night.

As he emerged from the forest, his thoughts were only of dissecting the recent revelations. Firstly Peter the pirate, then the chilling story from Roland Fane, and now another unexplained mystery!

"Pearly eyes!" said Edward aloud. "Benjamin Blackwood?"

A very strange sense of foreboding began to bubble inside of him. Could that have been *him*? Edward was completely fixated. The blood in his heart pumped with vigour and he spent the entire way home searching it for what was left of his morality.

Chapter 5
As the Balance Shifted

After a very troubled night's sleep, the day had finally arrived – Peter's trial. Edward was to make sure he would be present, as this seemed like the only true hope in his pursuit of the Black Diamond. The pirate seemed to know enough about the diamond to make him a useful asset and after Edward had woken from troubled dreams with the undeniable urge to go and find it, the question he asked himself was, *is this pirate worth saving from the gallows, at least until the diamond is found? Surely not, Edward Clavell, what are you thinking, you fool! He's a pirate!*

The morning began as usual, yet Edward's early getaways were starting to become a normality, much to Charlotte's concern. She began to wonder if he really had returned a different man.

Dressed in his parade uniform, now smartly brushed and free of creases, he could barely contain himself – with the Plummet his purpose. He arrived at the fortress-like structure, a fearsome construction of stone suspended between two cliff faces, high above a rugged brook that split the hillside. The prison had only one entrance and was accessed by a winding path that was built into the rock's edge. The main door was manned by a guard, armed with a sword and musket, the latter donning a bayonet on its muzzle. This officer wasn't about to question another man in uniform and let Edward pass without hesitation.

Inside it was a haunting place, where evil men lay in wait for their call to the hangman's noose. The birds outside didn't sing, the sun barely shone on the stones and there was a wickedness that encompassed every space from ceiling to floor. He entered a large, bleak room and on one side there stood a spiralling, steel staircase. The cells that lined the room were teaming with the stench of sickness and inside them were murderers, pirates and all kinds of malevolent sinners.

Barely able to think from all the shouting and that awful stench of unsanitary men, Edward ascended the stairs, entering the third floor to find Peter in the furthest cell, shivering.

Peter's cheeks had sunken into his skull, the skin around his eyes now blue and swollen. The cold stone beneath him was beginning to bite away at his body, yet the weariness of his mind was the most agony.

"Are you here to check on me, Officer?" laughed Peter. "Makes a change, it's the birds that have kept me company; although they're more miserable than I am."

"As you are already aware, I possess the scroll, I'll cut straight to the chase," said Edward sharply. "Looking around this dungeon of misery, it doesn't appear you're in any position to bargain, so listen carefully. You will be trialled later today and without my help you will be hanged by the neck."

"You're trying to intimidate me, Officer, yet I see you are just as helpless," said Peter. "We both know you need me alive as much as I need the court's pardon, otherwise, why would you have come?"

"The court will show no mercy to pirates, so you better hope they believe otherwise," said Edward. "If not, you will find yourself becoming ever more friendly with this cell."

"Who's to say that whatever they perceive me to be, is in fact the truth?" said Peter. "Or instead, will their judgement be darkened by what they really *want* me to be?"

"Save it, Peter! Innocent men tend not to meet their end by execution," said Edward, balking at Peter's conspiracy. "But I don't suppose you *are* entirely innocent; an adventurer maybe, but you fell afoul of the wrong people and I have my suspicions. Yet I see no branding on your skin–"

"If you could cut straight to the point, as you said you would, I'd be most gracious!" said Peter. "As you can see, my situation is a little precarious."

Edward glanced over each shoulder before leaning in towards the prisoner.

"My intentions are very simple," he whispered, his eyes tightening. "I want peace in Graelind. And you say this diamond truly holds the power to give this great nation said peace?"

"If that is what you seek, then yes," said Peter.

Edward pondered over the thought of such a time. It warmed him, but the thought couldn't slow the beating of his heart. "What would you do with it?" he scoffed.

"I want to see the world, Edward, and escape to the lands deep within my dreams," said Peter. "But a world without any of those things would be better than a short life in this cell. You were right about one thing; it's not likely I'll strike a bargain from behind these bars. If you help me break free, I'll help you change the world – as long as you can promise me an untroubled place within it."

"How can I be sure you won't stick a knife in my back?" asked Edward. "At the very first opportunity you get?"

"You can't be sure, yet here you are," said Peter. "You know there is more to this tale, more that I'm not telling you. But that's the chance you'll have to take."

"I'll do what I can … your fate lies in their hands, after all," said Edward.

"I could see it in your eyes, Officer Clavell," said Peter. "From the very first second I spoke of the scroll. I knew there was something stirring inside your heart, something rebellious."

"You know nothing about me!" snapped Edward, before making a swift exit.

Peter lay still in his cell, smiling from ear to ear; a smile which gently turned into a quiet, callous laugh that was drowned out by the tumult of the other miscreants that surrounded him.

The noises that broke around this bedlam were from criminals of the most utter vulgarity; crazed savages fraught with sickness of the soul. The entire structure reeked and the foul waste that seeped from it poisoned the brook below. If the inmates inside hadn't already been given the conviction of a mad man, this place certainly assisted in making them so. The guards rarely entered the chambers, only to bring food and water; but when a man is so weak in his mind and body and lacks the strength to eat – the food goes rotten, the stench grows and the rats flood in.

One by one the guards of the Plummet circled Peter's cell. He was dragged from within it, to the very top of the prison. His feet barely touched the ground as they climbed upwards to the hall where his fate awaited.

A vast broad hall it was, where even the smallest of sounds echoed. Boasting huge, stained-glass windows, draped in long falls of silver thread, finished with a large oaken table as the room's centrepiece.

Peter was seated, overlooked by the court Judge Farley. A stout man with a plump chin, bewhiskered but still smart. Appearing as superior as his position suggested, he was dressed in a red and gold robe, finished with a wonderfully embroidered white necktie. He sat beside an assemblage of witnesses. Among those were Captain Galaway, Lord Harrington and Edward himself, at his insistence.

"State your full name to the witnesses," said Judge Farley, scribbling onto a page.

"Peter Beaumont, from the town of Court Marsh."

"And the charges against you today are of piracy, do you understand?" said Judge Farley.

"Yes, sir, I do; although I am entirely innocent of them."

"You were found on board a vessel named the *Venturous*, is that correct?"

"Yes, sir."

"Tell me exactly how you landed yourself in such a struggle, Mr Beaumont."

"My path regrettably crossed theirs. Both looking for the same thing I would imagine, sir."

"Oh, and what might that be?" said Judge Farley humorously, looking round at his peers for validation. Lord Harrington obliged him deliberately. Galaway remained stone-faced.

At that moment, Peter caught sight of Edward trying to conceal the shaking of his head and he began to somewhat stutter - seemingly revising what he was about to say.

Judge Farley looked inquisitively from beneath his unkempt brows, staring directly into Peter's eyes, waiting for a flinch.

"Judge Farley, if I may?" interrupted Edward. "I told Lord Harrington the same thing; this man was in the wrong place at the wrong time and unless he bears the mark of a pirate - which I believe he does not - we surely don't have any grounds to keep him here."

With a contemptuous look of scorn filling up his face, Judge Farley almost spontaneously developed an anxious twitch in his left hand, very much in time with what he thought to be a brash intrusion from an officer far beneath him.

"In this instance, Officer Clavell, you are quite right. But I'm not yet entirely convinced," he spat, continuing to tap his fingers on the table to no distinct rhythm. "However, having spent a great deal of time in Court Marsh myself down the years, I've never heard of the Beaumonts, before now."

Captain Galaway cleared his throat. "If my memory still serves me correctly, Judge Farley," he said, "the Beaumonts hail from Little Brace and unless I'm mistaken, they brand their villains under the tongue."

On hearing this, Farley called upon a guard with a gesture of his hand, who pulled out a short blade and held it to Peter's cheek, twisting back his head with a fistful of hair grasped tight. Peter had no choice but to obey. Clenching the chair arms, he closed his eyes and reluctantly opened his mouth, revealing a star within a star branded onto the underside of his tongue.

"Ha! Your deceitful imitation has failed you, Mr Beaumont," snarled Judge Farley. "One more word and I'll have him remove it from your head!"

Edward had himself been tricked as this brand was unquestionably the mark of a pirate. He held back and refrained from showing the feeling of frustration that rose from his stomach. Galaway and Harrington only saw this as justice served and were anything *but* secretive about their pleasure, watching a rotten soul being dealt the harrowing news of his execution.

"A sentence of death shall be passed upon you for your wicked ways, Peter Beaumont!" shouted Farley, standing up. "You'll see out the rest of your days in the Plummet!"

The same guard flung Peter from the chair to the ground, as they all looked down upon him in shame. Smiling, Peter climbed to his feet to watch his hands become shackled once again. No tears, no words; emotion held firmly behind a grin.

Edward leaned over to the table, fetched his cap and then left in a hurry, each step closely watched by the wary eyes of Galaway.

The crash of the prison bars as they slammed behind Peter could be heard far down the valley, and now the stone beneath him gnawed away at his cracked skin once again.

Moonlight covered the Plummet's stones now the sun had set. A calm night with little wind but still a sharp nip. With the courtroom vacated and in darkness, the nightly guards manned their posts, as all manner of creatures began to murmur.

Bats in their thousands, fluttering and clicking, hung from the ceiling using the fortress as a refuge. The wild dogs around the hills and in the caves would call out for hours with rallying cries that spread far over the terrain. Huge deer, with wide and proud antlers, would settle under clusters of pine trees further down the brook. Summer's Reach now glowing like flames in the distance, as rich and vibrant music came rolling over the hills from Bardrain's Square. Amongst it all, Peter sat in silence, staring at the cold, rocky floor where he'd be sleeping that night.

Edward was at home in his chair whilst a rather angered Charlotte prepared supper in the kitchen. She brought to the table a large bowl of pottage, with warm bread she'd baked that day. This was followed by a plate laden with pork belly, the skin still crackling, and wine from the vineyards of Deepmont served in a crystal glass.

Charlotte was silent but visibly frustrated by the fact that her husband had yet to notice all her efforts and had proceeded to stare into the fireplace. His absence over the last few days was beginning to creep up a concern within her and she was about to make this abundantly clear.

"Edward! You'd better start explaining yourself, right now!" Coarse words to which he jumped as if woken from a lazy slumber.

"I'm sorry, Charlotte, you're quite right. I haven't been myself, have I?" said Edward, noticing his supper on the table. "Thank you, darling. What's become of my manners?"

"Tell me now, what is the matter?" she said, walking over and sitting down in his lap. "What are your misgivings? I don't think I can go on another minute without knowing!"

"I can no longer continue being the man I am," said Edward, all at once, as if it had all been bubbling inside him. "Always far from home, alone, not knowing if I will return to you. The sea has finally torn away the desire that I once had."

"You mean to leave the navy?"

"Maybe ... but I must see to a number of important matters before I make it final. I'd hoped to be more than just a turnkey, Charlotte."

"You have everything, my love," she said, stroking his cheek. "A respected position, enough coin to see us into the next century, a loving wife at home who cares for you dearly and a son who someday might well follow in his father's footsteps."

"He's better off selling his fruits," said Edward despondently. "I wouldn't see him in a grey coat for as long as there is life in me; no man should endure the horror of the seas. It's a wonderful yet toxic world full of evil and I wish to put an end to all that at the very soonest moment."

"You already do all you can, my love. As long as there is wealth throughout Graelind, there will always be those who try and take it."

"What if there was a way to end the chaos and kill the rats that torment us?" said Edward, in a whisper.

Charlotte was growing concerned.

"If there *was* a way," she said, trying to rationalise. "I hardly suppose it'll be a very attainable prospect. Now what are you talking about?"

"Today the balance shifted, Charlotte, as I watched what I thought to be a half chance crumble away."

"The pirate, he's had your attention. Why?"

"I never told you about the pirate, Charlotte," said Edward, flummoxed.

"You didn't need to; I saw the captain's wife in the market," said Charlotte. "Apparently he speaks to his." She was quick to her feet.

Edward puffed out his lips, took a deep breath and then continued.

"The pirate spoke of a great power, one which could be used to bring peace to our lands, forever."

Charlotte's expression changed from one of understanding and reasoning, to a puzzled look of scepticism. She was beginning to lose her composure.

"Edward, this is absurd! Surely you know better than to trust the dishonest word of a damn pirate? I can't believe this; you've fallen for his tricks like a dog for a bone, haven't you?"

"There is more to it than just his word, I know it," said Edward, shaking his head rapidly, trying to reason with himself at this point.

"What has become of your sanity, Edward? If this isn't just a scheme by a villain jostling for his freedom, what could *possibly* hold such power? Go on, tell me, tell me what on earth you are talking about?"

Edward reached into his pocket and pulled out the scroll, placing it in his wife's hand. She read the words on the parchment.

"The Black Diamond?" she snapped. "These are just old tales told to children, Edward!"

"There's more to it, Charlotte, I can feel it!"

"You must've gone mad!"

"Listen to me. I don't need you to believe the diamond is real, I just need you to understand this is something I *have* to do. It's for the future of Graelind!"

Charlotte began to cry quietly. She couldn't bear a world without Edward in it. The fear of losing him was too great a pain, yet after seeing how delusional he had become, perhaps he was already lost. Edward knew the idea would sound ridiculous to her, but she hadn't seen what he had seen - the anguish and the suffering of the world beyond the city. Seldom did Edward discard the advice of his wife, but this idea was now branded into his mind deeper than the stars under Peter's tongue.

Chapter 6
The Clock Won't Wait

Taverns for the common folk and taverns for the rich. A truism that outlined the contrasting way of life throughout Summer's Reach. The working men and women would frequent the areas close to the harbour, in Bardrain's Square, whilst the privileged could be seen attending the more lavish gatherings in the villas of the Old Carry. Such divisions dated back for generations, with the poor and privileged hardly crossing paths. The latter welcomed merchants from afar who came bearing gemstones fit for the royals, along with fine silks, spices and exotic liqueurs. Yet down by the harbour, the docks flooded with ships carrying nearby islanders, who came selling pelts and ale and vegetables that Graelind struggled to grow through its cold winters. The city owed a great deal to the men and women who had little, because they truly were the beating heart of the capital. From the smithy to the boat yard, the fishmonger to the cattle market and in each and every tavern, the city's true colours blossomed like the daffodils that filled the fields in spring.

James Percy often visited the markets of Bardrain's Square when not at sea, selling his own acquisitions directly to the local fishmonger, caught from the lake and river aboard his battered old wherry.

A young man with a radiant charm that gleamed over his subtle, boyish countenance. A lover of trinkets and treasures; one of which was a small silver pocket watch he wore hanging from the lapel of his waistcoat. His prevailing traits were his heart and an ability to see the good in all things – wicked or otherwise. Yes, maybe there was an air of naivety in him, but whose place was it to deem such a peaceful mind an unwise one?

James had once again found himself strolling the square – only this time his intentions were different, after recently making the acquaintance of Adeline Dawson.

That night in the Drum & Fiddle after his uncle had urged him to set aside his nerve and speak to her, she had briefly mentioned working as a waitress at the Prince's tavern in the Old Carry. He hoped to see her again, hoping this time he would be blessed with a little more luck than on their first meeting. Walking eagerly, he arrived mid-afternoon and after giving the exterior of the Prince's tavern the admiring glance it well deserved, he entered.

Paintings wrought in colour and framed in gold lined each and every hallway. Maids and butlers scurried to and from the kitchen in a hasty fashion, carrying platters of all things fine and sweet, and wines of unmatched quality. The dining room was clad with more paintings and furnished with tables laden in white cloth that draped to the ground, finished with floral embroidery around the edges. The chairs were wrapped perfectly in leather and stood tall, six to each table.

Before he realised, James was stood directly in the doorway, staring around at all the opulence before him. After a few more anxious steps, a sharp nudge against his shoulder from an eager butler was enough to move him onward, over towards a table where he hesitantly perched himself.

Walking across the room was Adeline, possessing every ounce of elegance he remembered. Sitting tall, with his chest proud, he appropriately straightened his waistcoat, taking one last look at his pocket watch, just waiting to catch her eye – which he did.

Adeline smiled apprehensively, her cheeks beginning to blush, wondering what business a sailor might have in such a place.

James smiled back at her, rather bashfully – to which her own expression changed to one of a concealed fluster.

Going about her own work was now ever more difficult, much to the dismay of the ornately dressed diners as she began to misplace herself. Eventually, Adeline was able to slip the merciless grip of the rich folk and came over to the table where James was sitting – and in all her candour, she said, "This is hardly the place for a sailor, Mr Percy."

"And I dare not stay long, my lady," said James in return. "If I could escape the gaze of these rich folks for just one second, I'd maybe blend in."

"Perhaps you would," said Adeline, "had you not trampled in all that dirt on those boots."

Adeline chuckled, watching as James looked down in disbelief at the mess he'd unknowingly brought in with him. A peaceful mind indeed but often an absent one. She found him rather endearing.

"I came to see if you would be so kind as to join me this evening at the Drum & Fiddle?"

Adeline gently smiled as the innocence of James Percy shone brightly. His longing eyes sang in admiration for her.

"I'll meet you there, Mr Percy, before the sun sets," she said sweetly, without much hesitation.

James' obvious delight was clear to see as he shuffled excitedly for a few more seconds, beginning to address his waistcoat again. Eventually standing to his feet, he bade Adeline farewell, bumping into the same unimpressed butler on his way out.

A sudden confusion gave way to a quick shake of Adeline's head as her fluster grew to excitement. Her obvious misplacement was interrupted by the arrogant clicking of a guest's fingers, demanding her assistance.

Adeline stayed true to her word and arrived at the setting of her invitation, decorously dressed. James had spent that afternoon pondering his options of exactly how to greet this wonderful lady now that he had her curiosity – a circumstance he was altogether unprepared for.

Much alike to their first meeting, he thought the idea of a pint of ale and a dance was rather appropriate but the charm of the boy was about to overcome the actions deemed traditional in these parts.

As she was about to step through the tavern door, James pulled Adeline's hand and led her away through the streets of the city; at times with a leap in his step, intermittently switching between a walk and a skip. She called to him, "James! Where are we going?" She couldn't help but giggle and she almost fell on more than one occasion. They came to the harbour where James' wherry lay bobbing in the calm water, moored to the edge. Adeline looked at James and her face said it all. "I'm not getting in that!" she added, just in case her look of surprise wasn't enough of a tell.

"Trust me, my lady, you won't regret it," he said softly, reaching out a hand.

She sighed, thinking, weighing up her own options. Adeline looked out onto the vast lake, the snow-capped fells beyond disappearing into the approaching dark of the night. She felt nervous, perhaps scared. She hardly knew the man. Yet there he stood with a proffered hand and a beaming smile she couldn't look at for more than a second without her face flushing up. "Very well, but if I fall in, I'll never forgive you!" she snapped, scarcely able to believe what she was about to do. But something just felt right. His hand was warm and comforting, her shaking fingers brushed over his palm before he held her tight.

Having been helped aboard, she perched herself ungracefully on the seat at the stern, tucking her dress neatly behind her knees, sitting curiously. James gathered his paddle and began to row, occasionally looking back to give her a smile.

Not half a mile from the harbour they approached a break in the trees by the edge of the lake. He continued to row on in that darkening direction, watching as the winter sun flickered behind the bare branches above them.

They came aground on a narrow bank and again, taking Adeline by the hand, he helped her to a steadier footing amongst the shale beneath his feet.

Beginning to guide her through the trees, his evident knowledge of the woods matched the puzzled look on Adeline's face and she kept asking him where it was they were going.

"It's a surprise. You'll see, soon enough!" he responded each time.

Looking back to see a rather confused look on her face, James tightened his grip and smiled with a sincere glance of reassurance, which she was heartened to have seen.

The bushes began to lose their denseness; the taller woods making way for shorter growing heather that boasted rusted wintery colours. A light sheet of dew now covered the heather that brushed away at the touch of James' fingers, leaving his knuckles suffused in blue from the frigid air. The trees again grew taller around them as they entered an expanse of pines, damp upon the bark. James turned and faced Adeline. "Wait there and be very still," he whispered, before turning away again, walking tiptoed into the near distance.

The sun had now almost fully set, leaving behind only pink glows beyond the heights of the canopies; an almost surreal spectacle that held the life of the world within it.

As Adeline's lips neared to speak, James reached into his waistcoat, took out his pocket watch and held it at arm's length.

He then lifted his blade from its sheath and grasped it in his fingers around the pommel, before gently tapping the steel against the silver of his watch.

The bright sound reverberated through every bush and tree, and within the blink of an eye the entire woods lit up, becoming a vista of a million fireflies that shone with a hue of speckled gold all about the place.

Adeline felt the world around her disappear, as if all else was worthless away from this exact place, at this exact moment.

Her dress swirled as she turned to catch each and every light that passed flawlessly within the branches. Her eyes at last found James; she stared intently into those singing eyes - and he was smiling back, hoping with every ounce of his heart she felt the same way he did. The lady who he so hopelessly desired was standing before him, alight amongst the fireflies - in that moment, he was utterly awestruck.

With James' wherry again afloat, he rowed them back to the harbour. Neither of them could keep from smiling. Adeline no longer had any apprehension; her heart beating like crazy, the very tips of her toes tingling with happiness.

Back at the harbour, James helped her onto the edge before the two of them walked hand in hand to the Drum & Fiddle, just in time for the music.

They spent that evening laughing together; the night was everything James Percy wanted it to be. It was perfect. And for Adeline, it was beyond magical.

When the time came for them to part, James reached into his waistcoat, grabbing his pocket watch. "I'll need this back before I set sail again, my lady, so see it's safe. I'll return for it soon. Goodbye, Miss Dawson."

Chapter 7
An Empty Bottle

Down by the river and in front of a hearth packed full of crackling logs, Edward sat washing a whiskey around his glass - as unsettled as he was now drunk.

That same stare, that same anguish, bled from him and poured all around him, filling the room. He was paddling for his life within his own thoughts.

He had to seek his desires alone. That was the only way; to part himself from his position of respect, no longer able to keep on questioning his morality.

The lure of the Black Diamond had him firmly gripped. He kept on trying to justify his intentions, over and over again, arriving at the very same outcome each time. Imagining a world in which the rotten souls would not be free to roam and where the people of Graelind could live in harmony. A world rid of pirates!

That night, Edward slept deeply; so much so, the glass that fell from his hand, smashing onto the hearth, woke his wife but it didn't even tingle his senses. Sitting bolt upright, Charlotte held her breath for an uncertain moment, to take in the disturbed silence of the night - only to hear nothing.

She stood, thrust a blanket around her shoulders and peered into the living room to find Edward slumped on his chair, glass shattered beside the fire.

A blank look of helplessness settled on her face. The recent days had shown a side of Edward she had never seen the likes of before. Her heart was hurting.

Daylight brought rain and with it the patter of drops on the windows. Edward woke from his slumber, his head thick like porridge. A new morning, yet one that began in a way that Edward believed could not have been a coincidence - with voices, chattering in another room.

Edward investigated; tense strides helped him to the kitchen – and yet again there was nothing. He walked to the window to find an old fox nosing around the garden, its red fur drenched.

This time he stayed put, deciding against facing the rain, feeling his fingertips tingle in the morning cold, urging him to reach for a few logs from under the table.

With the logs stacked against his chest, he walked back to the living room to find the dark figure of a man sitting in his chair.

It was Peter Beaumont, free from his bonds, armed with a small axe. He wore a cold smile that accentuated his piercing eyes as they stared intensely from beneath his brows.

"The wrong place at the wrong time?" said Peter. "Is that all you could come up with? Anyway, aside from the small matter of my miraculous escape, might I trouble you for a glass of whatever it is you drink in this wonderful cottage? In keeping with your own customs, of course."

"Firstly, you'll stay firmly put, you swine," snapped Edward, in a hush of anger. "And then you'll tell me how you escaped the Plummet and why you crawled your way *here*, to my home, where my wife sleeps in her bed!"

"For the love of the sea, calm down," said Peter. "I have no intention to harm you or your precious wife ... but I'd like that drink though, if I may?"

Edward paused in horror at this rudeness then carefully placed the logs on to the floor, glancing over to the table where his pistols were resting.

"I can assure you, Edward, that won't be necessary," said Peter. "Now please, I'm absolutely parched!"

Madly, Edward opened up a chest close by, taking out a bottle of ale before handing it over. Peter bit off the cork with his teeth and spat it into the now dormant fireplace. He began to chug at its contents, his hand shaking.

"Do you expect that not a soul in this city saw you come here?" said Edward. "This cottage will be surrounded by guards before you can finish that bottle."

"Well, it's high time we left then, isn't it?" said Peter, smiling mischievously. "I do believe we have a certain treasure to acquire!"

"No man has *ever* escaped the Plummet! I wonder how many officers had to die for your, what might turn out to be, temporary freedom?" said Edward, his hands meeting his cheeks in horror.

"I'll need a fresh set of clothes, if you'd be so kind," said Peter. "I doubt our forthcoming adventure will be too generous to us and these rags I wear, well, it'll not be long until I catch my death!"

Edward was astonished. Chiefly at Peter's complete disregard for the severity of the situation. The pirate didn't appear to have taken heed of a single word that Edward had said and the officer wondered how a man could be so brazen in light of it all, quickly remembering this man was nothing but a scoundrel, a pirate scum.

The inevitable knock at the door sounded with a *thud, thud, thud*. Peter didn't even flinch. Edward walked over to the front door, meeting a startled Charlotte in the hallway who had been awoken by all the commotion.

The Kingsguard had surrounded the whole building, armed upon horseback. Edward could see the host of greycoats gathering outside the garden as one after another began to dismount. He spun and was about to speak but Peter was gone. Then the door came flying open, crashing into the wall. The entire cottage was searched high and low by some twenty men. The kitchen was ransacked for no apparent logical reason. Tables were toppled. The logs that Edward had been carrying were now scattered across the ground. Charlotte watched in terror as her home was disfigured.

Edward stood helplessly, knowing good and well that harbouring an escaped criminal would certainly lead to his own execution. Yet throughout this entire ordeal, not one of the guards emerged from any crevice of the cottage with Peter Beaumont in toe. They found nothing. Not a trace, to Edward's disbelief.

Colonel Eustace Gürad was the leader of this regiment and he entered the living room vexing in frustration. He knew well enough that Peter Beaumont had taken refuge here. He viciously kicked over a table, swung on the spot and held his rapier to Edward's throat.

"If it comes to light that you aided his escape ... I'll see to it you are hanged for your treason, Officer Clavell," he snarled before marching out his men.

Charlotte left for the bedroom, slamming the door shut behind her. Edward knew there were no words that could ease her anger, so he made for the open window through which Peter *must* have escaped. His gaze was cast far down the river but there was nothing - Peter was gone.

He turned and faced the door to see the Kingsguard galloping away astride their horses, leaving only wet and trampled ground behind them.

Then ... a second, gentler knock sounded at the door.

"Captain Galaway!" whispered Edward, letting him inside.

"I heard Gürad and his men had been sent here," said Galaway. "Tell me why, Edward, and I won't take anymore *lies!*"

"He came here, Captain, the pirate. But I know not why; he fled as soon as he heard Gürad's men outside."

"I have sailed alongside you for over twenty years, Edward," said Galaway. "And for each and every one of them you have given me your loyalty and more importantly, friendship. Now, you look me in the eyes and lie? Your services to the *Baliant* are no longer required. I regret to say it, my lad, but you've left me with no choice!"

Edward took a moment, gathered his emotions and fell into a trance of regret.

Galaway placed his hand on Edward's shoulder. "You have goodness in your heart, Edward; for King and country, always," he whispered. "Yet the man I knew would have cut that pirate filth to the ground the first second he stepped foot in this cottage. That's how I know."

"Captain, I can explain. Allow me to-"

The captain huffed in anger and left. Edward upturned his chair then fell into it. He was dejected. He stared down at his feet, wondering how he had found himself in such a mess. His whole world was beginning to fall apart and it was entirely by his own doing.

Then, from the corner of his eye, he saw a little roll of parchment sticking out from the top of the empty bottle Peter had drunk from.

A handwritten note that read,

Meet me at the drover's tavern in Court Marsh.

Chapter 8
Court Marsh

Torn and indecisive. Should he meet Peter Beaumont? Charlotte would surely be scorned and never forgive. Edward thought long into the afternoon, his loving wife staying put in the bedroom without a whisper. At least she was once a loving wife, as Edward was once an admired man - but times had truly changed in the blink of an eye. There wasn't a single soul on earth who cared for Edward the way his wife did; and now he'd betrayed her trust and all that he stood for as an officer of the *Baliant*.

Maybe it *was* time to leave. The thought of which he pondered over in great detail. Perhaps this could be his redemption; to find the diamond and bring forth to Graelind the power and the peace that would follow? His heart skipped many beats as he succumbed to the temptation, the lure - he *must* find Peter!

Quickly gathering some items, he stuffed them into a large satchel. Sheets, a compass, a knife, a water pouch, a bottle of whiskey and a big drawstring bag of silver spinnels. He figured he would acquire something to eat along the way. He slung a heavy, leather jacket over his shoulders then the satchel strap over his head. He looked down to see his bandolier on the table, equipped with his two pistols. Hesitantly, he grabbed them, fixing them carefully in place before unhooking his cap from the wall.

He wrote these words on a piece of parchment and slid it under the bedroom door,

I hope you can find it in your heart to forgive me,
my dearest Charlotte.

Edward took the ten-mile journey to Court Marsh by wagon, paid for with six silver spinnels. A town so near, yet never had he ventured there. Let's just say, he wasn't missing anything.

"Court Marsh," he said quietly to his unknowing accomplice.

Court Marsh was an unfriendly and inhospitable place; a dark and callous little town with a bubbling temper, filled to the brim with the regret of the disreputable individuals within it.

Upon Edward's arrival, Peter was precisely where he said he would be. The pirate was tucked behind a table in a bleak-at-best establishment called the Drovers tavern. The officer, far from any of the cordial comforts he was used to, stepped through the noise and mayhem holding his slightly shaking hand over one of his pistols. He sat and pushed the scroll under Peter's nose, along with the letter he had left in the bottle. "I didn't think pirates could read and write," he said, mockingly.

"I've told you, I'm not a pirate, Edward," said Peter, looking quite surprised to be seeing his new acquaintance.

"Spare me," said Edward, sharply. "I know what you are, pirate. I'm not here to be your friend, I'm here to find this jewel – you're a means to an end and that's it. What it was that convinced me you'd be of *any* help at all, I've yet to discover. Now, where do we start?"

Peter started laughing loudly.

"Something funny?" asked Edward, regretting his decision already.

"Come on, Edward. You've got to see how hilarious this is?" said Peter, taking a swig of his pint; his hands no longer shaking now the alcohol coursed his bloodstream. "We've got to be the most unlikely of accomplices in the history of Graelind."

"A means to an end, remember that," said Edward, sternly.

Peter smiled. "Very well, Officer."

Then, the two of them began arranging the pieces of the puzzle through the power of speech and strong ale.

"So ... you say there's more to the tale?" said Edward. "I'm listening."

Peter froze. "Well," he began. "That might have been a slight exaggeration," he said, his expression of guilt beaming. "How else was I meant to get you to help me?"

"You son of a bitch!" said Edward. "I should have known."

"Listen, all I know, is there's power in that diamond," said Peter, defending himself. "My captain never shut up about it. He seemed absolutely convinced he'd rule the seas should he ever acquire it."

"I'm beginning to question coming here," said Edward.

"I'm going to save you the trouble here and now, Officer. Do not rest any hope on me never disappointing you."

"The scroll says, in a crown only fit for a king?" said Edward, scratching his chin, moving away from the subject before it angered him anymore than it had already. "Every Graelinder knows the King has *never* donned a crown, nor did his father or his grandfather."

"Yes, but there *is* in fact a crown, as I have seen it," said Peter, rather proud of himself.

Edward smiled sardonically. "You've seen the King's crown, have you? Ha, I'll enjoy this tale."

"I was captured back in Summer's Reach, some years ago," said Peter. "I'd become friendly with a girl, turned out to be the wife of a damn Kingsguard. My luck, ey? Rosanne, I think her name was. Anyway, after I had given them the slip, I found myself hiding behind the stables, just outside the palace walls. And there it was, as the drapes of a golden carriage blew open in the wind – it glistened. At least fifty guards followed, so I couldn't get any closer. I might have tried snatching it, had it not been so well guarded."

A waitress brought Edward a pint of ale, plonking it on the table without a single ounce of grace.

"You're very much as slippery as you seem, pirate," said Edward, taking a sip. The ale tasted oddly like bananas.

"That's not all. The guard hadn't quite forgiven me since last I saw him," said Peter, rolling his eyes. "He's no more pleasant now than he was back then … they've only gone and made him a colonel. Pah!"

"Rosanne?" Edward pondered over the details, taking another sip of ale. "Not the wife of Colonel Gürad?"

"That's him! The bastard beat me senseless when he got his hands on me," smirked Peter. "And I mean *senseless!*"

Both men shared in the laughter, caring equally little for Colonel Eustace Gürad.

"You did well to survive!" said Edward. He was rather impressed. "Gürad is a ruthless son of a bitch in the best of his moods."

"Yet, here I am," smiled Peter, his bruised eyes and cheeks no longer covered in purple blotches – the injuries now brown and fading.

Edward quickly returned to a serious note. "If it truly was the crown of the King … then I might know where to find it," he said, his intrigue boiling. "In the palace armoury. Keeper of the King's jewels and secrets."

"I'm listening," said Peter, narrowing his gaze.

"Well, you can start by smartening up," said Edward, looking Peter up and down. "You'll need a uniform, my uniform – I'll return home for it. The guards should think you're attending to naval business if you don't bring too much attention to yourself, which is exactly why you'll be shaving that beard! I'd go myself but I'd be recognised."

"Well then, that settles it," said Peter, puffing out his cheeks. "Thought there might have been a little more careful deliberation, though, perhaps to discover who was better suited to such a task."

"Then you thought wrong," said Edward smiling.

*

Captain Galaway sat amongst Lord Harrington and a few of the other officers, contemplating the consequences, all having heard of Edward's disappearance.

Charlotte Clavell had been summoned to the Plummet's courtroom. She was in tears, clutching a handkerchief, occasionally wiping her face clean.

"Tell me, Lady Clavell, *where* is your husband?" said Harrington, his demand made Charlotte jump.

"I don't know, sir. Edward hadn't been himself of late but I never for a second thought he would … do you think he's in any danger?"

Charlotte observed the room to see Lord Harrington standing by the window, peering far down the valley. Judge Farley was sat tapping his fingers as always. Captain Galaway sat staring at his feet and he didn't look overly present. After composing himself, he managed to muster up some words of his own. "A pirate has escaped the Plummet, Charlotte," he said, coldly. "And we have reason to believe that Edward helped make his departure from the city a swift one. He could be hanged for this treason, my lady, if there is *anything* you can tell us, please?"

"I know nothing, sir, truly, nothing."

Lord Harrington lost his patience, waiting for the truth he somehow knew she would never tell. He could see it in her eyes. "That will be all, my lady, you may leave," he grunted. *I will see you again!* he thought to himself.

Galaway dipped his head low. He was worried.

"Guards! See this lady home safely," snapped Harrington crossly.

"Wallace, could you?" asked Charlotte, desperately.

"With pleasure, my lady."

Galaway escorted her from the courtroom and down the stairs, her hand joined to his arm. She gained more speed as if frightened of her surroundings. After all, the Plummet was a wretched place with nothing but evil within it - no place for kind folk.

Galaway left her by the door of her cottage, smiling hesitantly. He too knew very well this was a lady with a secret. His heart ached.

"Emily and I will always be here, Charlotte - always," he said, his smile a comfort to her.

Inside, Charlotte set down her things and for a while, she cried silently. The thought of the Plummet sent a shiver up her spine. She rubbed her smarting eyes, took a deep breath and walked into the living room, where she hoped to find Edward slumped in his chair. She strained her mind, willing him to be there, but the chair was empty. In her heart she believed his intentions to be pure but this was beyond a doubt a reckless act of disloyalty. Charlotte hadn't come to terms with it yet, and she wasn't sure if she could find it in her heart to forgive Edward for what he had done.

A series of thudding sounds came from the bedroom, like measured footfall on the wood floor, growing closer. Edward stepped around the corner, his officers uniform slung over his arm.

"You fool, Edward Clavell!" she screamed.

Edward brought a single finger to his lips to shush her. "Charlotte! There's a guard outside, please!"

"If you've dared to bring that pirate here then a Kingsguard is the very least of your worries!" she growled, absolutely beside herself, fighting for her breath. "They took me to the Plummet, Edward. Me! I don't deserve this burden."

Edward embraced her in his arms, speaking in soft whispers. "He's not here, I promise. Please, let me explain." Edward did explain. His words offering her no solace. Was she to watch him leave a second time? Did she have any choice?

Charlotte barged him away and fled to the kitchen, bleeding with emotion. She disappeared down the hallway. The bedroom door slammed, shaking the casing.

Edward quickly grabbed his uniform, walked up the hallway and rested his palm against the wood that now separated them. There was a brief moment of silence.

"Charlotte? You don't need to answer me but I hope that you're listening. The world beyond the capital is dark and the people here go on oblivious; it's only a matter of time before the enemy lands on our doorstep. If there's one flash of a chance that I can prevent that, I'll stop at nothing. I would die to protect you."

Edward heard his wife touch the door on the other side. "I love you," came a whisper.

"And I you, my love," said Edward, as tears permeated his eyes. He asked himself the question then. *Am I doing the right thing?* The look in Charlotte's eyes had seared into his mind and he couldn't shake it off. She was crestfallen by his actions and he feared losing her.

"I will not return empty-handed, my love. I will not waste this chance!"

"I understand the man you are, Edward; for King and country, always. But if you leave, I might not be here when you return," she said sadly. Edward's fears had been realised. Now he had to choose between the conflicting desires of heart and mind. The decision almost felt easier to make without looking at her face. This opportunity was far bigger than his own little journey through the cycle of the time; but in that moment he failed to muster the courage to tell her that was how he felt. He just couldn't formulate the words in his mouth.

"I'm sorry," he whispered. "I will look to the stars every night in the hope that when I return, I will not have lost you."

The bedroom was deathly quiet.

Edward smothered the sense of swelling dread inside him and moved into the living room; the drapes on the window he came in through fluttered in the breeze as he climbed out and departed. Peter was waiting a quarter mile down the riverbank. The pirate noticed Edward's deeply forlorn expression, deciding against any unnecessary chitter chatter.

Upon the heights of the bank stood James Percy, watching down on them as they fled into the forest. The young crewman had been fishing the river as Edward and Peter emerged from the trees behind the Clavell cottage. They hadn't seen him standing there, rod cast into the shimmering winter flowing's of icy water.

An old shabby room at the Drovers tavern was their resting place for the night. A maid knocked at the door and brought inside two bowls of pottage and some manky, stale bread to accompany it. Edward looked downcast at this miserable looking fare. The two thanked the girl – Edward did so loathingly – and they polished off the supper quite quickly. Peter Beaumont, with absolutely no table manners of any description, scooped the contents of the bowl into his face aggressively, for this had been his first warm meal in quite some time.

"Tell me, Edward," he muffled, mopping his face with his dirty sleeve. "This diamond. Is it truly worth all the trouble?"

"I'll have to let you know if we ever find it!"

"You never did tell me what you'd do with it?"

Edward paused for a second and looked at him. "I've told you, I want peace in Graelind."

"Just say it!" snapped Peter.

Edward sighed. "Very well," he said, moving closer to the pirate to emphasise what he was about to say.

Peter's ears pricked in preparation.

"I've been an officer for many years now and I've seen my own men, friends and family torn apart in ways one couldn't imagine. Towns destroyed, ships torched, women and their helpless children murdered in cold blood – all at the hands of pirates. I'd see the world rid of every last one of them."

Peter nodded, shocked but understanding.

"Well, I'd like to think you'd spare me when the time comes," he shuddered, nervously. There was something about Edward that unnerved him, although he didn't show it. "After all, I am walking into almost certain death in aid of our requirement."

"Have faith," said Edward. "A gentleman in uniform shouldn't be questioned, so long as he keeps himself to himself and avoids rousing too much suspicion."

"And how do you suppose I acquire the King's crown without rousing *too* much suspicion. I'm in the right mind to think you're setting me up!"

"If you get yourself caught, Peter, it'll be none of my doing!" said Edward coarsely, caring little for the accusation. "There's a vault within the armoury and I know a way in. I believe it holds all the royal regalia."

"How did you come by this detail?" asked Peter, turning up his nose.

"Many years ago, when the palace was built for the second king, he had a series of passageways built beneath the grounds," said Edward. "No doubt to sneak around his mistresses. Anyway, after the work was completed, he had all the workers killed; easier to keep a secret when you're dead!"

"Not everyone I'm guessing?" presumed Peter.

"Indeed, his most loyal advisor to be precise," said Edward.

"The Lord Chancellor?"

"Yes, and his name was Clavell, too," said Edward. "His great grandson was William and he had a daughter named Mary. Her youngest son is sat before you in this room."

"Wait a minute. You're a descendant of the loyal advisor to the second King of Graelind?" said Peter, wide eyed.

"In the flesh. And you are the only one alive that knows that, besides my wife, of course," said Edward. "When my grandfather's mind had long left him, he told me of two remaining passageways. One could be found from within the palace, and the other from outside it. The outer tunnel has since collapsed so you will have to take the route from the inside. It's located under the Peace Monument in the courtyard - you'll have to hide until nightfall."

"But how can you be sure this armoury exists?" asked Peter.

"Well, as a once curious young officer, I had to take a look for myself!" said Edward.

"Not just the tales of an old senile then?" said Peter, giggling.

"You'd be wise to mind your tongue, pirate!" snarled Edward. "If you must know, my grandfather also told me that there happened to be an item belonging to our family that had found its way into the King's collection. I felt it was right it came back to us. Attaining it wasn't that difficult either, especially when the locksmith who'd only recently forged new locks for the armoury came waltzing into the Drum & Fiddle blatantly boasting about it. He saw a man in uniform, took a heavy handful of spinnels and cut me a key."

"Well ... what did you find?"

"Ha! More jewels than even you'd know what to do with," remarked Edward laughing. "I didn't see a crown though."

"I'd know just what to do with them," scoffed Peter. "Have faith in that!"

Edward shook his head disappointedly. "I can only imagine the debauchery."

"You truly see me as nothing but a dirty scoundrel?" said Peter, vehemently shaking his head.

"Precisely. Now, listen very carefully," said Edward. "Surrounding the Peace Monument is a pool of water, and the way inside is located under its surface through an opening at the very base of the King's Unison. I'm assuming you can swim? When you resurface inside the monument, you'll enter a chamber containing stairs to the lower passageway. Follow that to the armoury. Clear enough?"

Peter's face tightened. "And when I reach the armoury, what of the vault?"

"You're going to open it with the key I have. You don't follow on too well, do you? That leads me to our next problem; you'll need to steal my ring of keys back."

Peter looked on, puzzled. "What part of this deal sees me as the errand boy?" he said, visibly irate. "You steal the keys and I'll steal the crown and that's that!"

Edward didn't take any offence to his strict words.

"It's better I see to it anyway," he said. "My keys will be aboard the *Baliant* and I'll be damned before I see a pirate loose on that great vessel."

"I'd spit on its hull before stepping upon it."

"I could gut you without feeling a thing, Peter."

"For the love of the sea, Edward, you really do need a sense of humour," said Peter, scoffing back. "Hopefully you can acquire one along the way!"

Edward shrugged off his comment.

"You know, I truly have nothing to lose; so really, why all this trouble?" asked Peter.

There was a long silence.

"What I have to lose is already lost," said Edward seriously. "I threw it all away the minute I came here. I hope it's all worth it in the end."

"Me too," said Peter. "Me too. Anyway, maybe it's time we scour this town for a barber."

Edward chuckled. "If there's someone alive in this town who's willing. I'd wager that thing has mites!" he mocked.

Both men shared a moment of laughter that was cut short by another – yet this time – *thudding* knock at the door.

Edward took a quick stance, remembering that no more assistance had been called for. His heart raced at the thought of who it could be. He called out to the hallway for the culprit of the knock to speak up – no response.

He stepped outside and peered into the quiet hall, and as he looked left, he saw a door creeping closed, and through the gap there was a figure that seemed to be quickly fleeing. He pursued it down the flight of stairs and into the rowdy tavern hall.

Nothing suspicious at first, until across the room he caught a glance of two pearly eyes staring straight at him; eyes which he had seen before. Benjamin Blackwood?

Edward gave chase onto the street. There stood the being, unmoving in the middle of the road, just staring back at him.

Edward called to it, "Who are you? Show yourself!"

He gained more speed towards the dark figure who darted around the corner of the next tavern, its shadow cast up the wall from the moonlight.

Edward came out onto the main street revealing the shocking sight of Colonel Gürad and twenty of his men. He took to the wall for cover, beginning to peek around it to observe.

The Kingsguard began to enter buildings - taverns, smithies, butchers - in search of the disgraced officer and his accomplice. In quick judgement, Edward ran for it, back into the tavern, up the stairs, slamming the room door behind him. But the pirate was gone.

Edward laughed, letting his head fall softly into his hands as he contemplated what had happened.

"You fool," he whispered to himself.

A moment of clarity and regret, having just placed the whereabouts of the King's armoury into the palm of a pirate's hand, only to find he had hightailed it without him.

Peter barged through the door holding two huge glasses, completely unaware of what had happened.

"Are these not the biggest ales you have ever seen?" he said, so happily. "And who came knocking? I followed you down but you'd gone. Thought you might have had a change of heart!"

"Here's me thinking you were the one that had fled," said Edward, shaking his head. "Just looking for your next drink, ey?"

"Edward. I'm not sitting around here with nothing to drink."

"Then pass me one." A look of relief had settled on Edward's face.

"For the first time, Officer, you looked pleased to see me," said Peter, passing him the heavy glass.

"I'd use the word *pleased* lightly," said Edward. "I'm more relieved really, now I don't need to kill you."

They both laughed. Peter was still smiling, taking a few gulps of his ale. That was until Edward informed him that Colonel Gürad was lurking the streets below. Peter nearly choked. Edward blew out the lanterns and they both crept through the window onto the balcony. The rumblings of the Kingsguard began to build. They waited in the cold until the door to their room swung open. In walked a Kingsguard, peering around, clutching his musket in both hands, his gaze determined. To his eyes nothing seemed suspicious. The tavern landlord must have kindly kept his lips sealed. Edward and Peter were in luck.

Chapter 9
An Unwelcome Guest

It was the early hours of the next morning when Gürad returned to the capital – cold, tired, empty-handed and overwhelmingly displeased. He dismounted his horse in the palace courtyard and marched for Lord Harrington's council chambers where Captain Galaway was awaiting his own summons by the door.

"Captain Galaway? Are you sure that nephew of yours wasn't dreaming?" snapped Gürad. "We found *nothing* in Court Marsh."

"Well, Colonel. Either the pirate wasn't there or you didn't look hard enough," remarked Galaway. "And let's be clear. My nephew only informed us of which direction they fled. You chose to ride out to Court Marsh on a fool's errand as if the pirate would simply hide in plain sight in the next substantial town along the trade route!"

"No! You're mistaken, old man," said Gürad, gritting his teeth, edging closer. "I'm not searching for that pirate. I'm searching for that despicable worm you once called a comrade. And when I find him, you mark my words, I'll make him beg for the gallows."

"You do that, Eustace," said Galaway, his brows beginning to curl. "Now take a stride backwards, lad, or you'll regret it."

"Gentlemen, in here, right now!" snapped Harrington, as he stood peering from his doorway. "Any news, Colonel?"

"Nothing, my lord," said Gürad, a little shaken up. "My men searched Court Marsh and amongst all the nearby land. There was no trace."

"Have they vanished from all existence?" quipped Harrington, sarcasm not normally his way. "Leave us, Colonel, and do not return to me without them!"

Harrington was beaming around his cheeks in anger, taking deep breaths to control it. "Tell me, Wallace," he said, calming, as Gürad stormed out. "Did Edward Clavell ever show a side to himself you deemed at all rebellious?"

"Never ... he is an exemplary officer," said Galaway.

"He will be hanged for this. So, if there's anything you know, anything at all?" said Harrington.

The captain paused for a second or two, exhaling slowly through his nose. Something had come to him. "I've never had a reason to doubt his loyalty," he said, stroking his beard. "But I am certain something has his heart. I fear it has blinded his judgement."

Captain Galaway was ill at ease. He felt embarrassed and ashamed that one of his own officers had behaved in a way so detrimental to the integrity of his leadership.

"What do you think it could be?" asked Harrington.

"It seems a ridiculous thought, I know, but Edward wasn't the same since that night," said Galaway.

"What night?"

"The night we boarded the *Venturous*. He told me he'd found something, yet pulled only tobacco from his pocket. I just didn't think anything of it at the time. I might be a fool but perhaps my fondness for the lad has blurred my judgement too."

"I'm not following, Captain?"

"I'm saying, that whatever it was Edward found, he intended to tell me ... until the very last moment."

There came a heavy knock at the door. Harrington pulled it open, revealing one of his guards, pale in the face.

"You need to see this, my lord."

Harrington turned towards Galaway, confused. They both left together, following the guard back down the steps, through the main hall and into the courtyard.

Galaway focused his gaze into the distance to see a man standing amongst a parted crowd in the middle of the courtyard.

Clothed in black, from a feathered black hat to heavy boots. A face that was pitted and weathered. Hair that was brown and straw-like and a messy, greying beard that scarcely covered his cheeks.

The man walked towards them, meeting Harrington halfway – who by now had realised something wasn't right.

"Who are you?" he asked. "And why are you here?"

The man spoke firmly and with an unhinged smirk.

"Who I am is no business of yours, old man," he said. "I merely request that you grant me a few moments of your time."

"Forgive me. I cannot help but think you might be a pirate," said Harrington.

The crowds around were silent as they looked upon the conversing duo. The strange quiet in the yard and a hundred pointing muskets gave Harrington his suspicions.

"Dreadful of you to assume such a thing, Augustus," said the man.

"You know my name?"

"Yes, I do. And we can become equally acquainted if your men would kindly lower their weapons."

"We give no such courtesy to pirates."

"Perhaps I haven't made myself clear enough," said the man. "We will speak in private, or the order will be given for my men to discharge our cannons upon your precious city; and you will watch as the streets flow with the blood of its people."

As if on cue, a guard ran in through the gates, startled and stumbling.

"My lord!" he screamed, almost falling. "Four ships on the lake; pirates if I've ever seen em!"

"Kingsguard!" called Harrington. A command that triggered ten greycoats to form a tight wall behind the pirate. "Escort our unwelcome guest inside the palace, immediately."

The guards did as commanded, clinching both the pirate's arms roughly, forcing him from the view of the people to the inside of the palace.

The towering entrance door was slammed behind them, the boom echoing through the main hall; a room so decadent, for a split second the unwelcome guest lost his smirk.

The whole place was made of solid white stone, but the ceiling was painted exquisitely with all the memories of Graelind's history; the ground beneath their feet a sea of detailed marble patterns wonderfully arranged.

About the hall's entire perimeter stood archways beneath which many alleys ran off – and beside each of them stood statues of warriors, clad in amour beset with thousands of gems. The pirate was beyond impressed.

Lord Harrington came charging up behind them, as the Kingsguard saw the pirate to his council chambers atop the branching stairway.

"Thank you, kindly," said the man, grinning proudly as they were left alone. "I've come for a prisoner you hold, Lord Harrington."

"We hold many prisoners in this city, pirate," said Harrington closing the door.

"Yet only one of them is of any interest to me. His name is Peter Beaumont, he was captured aboard the *Venturous*."

"He isn't here."

"Hand him over, and there needn't be any trouble here!" snapped the man, growing angrier.

"Even if we did hold him prisoner in this city, it's *me* he will answer to," growled Harrington, pointing at himself. "Not some rotten soul that's clambered his way onto our land. Who are you for that matter?"

The pirate smiled and slowly walked around Lord Harrington. "That's none of your concern," he said. "Now bring the lad to me and I'll be on my way."

"I've already told you; he isn't here."

"But he was ... I know it."

"How so?"

"We were a mile north of the *Venturous* when she was toppled and torched. One of my own fleet, she was. I'm sure the officers thought they'd efficiently dealt with everyone on board. But a boy was hidden in Captain Delaine's cabin. We found him almost dead. He told us what he saw."

"Tell me what it is you want with Peter Beaumont?"

"Captain Delaine and his crew were bringing him to me," said the pirate. "He was in possession of an item of extreme value, and I know it didn't go down with the ship. One of the *Baliant*'s officers is now the keeper of said item."

"The lad escaped. Yesterday, in fact."

"From the Plummet? Ha! How many guards had to die for that?"

"None ... as a matter of fact."

"Always was a sneaky little bastard," said the pirate, shaking his head.

"My men will find him," said Harrington. "Then you can watch if you like, when we hang him from the *Baliant*'s yardarm."

"You mistake this man for someone I regard, Lord Harrington. The man is a thief and a traitor. His death will mean less than nothing to me. I merely sought to question him."

"Do thieves and traitors get off so lightly amongst your ranks, pirate?" said Harrington, smiling, knowing good and well that Peter Beaumont was a dead man walking. The pirate's face was blank.

"Like I said, the pirate isn't here," said Harrington. "Now, I'm sure you don't need me to show you the door?"

"Well, if this is truly the case, I just have one more question. The officer who stole that particular item I was talking about; well, I'd like to request he return it to me. Then, you have my word, my lord, that I will take my ships abroad and never return."

"I'm not sure you understand me. I do not strike bargains with pirates," said Harrington. "Nevertheless, it has come to light that the officer who appears to have stolen your item, was the same officer who aided the pirate's escape. He will also be hanged for his treason. Now allow me to make myself very clear! We have of our own cannons, pirate, and unless you wish to watch as your ships are blown to the deep, I suggest you leave!"

The man's face grimaced angrily. "I'll be sure to kill the officer for you, if our paths ever cross," he snarled back.

Words that quickly cut the conversation stone dead.

Harrington watched on as the man flung open the door, charged down the stairway and screamed at a guard, who with a grimace, opened the main gate to the courtyard. Harrington stood boiling on the balcony with nothing but a cold lump in his throat. Colonel Gürad burst into the main hall. The Lord-Commander of the Kingsguard screamed at the height of his lungs. "Eustace! Here, now!"

Gürad joined him on the balcony. "My lord? When ... who ... what did I miss? There are four ships on the lake, my lord. I came straight back once I heard the commotion. Who was that man?"

"I fear I've heard of this scoundrel, Colonel," said Harrington, quite shocked. "I had always imagined he would have the head of a snake! The evil they call the Murderous! Find Peter Beaumont and Officer Clavell before he does. Let's make certain we have something to bargain with should he return."

"Yes, my lord," said Gürad, leaving immediately.

Harrington turned to his advisor who had ascended the stairs. "Find out how four pirate ships made it past Byhollow unscathed!"

Chapter 10
The Armoury

Peter wasn't fazed by today's undertakings, that was just the pirate in him. After all, he was facing almost certain death whichever way he looked at it, so, *what's the difference,* he thought.

The armoury was to be quietly parted with the King's crown, so to acquire the Black Diamond from its helm. They packed up their belongings in the late afternoon and left the town of Court Marsh, hastily slipping through the dirty streets to catch a wagon back to Summer's Reach.

A trip to the capital, that this time would cost the inflated sum of eight silver spinnels, for the driver knew well enough who the two of them were, from his own deductions. Words travel fast. Yet he wasn't about to allow the search for the two fugitives to be brought to a successful conclusion, or aid it in any such a way; especially when the sum of eight spinnels demanded was bumped to ten for the promise of tight lips.

Edward sat opposite Peter with a heavy feeling in his stomach, almost like he had swallowed an anchor. It felt tangled, deep in his gut and up through his chest to where the knot choked his throat.

The wagon pulled onto a wide river barge, an array of which scattered the entire length of the Green Hollow River and could easily take a horse wagon, providing the water remained relatively still.

They disembarked after the short journey across. Peter sat calmly. His newly shaven face beaming red from the wind that rushed through the wagon as they made great time to Summer's Reach.

They drew up to a stable just outside the city limits. A safe bet, considering how imperative it was to go on without being seen. Edward shuddered at the thought of a noose being forced over his head. He doubted he'd ever been so daring or more precisely ... damn stupid!

After unloading the wagon of their belongings, they tipped their caps to the driver and dropped down a banking, out of sight. This would lead them into the forest, east of the city.

Even an officer wouldn't fair too well trying to enter the palace after nightfall, and the light was fading, so time was now precious.

Peter took the uniform from Edward's proffered satchel and quickly donned it. It just so happened to fit like a glove to a hand. A garment that he had never been so privileged to have worn before and it took him a little while to stop admiring himself. Edward reminded him, "Don't you dare get comfortable in that! Now, wait for me here. I shouldn't be too long."

"There she is, ey?" said Peter, looking over onto the lake where the *Baliant* sat at anchor. "You sure those keys will be on board?"

"I haven't been sure about a damn thing ever since I met you, Peter," replied Edward, plotting the easiest path through the trees. "My keys will be hung up on the porthole in my cabin, all being well."

"Very well then, let's be getting to it."

Edward slipped through the trees, out into the open, pricking up his collar and tipping down his cap – a disguise only to anyone who didn't know of him.

Now the plan had begun, Edward started to realise how foolish he might have been. Stealing a wherry from right under the harbourmaster's nose might well prove to be far trickier than he had imagined. Peter suggested simply paying the man off but it posed too great a risk. Edward was to use the art of sneaking. "More of a job for a pirate," he kept muttering to himself.

Sneak he did, quietly along the lakeside, careful not to rouse any suspicions.

Edward untied an old wherry he found bobbing by the decking, then gingerly stepped aboard, thrust a paddle into the water and began to row. The harbourmaster, clearly not up to the task, sat with his face buried between the pages of a book, occasionally lifting an apple to his mouth for a bite.

Edward boarded the *Baliant*, the sound of his footsteps reverberating through her hull. He flinched for a second as the subtle sound of chatting passed through his ears.

A light flickered, a small lantern. It was James Percy sitting beside a woman.

They were laughing together, thoroughly engaged and wouldn't have heard his approach.

Edward ever so slightly peeked from his hiding place and gazed upon the smiling faces of the couple. He smiled, turning away. Maybe it was the first moment he had thought of just ending this whole thing. He thought about Charlotte. Should he turn himself over? No. The thought of such was quickly set aside as he made for his cabin. It was too late to back out now.

There they were; the rusty effects of a turnkey, hanging from the latch on the porthole of his cabin. He snatched them away, placing them inside his jacket.

James and the woman sat unaware as Edward crept past them once again, down into the wherry. After a few minutes of tiresome rowing, he bumped into the shallow ground near the forest. Peter came over to lend him a hand.

"Well, that was easy," said Peter, grinning.

"Yes, without a hitch," said Edward, finding his feet. "Now, here you go, be off with you. I'll be right here when you get back."

Edward flicked through the bunch to acquire the correct one, never did any escape his memory. Each key embellished in a story he never forgot.

"I can't help but think it'll be my demise I find in that armoury," said Peter.

"Worry not, my new pirate friend, it's only the gallows that awaits. Anyway, if we're caught, they'll hang me right next to you - if that makes you feel any better?"

"Not at all," replied Peter, as he left for the palace.

The palace of the King. A huge fortress surrounded by thirty-foot-high walls, guarded and armed.

Peter Beaumont, the pirate clad in military grey, dreadfully ill-equipped for such a daring and reckless undertaking, stepped through the gates into the courtyard, hoping his ruse would be successful.

He walked for a while, searching for a place to lay low until nightfall. Guards prowled the whole place, various dignitaries nodded in his direction as he went by. "What the hell am I doing?" he whimpered through his teeth.

Time was running eagerly by when he found himself looking upon a stable. It was dark and broad and full of hay - perfect for hiding. That is where he waited, until the night consumed the palace and all but the guards on the outer walls had left.

The palace gates were locked tight with long iron bars that stretched all the way across them. Peter closed his eyes, took a giant, calming breath and longed for good fortune. Across the way, the King's Unison towered into the night sky. A huge mass of stone that protruded from the water that encircled it. Upon the stone stood two giant King's embracing hands in a show of unity between the nations of Graelind and Karlün. A celebration of past troubles now forgotten.

Peter lay in wait for the planned distraction. The guards who were scanning the scene saw what seemed to be flames flickering on the lake. Edward had set the wherry ablaze to give Peter the precious seconds he needed to make it to the monument. The time had come.

Peter set off, keeping low, moving swiftly, having already dropped the grey coat behind him.

The murky water was bitterly sharp against his skin and he nearly bellowed a great yelp as he quietly submerged.

He swam with desperate strokes of his arms and kicks of his feet, feeling his way to the bottom where the opening was situated. At first he couldn't find it, the visibility was non-existent and the cold was crushing him. He rubbed his hands across the stone desperately, reaching in all directions. He was about to resurface for a breath when his hand rushed forward into nothing but water. Finally, he had found it. He pulled himself inside, knowing he only had a few more seconds before his lungs gave out. Peter kicked off the ground and sprung out into a chamber. The air was thin and rancid, but when he breathed it in, the feeling was pure ecstasy. He caught his breath, tucking back the strands of wet hair that draped his face. His eyes adjusted to the darkness as he treaded water there.

There was a soft, orange hue to his right, beyond what looked like a ledge. He climbed onto it and looked down over the brink. The passageway Edward had spoken of lay beneath him.

Peter let his body hang from the ledge, then he dropped into the passageway. The entire length of it was lit with lanterns. He felt the warmth on his skin but he still shivered frantically.

The armoury door was in sight; a coat of arms carved into the stone shone in silver and gold detail. He pulled out the key from his pocket and walked eagerly towards it. The water fell from his soaked garments as he slid the key into the lock, twisting it in a half motion. He pushed open the door to reveal more gold and jewels than he had ever seen in his life. Sapphires, emeralds, silver spinnels and gold chalices. Shields of steel and swords from past wars and ages. Heaps of diamonds brighter than stars, boxes brimming with pearls and shelf upon shelf of other treasures he couldn't even begin to name.

The royal regalia stood assembled at the very centre.

"In a crown only fit for a king," he whispered, lifting off the golden headpiece, pulling it close to his face. Nothing. It was empty, save for the twenty red rubies that encircled its golden rim. This one moment that had been lingering so heavily in his thoughts was destroyed. Yet as he scoured the crown further, his eyes fixed upon some words that were engraved into the gold.

In the dark, the forest breathes.
Above the soil, beneath the leaves.
Ensnaring light, concealing thieves.
The jackal.

He stuffed the crown into his satchel and made for the door. Then, shutting it behind him, he used the key to lock it. "Like I was never here," he whispered. The plan was almost complete. With the crown acquired, he just needed to escape unseen. But there was a problem. He had walked only ten strides before a Kingsguard stepped out from the adjacent door unexpectedly and locked eyes with him. The satchel that held the crown was swung from Peter's shoulder as it struck the guard across the face. A quick reaction, the only one that came to him, the only one that made sense. It offered him precious seconds.

Reaching the ledge, Peter tried heaving himself into the chamber. The guard grabbed his leg as he wriggled to his getaway, writhing at his clothes to try and drag him down. Peter threw another instinctive strike, yet this time it was his boot the now frantic guard endured to the face. The guard dropped to the floor beneath, landing with a heavy, blood-curdling thud, cracking his skull on the stone. He was unconscious. More precious seconds gained, but was the guard now dead? It looked that way having seen his head hit the stone the way it did. The plan was ruined. Surely more guards had heard the encounter. Someone would stumble across this mess and Peter would be locked in the palace when the hunt began.

He let go of the ledge and dropped into the passageway; the guard unmoving on the ground, the blood pooled around his head. He looked to be breathing, to Peter's amazement.

Stealing the clothes from his back, Peter left the man half naked against the stone. The coat was of course grey, this time with golden buttons. The trousers the colour of sand. The bandolier was a brown leather, holding a pistol and two daggers and the hat was peaked in feathers. The musket he acquired. The boots he left behind.

This was his only chance. He burst through the same door from which the guard came, hoping it would lead him out into the open air. But Peter had found himself lost within a series of passageways he had no idea how to navigate. So, he just picked one, and at the very end of it he came to a structure of steel, like a cage door, that reached from ceiling to floor. The lock was open.

Quietly swinging open the bars, Peter continued, when by a stroke of luck, he emerged into the courtyard.

At each of the palace's four sides there were steps up to the walls. Heavily guarded. Some noticed him, but the disguise seemed to be working.

"There's an intruder in the armoury!" he bellowed at the height of his lungs. "There's an intruder in the armoury!"

The guards came running swiftly by and didn't even offer him a second look. Peter fell in behind them and after a few painstaking seconds he disappeared into the shadows out of sight. The plan was working.

His chance had arrived, so he took it. His knees were now trembling, his brow dripping in sweat and filthy water. He dropped the musket and made a run for it, leaping up the steps to the top of the wall. His only option was to jump off. He would surely break every single bone in his shivering body, but it was either that or the gallows.

"Stop!" came a desperate voice. Peter halted; a sudden spike of fear hit him in his heart. A few paces along the wall stood a Kingsguard.

"You need not die today, guard. Please, allow me to pass. I beg of you," said Peter, his voice breaking.

"Not as long as I bear the mark of Graelind!" answered the man, his pride oozing from him.

"Very well."

Peter, shaking with panic, took the pistol from his bandolier and discharged a single shot that split the guard's chest.

"I didn't mean for this. I'm sorry!" he gasped in horror, watching as the man dropped to his knees, clutching the wound that would kill him.

Peter jumped, crashing through a stable roof, landing all twisted. The air left his lungs and he gripped his body in both hands, suppressing his screams. He heaved his chest to draw in the air before taking a stance.

Stuffing the grey coat in the hay, he limped off into the city streets, as quickly and inconspicuously as he could.

Chaos ensued. The alarms sounded out around the palace. A robbery turned sour. At least one Kingsguard now dead.

Chapter 11
Two Shires

"Peter, you damn fool! What the hell have you done?" Edward was furious beyond measure having heard the alarm.

"I never meant for this to happen!" explained Peter, struggling to speak. "I just …"

"I heard a gunshot!"

"I had no choice, Edward, it was me or the guard!"

"You shot a Kingsguard?" blasted Edward, who was pacing between the trees boiling with rage.

"I'm sorry! What would you have me do, let him gun *me* down? I'd do the same thing again to spare my own life."

"That's because you know nothing of morality; you're just a filthy pirate!" screamed Edward.

Peter bawled back at him, "Morality? Coming from a disgraced officer who had everything? You know nothing of the suffering I have endured. I have forever been fighting for my life!"

A noise came from the trees. Boots heavily trampling the fallen branches. The hunt was on. "Run!"

They set off at pace and escaped the forest with the guards still tight to their tails. A wall of stones, adjacent to the field they were now crossing, was leapt - two desperate men with their lives hanging in the balance, sprinting with everything they had.

Finally, a break in the trees became clear when the crest of the next field was passed over. Never looking back. Shrouded by fear. Whistling over the swaying grass. Musket fire tainting the calm of the night.

Peter grimaced with each stride, his legs searing in pain, tingling against his soaked trousers. They came to a small river barge, the man who handled it was nodding beside a fire, blind drunk by the look of it - empty ale bottles scattered around his feet. The men pushed off from the edge and slowly floated into the darkness. The Kingsguard surrounded the drunkard who jerked into motion. He was clearly missing a barge but the man had no recollection of who had taken it. The dark, moonless night made the water indistinguishable from the sky. Edward and Peter were out of sight.

Shivering, they arrived in Deepmont after battling the cold contours of the hills, glistening in sweat that the winter wind chilled as it blew over their skin.

"Listen to me, Peter, there are two horses in a stable at the other side of the village. We need to be swift and we mustn't be recognised. We'll ride to Court Marsh."

"There isn't anyone around here familiar with me, I wouldn't imagine," said Peter, his hands on his knees, gasping his words. "I need warmth, Edward."

"Just keep your head down. I cannot be seen," said Edward. "There are folks in this village who know my face. Let's hope the cover of night disguises us. We cannot light a fire here for that exact reason. Here, put on your jacket."

They reached the stable, where the two shires stood lapping up water from a trough beside them.

"We need to saddle them, and quickly," said Edward in a quiet voice.

The horses were mounted and with a click of their heels, they burst through the stable doors and out on to the village road. As quick as they came, Edward and Peter disappeared into the night, leaving the host of Kingsguards chasing nothing but shadows.

Court Marsh stood nine miles northeast. There wasn't a second to spare. Peter tried to explain everything in detail, yet Edward never spoke a word the entire way, he only scowled in disdain.

Back in Court Marsh only provisions were gathered. A roll of sleeping furs for Peter: water, whiskey, biscuits, a couple of tins of gunpowder and a small iron pot that Peter had stolen from who knows where.

He met with Edward beside the horses.

"A guard needn't have died today, Peter," he heard spoken from behind the beast. There was dismay in Edward's voice.

Peter had wondered when he might speak up.

"If I can live with the guilt, then I'm sure you can live with the grief, Edward. It was me or him ... and I chose me!"

Edward scowled and packed the remainder of his belongings into the saddlebag before jumping on. Court Marsh was then a memory.

Their horses trotted alongside one another. The men hadn't spoken for an hour when at last the excruciating silence was broken.

"Are you going to show me the crown?" asked Edward finally, his grimace just visible now the moon had peered around the clouds. Peter reached into his satchel then handed it over. After a few more silent moments, Edward pulled back on his horse to a halt.

"The Jackal?" he whispered.

"What is it?" asked Peter.

"I've heard of this creature."

"What do you think it means?"

"I can't be sure … but we're going to find out."

"You say, *creature*?" said Peter, digesting the words. "Why does that unnerve me somewhat?"

"If my memory serves me correctly and I recall the tales true enough, then yes, you should be unnerved."

Peter shuddered. "Friend or foe?" he asked, trying to act as calm as Edward, when really he was beginning to regret his own part in this adventure.

"I wouldn't bet on either," said Edward.

"Where do we find this … creature?"

"Somewhere out near Bidle's Edge," said Edward. "We'll set up camp here for the night and head out in the morning. I'll start a fire."

Edward jumped off his horse and secured him to a tree, running his hand across its nose and behind the ear.

"This is a good horse," he said heartily.

"I wish I could say the same about mine," laughed Peter, jumping off. "Might well be the most ignorant beast I've ever come across."

"Perhaps if you plugged his nose, he would think more of you," said Edward, enjoying his comment.

Edward started preparing the fire, quite proud of his last quip. The two shires were restless on their ropes. Peter let them loose and they both sauntered off down to the waterside for a drink.

"For the love of the sea, Edward, I'm freezing here."

"Be quiet, I'm almost there."

"I'm going to die in these woods, aren't I?"

"If only you would keep your mouth shut for a moment, I'd be able to think straight," snapped Edward before blowing gently into the kindling; the small flame bursting into a big one, illuminating the trees.

"Shame there's nothing to eat around here," said Peter, tucking up near the heat, huddled inside his sleeping furs. "I'd give anything for some roast pig."

"Then you should make good use of that pistol tomorrow," said Edward.

"This thing saved my life, Edward. No better use for it!"

Peter reached over to his satchel and lifted out a green bottle, along with a pan and two mugs. "I'll get some whiskey on, that ought to warm us up."

"Where did you get those?"

"A stall back in Court Marsh, they won't miss em."

Edward shook his head, his blood still boiled to whistling. Peter felt the sharp sting of Edward's resentment as it manifested itself in every single word. Peter felt ashamed of himself. He had taken a life, and an innocent one at that. Never had he slumped to such lows, but what choice did he have?

Edward stopped dead. "Peter, my coat, where is it?"

"What coat?"

"My uniform, tell me you have it?"

"I was hardly in a position to go back for it!"

"Well, that's just wonderful, isn't it?" said Edward, bitingly. "Harrington's men will know it was us, should it be found."

"We cannot change what's happened, Edward," said Peter. "We're going to hang nevertheless and you know it! You can add impersonating a Kingsguard to *my* list of crimes."

"The thought of dying alongside a pirate truly haunts me," said Edward in a long and sighing tone.

Peter sipped his warm whiskey, shaking his head. Edward's remark had cut him a little.

"This Jackal creature, it can help us, you think?" he said.

"Hard to say. I don't suppose we'll be welcomed with much hospitality."

"How so?"

"You try living alone with only the rats for company!"

"Sounds like a mad man to me, this Jackal! How are you so familiar anyway?"

"I've heard a tale or two through the years. And I'm pretty sure the Jackal is a woman."

"Strange name for a woman, strange name for a man! The *Jackal*; a bit eerie if you ask me. I don't like the sound of it. Yet, I'm sure I've seen stranger things and made acquaintance with stranger folk on my travels."

"I wouldn't count on it, if I were you. Now, perhaps another whiskey, I don't wish to remember this day."

Peter swallowed his last drops, savouring the taste. "Yes, its mind-numbing qualities are most satisfying, but we mustn't waste it all in one day. Even a day as hopeless as this one." Peter stood up and dropped the bottle next to his satchel, walked over to his horse and started to rummage around what he had stored by the saddle. A long sharp blade with a strong wooden hilt is what he withdrew.

"I hope you never need to use this, Edward, but may it fare you well in time to come." He placed the blade in Edward's hand.

"What's this?"

"I noticed yours was missing ... after the chase."

Edward looked down at his sheath – it was empty – then turned the blade in his hands to look over it.

"I suppose you stole this too?"

"Spare me your insults for just a moment, would you? I made it myself."

"You?"

"Indeed, the pommel at least. I'm no blacksmith, but I can work timber into some fine shapes. Found it in need of a good stoning and I fixed up the hilt; thought it might come in handy some day."

"This is some blade," said Edward sitting up straight, pointing it out in front of him. "Thank you, Peter."

Chapter 12
Bidle's Edge

The next morning dawned bright; the journey to Bidle's Edge the day's matter at hand. It was a short ride east of eleven or so miles, into the land of caverns, where the town sat beneath the ground in a huge gaping expanse. The town was once a mine and the cavities that had been chipped away over time were now inhabited by settlers from all around. They carved out their own homes in the walls, and when each fire roared, the mine lit up like a giant beehive, and each glowing domicile could be accessed from a spiralling stairway that jutted out from the rock face. It was spectacular.

In all colonies, there is a queen, and Bidle's Edge was no different. Her name was Lena. She sat at the head of the council table, or at least around the campfire, where all was discussed regarding her ladyship's town in the ground.

Upon their arrival, later that day, it took a few knocks on the gate before a pleasant-faced man poked his head from a hatch in the door.

"Good afternoon! How may we be of service to you?" he asked heartily, with the kindest voice Edward had ever heard.

"A place to sleep and some warm food, if you would be so kind, sir?" said Edward.

"Five spinnels each and we'll make sure you're all cosy, don't you worry about a thing. Just tell us yer names," said the man, letting them in.

"My name's Edward, sir, and he's … gone."

Peter had rushed straight over to the huge fire that blazed in the centre of the town. His ice-like fingers were thrust in front of the flames.

"His name is Peter."

"Ah! Excellent! I'll see to it you're looked after, sir. Please, go and get warm."

The gatekeeper returned with two bowls of pottage. He passed them over; the meat-scented vapour drifting skyward, arriving under Peter's nose, urging a sense of vitality into him. Along with a small loaf of bread the gatekeeper had wrapped in a little handkerchief, the men wolfed down the bowls in complete silence. Once they had eaten, they were shown to their own 'home' in the wall – be it only for one night. In fact, it was a very comfortable spot to stay, truly a far cry from last night's woodland slumber. Peter beamed at the thought of the night ahead.

Edward took off his jacket and folded it neatly beneath his head. He slumped into relaxation until the silence was disturbed by a quiet sound coming towards them. The gatekeeper with a delivery of wine in a woven basket; a small bottle and two glasses that chimed together with each step he took.

"Here we go, men!"

"Please, sir. Tell me your name so I can thank you properly?" said Edward.

"My friends call me Obi, sir, so Obi's just fine."

"Would you sit with us a minute?" asked Edward.

"I suppose I could rest my legs for a short while," said Obi, filling up the glasses. The old man wore a fur-lined hat that stretched down over his ears and was tied under his chin with two strings – a pair of leather gloves hung around his neck. He looked to have a permanent happy glint in his eyes; Peter wondered if he had ever seen a man look so chipper.

"How did your people come to live here?" asked Peter, admiring the place.

"As a matter of fact, they're not my people, sir," said Obi. "The kind folks just took me in when I needed it the most. This place has been our home for ten or more years now."

Edward took a sip of his wine. He recognised it from the very first second it washed over his tongue – and that's not all he recognised. "Obi, who's that lady down there?" he asked.

Obi turned his head to see. "Why, that's Lena Hoster," he said. "Lady Lena, to us."

"What's she doing?"

"She helps people; cares for them. Without Lena around, I doubt Bidle's Edge would be quite the same."

Edward stood, then walked down to the fireside to greet her, still holding his wine. Lady Lena had her back turned as she moseyed about her daily business. Edward fixed his mouth to speak.

"Born from the soil of Graelind," he began with a smile. "A fruit so pure, that should it ever pass the lips of a common man, it would save him from his past and promise him his future."

"A notion that is utterly false," said Lena, without moving. "But it makes a bloody fine wine!"

"How are you, Lena?"

Lena jerked around in hopeful anticipation. "Edward?" she gasped, lost for anything else to say. She rushed over to embrace him. "How is my sister?"

"Charlotte is well," said Edward. "It's good to see you, Lena."

"What are you doing here?"

"It's a long story."

"Well, this is quite the surprise! Follow me, let's talk!"

Lena walked Edward through the town; the officer could see how the people admired her as she offered out words of comfort and kindness to each family they passed.

"So," said Edward, stepping through an opening that blossomed into a large room; the warmth within kissed his cheeks. "A lot seems to have changed since last we saw one another. It appears you have quite the influence around here?"

Lena took a seat and brushed her gown over her knees. The room they were now sitting in was lit with candelabras that sat upon any surface big enough to balance one.

"I just help them, that's all," she said. "I became a part of their people fifteen years ago, after I left Summer's Reach. We didn't live here back then, of course. Fort Gaze was our home, but after what happened we had to flee - eventually ending up here."

"It's some place!" said Edward, staring around.

For a room carved from rock, with no true sense of symmetry or definition at all, it was really charming. Take away the modest arrangement of furniture and candles, and you were left with a black hole of nothingness. Yet with it, it was perfect; elegant in ways Edward couldn't quite put his finger on.

"It is some place, indeed," said Lena. "Now, tell me, what brings you here?"

Edward swallowed the whole truth. "I'm doing what's right, or at least I think I am," he said, looking through the opening at the huge fire that cracked and spat in the town's centre.

"Where's Charlotte?"

"Back home. She knows the reason I had to leave."

"I don't know if I dare ask," said Lena, sceptically.

"It's better if you remain none the wiser, I'd say. That way you needn't lie if anyone comes asking." Edward quietly tittered nervously; he had already said too much.

"You wouldn't be doing anything foolish now, would you?"

"Some might say so."

"And for what cause, exactly?"

"A better future for my country, all being well."

"No harm in that, is there?" said Lena.

"You would think not."

"Whatever it is you're up to, Edward, my sister best be safe in all this – that's all I can say. Anyway, I'm sorry; it's not my place to pry. I lost the privilege of opinion regarding my sister and yourself many years ago. However, I'm sure you can understand. After all, you're rubbing shoulders with pirates. I'm bound to ask questions, am I not?"

"How did you know?" asked Edward tensely.

"Obi has quite the talent for picking out the particularities of one's character," said Lena. "Although, he says that he's never seen a pirate like him before. You make certain that man brings no harm to my people, Edward! The guards are watching. Now, shall we drink? I suggest a tickle more of the Deepmont draught?"

"Please," said Edward, thankful the talk had turned. "Lena? What happened with Harris?"

"How did you know?"

"Obi. He called you by your maiden name."

Lena paused the pouring of wine and squirmed at Edward's question. "The matrimonial ties that once bound us were no longer strong enough," she said sadly, finishing the top-ups. "I don't really want to discuss it, if that's–"

"Say no more," said Edward, taking back his glass. He changed the subject.

"No matter where it was in the whole world that I stumble across it, I could never mistake the taste of Deepmont's finest."

"Nor should you drink too much of it," said Lena. "Perhaps your friend over there would fare well off that advice."

"He's not a friend; more of a chance encounter, if the truth be told."

"I feel that's the *only* truth being told here, Edward," said Lena, curling her brows questioningly.

"Like the matrimonial ties that bind?" said Edward. "You're a very poor liar, Lena, rather like your sister."

Lena smiled. "Very well then," she said, lowering her defences. "Harris found himself another woman."

"I'm sorry to hear it."

"Don't be, the man was a scoundrel."

Edward watched Peter, who had sneaked past some of the locals to acquire a goblet more of wine.

"We have a different idea regarding the definition of a scoundrel," he said.

Edward and Lena talked long into the night. Lena would occasionally drop a suspicious remark into the conversation but Edward stood firm in keeping his mouth shut. Eventually, Lena seemed to relax and spare him any more officious attempts to get him to spill, settling for the simple talk of old times and the very well received good tidings regarding her little sister.

"Well, Lena," said Edward, noticing he had been sat talking to her for hours now. "I should head back and make the most of a warm place to sleep."

"You're most welcome here, Edward," she replied. "If you need anything, just ask. Obi doesn't get much sleep these days. He'll be around most of the night should you need him."

"Thank you, Lena, for your people's kindness. Let's not leave it fifteen years next time, ey? Charlotte would love to see you. What happened, is in the past."

Lena nodded stoically. "You're right, Edward," she said. "In the past."

Edward returned to find Peter in deep conversation with Obi, who was now sharing a glass with him. The gatekeeper had removed his fur hat, his almost entirely bold head shining in the firelight.

"Well, gentlemen," said the old man standing up, surprisingly nimbly for a man of his age. "I'll leave you to your night's sleep. Be sure to ask if you need anything, anything at all. I don't get much sleep these days. I'll be wandering about, keeping the place going."

Edward took a seat beside Peter as Obi slipped away.

"Found a friend, have we?" asked Edward.

"I'm fond of the better conversation, as it goes!" said Peter casually.

"Then allow me to oblige ... I've a question I'd like to ask."

"Feel free," said Peter, adjusting his jacket pillow.

"How exactly did you escape?" said Edward, quietly. Peter could tell Edward had been holding this back for some time now.

"I'm a pirate, how do you think?" Peter joked.

Edward gave him a stern look. "Listen to me!" he snapped. "This isn't a game to me, Peter. Tell me how many?"

"How many what?"

"How many guards had to die? Like I said before, no man has ever escaped the Plummet and I can't fathom how you could have done it. How many?"

"None. I scuttled past them like a little mouse. No harm done. I've been told on more than one occasion that I'm a sneaky little bastard."

"You must take me for a fool, man. Tell me, and tell it true!" snapped Edward.

"Alright, alright! I gave one of them a bump on his head, that's all."

"You'd have me believe anything."

"Well, that's the story, whether you like it or not."

"There's not a story to be told without an ending, Peter!"

"I can assure you, Edward, that not a single guard ceases to breathe because of my escape. Truth be told, you're beginning to piss me off a bit with all the accusations. How about a little trust here, ey?"

"I put my trust in you once before, Peter, and the Kingsguard are now a man light."

"Do you think I don't feel the pain of my actions, Edward? Tell me, have you ever found yourself in such peril where you're forced to make a decision quicker than the blink of an eye? Yes, I'm sure you have. I can almost guarantee your conscience will be stained by one of those decisions, somewhere down the line, you self-righteous prick!"

Edward stared into the near distance and gulped. He had struck a nerve and now a desolate gloom had befallen the space between them.

"Do you have any family?" he asked, changing the subject.

Peter laughed sarcastically. "You've found a little compassion in there, have you? I'm shocked; it didn't take as long as one might expect to chisel such an emotion off your stone-cold heart!"

Edward recoiled. "Peter, I'm sorry, I just–"

"I'm suffering inside, Edward! Although I might not show it, I'm suffering! You judge like you had no part to play in it. We stole the King's crown; what did you expect would happen when I got caught? A ceremonial send-off? Here you are, Peter, take the priceless crown of the King. Do come back when you please and feel free to steal more of our precious shit."

"Have you finished?" asked Edward.

"As a matter of fact, yes I have!"

Edward took a moment to think. *Time to swallow your pride, you stubborn fool,* he thought. "I'm sorry, Peter. You're right. I knew the risks. I must be the most foolish idiot in Graelind, and to blame you is wrong. Now I'm certain this was all a huge mistake. I should never have started this."

The desolate gloom now a swirling storm of ambivalence, Edward rubbed his eyes, his shoulders dropped. A silence bursting with anxiety that seemed to go on for hours without rest. Too many emotions had been laid out on the table in one swoop and Edward found that hard to deal with. Peter shook his head, then proceeded to stare blankly at the stone ceiling under which he laid. The patterns scored into it grabbed his attention for a brief moment before Edward readied himself to leave, the officer was agitated at his own inability to rewind time and altogether change the events of the last few days. Edward concluded that his apology clearly didn't cut it, and maybe it was best he left Peter alone with his own thoughts.

"I have three older sisters," said Peter, finally breaking the tension. "I'm not too sure where they are now – which is a crying shame. My mother and father have both passed on, sadly."

Edward sat back down, relieved.

"A lady?" he asked, watching as a gentle smile crept upon Peter's lips.

"There was this one lady," said Peter. "She wasn't from Little Brace. She used to sneak into town on the back of the wagon her father would ride in. A farmer he was. The first second I saw her, my eyes lit up; I could feel them widen but I couldn't help it. This one day, I managed to find the courage to talk to her and we were friends from then on. We'd play tricks on the folks in town. We'd run the fields and splash the streams; there wasn't a tree in the entire forest we didn't climb together. But, one day, she didn't come back – and that was it."

"You've never tried to find her?"

"I've never stopped."

Edward smiled sadly. "What was her name?"

"Elizabeth. I just called her Lizzie, for short."

"Maybe you might see her again, someday?"

"I hope so," said Peter.

Edward shuffled and laid back on his elbows. "My father died at sea and I'm sure my mother died with him," he said. "She was never quite the same after that, spending the remaining years of her life pretty miserable. She hardly spoke, hardly ate. She simply grieved too much." Edward pondered over this. "I have a son named Jack. He and his wife had a daughter a few years ago but I've hardly been around to watch her grow. To tell you the truth, I've never really been there. I can't tell you how much that hurts to say out loud. In my defence, my duties have always come first and they no longer live in the city."

"Any siblings?" asked Peter.

"My brother's name is Arthur, but he's gone, too. Battle of Fort Gaze."

"And your wife's name?"

"Charlotte."

Peter sighed.

"What lives we have lived, ey?" he said, the sigh continuing. "Cooped up on ships with nothing but the vast blue of the oceans around us. We just fought for two different causes."

"Well, we're fighting for the same one now, Peter. Get a good night's sleep in," said Edward. "I've no doubt you'll be feeling sorry for yourself in the morning. I saw you sneaking that wine."

"Ey! It's been a very long time since I was afforded such luxuries," said Peter defensively. "I was only making the most of them. Anyway, sleep well, Edward, and let's hope breakfast comes quick; I can feel my stomach rumbling already."

Peter wriggled into his sleeping furs, then paused, having thought of one last question. "Tell me, Edward. What was it you retrieved from the armoury all those years ago? You know, the family heirloom?"

"A ruby necklace."

Chapter 13

The House of the Jackal

Early the next morning, as the winter sun beamed into life, Edward and Peter began to gather up their belongings. Obi had popped over to wish them a few words of good fortune, doing so with the delivery of two more fresh loaves. "Safe travels, men," he said, with a little wave.

"Obi, might I ask just one more thing?" said Edward.

"Yes, of course."

"Our journey will have us meet with the Jackal. You wouldn't happen to be familiar, would you?"

Obi paused, standing with his mouth wide open, stuttering his next words. "No. No. You mustn't!" he quivered. "I beg of you, stay clear of that creature!"

Hurrying over, Obi placed both his hands on Edward's shoulders. "You don't have to take my counsel, Edward, but consider yourself warned, yes? Many folks have never returned from the house of the Jackal. Oh, I'm so sorry! Who am I to tell … I do hope you could forgive me?"

Edward took Obi's hands in his. "Obi, there's nothing to forgive and your counsel is most welcome. I do wish there was another way, but this is what we must do. Can you help us?"

"If I said *yes* … w-w- what is it you would need?" asked Obi with the utmost reluctance, shimmying away a little.

"We just need to know the way, that's all."

Obi shuddered, grimaced, scratched his head and fiddled with the strings of his hat nervously.

"I do believe you're a mad man, Edward," he said. "But if that's all you need, then I can certainly help. Although, I'm not pleased about this at all!"

Peter walked over and slipped three silver spinnels into Obi's shirt pocket. Edward looked on deploringly, wondering which hapless soul he could have stolen them from. Obi pouted his lips in quiet satisfaction at the sound of coins landing in his pocket.

The three of them set off on foot, back down past the fire and out towards the front gate. The path ahead wasn't fit for the two shires so they were left behind in the care of the townsfolk.

Lena was standing by, watching, waving and she was smiling brightly. Yet, the second the three men left, Lena's smile quickly shifted and she began to silently follow them. The men remained unaware as she slipped out of the gate and around to the stable where her horse was tied. She leapt on, and the mare was away – to Summer's Reach she rode swift.

Obi was extremely tentative. He wanted this, rather, he *needed* this to be over and done with. They trudged on with his guidance, deep into the thick woods. This whole thing set his teeth on edge and the coins seemed to have lost their value all of a sudden.

"How much further might we be going?" asked Peter from over Edward's shoulder.

"A few miles ahead yet, do be patient, sir!" said Obi, his teeth bare to wind in a grimace.

It was hard-going terrain, and at one point, Edward slipped on the glassy mud and fell. Peter was amused. Obi helped him up.

The miles eventually passed by, their surroundings changing by the hour. A dense fog approached, thick and damp, hindering their vision at a distance; the morning sun struggled to pierce the sullen, grey blanket that now befell them.

"Be careful now, men," said Obi. "The footing isn't too steady around here. Plenty of hidden pools and puddles."

"How is it you know these lands so well, Obi?" asked Peter, whilst minding his step.

"I often wander up here to pick the mushrooms, huge things they are!" said Obi happily. "And from time to time, this is where I come to hunt. You know, rabbits, badgers, that sort of thing."

Obi tapped the bow and quiver that was flung over his back, stopping in his tracks, bringing a finger to his lips. "Stay quiet now, men." The dark, grey mist thickened; the moisture in the air had an almost rank taste to it.

Obi ushered them quietly through the undergrowth, where each bush looked to be connected, by web after web of spider's silk that glistened from the frost that settled upon each strand. Peter shuddered at the sight and threw back his head as if in retreat. As his eyes lifted to the distance, a tall, lonely gothic house standing in the middle of a clearing became visible.

"This is where I'll leave you, gentlemen," whispered Obi. "It has truly been a pleasure. Stop by on your way back, ey? Be careful."

A few handshakes and Obi disappeared into the trees. Edward and Peter each inhaled a long, damp breath, beginning to slowly walk on, taking great care of their steps, eagerly getting closer to the house. Edward held his pistol tight and Peter clenched his axe behind his back. The sound of faint rustling pricked their ears, as one noise became many. They both looked at each other in puzzlement, the grass seemed like it was moving all around them. Edward gestured towards the path that split the field.

"Something's alive in here, Edward," said Peter, his courage shrinking away as each agonising second passed. "The forest breathes. Above the soil, beneath the leaves?"

"The rats," said Edward chillingly. "Keep to the path."

The men were close now; close enough to smell the emerald-green growth of moss that covered the whole of the house. Edward stepped onto the decking, raising his fist then, *knock, knock, knock!*

Nothing, not a single sound; even the rats in the field had grown silent. He knocked again, this time louder, but still no life.

"Something doesn't feel right about this place," said Peter quietly.

"Hello!" shouted Edward, cupping his hand, making Peter jump in fright.

Peter looked at the sky. "The crows are circling us," he said, swallowing how uncomfortable he felt.

Edward reached out, pressed his hand on the door, then pushed. It croaked open. A gust of stench hit them like a fist. Water dripped from the ceiling inside, the smell was foul. The floorboards were rotten and unstable. The moss outside had grown within, covering the walls and now the paintings that were hooked there could no longer be seen for it.

They edged further into the house, slowly and tentatively, until they came to what seemed to be the living room. Inside it, the smell was even worse, and the rats scuttled here and there, squeaking and gnawing at the rotten furniture.

There she sat, in a rocking chair beside the window, staring out over the wet fields. Peter entered the room; Edward held a hand against his chest to gently restrain him.

"Pardon us," said Edward. "We mean no harm, just passing by. If it's not too much trouble, we'd be awfully grateful if we can help ourselves to some water, from your well out there?"

The woman was as still as stone, gazing motionlessly, without the slightest blink. Her dark, shredded gown covered her and the chair she was sitting on, flowing to the floor around her feet. She had no life in her face nor in her form. She wore a hood around her head and you could see the delicate, grey strands of her hair hanging from the hem.

Edward and Peter looked around to see dozens more rats climbing through the windows and upwards through the broken floorboards. Peter was growing increasingly uncomfortable and began to fret a little, when one of the rats nosed into his pocket and stole a handkerchief. "Little thief!" he whispered.

Edward spoke again. "Pardon us, my lady?"

He took one small step and the woman's head snapped left to the sound of it. Eyes of despair and anguish looked upon him. Edward's knees shuddered, his hands became stiff and clammy. A bead of sweat dripped down the side of his face from his brow.

Those eyes; those chilling, pearly eyes! The sight of them brought a pain over him, as if he'd been struck in the chest.

She turned away; the two men were lost for words. Peter shook his head and gestured to leave immediately.

Then a weak little voice spoke. "Who are you?" she whispered, colder than any wind in Graelind.

At first, Edward couldn't speak, for his composure had long abandoned him.

"I'm Edward … and this is Peter," he finally muttered.

"You need to leave," she snapped.

"We apologise for our intrusion," said Edward. "How rude of us to arrive so unexpected like this. But all we ask for is a little water, to see us on our journey."

Peter scowled toward Edward, wondering if he'd forgotten the true reason they were here.

"Take the water and leave! Run! As far away from here as you can," said the woman despairingly.

"That is very kind of you, my lady," said Edward. "We'll be on our way now."

Peter scowled even harder, thinking Edward must have lost his mind

... until the officer turned on his heels and spoke again.

"Oh and just one last thing," said Edward. "I hate to bother you with it ... but, do you know anything about the Black Diamond? As chance would have it, I believe you might have heard a thing or two?"

The woman looked to regain her wits, but still she sat staring blankly through the window. Her breaths became deeper and quicker as she began to shuffle in her chair. A single teardrop fell from her left eye, landing on her gown.

"I've told you, *you must leave, now!*" This time her words were delivered with anger.

"So, you do know something?" asked Edward.

The rats were restless now, almost angry; the whole house had come alive with them.

The woman began to weep into her hands. "He won't like that you're here!"

Peter stepped forward. "Wait, whose *he*?"

She turned her head again, her pearly eyes glistening behind the tears. "The *Jackal!*"

Then footsteps sounded behind them. The men armed themselves ready as the footsteps grew louder. Peter slid the axe from his belt. Edward unsheathed the blade Peter had gifted him. Then, the footsteps stopped dead. They looked around and the woman was gone.

A moment passed, when out of the darkness, a huge figure sprung from the hallway, screaming like a deranged psychopath, froth spitting from his teeth.

They couldn't lift their weapons quick enough before the fearsome man rode into them, knocking them both across the ground. Edward lifted his pistol and discharged a shot toward the centre of his chest. The bullet threw him back but the man didn't fall; he only wailed in anger. Peter rolled to the side and gained a quick footing, raising his axe.

The Jackal drew a dagger from his belt, grasping it tightly, with the blade pointing down. Peter swung his axe fiercely but it was parried by the much stronger man – the pirate's hand screamed in pain as his axe flew off into the distance. With immense, beastly power, the Jackal thrust his boot hard into Peter's stomach, dropping him to the rat-filth-covered wood. Edward stood to his feet, a trickle of blood dripping from his nostril. He circled the Jackal before attempting another strike. To no avail. Edward was sent crashing into the wall; he felt sick when he realised his second pistol had dislodged from his bandolier during the first attack.

Both men were laid out with this animal staring down at them. The Jackal held the dagger high above his head, his mouth frothing and biting. He walked towards the men, deliberately, with evil intentions. This was it!

All seemed to be lost until an arrow came whistling through an open window, sticking into the Jackal's throat - the bloody point appearing through the other side. The Jackal let out a long, wheezing groan of pain, his dagger fell from his wretched fingers. Edward leapt up, swung his arm in a wide arc and drove his blade clean through the man's heart, staring deep into his pearly eyes whilst he twisted the steel.

The Jackal fell, landing with a heavy bang. The rats completely freaked out and began to rush all around in a frenzy, until the room was entirely empty of them.

Peter was still lying on his back, his mouth agape. He gradually crept up and peered nervously over the windowsill. In the middle of the field stood Obi, his bowstring finger frozen beside his ear.

Peter curled back into a ball on the floor, still stunned and shaking, watching as gushes of blood poured from the Jackal's flesh. Their attacker was the biggest and most fearsome man Peter had ever seen in his life. His shirtless, pale body looked absent of a single hair. His eyes like two spheres of white that protruded from his raw-dough-looking head.

Obi hadn't moved an inch since his deadly arrow was let fly. Edward jerked the blade from the Jackal's corpse and rushed outside to meet him.

"I *had* to turn back!" said Obi, shivering. "Something didn't feel right letting you go in there alone. I had the strangest feeling, like I'd jumped out of my own body and started screaming, *turn back, turn back! Save them, Obi!*"

"Well you did so at the perfect time!" said Edward, not quite believing he was still alive. "I am entirely lost for words!"

"Come, quick!" called Peter.

Edward and Obi sprinted inside to find Peter standing over the now stricken woman; she was cowering in a corner, shaking back and forth on the spot.

"That diamond cursed us both!" she cried. "He never let me leave this rotting house. I've spent years here just dying slowly!" She wiped her face and looked up at them. "You listen to me! If you ever find that diamond, you must destroy it!"

"Would you tell us where to find it?" asked Edward.

"Your fate would be no different than any other," she snapped despairingly. "The diamond is pure evil; evil I tell you!"

"We intend to use the diamond to bring peace, my lady," said Edward, taking a knee. Peter and Obi stood with mystified expressions. She turned to Edward, shivered, then whimpered her next words.

"I cannot help you," she said. "I'm so sorry. The diamond will be your ruin. I will not allow it."

Peter reached inside his satchel and dug out the loaf of fresh bread that Obi had given him. He knelt down and placed it in her hand. The bread had been tucked away inside his sleeping furs and was still ever so slightly warm to the touch.

"My lady," said Peter kindly. "Please, would you tell us what you can? We believe the diamond can bring peace to this land. You could be the very catalyst that helps us find it; or the sole reason for our failure. Help us, please. I am already on my knees."

The woman unwrapped the handkerchief that covered the bread. The aroma brushed across her face and she smiled. Her feeble, shaking hands were not strong enough to tear off a piece, so Peter reached over to help. "If you don't mind, my lady?" he asked. Peter then ripped it into four pieces and filled her palms. Very slowly, she lifted a piece and ate it, sinking deeper in the corner in satisfaction. Obi brushed a tear from his cheek. Edward felt a lump rise in his throat. Peter unhooked his water pouch and helped her take a sip. The woman took Peter's hand and looked at him; he couldn't tell exactly where she was looking, because her eyes were void of anything but their pearly glow. They say pictures paint a thousand words, but in this instance, it was her expression that did the painting. Peter sensed her gaze was upon him.

The woman shuffled up a little and took Peter by the hand. "Thank you. It has been many years since I have tasted freshly baked bread."

Peter smiled and brushed his warm hands on hers. She nodded, like she was about to say something the men really needed to hear.

"You will find who you're looking for on Ridikus island," she said, coughing into her sleeve. "Look for an old man by the name of Leander. He might be able to help you. He came here looking for us a few years ago. He collects gems and wanted to see the effects of the Black Diamond for himself. I don't think he's a good man. I got the feeling he knew where to find it."

Peter smiled. "Thank you," he said, bringing her hand close to him. "Can we help you, my lady? Is there *anything* else we can do?" he asked softly.

The woman reached out and pointed at Edward's pistol that lay on the floor, just out of her reach.

"I'm no longer trapped," she said, beginning to weep. "But there's nothing for me here. Nothing at all. For too many years have I suffered in these bonds."

Peter's eyes became teary; he saw how she hurt and how she had suffered. Her frail hand brushed past his as she withdrew it. Again, Peter could feel how bitterly cold her skin was. He stepped outside, taking a moment to consider. Never had he seen anyone in such anguish and disrepair.

Walking back inside, fighting the voice in his head, Peter picked up Edward's pistol and checked if it was loaded. It was. Reluctantly to say the least, he placed the pistol in her hand and sat beside her.

"Is there nothing more I can do? Are you certain this is your wish?" he asked, resting his hands on her wrists once again.

"I am certain," she said, her voice sweet and restful. "Now, at last, I can be free. I really hope to see my husband again, free from his own bonds. Trust me, this is what I want. I need peace, and you could be the very catalyst that helps me find it."

Peter's emotions were about to spill forth and he was trying with all his might to stop from bawling – the tears formulating in his eyes.

"You can be at peace now, my lady," he said. "Your days of suffering are over."

Peter leaned over and kissed her cheek. The woman flashed a gracious smile at him; Peter returned one of his own, a smile full of all the sympathy in his heart. He stood, straightened his jacket, then left for the field, catching up with the others a little way down the path.

The sound of a gunshot shocked the forest, and the crows resting upon the house of the Jackal took flight.

Chapter 14
A Mother's Approval

The entire world around James Percy seemed to have stretched a little, which was unusual, considering he spent weeks at a time upon that giant blue blanket of water. You wouldn't think his world *could* be stretched, but after meeting Adeline Dawson, his world became bigger and brighter and warmer.

After he'd seen Edward, sneaking down the river with a wanted pirate in tow, he just couldn't keep it to himself. He was fond of Edward, but every chance to show loyalty to the King should be taken with both hands. At least that's what he thought he believed. Perhaps his loyalty didn't extend quite as far as he once thought. For that night on the *Baliant*, James Percy *did* see Edward on board, sneaking around the deck. Yet, he stayed silent and said nothing. Maybe James was one of the few that could reason with what Edward had done, and maybe he was changed by the love that coursed through his veins with every beat of his heart. All James ever wanted, was to be an officer. From being a little boy, he and his brother would fashion uniforms from sheets and stage battles down by the river. His uncle would bring home trinkets from his voyages, and each time it would ignite a great desire to sail the seas. The day his uncle requested his presence aboard the *Baliant*, his entire world changed.

He became a crewman, to his jubilation, on the first day of his eighteenth year and for five years since he'd served the *Baliant* with pride.

That was until he met Adeline. Never before had the affection of a woman so easily swayed him; but she was like no other he had ever seen. He dreamt about her on each night since they had met. Just the thought of leaving her behind seemed ridiculous to him now. He searched his mind for the right words other than, *Captain, I've met a lady and I shall sail alongside you no more.* He didn't think that would cut it with his Uncle Wallace.

In Summer's Reach, you can exist as a good many things: you can follow the path of honour to fight for your country and people, as an officer, a guard, or maybe even by taking up arms in the Graelind army. There is plenty of work for an honest soul down in the markets. Maybe you're the type who grew up on their family's farm and you're just following in the footsteps that are already trodden into the path that is life.

James Percy was beginning to wonder whether a life at sea was what he truly wanted, or just an inescapable fate his uncle had laid out for him.

James sat beside Adeline, their legs swinging over the side of the *Baliant's* hull. They were staring towards the harbour, the lights of the city flickering in their eyes. They were giggling. Adeline was sat with her hands on her lap, she was nervous. James equally so.

"James, would it be awful if I asked you to stay here with me ... in Summer's Reach?" she said, sheepishly.

James glanced at Adeline; the expression upon his face quickly gave away his feelings.

"I think this is the happiest day of my life," he said in his endearing, boyish way.

"So does that mean, *yes*?" she asked.

The sides of James' mouth stretched further up his cheeks than ever; a feeling of ecstasy, like his heart had burst into flames, only for a sobering thought to creep in there and douse it. It was at that very moment he saw Edward walking the deck. He took a few seconds to ponder over it, then brushed it aside in his thoughts and looked Adeline in the eye.

"I'm sorry, Adeline," he said sadly. "But I can't. I'm sworn to duty, I couldn't leave the *Baliant* now. I hope you understand."

Adeline did understand. The young sailor wasn't the only one to have fallen in love. She'd seen something in James; a rich spirit, bursting in charisma and gentlemanly charm. Hearing that he couldn't stay with her broke her heart. But she expected it, in a way. She cursed under her breath at falling for a sailor, then composed herself - she didn't want to show her pain, after all, they had only known one another for a matter of days.

"I'll be back before you know it," said James, making light of it. "I shouldn't be away for long." He took her hand. "Would you wait for me, Adeline?"

Adeline was truly discontented. "I couldn't live like that, James. Not knowing if I will ever see you again. I know what happens out at sea. I see the families of the men that never come home. They live in fear, awaiting ill news, given to them by whichever guard Lord Harrington has on hand!"

"Adeline; I give you my word, I will return to you!"

"You don't know that!" snapped Adeline, standing up straight. "You're not invincible!"

She lifted James' pocket watch from around her neck and passed it back to him. "I'm so sorry," she said woefully. "How selfish of me to expect this of you. We hardly know each other. I should have never said such things. Forgive me."

Adeline took off down the deck.

"Adeline, wait!" called James. "Will I see you again, before I go?"

"I don't think so. Sorry, James," she called back whilst climbing down from the ship into a wherry tied to the side.

She floated away from him, further and further with each motion of the oar. James felt a deep tumbling feeling in his body; he just stood there watching the girl of his dreams row away. He was motionless and weak. He gathered himself for a minute before turning to the other side of the ship.

There in the distance, he saw Edward, bumping up against the shale at the lake's edge. James believed deep down in his heart that the officer wasn't simply abandoning his life for one of a criminal - he *must* have had a just cause.

He was looking down upon a man who he greatly respected, taking a chance on something he believed in, and it triggered a rush of strong emotion within him. Knowing what he had to do, he ran over to the port side of the ship as fast as he could, calling to her, at the very height of his lungs.

Her eyes met his. Tears had now spilt down her face and the cold snap upon the lake had brought a chill to her cheeks.

James, shaking with excitement, climbed down into a wherry of his own and rowed off like a man possessed by desire. Adeline saw his intentions and was overcome with happiness. She barely stayed upright trying to spin round and row back to the *Baliant*.

Their wherries finally knocked together; James reached out and pulled her towards him. They gently twirled upon the water, locked in an truly amorous embrace that sent overwhelming feelings flushing through both their hearts.

"I won't leave you," he whispered. "I promise."

Adeline was delighted, yet she still had her doubts.

"James, I cannot ask this of you, surely not? All I know is the past few days have been some of the best I can ever remember!"

"I am not leaving you, my lady," said James, holding her tighter. "I can make enough money to get us by, I think, well … I hope!" The excitement had James stuttering now. "I'll sell the fish that I catch or the fruit that I can grow. I'm not leaving, not now."

The wherries were uneasy on the surface. The two of them couldn't keep from swaying in all the excitement and emotion. James leaned over again, this time a little too far, rocking and bobbling into a frenzy before tipping into the icy water. His chest tightened; his body dealt a shock from the piercing dark of the lake that punched the air from his lungs. Adeline coughed out a rather panicked laugh, but managed to upright James' wherry.

She steadied herself and grasped his arm, struggling at first as he flapped around from the shock. Eventually her will prevailed and the shivering young sailor was pulled up - his oar had been lost to the lake bottom.

Huddling into a shivering ball, James couldn't speak. Adeline tied the mooring rope over both wherries, so they were connected bow to stern. She plunged the oar into the lake and began to row, as quickly as her strength could move them. Once they had reached the harbour, Adeline leapt onto it, turning back to offer James a helping hand.

"Follow me, sailor," she laughed. "I'll have you warm again, soon enough. And I'm sure my mother would enjoy meeting you."

The shivering chatter of James' teeth was just about the only noise he could muster, save for his wheezing breaths, of course. Now, the simple, primitive action of putting one foot in front of the other felt like the most difficult thing in the world.

Not far from the daily happenings of the city, tucked away from busy life in the district of Harkness, stood row on row of cottages that lined cobbled streets, dotted with lanterns beaming warm hues onto the roads.

Adeline held James by his arm as she helped him between one of those streets, into a little house with blue shutters and ivy on the walls that reached to the highest sills.

James found himself inside with no sign of Adeline. He stared around, teeth still chattering, with his hands across his chest holding his arms.

A fire burned in the corner of the room. He rushed over to it, stretching out his hands against the flames feeling them tingle.

Adeline returned with a great woollen blanket.

"Here you are, James," she said, proffering it. "You'll need to take off those wet clothes first, though. I'll get them in front of the fire."

James was too cold for words.

Adeline left for the kitchen, allowing him his privacy. The young sailor laid out his wet clothes on the hearth, wrapping himself in the blanket - feeling the wool caress his wet skin. He sat beside the fire, waiting; a deep breath settling him down into the chair.

Adeline came back to the living room with a kettle filled with nettle leaves and sweetened water. She placed it over the stove and the smell of honey filled the whole place the second steam began to rise.

"Thank you, Adeline," said James, smiling forcefully behind his grimacing teeth.

"This shouldn't take long to boil," she said. "Hold on a little longer and we'll have you all warmed up."

Her words were so pure to him, kind and soft tones he could listen to all day. He loved her so much, and for a second the cold all but left his bones.

There came a sound from another room, and in walked a lady who looked just like Adeline - only a little older - her voice equally as warming.

"So then, this is James Percy, is it?" she asked inquisitively. "Why, Adeline was right - a handsome boy!"

James blushed, realising how hopelessly vulnerable he was.

"James, this is my mother, Evelyn."

"Very pleased to meet you, my lady," said James, standing to greet her.

"Evelyn is just fine, thank you very much," she said. "There's no need for such formalities here, sit down."

Evelyn sat beside him. "Now tell me why you're half naked in my living room, James Percy?"

"Mother!" gasped Adeline, uncomfortably.

"I like to fish, my lady, I mean ... Evelyn, of course; and the craftsmanship of man has begun to make a habit of betraying me," laughed James, nervously.

"So, you're a clumsy sod?"

He looked at Adeline, who was now showing telling signs of embarrassment. He then smiled, cheekily, knowing he wasn't being entirely truthful.

"I am rather a clumsy sod, yes!" he laughed. "The first time I met Adeline, I fell through a chair and made a fool of myself in front of the entire tavern!"

Evelyn chuckled. Her daughter had already told her all about it.

"Adi tells me you're a sailor?"

"I am, yes - aboard the *Baliant*."

"I do hope you're not the one steering it?" she said, turning to smirk at him, hoping he'd taken the joke well.

They all laughed. Adeline's smile slowly began to break through her unease.

Her mother stood up. "You're welcome to stay, James Percy, you get yourself warm. Adi, darling, pour the boy some tea and I'll see to a buttered loaf, right away."

Evelyn then left. Adeline moved over to the stove, dunking a spoon into the tea, mixing the nettle leaves before pouring two cups.

"Drink up!" she urged him; his hands still a little shaky as he reached to grab the cup.

James pursed his lips and took a gulp, followed by a gasp of air to cool his mouth. Evelyn returned with a plate laden with sliced bread, buttered from one side to the other, then dragged over a small table to lay them down on.

James could scarcely hear beyond the voice in his own mind, for his attention was truly fixed. Nothing else mattered in that moment. The rest of his world seemed a distant memory.

Chapter 15
After Obi's Return

Lena had ridden to Summer's Reach in haste and she'd arrived carrying her concern heavily on her shoulders. Her suspicions about Edward had her wide awake for most of the night. What endeavour could he have possibly embarked upon, in any regard other than his naval duties; and, more to the point, what business did he have in Bidle's Edge? Questions only her sister might answer.

Charlotte was out by the river, washing clothes in the shallow cut when Lena came galloping by. Charlotte's eyes lit up when she saw her, it was the friendly face she needed the most. That familiarity. That comfort.

Lena slid down from her horse and flung her arms around her younger sibling. Charlotte slumped into the embrace and began to cry.

"It has been too long, sister," said Lena, squeezing her harder.

"You don't say. Fifteen years!" said Charlotte, her voice muffled against her sister's shoulder, gentle droplets of tears falling from her eyes.

"It never seemed like the right time to come back," said Lena, stroking her sister on the cheek. "But now that I'm here, I wonder what purpose kept us apart for all these years."

Charlotte looked up. "I never knew where you were," she said softly. "I would have found you myself, if I did."

"It's okay," said Lena, sweetly. "I'm here now. Let's go inside. Come."

Charlotte took her softly by the hand. Inside, they sat down beside the hearth. Lena wasted no time cutting straight to the meaning of her visit.

"I have seen Edward, in Bidle's Edge," she said. "With a man he didn't seem overly willing to introduce me to. A pirate, nonetheless! They stayed the night and left at first light. He told me he had a good reason to be away, but if I knew him any better, Charlotte, I'd say he was lying. Is everything okay?"

Charlotte was poking the fireplace to stir the flames. "He told me he could bring peace to Graelind," she said, wiping her eyes. "Then he told me there was a diamond, and if only he could find it, he would hold the power capable of making change in the world … for good.”

“You surely didn’t believe such nonsense, sister?” said Lena casually.

“I have no idea what to believe anymore, Lena. Edward hasn’t been the same for many months now, and news of this diamond has corrupted his heart. But I love him dearly, and when I looked into his eyes, I just knew he had a good reason – so I let him go. He left thinking I wouldn’t be here when he returned.”

“On account of what?” asked Lena, regarding the latter.

“On account of me saying I wouldn’t be here when he returned.”

“Well, sister, I think you did the right thing,” said Lena. “Yes, he’s an officer and, well, they’re a very particular type of man; for King and country always, and all that! What I’m saying, Charlotte, is women like us have come to expect our husbands gallivanting around the world – but I sensed this was different, and it appears I was right.”

Charlotte took heed. “How’s Harris?” she asked bitterly.

“*That* is a story for another day, entirely,” said Lena, waving off the subject. “My husband is a scoundrel, there is no hope left for him – but Edward?”

Charlotte paused for a few moments and stared thoughtfully into the flames. She was sitting in Edward’s chair and the desire to feel him next to her was strongly present, even overwhelming.

“I meant what I said. Yet, I trust Edward. What troubles my sleep the most, is that *pirate*! Harrington thinks my husband had a part in his escape from the Plummet.”

Lena was the older of the two by a few years, and from the day Charlotte was born, they were joined eternally by blood and friendship. Nothing changed but the miles between them. Lena knew her sister, and despite their absence, she trusted her words were from the heart.

“Very well,” she said. “We’ve all made sacrifices for the man we love.”

“They will kill him if they ever find him,” whispered Charlotte.

“Edward knows that,” said Lena. “I’m almost certain he would’ve considered all the consequences. Although, one might deem his actions foolish – to aid a pirate, is to aid the root of evil.”

Charlotte nodded. “Yes. A fool he is, but a fool that would do anything for his people. He’s risked everything for that cause. What’s holding me together is simply my trust for him.”

"Charlotte, did you tell *anybody* about this?"

"No, I didn't; I was questioned by his captain and Lord Harrington, but I said nothing, to no one."

"Good, and it shall remain that way! It's the gallows if he's lucky. He'll do well to avoid the axe! Come and stay with me for a while, you shouldn't be alone."

"I just couldn't," said Charlotte. "If Edward returns, I need to be here for him."

Lena leaned in and rested her hand on Charlotte's shoulder. "So much for not being here when he returns, ey? Sometimes the virtues of a soul such as your own can be their ruin. I hope your loyalty doesn't land you beside him when the axe falls."

Cutting words, as sobering as a cold winter wind. Charlotte felt them sting, just as Lena intended.

The two of them began to wander into the past, to catch up on lost time and reminisce about the old days. Two sisters reunited after so many years had lots to talk about.

Yet, unbeknown to them, the words spoken on this day, didn't just fall upon the ears of two. Colonel Gürad had been hiding outside the window, scarcely able to hear, but the words he *could* make out stirred a great satisfaction inside him.

There was a diamond that Edward was hunting for. He had aid in the form of Peter Beaumont and he was seen in Bidle's Edge on that very morning.

Gürad grinned wildly, quietly sliding from beneath the window. He mounted his horse not far from Clavell cottage and cantered to the palace, to summon his guards for a pursuit.

*

Obi was shaken; flinching at the slightest of sounds. Jumping in fear at the groans of old trees swaying in the breeze and the branches that whistled under the canopies. What he had seen would *never* be forgotten. Edward explained everything: the diamond, the armoury and their business at the house of the Jackal. He and Peter owed him that much after all the trouble. Not to mention the courage, kindness, unwavering bravery and, of course, that perfectly placed arrow.

Obi was astounded and listened without saying a word. Edward shuddered as he remembered that frothing mouth and those pearly eyes. Peter couldn't bide how haunting it all was. He felt naked, like his fears were made bare to the world. The Jackal had looked deep into his soul and each time he blinked, he saw those eyes staring back at him – cold, like rocks of ice.

The forest had fallen darker, the trees thick and dense about them. The rain now tumbling from the grey clouds, dripping through the branches, drenching them down to the skin.

Ridikus island was their destination, and Obi had kindly agreed to take them as far as Fort Gaze – a great port city by the sea, with fortress walls and cannons down its entire line, almost as agile as the arrow of a compass.

A fortress at one with the waves that crashed against its formidable stones and the razor-sharp rocks that protected it. In days gone by, the city had been a stronghold of the Graelind navy, but after being left unguarded for a short time, the city was sacked by a pirate fleet – thereafter taking control of the land and the sea around it.

The thin strait between Ridikus island and the Graelind mainland was now forbidden for naval ships of any kind, and offered safe passage between the two for all manner of seafaring scum, under the careful watch of the fortress's new occupants. For years had the King demanded it be retaken, but the lives that would be lost was too high a price to pay. Simply, it was too heavily fortified to mount any large-scale attack; and with many of the city's people still residing within, the inevitable outcome would be the massacre of innocents. The King had learned this lesson once before; fifteen years had passed since the first and only time he gave orders to retrieve what was lost. It did not go to plan.

The forest opened up and revealed the grey, gloomy sky. There were now no obstructions between the rain and the men, their boots beginning to drown in the mud. Safer passage through the trees and fields was a must, for there was no doubt the Kingsguard would have all roads around eagerly watched.

From the house of the Jackal, it was an uncomfortable three-day journey over harsh terrain. The rain continued to pour down and the campfires they lit in any shelter they could find, barely dried their soaked jackets, let alone their stockings. Thus far, Peter had managed to complain the entire way. Obi simply shrugged off the pirate's childlike whining, for he was clearly an extraordinarily tolerant man. Edward, his mind was busy with thoughts. He'd never ventured to Fort Gaze from any direction other than the sea. The bad memories of the time the fortress was taken fifteen years ago, still circled bitterly his mind. He, aboard the *Baliant* as a younger officer, was part of the ineffectual attempt to reclaim the city. A fleet of four Graelind ships set out and only one came back. It was nothing short of a bloodbath.

The naval ships discharged their cannons from the shallow strait only to be met with stationary artillery of a much greater force. Tearing apart the ships and sinking them to a sandy bottom. All except the *Baliant*; as chance would have it, she escaped.

In the years since, Edward often looked upon the battle with great grief. His brother Arthur was taken from him on that fateful day. He sailed on the mighty ship, *Fortuna*, being one of the three that perished, along with all her officers and crew. The harrowing thoughts of such times never left him and knowing he was only a short journey from where it all happened, stirred them up like a steaming cauldron of recollection.

Graelind was scattered with old houses and sheds that had long since been abandoned. Settlers from many years ago had left their homesteads in search of better resources for their people. Never was there a shortage of shelter if you knew where to look.

The men had found themselves a windowless house just off a stream. It stood half in ruins and one of the walls had all but fallen in. Nature and time had worn away the past, but not entirely. You could still see where the stove once was in the middle of a bare, grassy patch outside. There was a saddle, tied to a tree across the way, that the children would have swung on. For a moment, Edward's mind slipped into a trance-like state, when a vision that didn't belong to him started unfolding before his eyes; the house seemed so recently departed it conjured a memory that for second he believed was his own. He snapped out of it and drew a deep breath.

It was agreed that this was to be the night's resting place. The men started to block in the empty spaces in the windowsills, using the stones that had fallen from the outside wall. It was perfect. The roof was miraculously still intact after all these years, and once all the windows were filled with loose stones, not even the light could peer through. The rain had now stopped for a brief time. The wind a scarce breeze barely rustling the whiskey-brown grass dotted across the forest floor.

Peter lit them a fire, promptly warming up some whiskey to improve their mood. He had managed to acquire a small pot of honey before they'd left the comfort of Bidle's Edge and he scooped out a huge blob with his finger.

"Try some of this here, Obi," he said, stirring the golden liquid with the same finger before pouring him a cup.

Obi took a sip and his face creased into a knot.

"Well that's one way of making bad whiskey taste better," he said grimacing, his lips curling up at the edges. "An apology for my frankness, but that's awful stuff, is that."

Edward laughed.

"Hold on," interrupted Peter. "This whiskey is of the finest quality. This is Court Marsh stuff! A delicate blend of spices you can't get anywhere else in the country."

"Stolen spices, no doubt!" quipped Edward.

"Oh, for the love of the sea, Edward, drink it and shut up!" said Peter. "Hardly matters where it came from anyway."

Peter was clearly offended by their aversion to his adopted town's beloved spirit.

"When all is said and done, I'll show you lads what real whiskey tastes like," said Edward. "We'll share a drink at the Drum & Fiddle. That's the spot for the best whiskey in the country."

"Nonsense!" said Obi, clearing his throat. "The best whiskey in Graelind sits right here in my pocket."

"I'll be the judge of that!" said Peter. "Pass it over."

Obi reached into his pocket and pulled out a small, debossed leather flask. He threw it over the fire. Peter uncorked it and took a sip. Obi had a proud look on his face as if he knew good and well it was quite the improvement to what the pirate had offered. Peter, wincing considerably, rather unwillingly enjoyed the taste of it. It was without a doubt the better option of the two.

"Let me see, then?" said Edward, intrigued. "But I doubt I'll have my mind changed."

He took a sip, smiled, coughed at the strength of it, then nodded in approval.

"This is sure to enrich one's spirit. It's much better than Peter's Court

Marsh filth, I'll grant you that, old boy!" he said mockingly, handing Obi the flask. "A familiar flavour that has long since passed my lips. That must be a very old vintage?"

"Indeed," said Obi. "Sure to spring a smile upon the face of any man; perhaps not the face of a man who's still scowling after a swig of Peter's."

"Then you'll both go without," snapped Peter. "I've more chance of becoming a colonel in the navy than you have getting another dram of this!"

Obi proudly nestled the flask into his pocket, patting the leather of his jacket.

"I think there's more chance of the latter, Peter," said Edward. "For there is no such rank in the Graelind navy."

"Well it's all the same to me. You're all up your own arse!" said Peter.

Edward laughed quietly, very much enjoying how his provocative remarks had offended the pirate. "Allow me to explain the ranks of Graelind. They're a little simpler than that of other nations," he said.

Peter huffed at the sky.

"In the navy, you will begin as a crewman, eligible at the age of twenty-one to become an officer. In any case, those promoted are few and far between and even less so before the age of thirty. Once an officer, your level of authority would only increase in relation to your service years, until the day comes when you're eligible to command your own vessel as a captain. After that, would be commodore, in command of a small fleet of vessels, again only progressing in authority in relation to service years. And lastly, Lord Admiral, the commander of the Graelind navy.

"The ranks of the Kingsguard are based on the same service years system, yet the titles are different. Beginning as a guard, you will work towards becoming the captain of your own regiment, onwards in time to becoming the colonel of numerous regiments. Lord Harrington holds the rank of commander of the Kingsguard.

"The Graelind army; now, again, same service years system, starting out as a corporal, then sergeant, then captain, and lastly, Lord Colonel, commander of the Graelind army."

"Don't think a lesson in military classification will afford you the privilege of my good graces. No more whiskey for you, no sir!" said Peter, his bottom lip protruding from his face.

"I've had quite enough of the stuff, for now," said Edward. "I'm going to the stream to fill my pouch. Make the most of the fresh water. I doubt we'll be privy to such things on Ridikus - that rotting hole of worms. You can smell the place a mile out!"

"Edward?" said Obi, with curiosity. "I mean this with respect, of course, but given your apparent age, how is it you aren't a captain yet?"

Obi needn't have listened to Edward's lesson. He knew such details well enough already.

"Oh, I could be, should I choose to," said Edward, standing up. "But rather alike to *my* captain, I chose to stay with the *Baliant*."

Edward dusted his trousers, leaving Peter and Obi chatting by the fire. They could still hear the officer mumbling to himself as he walked off into the distance.

Joining the waterside, Edward turned and could faintly see the flickering of the fire behind him. He knelt down and tipped his pouch into the stream to fill it, when a strange sense of foreboding came over him.

An awful feeling, as if something dreadful was about to happen. The trees around him seemed to close in and his heart began to beat quicker.

Taking a drink from his pouch he swilled his face, the shock of the cold water cleared his thoughts. Yet the feeling wouldn't subside and it kept returning, over and over.

He walked back to the camp. Troubled. Peter and Obi were chatting away but Edward's feelings of dread lingered and they were *not* irrational. For not a day's walk back, in that field full of vermin rats, where the birds no longer called and the sun barely shone ... the eyes of the Jackal opened once again.

Chapter 16

Hunted or Haunted?

The next morning, at the very first light of dawn, the men awoke to the ardent chirping of birds, loud in song. The dreary, tiresome mizzle from the previous day hadn't returned and the embers from the campfire still smouldered. Peter kicked them across the trampled, wet ground around him, dulling what was left of it.

Obi took the lead and Edward followed, then Peter. Two more days on the move were out in front of them, so to arrive at Fort Gaze on the third evening of their journey.

Their path headed a little north, up a steep hillock, away from the waterside, where at the top it was rocky and slippery underfoot; so much so that the men barely looked up from their feet, almost missing the wonderful view of the sea that presented itself.

They cast their eyes out afar, following the line of the coast north; and in the distance, there it stood - Fort Gaze. Then, only a little further beyond, across the strait, was Ridikus island.

Edward looked over at Peter with foreboding eyes, then turned to see Obi had already begun to walk on.

A long drop from the hillock took them deep into a ravine; the ever-slippery ground dictating their pace as they descended, eventually finding their way back to the stream at the very bottom. Edward began to feel rather strange and uneasy. He kept turning around as if he'd heard something clambering around the trees. *Probably just nothing,* he kept telling himself; but the noises were distinctively like the sound of branches and dead leaves cracking to the pace of walking feet.

He carried on, peering over both shoulders alertly, while trying to count the footsteps of the others out in front.

Peter stopped in his tracks; it appeared something had plunged into his boot leather, and he'd propped himself up against a tree to remedy the irritation.

Edward passed by, leaving Peter a way behind. Then *he* heard it. Out there in the trees, and it was getting closer. He caught up to Edward; Obi seemingly hadn't heard a thing and went racing on ahead, whistling in the hope that his attempt to mimic the birdsong would afford him a response.

This day dragged on much longer than normal. The forest seemed to stretch the hours and it was draining the men. Of course, it was merely the terrain that hindered them, but there was something else, something familiar - something heavily taxing their bodies. Edward kept on looking back but nothing caught his eye. Yet, there *was* something out there, he could hear it - and sense it. The footfall of another, the sounds of which were at a distance behind them.

Edward's state of unease began to quickly change, he was now defensive and tense, jerking his head left and right to any sound. Peter saw this, wondering if Edward was hearing the same sounds he was.

Then, Peter heard an even heavier crack of twigs. "We're being followed!" he said, drawing his axe, no longer able to bear it.

Edward called to Obi who came running back. "What is it, men?"

"There's someone with us in this forest, Obi," said Edward, fearfully, loosing his gifted blade from its sheath. The men circled back-to-back, scanning the scene around them for any signs of movement, any noises. The footsteps had fallen silent for the moment; as though whatever was out there knew they were now on watch. The birdsong had gone, a foul stench growing thick in the air all around them, thick like soot - a familiar, hot wreak of filth.

"Can you smell that?" asked Peter.

"Yes," whispered Edward, his nose curling, taking in the air.

"It cannot be?" said Peter.

"I'm not sticking around here to find out, men," said Obi. "We need to leave here, and fast!"

Peter was the first to run. The others followed tightly behind, knowing what evil followed that stench they now had lingering in their nostrils. They came to yet another old, abandoned house, this time completely in ruins. Obi climbed over the fallen stones and took cover inside. Edward split left and Peter right. Obi had found a dark corner to ball into; a single, thin beam of daylight shone through a crack onto his face. The others hid behind thick trees and were silent, save for the heavy breaths of cold air they drew.

Not long passed before that same stench once again entered their nostrils, the footsteps growing louder and gaining on them. Peter crept around the tree for a look; the Jackal was standing still amongst the trees, with crimson stains on his chest and froth pouring from his cracked lips, covered in blood.

How could it be? Peter saw Obi's arrow pierce his throat and Edward's blade pierce his heart – but there he stood before them.

The Jackal inhaled the air through his blooded nose, taking a huge sniff like a predator stalking his prey.

"I can smell you," he snarled, chillingly.

Obi quivered in his jacket, frightened beyond words. He was certain the likes of such he would never see again in all his life. He felt haunted by the Jackal, and it had caused a great aching throb in his heart. Only a crumbling, old wall stood between himself and this beast back from the dead. Obi looked through the crack and saw him; then, he slipped out of consciousness, falling helplessly to the ground. Edward could see through the ruins and watched him drop. He looked over towards Peter, who was wearing a dark scowl on his countenance, looking as if he was about to do something reckless.

Peter stepped out into the clearing. "Let's have it! You rat!" he screamed.

Edward joined him, and in unison they raised their pistols, aiming upon the Jackal's distorted, haunting face. For half a second, Edward wondered where on earth Peter had found such a weapon but he snapped out of it quickly.

Their fingers clicked the triggers and two shots were sent down the barrels, flying swiftly across the cold distance between them, landing right on the mark.

In that moment, the forest around them erupted into bedlam as the sound of dozens of firing muskets exploded from amongst what seemed like every last trunk and branch. The men fell to the floor for cover. Bullets whistled over their heads; the Jackal crashed to the dirt, clutching his chest and wheezing as blood spilled from his wounds.

The gunfire ceased. The men peered upwards to see a host of hooded figures leap into the open. One of them, appearing to be the leader, stepped across the Jackal's shuddering body, now riddled with iron, lifted his sword and severed the raw-dough-like head in one clean swoop. Edward ran straight for Obi who had regained his wits and missed the whole thing.

"I heard gunshots, Edward, in my dreams!"

"Obi, you're not dreaming!"

"What happened here?" said Obi, hearing the chatter of many men.

"We are lucky to be alive!" said Edward, thankfully. "If it wasn't for help, we'd be dead, I'm sure. Now, be calm and take some water."

"Is he dead, Edward? Tell me that beast is dead! *Tell me!*" cried Obi.

"Obi, be calm, *be calm!*" snapped Edward, shaking his shoulders. "He's dead, for certain this time. Now, rest easy for a moment and I'll be right back."

Edward joined Peter. The leader of the hooded figures addressed himself. A man as tall as an old oak, with a scar that covered his right cheek was standing proudly before them.

"The name's Jasper Montague," he said in an accent a little different to that of Edward and the like. "And these are my men. You're lucky to be alive, you know; the Jackal was a formidable foe. The bastard held these lands to ransom for far too long."

"How did you come across us?" asked Peter.

"We've been hunting him for weeks," said Jasper.

"We killed him," said Edward in disbelief. "I stuck him clean myself."

"Not clean enough!" snapped Jasper. "That was a being possessed, by what, I dread to think, and you only angered him. I doubt the bullet we found in his wife's head brought him any such joy, either."

"Now, that wasn't us!" shouted Peter defensively.

"Nevertheless," interrupted Jasper, "the foul beast will be no more trouble to anybody, bereft of his head."

"In any case, a thank you is truly in order, Jasper," said Edward, extending a hand. "I fear our time might well have been upon us, had you not arrived when you did."

"Where is it your journey takes you?" asked Jasper.

"Me and my companions wish to reach Fort Gaze by tomorrow evening."

"You'll be needing shelter, I would imagine?" said Jasper, returning Edward's gesture. "A place to rest this evening?"

"Only if it's no trouble to you and your men?" replied Edward earnestly.

"Fort Gaze, ey? Well, let's be moving then. We have a small camp not far from here," said Jasper, sheathing his sword.

Edward helped Obi to his feet, the old man swaying as the officer chanced his balance and let go. Obi was lightheaded and still shaking but trod on.

They joined the pack of twenty soldiers, now walking in single file, moving at pace through the forest. The birdsong had returned to the atmosphere; Obi felt a sense of solace rush into him at the sound of each woodland chirp.

Peter stayed behind and crept cautiously towards the headless body of the Jackal. His bones shuddered as he smelled the metallic tang of blood in the air.

Chapter 17
Jasper Montague

The soldiers' camp was rich in provisions and amenities. Peter's eyes widened at all the luxuries before him as he wondered how such things were acquired - by a little sharp practice is how *he* imagined it. He left Edward and Obi and then searched the place, ready to snatch something up from under someone's unsuspecting nose. Edward knew his intentions precisely and caught up to him, giving him a firm warning to act as mannerly as guests should. Peter denied all, but when Edward had walked away, he slid a smoking pipe down his sleeve and into his jacket pocket.

The camp was made up of many horse wagons, with long sheets drawn over them, stretched out to stakes to make tents. There were hay bales used as wind breaks that neatly formed a circle around the fire pit in the very middle, where a giant pot of stew bubbled away next to it, billowing gamey aromas.

There, under the clear, starry sky, everyone seemed to have settled down for the night; everyone except Jasper, who was now the only man standing, pacing the camp from one side to the other. He was a strange-looking man; having no colour in his eyes and a rather oddly shaped face, thin and stretched. A scar running the full length of his right cheek stood out evidently and he wore it with pride - a consequence of battle. He was tall and gangly, but strong in hand and mind; the leader of the Soldiers Slain. He approached Edward, who was laid out under a tent, burrowed into his furs with his hands folded across his chest.

"Edward, is it?" he asked.

"Aye."

"You look like a man of rank?"

"And why is that?"

"The starling on your bandolier."

Edward looked down, realised he wasn't entirely inconspicuous, then smiled. "Only a man of rank himself would have noticed," he said curiously.

"Soldier," said Jasper.

"Officer," said Edward.

"Thought as much; what's an officer doing travelling with the likes of those fellows? Not to mention all the way out here in the forest."

"I'd prefer if our business remained our own, if you don't mind, sir?"

"Of course!" said Jasper, sitting down beside him. "No more questions shall be asked, certainly none in need of an answer, anyway."

"I'm an officer of the *Baliant*, under Captain Wallace Galaway."

"Ah! The *Baliant*?" said Jasper inspiringly. "A spectacular vessel, so she is. I was lucky enough to see her once, docked at Fort Gaze, many years ago. I was astonished at her size and beauty."

"There are many great vessels that have sailed our waters, but none with such charm," said Edward proudly. "Which company do you and your men belong to, might I ask? I see no military embellishments?"

"We are the Soldiers Slain," answered Jasper, showing a burst of pride of his own.

"Slain?" questioned Edward. "You all seem alive and well if my eyes haven't forsaken me?"

"You're quite right, Edward," said Jasper. "We belong to the name because it is believed we are dead. You see, five years ago we set out with the objective to assassinate Lord Becker of Rushing's Hall. He was poisoning his own people, having gone completely mad. Hard to believe, isn't it? Well, there weren't the tools to topple him and his guards obeyed his every command to save their own skins. Word spread, until the news came to Guntrick Castle - our town. Lord Billian couldn't just stand by and do nothing, so he ordered our march to Rushing's Hall, with a plot to remove Becker's head and display it for all to see. The bastards were waiting in ambush ... silently in the shadows. Then we were captured, tortured; many terrible things happened in that dungeon that I don't wish to speak of. Becker had told Lord Billian he'd had us all killed, yet we were taken north to only the wind knows where."

"How did you escape?" asked Edward with a morbid interest.

"We fought our way out at the opportune moment," said Jasper. "You see, in a cell with no features but its dark walls and cold floors, you'd be surprised just how keen your senses become. The guard sees only what he *wants* to see, and that's a man enclosed in steel, helpless and cold. But what *cannot* be seen, so deep in the darkness ... is one's spirit. A man with spirit, and everything to lose, can always find a way, should he find it in his heart. That's what we longed for, day after day and night after night – the way! You could hear it: the slightest footsteps or the most inconspicuously spoken word. A guard farts and after all that time in the darkness you'll start figuring out whose arse it came from. Damn it, I was sure I could hear the bastards blink, sometimes! In the end, the only thing to do, is think and listen and plan. Learn a man's patterns and you'll soon learn which door to run through when the time comes. One of the guards stepped too close to the bars, underestimating our resolve and the power of the men he saw only as helpless prisoners. Then, I strangled that bastard with the tattered shirt from my back! A guard had to die; I just made certain it was the guard with the keys. We killed them all, Edward, then marched to Rushing's Hall and dragged Lord Becker from his bed, torching him alive – on his own porch, I'll add."

"Seemed the world needed rid of him?" said Edward.

"Indeed," said Jasper, grimacing. "Although we fought back our freedom, we never returned to Guntrick Castle. To their knowledge we had perished, and henceforth became the Soldiers Slain."

"And for what cause do you and your men now fight for?"

"Well, it came to our ears that the Lord of Guntrick had planned the ambush all along. He's just as mad as Becker was! Me and my men feel it's time to set the record straight, once and for all. Lord Billian dies next!"

"What was Billian's reason for wanting you dead?"

"He had reason to believe we had the intentions to usurp him."

"Were his suspicions correct?"

"Of course!" laughed Jasper. "The man's a fool, a fraud, a cheat. I curse the day he was given the power and freedom to desecrate our great town with his injustice and vile antics. Guntrick is my place of birth, all of ours. We meant only to dislodge his seat by means of a vote. He deals in a different manner, as we found out. I dream of the moment when we are face to face; it's only then a matter of *how* he dies and not *if*."

Edward listened with rapt attention; Jasper seemed to have divulged all that he intended and looked at Edward in anticipation of a response. The soldier, in his own clever way, had baited the officer quite successfully into telling him a little more about himself.

"There are many men who deserve such fates," said Edward. "For me, I'd see Ridikus burn. They seem to breed them there, those rotten souls." He shuffled to face Jasper. "There's a pirate, one whom I am yet to meet. The commander of a fleet of vessels, bent on leaving nothing but ruin behind them. He captains the *Dürlarain*, his true name I do not know. The other miscreants of the world call him Bill the Baneful, or the Murderous. The man values the lives of others little more than cards in a deck, and I hope that someday … it is I, who deals his final hand."

"The *Dürlarain*; wasn't that once a naval vessel?"

"Yes, but now the spoils of battle," said Edward.

"It pains me to hear," said Jasper. "If the stories are true, the *Dürlarain* is the mightiest ship on the seas?"

"Of unmatched proportions, indeed," said Edward.

"Well, Edward, we both appear to have a just cause then," said Jasper.

"At least that's what I keep telling myself," laughed Edward.

Jasper smiled and then a memory struck him.

"The *Baliant*?" he said, scratching his chin. "The only ship to make it off from Fort Gaze intact, yes?"

"Besides the scars we have to show for it," said Edward, sadly recollecting. "We should have never attempted the attack. Hundreds of men died that day, my brother being one of them. He sailed aboard the *Fortuna*."

"I'm sorry for your loss," said Jasper, standing and dusting the dirt from his trousers, lifting a pouch of tobacco from his breast pocket. "Tell your friend that thieves are no better than dogs amongst my men. Yet, perhaps it works out all the better for me, not having a pipe to smoke. I'm beginning to wonder if it's any good for me, after all."

Jasper laughed and tossed the tobacco high into the air for Edward to catch. "And remind him," he continued. "Peter might have lost a finger or two, had I not been so forgiving."

"I'll see to it he's aware of your clemency, Jasper," said Edward thankfully, tipping his cap then pulling it down over his eyes, laying back to rest.

Jasper returned to his tent, entered a deep state of thought and flinched when something grabbed him, something crazy; a thought he couldn't help but see through. He left his tent and ambled back across the camp where Edward was by now half asleep.

"Officer?" he whispered. "I might have a proposition for you."

"Go on?" said Edward, lifting his cap sleepily.

"If you join me in taking Guntrick Castle, I'll make sure my men fall under your command, should you ever need them."

"You're asking me to-"

"It seems crazy I know, but we could use a man of your military experience. Then, I give you my word, the Soldiers Slain will help you take Ridikus."

"It will take a host of more than twenty men to sack Ridikus island!" said Edward, thinking this was all a big joke.

"My soldiers will follow me no matter what and this world will never be short of things worth fighting for. No, you're right, twenty men can't take Ridikus, but you've more chance with us than without. What do you say?"

"You think the will of three men will change your fortunes?" asked Edward.

"Perhaps not," said Jasper. "But the will of twenty might change yours?"

Edward took a brief moment to digest the words, realising Jasper was in fact entirely serious. "If you'll allow me to sleep on it?" he said politely.

"Of course. You know where to find me should you come to a conclusion."

Then, Jasper left again, and Edward entered a deep state of thought of his own, silently caressing the newly grown hair on his chin. *I shouldn't trust this man,* he thought. *If he finds out about the diamond, he'll surely want it? Then you'll see precisely what the will of twenty men looks like. Don't be a damn fool, Edward Clavell! Yet ... he never needs to know about a thing. Keep the true meaning of your journey between the three of you ... and how could he ever know? Is the sacrifice worth the reward? How valuable are twenty soldiers should the diamond worth a thousand times that be found?*

But in that moment, Edward realised something. *I would be dead had it not been for these men. Would our part in this just be payment for saving our lives? If the road ahead is as bleak as the road behind, we could certainly use that firepower.*

He crept to his feet and gestured for Peter to join him away from camp. Obi was sat beside the fire, listening to it crackle, staring at the stars.

"This better be good," said Peter. "Just about to pull that rabbit off the spit there."

"Sir Jasper and his men are going to attack the town of Guntrick not far from here," said Edward. "He has his reasons and I believe them to be just. If we help him, he's given his word that his men will fall under our command. And when the time comes, we might just need a little help, what do you think?"

"You would risk your life for another man's cause?" said Peter, shaking his head.

"I would risk my life for safe passage to Ridikus. Allow me to remind you, the three of us would cease to exist without them."

Peter glanced over each shoulder secretively.

"And what if they find out about the diamond?" he whispered. "Have you thought about that?"

"They will *never* know," said Edward. "I'll insist their side of the bargain ends should they see us to Ridikus in one piece and that we mean to part company at a crossing near Fort Gaze. Sparing them any more of the details."

"I'll need to know the exact matter at hand before I can make an honest call on this, Edward. You can't just spring a siege onto me whilst I'm all cosy and warm and up to my cheeks in roasted rabbit. A man needs to hear the ins and outs before a decision is made. Yes, *you* are a mad man, but *I'm* a pirate and I love a good fight - if it's for the right reasons."

Edward smiled and told him Jasper's story word for word. Peter listened on with curled brows.

Then a noise came from the wagon beside them. The men shared a confused look before each taking hold of a handle, pulling the doors wide open.

"I hope you haven't promised that fellow over there that I'll be running into some castle for a tumble?" said Obi, sitting there in the darkness. "I'm too old and I'm not partial to it, you know, this fighting business. I'll be waiting outside, sat upon one of these wagons ready for a sprint, should this endeavour of yours take a turn for the worse."

Edward looked on, tilting his head questioningly. "Eavesdropping, Obi?" he asked, as a warm simper crept upon him.

Peter enjoyed the mischief. "I will forever fear what might have become of us, had you not turned back to help us, Obi," he said thankfully. "A gatekeeper, with the heart of a lion, and bow-wielding fingers as light as feathers. My new friend, we couldn't possibly go on without you."

Edward reached out to help the old man down. "It's the three of us now, old boy," he said, as Obi landed beside him. "No more secrets, ey?"

"Let's eat, then!" cheered Peter, rubbing his grubby hands together. "My belly aches, and I smell that rabbit burning. Who's joining?"

Edward halted him with a firm grip to the arm. "If you think I don't know what you've been up to, then you're more stupid than I thought, Peter," he said sternly. "Return that pipe at once! Before our host sees fit to change his mind. He knows you've taken it, and I'd sleep with one eye open, if I were you."

Chapter 18
Guntrick Castle

Edward lay sleeping as the morning sun inched over the hills, shining beams of golden light across his face. He was dreaming of the summer, when the grass turns emerald-green, and the flowers bloom into a profusion of vibrant colours and shades. Charlotte was of course there; the gentle warmth of the sun that shrouded him made his dreams feel all the more real. He reached out to touch her, then woke.

The smell of roasting meat travelled with the wind as Peter jumped to his feet to try and find it. Edward's eyes flicked open and the blurry figure of Jasper Montague stood above him, shiny and dazzling.

"A fine morning it is, Edward - will you be joining us?" he asked.

Edward tiredly glanced around the camp at all the commotion, slipped from his furs, stood to his feet and reached out his hand.

"The deal seems fair to me, Jasper. It will be an honour to serve alongside a fellow Kingsman."

"The honour will be all mine, officer," said Jasper. "Your comrades over there, did they take much persuading?"

Edward dusted himself off. They began to walk together.

"Pirates aren't known for making rational choices," he laughed, watching Peter fill his face with a slice of bacon. "Many of them just follow the chaos. Perhaps I'd be a fool to believe Peter was any different. The talk of a good fight pricked his ears quick enough. And Obi, well, he might be the bravest amongst us, although he remains entirely unaware of his own virtues. He seems bound to us by the sincerity of his own promises."

"There is much strength in a man who honours a promise, so there is," said Jasper. "Soldiers!" he called to his men. "Today we march for Guntrick Castle. Our time has come for revenge and we will *not* be denied it! At any cost shall Lord Billian hang from the walls for the town to see. Tomorrow, we storm the gate! Move out!"

The men sauntered alongside the now moving wagons. The wheels bounced and fumbled over the rocks in the road and the soldiers that sat upon them lifted from their perch at each bump. Obi could barely keep up, being so easily distracted by the birds that chirped and whistled all around him. Peter was still considering things and kept on looking over to Edward to see if his spirit about the matter had waivered at all. It hadn't; Edward looked devoted to his decision to help perpetrate an attack upon a castle and town he had no allegiance to. Another thought that began to creep into his mind, was the wonderment of which his wild imagination ignited – what exactly would be the resistance? Was it just a clan of low-level soldiers, or an army of formidable brutes loyal to a fault? How would the people react to an attack; the people who swore fealty to this, by all accounts, callous Lord Billian? He couldn't continue on this path of uncertainty, and needing answers, he caught up to Jasper at the front of the march.

"I've just a few questions, Jasper, or concerns, depending on which way you slice it."

"Peter? What is it that troubles you?"

"I hope it's a very small castle you plan to besiege?" said Peter, his shorter legs working nearly twice as hard as Jasper's.

Jasper laughed. "Peter, there are many loyal soldiers that follow Lord Billian, and there are many that do not. Once we arrive, the mere beating of our hearts will be enough to afford us the advantage. I have a plan – worry not!"

"I'd sure like to hear that plan, you know, to ease my nerves a little."

"And hear it you will, my new friend, but all in good time," said Jasper. "I will summon my men, speak of what I have devised, and we shall share a drink to toast the occasion. But tell me, surely you must have seen your fair share of engagements like these, what would you do?"

"I'll spare you the worthless opinion of a pirate," said Peter, a little ashamed.

"I've never met a pirate quite like you before," said Jasper. "The only pirates I've ever come across, I've been staring at over the barrel of a pistol; never did get much chance to make any of their acquaintances."

Peter's head fell forward in sadness. "I wasn't like the rest of them. I spiralled my way into the clutches of that miserable life, and looking back, I don't *really* know how. I always did just enough for them to believe that I was every bit as despicable; you know, to make it seem as though I was one of them. Yes, I have done terrible things and seen far more than any man should – but an innocent never perished at my hands. At least there's that to reassure me."

The guard atop the palace walls flashed before his eyes; the thought twisted his stomach.

"And you left the pirate life behind, for what?" asked Jasper.

"For a chance to someday redeem my transgressions," said Peter, shaking off those harrowing thoughts.

"And so…you met the officer?"

"I was found aboard a ship named the *Venturous*. The navy torched her to ashes, and it was Edward the turnkey, to whom I became acquainted."

"I see. And by what stroke of luck had the both of you searching for the same thing?"

"I asked for help and Edward obliged. I guess he saw the little good left in me. Although, it mattered little; the judge paid him no mind and saw fit to see me hanged, anyway."

Jasper silently acknowledged Peter's dodging of his question.

"For what crimes?"

Peter lifted up his tongue to reveal the star within a star. "You knew I was a pirate, didn't you?" he asked a little shakily.

"From the very first second I saw you, yes," said Jasper.

"Then why all the kindness?"

Jasper shrugged.

"Well, I ceased to hold a grudge the day I was betrayed by a man I thought to be honourable. I've kept a close eye on you, sure enough, my new friend, and I will *not* hesitate in removing your head should I need to. Yet I see no malice in your eyes, so my sword shall remain sheathed until you cross me."

Peter shuddered. In that moment, Jasper's dark, forbidding eyes lacked any compassion at all, and they told the whole tale, or at least enough of it. *Do not cross this man!*

"I think it's about time I gave this back then," Peter quivered, removing the pipe from his jacket.

"Keep it, Peter. I do not threaten you over a stolen pipe."

"I couldn't keep it, sir. You must think I'm little more than a worthless pig. I harp on about making amends for my sins, yet I steal the first thing I can, the first chance I get. Here, take it."

Jasper looked over and took the pipe from Peter's outstretched hand.

"Here you go, Peter. A gift for you," he said gleefully, handing it back to him. "Now you can smoke and smoke and smoke, knowing that you didn't actually steal it. Call it a transgression redeemed."

Peter couldn't help but smile in appreciation.

"Thank you, truly," he said, nestling the pipe in his pocket.

"Your friend, Edward," said Jasper. "He desires a world rid of pirates, so he does? It seems Ridikus is where he will begin?"

"Indeed, it is," said Peter, cautious not to mention any words like: diamond, scroll, armoury or crown.

"With the might of Fort Gaze peering over its rancid shoulder," said Jasper, "he'll need a fleet of twenty ships to topple it. Yet I sense he has something far more inconspicuous up his sleeve. One doesn't simply walk amongst those rotten souls unnoticed, like mice in the dark. Folly, if you ask me! Either that, or the three of you have the bollocks fit for an ox!"

Peter laughed. "I know well enough how thin the line is between bravery and foolery, Jasper; ironic how that's never stopped me stepping on either side of it." Peter paused to collect his thoughts. "On that note, I should be heading back - see to the old man."

"Here," said Jasper. "Tell him to ride my horse for a few hours, rest his weary legs."

"A kind offer, sir."

Peter led the horse over to Obi and helped him on. The old man looked deeply thankful and sunk into the saddle with a relieved deep breath. Edward moved to the side of Peter. "So then, do you return convinced?" he asked in jest.

"Convinced of what, exactly?"

"That our forthcoming escapade won't lead to our untimely demise," smiled Edward.

"There will be nothing untimely about it!" snapped Peter. "I can only imagine what lies ahead, and it ain't good! No, I do not return convinced, Edward."

Peter began to mumble soft words under his breath, the odd curse scattered within. "Let's besiege a castle, ey? What could possibly go wrong? Damn fool you must be, Peter Beaumont."

"What happened to loving a good fight?" laughed Edward.

"I like fights that I can win!" said Peter. "And I know what I said last night, you needn't remind me again, but I was delirious on all that rabbit and wine."

"What did the two of you speak about, anyway?

"I asked about the task at hand; he told me absolutely nothing. I'm sure he's hiding something, you know, but I can't quite put my finger on it. Trust no one, I say."

Peter's words were not entirely true. In fact, he did trust Jasper; he trusted that the soldier would slit his throat if he stepped half a toe out of line ... again.

"I think you're being a little hasty in judging the man," said Edward, unsure if he could keep up this lack-of-concern ruse; only doing it to discover the point at which Peter's nerve would snap. "Although, the only folk to be trusted around here are the three of us, and unless I'm proven otherwise, the three of us it shall remain. But his men will prove valuable to us, if we don't die out here, that is."

Edward looked towards Obi. "I've been meaning to ask, old boy. Why have you stayed with us, all this time?"

"To see you safe to Fort Gaze, Edward," replied Obi, proudly.

"That we know; but do the deep and dark of these woods not make you long for home?"

"Oh! For certain!" laughed Obi, trotting steadily by on his borrowed mount. "I really don't know why I'm here. Or maybe I do, who knows? Although, after seeing what I have, these past few days, I'm not entirely sure I'm still sound of mind. Strange business was that Jackal, and now this Jasper character. If I do return to Bidle's Edge and start telling tales of pearly-eyed men who rise from the damn dead, they'll have me out on the road to fend for myself in no time. So, perhaps *that* is why I'm here, because I couldn't keep my mouth shut. No place for a mad man amongst folks like that."

"If all the unbelievable things a man sees makes him mad, there's no hope left for me!" said Peter, deep in contemplation. "Surely there are more folk who knew of the Jackal?"

"Of course, but none that were ever willing to admit as much," said Obi. "I've travelled many a mile in these lands whilst out and about and it quickly became clear that I wasn't the only one out here hunting – or killing to be precise. He was out there, sure enough, and perhaps the reason he'd never been seen much was that many of the poor souls who laid eyes on him never lived to speak of it."

"Yet, you knew just where to find him?" shuddered Edward.

"Curiosity!" said Obi, looking back on his choices in regret. "I was the only sod daft enough to go looking. The beast stayed clear of the townsfolk, so it was me who ventured out to find him. I must have been so foolish! Some days I'm frightened of my own bloody shadow, so who knows what possessed me to go searching. All I found was the lady, rocking in a chair on the porch, with rats scuttling the field around her. But I knew there was more to it, so I returned, again and again. Then I saw him, just the once, striding the woods; a young buck slung over his shoulder, blood dripping from his filthy mouth.

"Forgive me, men, I didn't mean to guide you into such danger, but I quickly convinced myself it wasn't my place to argue, and that you'd surely have a good reason. I'm a gatekeeper, the helpful kind, and the two of you seemed like you could damn well look after yourselves. These spinnels in my shirt pocket sure helped me along, I won't lie about that."

Obi tapped the coins, *click, click.*

Later that day, when the sun had all but fallen, and the crisp evening chill had crept in, the march stopped. Camp was again set up, the smell of the evening's fare a blossoming redolence of honey-smothered grouse and buttered potatoes. Yet on this night, Edward observed, the camp felt a little different; edgy, ill at ease, at best. The only words to be heard were the simple grunting thanks after the cook dropped the morsels of grouse into each soldier's bowl. Peter thought about cracking a joke, but there was something unnerving about the sombre look on each man's face. The Soldiers Slain, although clearly formidable, hadn't managed to intimidate him much, until now. He looked over at Edward who was taking in the aromas of his bowl, keeping his head firmly where it belonged - in his own business. Obi had wolfed down the meal and had already curled into his sleeping furs, hoping to slip seamlessly away from his consciousness. Peter stared up at the sky thoughtfully. It looked to split in two, like anger and delight; the faintest pink hue at one side, and a black abyss at the other. He hoisted his own furs to his chest, lit Jasper's pipe, and blew a long, grey stripe of smoke into the night, splitting the sky into three.

Edward woke to the sound of Peter muttering beside him.

"I've heard we'll be there by late this afternoon, Edward. Look sharp!"

"Do allow me another minute before you continue talking, Peter?

Your voice, it cuts right through me, so early in a morning."

Peter raised his middle finger and slunk off into the distance. Edward sighed tiredly, crawled from his furs and proceeded to roll them up and tie them to his satchel. He lifted his gaze towards the camp. Jasper's eyes caught his and they both shared an apprehensive look, then, an acceptive nod. The time had come.

Onward into the day they marched. Peter took a calming gulp of his whiskey, observing the sky again, which still looked to be in conflict with itself; the clouds growing darker with each passing minute. Obi whistled away songfully; Edward found himself hard pressed to remember a time when he'd been as nervous as today. His heart thumped; the anxiety exhausted him, a flicker of regret leapt around inside his stomach, occasionally slithering up to take a grip of his throat. Had this been a mistake? He spent the entire day contemplating that thought.

Evening approached and the wagons had to be set aside; they were too big and not nearly quiet enough to ride too close to town, so the final push was to be made without them. Jasper summoned Edward and Peter; he was standing beside one of the wagons that had been flung open at the back. When they came closer, the leather covering Jasper had held open revealed an arsenal of weapons stacked from side to side: axes, swords, muskets and barrels of black powder. A deadly assemblage of arms, collected for one purpose – death.

Jasper called them all in. "Listen up, boys! There will be some who still fight for Lord Billian. He didn't act alone. But in my heart I know our people will rally beside us. We will break into the courtyard and tell them all what truly happened. Any who oppose us will die, any who yield, will live. I expect nothing less than bloodshed here today. We are the Soldiers Slain and we shall have our long-awaited vengeance! The first man who captures Lord Billian can take the honour; but I ask that I'm the one to slip the noose around his fat neck!"

The soldiers cheered and set about the trees with haste. Edward and Peter had taken a few items from the arsenal, then followed. They looked back at Obi who was sat atop one of the wagons, waving back, with a huge, nervous smile shivering on his lips.

"Come back in one piece, my friends – be safe!" he called to them, his smile turning upside down in a slow movement. He was scared for them.

Peter looked astonished. "Edward? Jasper made it clear that he had a plan, yet he means for us to storm a castle in the hope they don't start firing?"

Edward noticed the knot in his stomach grow tighter with each breath.

"He trusts his people, Peter, so perhaps we should trust them too," he said, trying to reassure himself – but that seemed futile.

Before the sun had slipped over the hills, they came upon Guntrick Castle; a fortified town that jutted from the hillside, standing high in a sense of majesty, peering down over a massive plain of wide, grassy cattle fields. The castle was huge and shaped with many sharp, patina-covered spires; and in the middle, one central tower stood higher than all the rest. Peter craned his neck at the huge stones and the beautiful copper roofing, then smiled. It was by far the most enchanting building he had ever seen.

The soldiers found a vantage point in the trees, laid low and waited for Jasper to make the next call. Jasper looked out, counting the guards on the ramparts and down in the courtyard. *As if an exact count makes a difference,* thought Peter angrily. He looked down, lifted his hands to his face then pondered over them. His skin felt more penetrable than ever, and nothing could change that; nothing could transform his flesh into iron. He felt exposed ... again, and he cursed madly under his breath at the frailties of the human body and just how hopelessly useless it was at stopping bullets. "*Damn it!*" he snapped quietly.

Jasper's hand landed firmly on his shoulder, making him jerk around. "Are you ready, Peter?" said the soldier, pointing down towards the gate where two guards stood watch. "Now, this is where you and Edward play your part," he whispered. "I know those guards and they'll know any one of us. Distract them, then make sure they're dreaming about the butterflies by the time we get down there."

Peter sighed apprehensively. Edward slid a musket off his shoulder, closing his jacket to cover the starling on his bandolier. "Let's go, before I change my mind," he whispered to Peter.

They dropped down onto the road.

"Just follow my lead," said Edward sternly, as he began to stumble just as a drunkard might.

Peter looked on befuddled. "For the love of the sea, Edward, what on earth are you doing?" he chirped from the corner of his mouth.

"Shh! Just follow my lead, Peter," snapped Edward, tripping over his own feet.

Peter joined in with the charade, reluctantly; what other choice did he have? Lifting out his whiskey flask he knocked back a giant swig. "There's no need for pretending!" he mumbled.

They were close now. The guards looked over them disapprovingly. One of them nudged the other, his eyes rolling. "The local sots?"

"Evening, gentlemen of the guard," slurred Edward, stumbling again. "I've heard–"

"Step back! We don't want any of your kind around here. Now be off with ya!" said the ugliest one of the two.

Peter fumbled forward and faked a trip, letting the whiskey spill out to douse the pair of them.

"My handkerchief!" he said, reaching down into his pocket. "It's gone! Those rats must have taken it!"

The guards were now furious, having seen enough. The ugly one raised his musket, clicking the hammer into place. "I'm warning you, boy. Step back!"

"Allow me," said Edward, lifting a handkerchief with his left hand, swinging the clenched fist of his right to land four cold knuckles flush across a guard's jaw. The guard hit the ground with a dull thud. Peter dealt with the second the very moment before he squeezed the trigger.

The plan had worked. The soldiers moved down to join them. Edward and Peter fell in behind the stone walls for cover, their hearts beating like mad.

A case of black powder was placed against the gate and the fuse was lit. They stood back, then *bang!* The gate was compromised; Jasper kicked it through, and with the most immense show of fortitude, he strode out into the middle of the courtyard with his sword raised high in the air. "We are the Soldiers Slain, and we are here for Lord Billian!" he growled, fiercely.

The guards and the people of Guntrick Castle could scarcely move, having just seen a host of men once thought to be dead, standing before them. The rest of the soldiers stepped up behind Jasper in a formidable formation, their aims cast all around. The guards were unnerved and did nothing. The trees whistled above them. The breeze toppled the wispy dead hay off the courtyard stones, and it was cold – so very cold.

Noises echoed through a tunnel at the north side of the courtyard, from which more guards spilled out, drawing their muskets. Lord Billian followed with an anger in his heavy steps, his eyes bulging, his sharp chin leading the way. Then, those bulging eyes sunk back into his skull in fear.

"Montague? I thought you were ... dead?" he quivered, taking a huge gulp.

"Yet here I am!" said Jasper coldly.

"It is so good to see you alive and well!" said Billian, in a tiresome, satirical manner, albeit a front.

Jasper's lips curled in rage. "Tell the people what you did to us. *Tell them!*"

"Forgive me, soldier, but I have no idea what you're talking about."

Lord Billian was a fat mess of a man, who'd grown rotund from all the years sat before a banquet table. Jasper sneered at the man; he made him sick. The guards on the walls all shared looks of wonder. The people longed for answers. The dead men before them looked as alive as ever.

"You always were a coward, Lord Billian. Allow me to speak the truth of it to the people."

Jasper turned to face the townsfolk. "It has been five long years, and now I look upon you good people with much joy in my heart," he said eagerly. "Yet I fear you know little of the foul swine who rules you. This traitor banished us to a cell and left us all to die!"

The questioning eyes of the people pierced through Lord Billian with a sharp demand for answers. The fat lord just chuckled away to himself, running his clammy fingers down the length of his golden robe, admiring the softness of the silk, ever indulged in his own cupidity. The townsfolk began to murmur.

"For what crimes?" one called as she stepped up.

"You call that King's justice?" said another, followed by cheers.

"We beg of you to answer, m'lord," said a third.

"It is *this* scarred beast and his rabid clan of dogs who are guilty of treachery!" snapped Billian, shaking his fist, his fat jiggling. "I am no coward, Montague! Perhaps I am a fool for allowing Becker to have his way with you. I should have seen you hanged in this very courtyard for trying to usurp *me!* Fools! And now, you're back to face justice! Guards!"

The guards atop the castle walls lowered their aims. The loyal that remained stood trembling in their boots, gripping their muskets, as a fear rose from deep within them. They knew they were all alone in this ever-darkening courtyard.

Billian's nerve betrayed him and he ran for it, as quickly as his obscene shape would allow. Jasper watched as he disappeared into the tunnel and out of sight. He could smell the stench of fear on the guards left behind. There was a silence. A few agonisingly anxious seconds of it before Jasper jerked up his musket and fired.

The Soldiers Slain unloaded their guns, and Billian's remaining loyal guards were riddled with five years of revenge.

Jasper walked pressingly past the dead, onward through the tunnel into the central tower of the castle - his eyes slowly adjusting to the darkness. He could hear Lord Billian running frantically, his quivering voice fading with each step he ascended.

"Billian!" screamed Jasper. The echoes went surging past the fat lord. Jasper climbed the tower to find the man cowering in the corner of his bedchamber, pleading hopelessly for mercy. Billian's wrist took up the whole of Jasper's hand as the soldier grasped it viciously.

"Have mercy! Please, have mercy, Montague!"

Jasper barged through the door onto the courtyard halfway up the tower, dragging Billian, kicking across the cold stones. Four other soldiers joined him in securing the noose as the fat lord fought fruitlessly to escape. Jasper reached for his legs and heaved him over the parapet, the rope tightening with an eerie crack as it took the weight. The people below gasped in shock.

Once the leader of a town in the east, now hanged by his neck from the very tower he ruled from. The Soldiers Slain had finally delivered the people they strived to save, the long-awaited justice they so rightfully deserved.

Chapter 19
Hot on the Heels of Justice

Gürad had summoned all his men into the palace courtyard. Lord Harrington looked down at him from his chamber window, grimacing. Gürad grit his teeth through every order that was given to him. He wasn't loyal in that way, but he was effective, and sinister. He longed for the power Harrington possessed, and perhaps, that was his most wicked vice.

"Right!" he snapped. "That filthy pirate-loving bastard was spotted in Bidle's Edge just this morning. I have it on good authority that is where he spent the night. However, it appears their hosts knew our fellow Kingsman had taken a pirate accomplice, and they did absolutely *nothing*! That is a crime in itself and I'd rather like to ruffle some feathers about it. Now, mount up, and you'll ride your horses into the damn ground before our chase slows. GO!"

The Kingsguard burst out from the palace gate, the deafening sound of horse hooves thrashing the ground. Colonel Gürad rode as if he had a score to settle. He had taken this matter personally; the immense rage that brewed inside his soul had no means of concealment. He brandished it, wearing it like a badge of honour. The sound of the horses cantering in pursuit excited him madly; the wind rushing past his ears stimulating his desires. No man was above the law and Colonel Gürad was to make certain Edward Clavell hanged for his treason.

Upon their arrival at Bidle's Edge, the horses were exhausted, steam pluming from their coats as they gasped for air. Gürad leapt down first and hit the gate with three echoing knocks, *boom, boom, boom!*

A short moment of silence was followed by the appearance of two brown eyes through the hatch, eyes as gentle as a spring breeze.

"Open the gate!" he snarled. "Now!" The young lady noticed the greycoats and jittered. Creak went the gate; the guards slowly walked in.

Gürad strode right past her, glaring menacingly, deep into her soul. The lady stepped back in fear and let them pass.

"There were two men here," he growled. "This very morning. Tell me where they fled. That is a direct order from Lord Augustus Harrington of Summer's Reach!"

The town remained silent; only the flickers of the fire filled the space between those beehive-like homes.

"Speak! And speak now!"

He rushed over to the lady at the gate, clenched her by the throat and forced her against the wall with a crack. He drew his face close to hers and whispered, "Tell me ... sweet little thing."

The people of the town flinched at the sight of it. Some of them stood, some whimpered, many pounced to protect her. Gürad never flinched; his men drew their blades. "*Stand down!*" they all called in unison.

The lady's throat was reprieved of the colonel's tight grasp; she choked and fell to the ground, clutching the pain. Once again, the colonel asked and once again the people remained silent.

Gürad began to vex, shuddering in anger, for he knew not why these people protected them. But his patience had run thin. He grabbed the lady by the hair, dragged her to the fireside and threw her to the ground by the burning logs.

"Tell me!" he screamed, striking her with the back of his hand.

Then a voice. "Stop this madness!"

It was Lena, she had returned from the capital. Gürad spun on the spot and smiled – he recognised her face.

"I beg of you to stop this!" she cried. "Stop this, now! What do you want with my people, guard?"

"I want nothing with your people, Lena Hoster!" snapped Gürad. "Tell me what I need to know, and I will leave you all to rot in peace, in your filthy hole in the ground. And you will address me as Colonel, next time."

"A colonel who would strike an innocent?" scoffed Lena in disbelief. "Is that how you've earned your authority?"

Gürad lifted his pistol and sniggered. "You don't *earn* authority, bitch ... you *demand* it! Would you like me to demonstrate?"

Gürad turned his aim upon the lady by the fire. The townsfolk gasped. Lena couldn't take it another second and spilled the truth.

"Edward left Bidle's Edge, heading east. But where exactly, I do not know. Our gatekeeper left with them and said something about a place not far from here, a house, in fact." Lena shuddered as she spoke. "Now ...

lower your aim, Eustace. Do not force me to do something reckless." Lena casually revealed the pistol she had stashed in her coat.

The colonel smiled widely, holstering his weapon. "Now that wasn't so hard, was it?" he said haughtily. "Oh, and give my regards to your sister. You'll find her at the Plummet, awaiting trial ... for treason."

The Kingsguard searched the forest high and low for any sign, but there was nothing – not yet at least. The colonel knew his assailants wouldn't have taken the road for fear of being seen, but rather the simplest route through the trees. The guards were looking for a house, east of Bidle's Edge, and Gürad, knowing the lay of the land as well as anybody, had a strange hunch where they might have headed. He himself knew there were no nearby settlements, and having heard a strange tale of a strange house, located in the lands east of Bidle's Edge, he wondered if it could be possible. "The Jackal?" he whispered to himself.

The guards became increasingly frustrated, cursing and complaining; their mounts groaning and puffing as they struggled over the cragged terrain.

A camp had to be made, with the misty bite of the evening drawing in; the Kingsguard tired and restless. Gürad didn't sleep a wink that night; he just sat there plotting. At this point, there was nothing else on his mind; even the touch of his wife's love didn't register on him. He was utterly consumed by his duties. The thought of seeing Edward hanged, and how he would be content watching it whilst Edward breathed his final breaths, put a wicked smile on his face.

They awoke from the cold ground that next morning and cleared up the camp. Then, they were off, yet this time the light of a new day was in their favour. The morning dew on the grass gleamed as their horses trampled it to mud. Gürad, an ever-dedicated force to be reckoned with barked orders, his men enthused with a renewed vigour.

The trees and their branches never left the colonel's gaze. He was looking for a sign, any sign. Just a boot print can tell a thousand stories in forests like these, if you knew what you were looking for. One of his guards pulled up on his horse after catching a smoky aroma in his nostrils. "Colonel ... I smell a wood-fire."

Gürad signalled for the rest of them to halt; the guard jumped down from his mount, quietly ascending the adjacent banking. And there it was, the old, ruined house, deep in the trees, with a saddle tree-swing out front.

"The embers are still warm, Colonel," said the guard, looking to his superior for approval. "Whoever was here, can't be more than a few miles away."

Gürad walked about the grass, examining the prints in the trodden dirt.

"Three set of footprints," he said, feeling around, brushing away long strands of grass. "Very interesting. Our slippery friends have indeed an accomplice. Tell the others to bring up the horses, we ride this way!"

The tireless legs of their mounts held up steadier than castle walls as they trudged on. The boot prints telling the story Gürad so desperately wanted to hear. Onwards they rode, until a shivering sound of gunfire pounded their ears. They halted then gained formation. Gürad placed a finger to his lips, urging silence. The Kingsguard stood quietly amongst the gentle gusts that blew past them. He gestured for two of his men to follow him, deeper to where the forest thickened. They pressed on with their weapons drawn, quietly through the thickets - the sound of voices began to grow and grow.

Gürad crouched down, almost crawling and then rose to find cover behind a thick trunk. The others joined him, and from there they could see a beastly pale man laid on his back - headless - the forest air thick with a grey haze of gun smoke. And there, amongst the maelstrom. "Edward Clavell," snarled Gürad.

The guard beside him discreetly tried to draw his musket, until he felt the firm hand of the colonel force the barrel into the ground. "Are you some kind of fool?" he quietly snapped at the guard. "Fire, and you'll get us all killed - can you not see they are armed to the teeth?"

"But Colonel, we have the traitor in our sights, should we not–"

"Back to the horses, before your insolent mouth meets the butt of my pistol."

Gürad and his men re-joined the others. The colonel untied the satchel from his horse. "Like a dog to a rabbit!" he chuckled to himself. "Guards! I will follow them on foot, alone. Ha! It seems they have acquired friends in the dark of the woods. They outnumber us two to one. Meet me at Willow's Pass. That seems the most logical rendezvous on our current course."

"Surely they will halt for the Kingsguard, Colonel? Turn over our prisoners?" questioned one of his men.

"I wouldn't count on that!" said Gürad. "Those men look as wild as the woods itself if you ask me, and I'm sure I've seen one of them before – that scar?"

Gürad caressed his chin, searching his memory, then vanished.

He stalked them through the woods, watching them at every turn. Sneaking, lurking behind the dark layer of branches around the camps they made and the roads they travelled. He couldn't get close enough to hear the words spoken, but through the night he spied and through the light he followed.

Two days had passed when the Soldiers Slain took Guntrick Castle; Gürad watched on. He'd devised a simple plan that would surely change his fortunes. A plan to take the old man that Edward and Peter seemed so fond of.

He climbed on the wagon and pressed his blade against Obi's neck. "Don't you make a sound. You're coming with me, quickly!"

Obi jumped in fright then froze, then whimpered for mercy. He stepped down from the wagon and Gürad dragged him into the forest, gun to head.

They would walk to Willow's Pass to meet the rest. Obi was now a prisoner of the King.

The light had faded into darkness, the Kingsguard were stood waiting where ordered. Gürad hurled the old man to the ground, and there in the dirt, he was bonded.

"They've taken shelter at Guntrick Castle," said the colonel. "With much force behind them. We are outnumbered; trying to take them with a fight will get us all killed. This man here is of worth to those worms and at first light we'll use him to tempt Edward Clavell from his hole. I will not leave this forest without him, and I will have no mercy!"

*

Guntrick Castle was still and quiet after a day now carved into its history. Lord Billian was the rotting tooth that had to be extracted and Jasper and his men dealt the blow. It was a time for reflection, a time for resting, a time for peace amongst the people.

Jasper took the dead lord's chambers for himself, and there, with the sweet feeling of vengeance ablaze inside him, he wept. Tears of joy spilled down his scarred cheek as he stared at the stone walls left utterly bleak from neglect. Yet there was comfort. Finally, after the long wilderness had they returned. Jasper stepped out onto the high courtyard to breathe the air, looking down upon his men who had set off to retrieve their wagons.

Edward and Peter had walked out behind them to meet Obi. But their companion was nowhere to be found.

"Edward … he isn't here!" Peter called, whirling around in search. "Where is he?"

Edward leapt onto the wagon and cast a lengthy investigative stare down the road and then back again, his thoughts jostling with one another.

"Maybe he's just left us, Peter?" he said wistfully. "Perhaps he'd seen quite enough strange. I can hardly blame him."

"No, something isn't right here," snapped Peter. "He wouldn't have taken off like this, I'm certain."

"Peter, try not to worry," said Edward. "We can't be sure he wasn't sick of all this and just headed for home. The whole thing will have spooked him, that's all."

"In any case," said Peter, gritting his teeth, "I'll ask Jasper to lend me a horse and I'll ride out to find him; he can't be far, and I'll see to it he gets home safely. This forest is no place for a man wandering alone. There might well be stranger things than the Jackal lurking about."

Edward became frustrated. "Just being here has added days to our journey, Peter. How much more time will we waste before we take our leave?"

Edward took a deep sigh having seen the chilling scowl on Peter's face.

"Waste?" snapped Peter. "I really ought to smack you in the face for that. Tell me, what happened to the *three* of us?" Peter was right in Edward's face now.

A stabbing pain of guilt hit Edward hard. "I'm sorry, Peter," he said, shaking his head fervently. "I don't know what has got into me. You head off and find him, hastily, and make sure you return in one piece. Give Obi my best and tell him goodbye for now. Be careful, Peter. I'm almost certain the Kingsguard will be in pursuit; do not get caught."

Peter came back to the road after speaking with Jasper, who'd kindly offered to have one of his men accompany him. The soldier walked two horses up the road, and together, he and Peter jumped into the saddles and were off.

Jasper summoned Edward from atop the castle walls; the officer, grabbing a few sacks to take with him, walked back through the gate to meet the leader of the Soldiers Slain in the courtyard.

"This place looks better already," said Jasper. "Wouldn't you say?"

"Indeed, it does," said Edward, taking in the beauty of the spires that looked to hover above him like sharp shadows in the night sky. "There is joy in your people's faces. I was right to trust you after all."

"And I will honour my word, Officer," said Jasper, seriously. "When you need us, you only need ask."

"There's no way I can thank you, Jasper," said Edward. "And I hardly believe we have earned what you offer. I feel like the deal we made weighs heavily on your men."

Jasper smiled and looked upon his people.

"Things could have been very different here today," he said, taking a breath, his eyes scanning around at the remnants of his old town. "The people needed to hear the truth. From then it was theirs to do with as they saw fit. They'd seen enough of Lord Billian's antics, it turns out. I can only imagine the sadness that dog brought upon our town. I will endeavour to make this castle as formidable as it once was. A true power. Just by the fact that you and your friends had any part to play, is enough to hold your end of the deal, Officer.

"The Soldiers Slain are castle guards no longer, nor have they been for many years now. We stayed true to our country and those within it, although many of them betrayed us. For some time, we have fought on many fronts, wherever our swords and muskets have been required. I'll see to it that you're well fed tonight, Edward. Peter was sent off with some provisions. I do hope they serve him well. You're a guest here now, so put down those sacks and see yourself to a chamber. I'll have something warm sent to you at once."

Jasper strode off through the crowds. Edward's feet remained planted on the stone, his thoughts switching to that of Peter and Obi. Had he made a mistake allowing Peter to leave? But then, the pirate's words echoed in his ears. Edward again glanced at the sharp shadows in the sky, before his gaze fell to the forest beyond. It looked alive in the wind; like creeping black tendrils, dancing under the now looming, milky white ball, set within the twinkling stars. The hairs on his arms pricked up; he couldn't shake this new feeling that something bad had indeed happened. He then realised how fond he had become of Obi; and even Peter, despite all his flaws. Edward shook his head dismissively, which seemed only to urge new foreboding thoughts into his mind. Of his wife, Charlotte, and the words she had said to him before he left.

Chapter 20

The Clue That Was Missed

Peter stayed upon horseback for a few miles before continuing on foot. His plan was to gain some distance and then cut back onto the trail he thought Obi might have taken, hoping to meet him face on. He called for him, but there was no response - they searched the thickets for over an hour. The soldier had been scanning the ground but it gave nothing away, and what little hopes they had began to fritter into the evening sky.

"Something isn't right," Peter kept saying, over and over. "He would have left word of his departure, in some form or another, I'm bloody sure of it. We may be searching for something that isn't here. We will ride back to the castle, sir."

They galloped back into the castle grounds. Peter dismounted and climbed the stairs in the central tower. Edward had seen him ride in and went to meet him on his way up.

"There's no sign of him anywhere," said Peter, gasping. "We've searched to the very reach of the land he might have covered. There's no trace! Obi has the stamina of a man far younger, but not that of a horse, Edward. I'm telling you, there is foul play here!"

"Peter, follow me," said Edward, calmingly. "Take rest, and we shall have this matter dealt with. Jasper has set out some clothes for us to change into. Come, I'll show you."

Peter followed Edward into the tower, stopping outside the rooms Jasper had offered them for the night. "Now, clean yourself up and rest a while. Let me see if I can figure this out, yes? Peter?"

Peter nodded nervously and closed the door behind him.

Edward found himself on the courtyard halfway up the tower, peering over the edge which Lord Billian still hung from. He could see out for miles down the hillside, where another town shone in lights. *That must be Rushing's Hall*, he thought. It was now dark and eerie, the branches above him cracked in the wind as it swept through the tower. The people went about their own business down below as if nothing had happened. What awful things must they have endured for their spirits to seem so revived at the sight of their leader's death?

A lantern burned away next to him; and when the wind subsided, he could hear the oil igniting inside its copper case. Grabbing its handle, Edward walked down to the main courtyard and out through the gate. He stopped beside the wagon where Obi was last seen, and lifting the lantern out in front of him, he began to observe. There were footprints everywhere; yet too many to form any kind of distinct pattern. He lifted the light to the footrests, squinting his eyes to see if the muddy marks could tell a tale, but they were only smeared and dry. He cursed under his breath. Then he saw something. A bow, leaning against the rest behind the seat. It was Obi's.

Edward had only known the old man for a matter of days, and not once had Obi struck him as a fool; but to leave your only means of defence behind and go wandering off alone was foolish indeed. Edward snapped into an immense realisation. Peter was right. Something bad must have happened here.

Edward sprinted back to the castle to find Peter.

"Obi wouldn't leave without his bow!" choked Edward, barging through the door of Peter's bedchamber.

Peter shot up, startled. Jasper saw Edward come flying in and came down to see them.

"Jasper, are there beasts in these hills?" asked Peter deliriously. "Wolves or bears?"

"No. Not for many years," Jasper answered. "They were hunted off the island decades ago. Now calm down! Are you sure this bow is proof enough that he hasn't just ... left for home?"

"I'm certain!" snapped Peter.

"If only this was found when we had the light with us," said Edward, sitting down, trying hard not to despair.

Peter fumed. "We must set out at once! He could be in danger and I will not sleep a wink in this castle until he is found!"

"You will find nothing in this darkness, Peter," said Jasper. "At first light, I'll have my men dispatched to find him. Is that good enough, for now?"

"No, it isn't good enough!" blazed Peter. "He was safe with us! Coming here has landed him in this mess. If we'd set about our intended path, none of this would have happened."

Edward stood to try and console him but he was pushed away.

"I'm sorry," said Jasper. "I truly am, but there is hope yet that we will find him. But *not* in the dead of night! And might I remind you, had we got to the Jackal a minute later, you'd have all been dead! So, please, spare me the blame."

Peter recoiled a little, realising he'd overstepped the mark here. He fixed his frown and his gesture was that of an apology without words. After a few silent moments he started again.

"He saved our skins, too," he said. "But he is *not* a soldier, or an officer or a pirate. He's an old man, who in the midst of trembling fear, loosed an arrow that pierced the Jackal's throat. Perhaps had he not taken that shot, the beast wouldn't have been so easily defeated. He is of as much worth to me, as any of your men are to you!"

"I cannot be clearer. You will find nothing in these woods until dawn," said Jasper. "My men will be of service to you then. Peter, I know you care for your friend, but if you go out there tonight, you'll be going out alone."

"Maybe not alone," said Edward boldly. "I'll come, but only to search the land nearby. We cannot venture too far from the castle at this hour. Jasper, are there any villages or towns close by? He knows the land well, perhaps he might have taken refuge somewhere close?"

Jasper sighed in frustration. "Nothing out east until Rushing's Hall. The only folk you might find around here are at Willow's Pass, but that's only a traveller's rest. It's about a mile from here, but be careful; you're rather likely to find only strange people lurking about down there – another reason why it's best to wait."

"I appreciate your counsel, Jasper, I do, but that's not going to stop me," said Peter, readying himself.

"Very well," said Jasper. "Then I shall take my leave." Jasper shook his head. "Oh, take a left at the end of the road and keep going. You can't miss it. Be safe."

Peter's wild imagination began tormenting him. He kept on thinking he could see the glowing, white eyes of wolves gathering in the distance. He had to shake off the thoughts and concentrate. He and Edward had stayed close to the road, and so full of nerves, had only been walking for what seemed like seconds when Peter looked ahead at a point in the distance where many lights began to pop, one after another, in various places beyond the treeline. He tried to blink them away.

"That must be Willow's Pass," said Edward, pointing in the same direction. "We cannot simply walk straight in; we need to climb that ridge, it should offer us a better look."

Peter agreed and, keeping low, they climbed, halting where the trees stopped and a small rocky cliff fell off in front of them. The cliff spread far across to their left, the moonlight illuminating each sharp, cutting stone clearly. A treacherous drop beneath for a misplaced boot. Below stood Willow's Pass.

Edward pulled Peter down by his sleeve. "Look, I see people and horses," he whispered quietly.

Peter squinted and, having the keener eyes of the two, concluded, "At least ten of them, in grey uniforms."

"Kingsguard?" asked Edward.

"We need to get closer," said Peter, leaping towards the next suitable vantage.

He stopped as Edward caught him up.

"Yes, Kingsguard," said Peter. "Gürad and his men. You can't mistake that prick, even from a distance. They look to have made camp."

"They must have found our trail?" said Edward, his face finding his hands.

"They could have taken Obi?" said Peter, shakily. "But I can't see anything for the horses. We should move closer for a better look."

"No!" snapped Edward. "If we are seen, Peter, they will kill him and then us. We cannot fight ten men!"

"If those bastards have taken Obi, I'll bring the fight to them myself," snarled Peter.

Edward yanked him back forcefully.

"No one needs to die!" he growled. "We will be safe at Guntrick Castle. If they *have* taken him, you know Gürad will bring Obi back to the castle to bargain with. Anyway, his presence here might well be a coincidence, and-"

Edward's words simply didn't work; he turned to find Peter sliding down the hill into the danger of the camp, determined to take the closer look that would satisfy his suspicions.

He slunk around the place, at times nearly crawling. Fearlessly, he searched amongst the horses. The guards circled the fire and all looked to be dozing off, sleepy, yawning, some were snoring – a few of them were sitting in the shelter of the many huts plonked here and there throughout the rest.

There was Obi, his hands in bonds, tied to a tree trunk. Peter tried to gain his attention by waving his hand gently. Obi's mouth was gagged. When he saw Peter, his eyes filled with joy and leaked with tears. Peter checked around himself, readying his next movement, but he had no idea what to do. He had made a big mistake, that was certain. He willed his heart to stop beating so loudly; he felt like someone else might hear it pounding at such a thumping rate. In that precise moment his fear peaked, his senses heightened, his eyes capturing every detail laid out before him. The skin on his neck stung and it made him jolt on the spot. But the stinging began to gradually subside. And then he realised. The stinging sensation wasn't from fear, but the cold bite of a blade pressing against it.

"What do have we here?" said Gürad, with a vicious smile planted on his lips.

Edward's heart sunk into his boots, he was frozen stiff looking down on what had unfolded. For a second, he thought to fight, but he knew any act of bravery would only get himself and his companions killed. So, he ran for it, so fast that his cap flew off behind him into the forest. His weary legs struggled over the uneven ground and at times he stumbled, but he didn't stop. He reached the castle, each broad stride gained him precious seconds. Jasper was smoking a new pipe and reading a book when Edward burst through the door. "Jasper, I have no time to explain, but I need your help!" he gasped.

"What is it, Edward, where's Peter?"

"He's been captured by a colonel and his guards. I think they have Obi too."

"How did this happen?" asked Jasper, shooting into a stance. "Why?"

"I have no time to explain. Please, I just need you to summon your men."

"What business does a colonel have with you?"

"I really have no time to say!"

"Well say you must! How is it you expect me to deal with this problem … with violence? By fighting the King's men? No, Edward. I cannot risk my integrity. You must understand."

"Integrity?" said Edward. "I just watched you gun down near on a dozen guards, did I not?"

"Now that's different, Edward, and you know it! How dare you compare the two. I ought to-"

Edward looked down at his feet dispiritedly, knowing that Jasper was right. "Forgive me, Jasper," he said quietly, deciding that it was time to relay a little more of the truth. "Peter was trialled back in Summer's Reach and he was found guilty. He escaped the Plummet and for a particular reason I followed. I do not wish to confess the reason why, but that's the truth of it. Colonel Gürad and his men must have tracked us out here. They're now waiting at Willow's Pass. Peter entered their camp in search of Obi and he was caught. It's me the colonel wants. Not Peter, or Obi, if they have him, that is. He wouldn't spare a thought if either of them lived or died, but he'll see me hanged from the palace walls, of that I am certain."

"Gürad, you say?" asked Jasper, scratching his sharp chin. "That is a name I haven't heard for many a year. Of all the guards you could have chasing your tail ... terrible news it's him. But I cannot help you, Edward, I'm sorry. I will not meddle in the business of those so loyal to the King. If I act, the full force of Summer's Reach could be thrown at Guntrick Castle and I'll hang beside you. My men and I have come a long way and have gained the power I will not so willingly forfeit."

"You're quite right," said Edward. "I don't know what I was thinking, asking such a thing of you. I have a feeling Gürad will bring them to the castle; then, I will turn myself in. I won't risk the lives of my companions for the sake of my own. If there is still any honour within me, I'll do this, and by some I might be forgiven."

Edward left and walked out onto the yard, kneading his hands over his face in disbelief. His hands fell, landing on the wall, his fingers brushing against the rope that Billian hung from - the feeling sent a wicked chill up his spine. He had never felt quite so alone in his whole life.

Chapter 21
An Unexpected Gift

Gürad jumped down from his horse, beginning to lead it by its collar rope to Guntrick Castle's front gate - or at least what was left of it. Obi and Peter were tied to the back of his mount and had been made to walk the mile from Willow's Pass, stumbling and falling behind. The castle guards recognised the uniforms and stepped aside.

The colonel considered the townsfolk with his cold, questioning eyes, then halted in the centre of the courtyard, a beaming red scowl spread wide across his countenance.

"Would the Lord of Guntrick come forth?" he called, ensuring his voice would travel all the way up to the peaks of the patina-covered towers.

Jasper caught the rumble of Gürad's hoarse voice and descended the central tower, emerging from the tunnel with speculative hesitancy.

"I am not the lord of this castle," said Jasper, approaching him. "But I speak for these people in his absence."

"Montague! It has been a while ... hasn't it?" said Gürad.

"It has indeed, Eustace," sneered Jasper, clasping his hands behind his back. "Pardon me, it's Colonel, isn't it?"

Gürad only smirked, and turning towards Edward, he snarled, "Clavell! How delighted I am to see you. I think we have much to talk about on our journey back to Summer's Reach."

The gag around Peter's mouth muffled his screams.

"Montague?" started Gürad. "By what rank should I be addressing you?"

"Sergeant," said Jasper, feeling a pang of pride rise up into his cheeks. For it had been many years since such a title had preceded his name.

"Very well ... Sergeant. Edward Clavell is to be hanged for treason. I ask kindly that you do not oppose me? Nay, I command it, as your superior."

"The old man goes free," said Edward. "He is of no use to you."

"If he is of no use to me, Clavell, perhaps I should kill him now, for knowingly aiding a fugitive?"

Gürad unholstered his pistol and forced it firmly into Obi's face.

"Colonel Gürad!" snapped Jasper. "A man so keen to deal in the art of King's justice should know that such actions would be murder? You'll let the old man go, or I'll be happy to accompany you to Summer's Reach? Oh, and you'll be in chains!"

The guards of Guntrick readied their muskets. Gürad slid out his blade and sliced Obi's bonds, then kicked him to the ground. "These days, people are too easily spooked! Where is the spine that once steadied this great nation of ours? You make me sick, all of you! Take your fat old man!"

"You shall have my cooperation," said Edward, painfully. "Jasper. Sergeant, to have brought such business amongst your people. Please, forgive me?"

Jasper proffered his long hand, and when Edward took it, the sergeant used a sleight-of-hand motion to slip a thin blade inside the officer's jacket sleeve.

Edward smothered his emotion and walked over to Obi, lifted him to his feet, and pulled the gag from out of his mouth.

"I'm so very sorry, Edward. He caught me unaware," said Obi, frightened, cold and catching his breath.

"You have nothing to apologise for, old boy," said Edward. "And I do hope I might see you again someday soon."

Obi had tears in his blue eyes, bruises across his left cheek, and burns from the ropes that had hung so viciously around the skin on his wrists.

Edward eyed Gürad; the colonel was grinning like a mad man.

"They will hang this filthy pirate beside you, Clavell," the colonel whispered, pointing at Peter. "I will ensure the executioner allows you a moment to ponder over your actions before that trapdoor is sprung. And let this be known, traitor. I wish I was the one pulling the lever. But I will be watching, no doubt about that."

Edward remained expressionless, offering a guard his hands so they could be bonded behind his back. His bandolier was taken and thrown to the ground. Peter himself had been beaten very badly. The pirate pulled at the horse whilst making a stance, immediately restrained by a Kingsguard who struck the back of his knee with a blow of his musket butt. Peter fell and more muffled screams sounded.

Gürad climbed onto his horse and shot Jasper a wicked smile; a smile filled with his own incessant delusion of supremacy.

Edward and Peter were themselves forced onto horseback. Obi followed out the Kingsguard for a few steps, his eyes bleak with sadness. The blood and the tears had smeared on his face and with his sleeve he wiped to clear his vision, watching as the galloping company hurtled up the road and out of sight.

Long into the morning did the Kingsguard ride without rest, and long into the morning did Edward wonder why Jasper had aided them. He kept his fingers firmly gripped to his sleeve so the blade didn't fall from his clutches onto the muddy road beneath him. It was torturous.

Many hours passed until the guards finally came to a halt, their new captives meeting the dirt with a heavy thud. Gürad and his men deliberately roughing them up at every opportunity.

Peter, with blood spilling from his nose, edged his way towards Edward and leaned up against him back-to-back. One of the guards stepped over and untied their gags. Peter inhaled the crisp air with a giant breath. Edward's fingers were numb like stone and ached badly. He was unsure of how much longer he could hold on to his sleeve before his fingers lost feeling entirely. A little panic began to murmur. This was their lifeline. He had to cut them both free or they hanged in Summer's Reach, it was that simple. It was imperative he held on. If that blade slid to the ground without him realising, then it was all over.

Gürad was searching through a satchel on his horse saddle and turned out a small, stale-looking loaf of bread. He tossed it in the mud in front of the men, swilling it around with his boot. The loaf was dripping in watery filth, sodden and spoilt. Edward found himself staring off into the trees. Gürad held out the bread in front of him. "Eat," he said, holding back his joy and satisfaction.

Peter could see from out of the corner of his eye and cast his head away in disgust. Edward ignored the colonel, who smiled wryly and turned towards Peter, proffering the same dripping loaf. "Eat!"

Peter hadn't the composure of his companion and spat onto the colonel's jacket. "Fuck you!" he snapped.

Gürad delivered a strike with the back of his hand that landed cleanly across his cheek. Peter returned with only a grin. "Is that all you've got?"

"You two filthy little worms thought you could escape me, didn't you?" said Gürad, shaking off the stinging sensation in his hand. "I knew I would find you out here somewhere. Now, I only wish I'd put a bullet in your fat friend's chest when I had the chance. Thinking about it, I really ought to have done. Maybe once you're both dead I'll return for him and kindly afford him the death he deserves."

"I'm going to kill you," said Peter very calmly.

The colonel let go of a great bellowing laugh, then a growl.

"Scum! Not even after you are dead will those bonds on your wrists be cut!" he snapped, the veins in his forehead blue in anger.

He flung the filthy loaf at Peter's face, leaving muddy water dripping from his brow. "Then you *don't* eat!"

The day went on, and more miles were ridden; the galloping of horse hooves hurrying by each tiresome minute. Peter was staring two deep holes into the back of the colonel's head with an excitement tingling up his spine and over his neck, simply at the thought of someday destroying him. That thought tasted sweeter than any fruit to be found, and certainly sweeter than the filth that had, by now, congealed on his lips.

The Kingsguard set up camp. The horses steamed from the heat that left their bodies as it met the cold forest air. The men were set down against the bushes by the roadside. Their trousers were spoilt, soaked, sticking to their legs and rears.

Peter whispered, "We need to get out of here, Edward. I cannot go on another minute in this filth!"

Edward remained silent. In the end, the only thing to do is think, and listen, and plan. Exactly what Jasper had said to him when they first met.

The camp lay silent, the restful night had shadowed over them, the day's wind now dormant and breathless. Peter had drifted off into a drowsy state, but was awoken when he felt something pushing against his hands, shuffling around behind him. He turned, found his wits, realised that Edward was cutting their bonds and froze. He knew not how or by what stroke of luck had Edward found something sharp enough to do so, but his spirits took a giant leap into the sky. His skin shivered until it was covered in goosebumps from the excitement. He inconspicuously checked about the camp whilst stretching the rope tighter; the Kingsguard looked to be fast asleep. Edward hurried his attempts. Peter had to shake away the visions of Gürad tossing the filthy loaf at his face. Yet at least it took his mind off the agonising wait for Edward to free them.

At last! When Peter's hands came apart, he felt the strangest sensation, like his arms weighed absolutely nothing. Blood ran back into the deep ruts the bonds had left behind. It was ecstasy, but he feared moving, even still. Until he heard Edward's voice that is. "On three?" whispered the officer.

Edward carefully took a stance having tapped Peter on his arm three times. Peter, through the burning pain in his freezing legs, crept to his feet. The camp still uttered nothing but snores and Gürad was propped up against a tree trunk with his head stooped down on his chest - he was quite obviously asleep. Every noise from under foot was received with deep anxiety, but the men walked on, knowing each stride was a chance taken.

After twenty or so measured strides, the edge of the road was reached, and when they stepped off the trodden ground onto the unspoiled earth around the tree roots, Colonel Gürad's eyes flicked open. Something had stirred him from his dreams. He peered around the camp, letting his eyes adjust. The blurry and dark outlines of the trees shrouded the place and the pale light from the moon shone amongst the stars. He stood and circled the entire camp, but could see nothing beyond the flickering hues of his own lantern. He walked to where his prisoners were laid to sleep; the ropes frayed and lying in the dirt was all that he found. An anger flooded from his heart. A scream ripped through the air.

His guards woke in fear of his grave cries and sprung to attention. "Find them at once, and kill them, *kill them!*"

The guards scattered, but Edward and Peter were already many rows though the forest and couldn't be seen. The darkness lay heavy around them and each hanging branch became a sharp obstacle to dodge.

Their footsteps were drowned out by the tumult on the road, the screaming colonel and his shrill demand for death echoed through the forest.

They came upon a small body of water with little cover, a few hundred yards north of the camp. Veering around it as fast as they could sprint, they ducked and dodged the trees hanging offshoots that were cast down into the water's edge. Edward stopped for a second and knelt to the floor bringing a finger to his lips. Peter halted beside him and they listened for any noises out afar.

Distant calls turned louder and louder as the forest behind them illuminated. "Keep moving!"

Climbing higher, the ground became denser and their boots didn't sink as deep into the earth and this hastened their strides. They found a thin opening in a fissure within a cliff side. It was gorge-like and roofless, seeming to stretch for some way. The chance was taken to enter, the path growing a little darker each second; even the apparentness of their own boots had disappeared from beneath them. They squeezed through tight gaps and splashed through pools of water that had gathered on the ground. The stark outline of the rocks either side of them gave the feeling the path was dragging them down into an endless abyss of misery and inevitably, death. The way was getting tighter, and if it was possible, darker. Now, the air seemed thin and suffocating. The walls beat like a giant heart, narrowing with each pump.

Then, the earth fell from beneath their feet as they were sent tumbling down a banking, landing in the open air, winded and disorientated.

Scrambling to their feet they bolted toward the only cover they could see, a forest atop the next hillside. It looked like a great, black cloud had taken rest on the ground, its peaks waving in the wind like darkly clad people all dancing in a row.

The forest swallowed them. They were safe here; this vantage offered them a moonlit view of the field and if anything was to stir down there, they would hopefully see it and have time to flee. Now, they needed rest. Peter fell flat on his back, the ache in his legs gradually subsided.

"I really didn't think we were getting out of that one!" he said, wiping the sweat from his brow. "Where did you get the blade?"

"Jasper," said Edward, panting like an old dog.

"Why would he help us?" asked Peter, having never been more relieved in his whole life.

"That I don't know," said Edward. "But I feel we are in greater debt to him than what we are ever likely to be able to repay."

"Well let's hope a simple thanks is enough because a thanks is about all we've bloody well got!" said Peter. "Maybe he'll let us stay for a while? I'm sure there will be some place to lay low in that castle."

"We cannot return to Guntrick Castle, Peter. That's the first place Gürad will search," said Edward.

"Then what are we to do without any provisions?" said Peter, questioningly. "Kindling, food, water, weapons, *my whiskey!*"

"That's already been taken care of," said Edward. "I left some things outside the castle when I realised Gürad would come. In there, is everything we need, including my blade and an axe I've acquired. I assumed you would have been parted with yours? Hopefully, Obi will have read the scroll I sneaked into his pocket and he'll bring our belongings to Willow's Pass."

"Fortune favours us!" laughed Peter. "But what if we hadn't escaped? You made the arrangements not knowing? I for one thought we were goners!"

"I don't intend to die at the gallows, Peter. I made the arrangements because I myself had another plan. Jasper only gave me a better one."

"What plan?" asked Peter, sarcastically. "Have we been practising some kind of sorcery? Learned to break bonds with just the swiftly spoken words of some spell? Or did you just imagine rolling off the horse, down a hill and out of sight?"

"I wish you'd be quiet," said Edward.

"I wish I'd have known about your little plan here," said Peter. "I might not have angered that bastard so needlessly. Someday, I'll kill that man, you mark my words."

"I'm sure our paths will cross again," said Edward, who turned up his collar, preparing himself for a night of no sleep.

Chapter 22
A Sight for Sore Eyes

It was still dark when the men stirred; they couldn't sleep right for the cold and dared not stay on the hillside for any longer. With no belongings, they were swiftly up and away into the morning.

Willow's Pass was today's destination and they set off with every faith that their companion, Obi, would be there waiting for them. Finding the road was the best chance to gain some bearings, having fled into the lands without any real purpose of direction. Once found, the roads were easy to follow, with signs in certain places giving direction to the nearest settlements. But the roads were now filled with danger, for the Kingsguard prowled and Colonel Gürad had a deep-rooted rage that boiled his blood.

On horseback they had ridden for a full day away from Guntrick Castle, so getting back there on foot would take them well into the next morning. Peter hadn't eaten in days and he was becoming weak and weary; save for the water they had scooped from the brooks they passed, the only nourishment to have passed his lips was a manky old pickle he was given whilst captured.

When they did find the road in the distance, they began to follow it, keeping well back and quiet. Peter was fatiguing quickly, misplacing his feet as his mind strayed away into fantasy. He thought so hard he could almost taste the roasted rabbit from a few nights ago; but that was just the taste of the sweat gathering around his lips.

Edward was pressing urgently on, glancing down at the blade he was turning between his fingers; the razor-like steel that had saved them.

Peter halted, having seen a little rabbit in the bushes. He stooped to his knees to take cover, then uncoiled like an adder trying to grasp it. No luck. No catch. And there he remained, flat on his face, absolutely exhausted. Edward slid his arms under Peter's shoulders. "Not far now," he reminded him. "Just hang in there for a little while longer."

Then, from the sky, there came a huge rumble that broke in the clouds and with it, a deluge that flooded the lands and drenched the men to their skin. A once charming day, now filled with a bitter, wet cold that burrowed down to their bones.

There was a break in the forest where a green row of huge furs towered above them. The ground underneath was almost dry and the men huddled in close to escape the falling rain. Peter kept dozing off, often slipping in and out of the same dream. He saw a woman, an elegant beauty, not in the darkness of the forest but from a house by the seaside. Her hair blew like soft silk in the wind and was as golden as the sand. She always turned to him and smiled. A smile that lived with him every single minute of his life; a smile that he held so dearly, it left little place in his heart for much else. In this dream, the sun always shone and the waves crashed white against the rocks nearby. It was vivid and real and beautiful, yet when he stood to hold her in his arms, the darkness closed in and he woke. Never did the dream go any further.

Edward sat shivering with his arms crossed over his body, silently listening to the patter of drops that fell from the evergreen needles. Grim colours spoiled the day and every now and then the wind would swoop the rain towards them with the odd gust. Edward sunk into the fallen needles beneath the tree, trying fruitlessly to keep warm. When across the way, under the trees afar, he saw a dark figure. Through the sodden lens of the beating rain the figure seemed to shimmer like a ghost as it moved. Edward examined what looked to be a man. His shoulders broad and he was tall. The second thought to spring to his mind was the question of whether this figure was the same being he had seen at the Drum & Fiddle, and again at the Drovers tavern? From this distance the eyes could not be seen but the feeling he had was familiar. A strange rush of emotion he couldn't explain. The being began to move. Edward tensed and jerked his head towards Peter who was snoring in soft rumbles beside him. He looked up again and swallowed his fear. The dark figure had narrowed the space between them, just enough for two pearly eyes to gleam from beneath its hood. Edward felt like screaming a demand for it to reveal its true identity, but Peter couldn't know. These unearthly experiences were personal to him alone and he feared sharing them with anyone. He did nothing, frozen stiff on the spot as the being strode off into the forest.

Tired, wet and cold, the two men started again. If Obi had read Edward's letter, the hope was that he would be waiting for them in the early hours of the next morning; and with the night drawing nearer, it was time to get moving. As the hours of darkness rolled in, Peter seemed to have gained a spring in his stride. Perhaps the thought of warm food and whiskey had sparked a burst of energy in him. Because it was close now, or so he hoped.

Through the trees, Peter could see a road sign sticking out from the ground. When he stepped close enough to see it, the carven words alight in the moon's gentle glow read *Willow's Pass*.

"This is it," he said. "It looks bleak."

"Indeed," said Edward. "Can you see our man?"

"Not yet."

"Wait here. I'll go and take a look."

Daring not to venture too far from the cover of the trees, Edward examined the scene. It wasn't yet dawn and the black sky was still densely arched above them. He couldn't distinguish any sure signs of life, until a gentle breeze blew across him that carried the smoky scent of tobacco on its back. As his senses jumped, he moved closer, beginning to hear whispers coming from inside one of the huts that formed a perimeter around this strange haven.

Edward retreated back to warn Peter. "Someone lurks here," he whispered.

"Are you sure?"

"Yes, I'm certain. I heard voices."

"And Obi?"

"No sign yet."

"For the love of the sea, I hope he turns up," said Peter, thinking. "How do you know he isn't already here?"

"I don't. But it's best we stay hidden until Obi shows his face. Now, keep your eyes peeled. Remember what Jasper said? We're likely to find only strange folk lurking around down here."

Peter laughed to himself.

"What's so funny?" asked Edward.

"This whole fuckin' thing! This quest, adventure, or whatever you want to call it. Doomed from the start. Not a single event so far has passed without a hitch, and I've been wondering when our luck might run out, Edward. I'm starting to think that time is now."

Edward smiled. "No. It appears we are very much *in* luck," he said, pointing into the distance where a man came scuttling from the trees.

Lanterns began to flash on from within the huts. Edward and Peter were on high alert. "I see shadows," said Edward. "And look, that's definitely our man."

Obi's face was now alight as he came panting into Willow's Pass. The strings of his hat swinging to and fro and a big sack of provisions was slung over his back.

"That's him alright," said Peter. "Come on!"

"Wait!" said Edward, when a strange vagrant of a man came walking out into the road.

"Where're you heading?" they heard him croak towards Obi with a knife in his hand. The man wore a long, leather coat that was stained in dirt and worn from time. You couldn't tell how gaunt his cheeks were beneath the foliage he called a beard, but he was thin and starving.

"I haven't eaten in days, old man," he said. "Could you spare me a morsel or two?"

"No, sorry. I'm afraid I've just enough for me and my friends," said Obi with regret. "Can't help you today."

"I don't see anyone else around here but you. Help a fellow out, would ya?"

Obi heard the creaking of floorboards coming from inside one of the huts and then another rodent-looking fiend came skulking out. "Open the sack!"

Before Obi could blink there were now three of them. "Open the sack!" He was surrounded.

Obi shuddered, yet quickly collected his nerve that had fallen crashing from his stomach and gripped his bow. "I will not!"

"And what are you going to do with that?" asked the first vagrant.

"Take a step closer and you'll find out." Obi shocked himself with that one.

He reached into his quiver and clipped an arrow to the bow string, his hands shaking like the petals of an orchid in a winter breeze.

"Get him!"

The arrow flew off, piercing one of them an inch above his kneecap, ripping through the man's flesh - the blood-soaked tip appearing crimson through the other side.

The vagrant wailed in agony. Obi stuttered back and spun on his heels to find Edward and Peter standing over two limp bodies lying on the road.

"We've got you, old boy," said Edward. "Now, bind these men. They'll slit our throats in the night should we leave them free."

"Help me you fools!" cried the first vagrant, fighting against the pain as he tried fruitlessly to extract the shaft that stuck him. "I'll die out here!"

Edward stepped over his body; he was now screeching like a coward. "You should have thought about that before drawing your blade," snapped Edward. "You didn't know who you were dealing with, did you? Well, perhaps next time you'll think twice. Now, run along."

Run he could not; but he limped, sobbing through each excruciating hop. He fell down by the roadside, streams of blood spilling from his leg. The other two came around, dazed, and delusional; the moment they realised they were both bound they began to plea helplessly.

"Are we to leave them here to die, Edward?" asked Peter.

"Places like this are monitored regularly and by the nearest authority," said Edward, impatiently. "That authority will be Guntrick Castle, I suspect. Should they die before they are found ... hard luck."

Peter raised his brows, aghast at the malice in Edward's tone.

"Thank you, Obi," said Edward, reaching for the sack on the old man's back. "Again, you have proven to be indispensable."

"I'm happy to help, Edward," said Obi, looking down at Peter who had now fallen to the ground. He rushed to him, lifted Peter's head and gently placed a water pouch under his neck. "We need to get this man warm, Edward. His lips are blue!"

"We need to get him off the road now."

Each grabbing an arm, Edward and Obi hoicked Peter on to his feet. The two men bound to the trees gave one final plea. The bleeding man had dragged his weight over to the roadside banking, his wounded leg a blank mass of fleshy nothingness.

The road was eventually out of sight. Peter took rest on the forest floor. Edward slid the sack off his back, setting it down in the dead leaves, rummaging around inside it until he found what he needed to kindle a quick fire. He brought out pans, a water pouch and two rabbits. Obi made quick work of skinning them. Edward broke off a handful of soft bread filled with brandy-soaked currants and laid it in Peter's hand. The pirate stuffed the bread into his face, trying to catch each crumb as it fell onto his jacket.

A fire was lit, and over the flaming tendrils, Obi began to sizzle the rabbits, warming water in a pan with his other hand. Edward unrolled a sleeping fur and wrapped it over Peter's shoulders, then popped the cork from a whiskey bottle and gave him a giant gulp to tingle his chest and cheer his spirits.

The fire crackled away, the rabbit fat dripped, hissing on the red flames that illuminated their expressionless faces. Edward took hold of Peter's jacket, and after breaking off a branch from a nearby tree, he stabbed it into the ground and hung the garment there to dry.

The smell of meat grew as the rabbits cooked away on the spit that Obi had conjured himself. Peter took a sip of the warm water he'd been passed, the near steaming drops slipped down his throat and settled peacefully in his stomach. The glint in his eye was returning, his mouth watering as he watched Obi carve off strips of meat and share them into bowls.

"Here you are men. Eat up!" said Obi, passing both of them a rabbit each.

"There's enough to go around for the three of us, Obi," said Edward, taking a bowl.

"No! Absolutely not, Edward," said Obi, patting his belly. "Jasper had me a huge supper made up last night. I'll spare you the details, but let's just say, it was fantastic. I couldn't eat until at least dinner. Now scoff away. I haven't been out in the wild for the past two days."

Peter began to liven and smile a little. "I dare say, old boy, I've never enjoyed the taste of rabbit as much in my whole life."

"I've got us something else," said Obi, grinning, searching his pockets. "I may have stolen them, but … oh well."

Obi brought out a cloth that was filled with dates and he offered them around. They went down a treat.

"Enjoy," he said, closing his eyes, pressing his face closer to the fire.

Edward poured them three large whiskeys. Obi shuffled inside his sleeping furs. "I'll tell you a story, men. One from when I was a young man," he said, warming his hands by the flames. "It's only a silly story, not heroic or anything like that. I was born and lived up in Mountpane; my father was a butcher, and sadly my mother died when I was young so there wasn't really anybody to take care of me. My father had a boy working for him, who helped him around the stall, and from time to time he'd help butcher the pigs and the other creatures. He was a dreadful little boy and perhaps around five years older than me. He'd often hurt the animals needlessly, and I'd see him doing it, but I never said anything because I kept telling myself that was just the poor fate of the beasts. Until one day I saw him beating this one little pig. My blood boiled and when he wasn't watching, I opened the latch on the gate and swung it open. The poor thing bolted like a horse right past my father and out into the town, never to be seen again. The boy came running out after it shouting and bawling. He got a beating off my father he would never forget. From that day on, I've always given my help to whoever needed it."

"I thought you said it wasn't a heroic story?" smiled Edward, pouring Obi more whiskey who smiled back. "So, is Obi your true name? It seems quite unusual for these parts," added Edward.

"No, that would be Oliver. Although it's been quite some time since I've heard that."

"And where might you find Mountpane?" asked Peter, filling his cheeks with dates, enjoying the sweetness.

"Oh, way up north. A land full of farmers really. With a resistance to the cold it would seem."

"You'll have to take us there some day," said Edward. "In the meantime, Peter and I will figure out how best to repay you for all you've done for us."

"Nonsense," laughed Obi, throwing out his hand as if to wave off the idea. "I shall guide you to Fort Gaze as promised, and from there, we'll go our separate ways. No reimbursement of any kind will be necessary. All I ask, is that you join me for a glass of the good stuff on your journey home."

"I'll drink to that, old boy," said Edward, swilling his whiskey.

"Me too," said Peter.

"So, where do we go from here? I seem to have lost my sense of direction," said Edward.

"Luckily for you," said Obi, rubbing his hands to warm them, "I know these lands rather well and if we can make it to Rushing's Hall, then it should be easy going to Fort Gaze from thereon out. Although, there's really no telling whether the roads will be safe, so it's best we keep to the trees. Rushing's Hall is around fifteen miles east and we should make the most of the day as soon as Peter can spare some energy."

The men sipped at their drinks and held a moment aside to think. Edward had something prodding his mind. "Jasper knew Gürad," he said quietly. "I'm starting to think that is why he helped us. I saw how he looked at me when I mentioned his name."

"The bastard's infamous," said Peter, stretching his jaw.

"He sure has left a lasting impression on me," said Obi, stroking the purple blotches on his cheek.

"Colonel Gürad is a dangerous man," said Edward. "One day I fear he'll take Lord Harrington's place and I'll have to answer to him myself. Well, that was until I helped a convicted pirate escape the city. If I ever make it home, it will be Judge Farley I'll be answering to."

"Have faith," said Peter. "That someday soon we will find this diamond, and all will be forgiven. The world will be a better place, and I'll be far, far away."

"Where is it you'll go?" asked Obi.

Peter smiled, brighter than he had in weeks. "To the seaside," he said.

Chapter 23
The Right Track

They marched the fifteen miles to Rushing's Hall. Peter yearned for the feeling of warm sheets caressing his skin, a hot whiskey in his hand and a stool upon which he could rest his feet. He wasn't quite sure if he could still call them 'feet', or just two deadly numb blocks attached to his legs that dragged against the ground as he stumbled under the archway into town.

Words would fall rather short when trying to describe the charm of Rushing's Hall. The streets were paved with white stones and each magnificent building stood as grandly as the last. The wagons that carved the roads were of the most exquisite design; adorned with golden arrangements of historic depictions. The horses that pulled them donned silver crowns, peaked with long, white feathers and were steered by reins of black leather, embroidered with many sinuous lines of floral patterns stitched in gold.

The men walked with an eagerness in their short and tired strides, admiring the decadence. Obi found himself looking up at the tallest horse he'd ever seen, and beginning to run his palm over its shiny brown coat, he smiled. From out of the corner of his eye, he caught a glimpse of the coachman scowling down at him. Obi, ceasing to smile for only half a second, lifted the cap from his head and then plonked it back on again. "Good day, sir," he said, before scuttling off to catch up to the others.

Edward and Peter looked a little flustered, for the whole place was heaving with people; yet amongst all the madness, there was an undeniable decorum about it. Edward looked down at his own filthy garments and winced. Peter puffed out his cheeks in response to a man that barged into him mistakenly.

"Ever so sorry, chap!" said the well-dressed fellow before turning up his nose and grunting at Peter's appearance.

Edward scanned the street as he walked on; the sack swinging from his back jingled with each advancing stomp, drowned out by the clopping of hooves and the chatter of many folks that came bursting in and out of taverns and stalls wearing the finest suits and extravagantly cascading silk dresses.

At the end of the road stood a great mansion with at least a hundred windows and beautiful green gardens scattered with leafless silver birches. Peter's jaw hit the ground as he crept towards the gate, taking the iron between his fingers, wondering who on earth lived in such a place.

Obi strayed across the road, finding himself staring at a huge sign that hung above the door of a rather suitable looking establishment. *Welcome to Whittle's Lodging House.*

Obi peered through the window at all the occupied tables, and from within his own reflection he could see the landlord waving him inside. Edward joined him over the road, studying the sign above the door, debating with himself whether the place looked adequate enough for three roughed-up fellows caked in mud. He smiled at his own humour, it wasn't adequate, it was perfect.

They opened the door, and the little bell above it rung out with a sweet chime. Peter came in behind them. The room was filled with folk of wealth, that part was certain, and many of them were unable to refrain from goggling at the three men all covered in dirt and filth, two of them battered and bruised. The landlord, as if on a current, came gliding towards them, queerly examining the men's strange choice of attire.

"Must you have walked all this dirt in, gentlemen?" he asked. "I hope it's not lodgings you're after? You look like three strays to me!"

The guests around all chuckled from behind their teeth, quietening when Edward dropped a heavy bag of spinnels onto the landlord's table.

"Sir! My companions and I have had a very pressing day," he said, pumping out his chest. "We would like a room for the night and three pints of ale brought to us at your very earliest convenience. Oh, and we'll be taking *that* table by the window, if you please?"

The landlord stood with his mouth agape, the embarrassment tickling up his neck. Peter and Obi joined in with the ruse and although they looked strangely awkward and out of place, they stood up smart and imperious as the room fell almost silent in a stare.

"Very well gentlemen ... take a seat!" stuttered the landlord. "I'll be out in just two shakes of a spaniel's tail."

Edward lifted the bag of spinnels from the table and the men walked to take a seat by the window. The landlord returned and placed three pints of ale out in front of them.

"Let me tell you a secret, gentlemen," he said smugly. "Here, we offer the best pottage in town, how about a bowl apiece? You don't half look like you need it."

"Sounds perfect!" said Peter, shuffling excitedly in his chair.

"Wonderful," said Edward in a snap, careful to maintain his dominion over the situation.

"Can we trouble you for some bread?" asked Obi.

"Yes! You most certainly can, sir," said the landlord. "Allow me a few minutes to prepare it. Oh, and just in case you're wondering, I'm Mr Whittle."

Mr Whittle brought over three bowls of steaming pottage and three slices of bread, buttered thick. The men didn't speak, just ate and smiled. Mr Whittle watched over as they cleared their bowls, then came skipping back to the table.

"Gentlemen!" he said, beginning to clear the mess of bowls and napkins. "I've put together a room that should be very much to your liking. More importantly, I never wished to cause any offence earlier today. I only judged you too hastily from your appearance. Now, I hope that is to be forgiven?"

Edward drew open the bag of spinnels.

"Mr Whittle, sir," he said, ignoring what the man had said. "I'd like to make payment for this fine fare you have provided us."

"Of course, sir. Well, the lodgings for the one night will be nine silvers, and three more for a second. The food, one each. A sum of twelve, if you please, sir."

"If I part with twenty," said Edward, "we would much enjoy a fresh pair of underclothes, and for our trousers and shirts to be given a thorough washing."

Mr Whittle was more than happy to take the money, urgently scooping the twenty spinnels into his purse. "I'll see you gentlemen to your room, and I'll have one of our maids run out and acquire you some fresh garments. Come!"

Mr Whittle escorted the men through the door beside the kitchen and out to the garden. There was a path running through the centre. Mr Whittle quickly skipped along it in a narrow, scrunched manner, gesturing with his hand in a 'this way' motion.

At the other side of the garden stood many doorways, flanked by two yellow shuttered windows.

"Enjoy your stay, gentlemen," said Mr Whittle, as the key to one clicked in the lock. "Should you need anything, anything at all, do call."

And on that note, Mr Whittle was off. Edward pondered over the man as he scurried away, back into the room of pretentious grins.

Inside, Edward set down the sack on one of the three beds, and at the far end of what was a very lavish room, was a window that looked out onto one of the town's streets. Beneath it, there was a beautifully decorous rocking chair with a view of the outside that Peter, without any hesitation, fell right into, kicked off his wet boots and put his feet up.

Obi whipped off his jacket and trousers and slumped onto the middle bed; he was asleep in seconds, snoring in long heavy rumbles. He woke with a jump when a knock sounded at the door. Edward, taking off his own boots, stood up to answer it. A lady, proffering both her hands, was holding a tall stack of fresh linen garments.

"Here you are gentlemen, as requested," she said, handing over the snow-white cottons. "You will find a chamber pot beneath each bed, and should you need a little more privacy, there is an outhouse by the other side of the garden. In the linens I have folded three night gowns, for if you do not wish to parade around in your unmentionables. Will that be all, gentlemen?"

"Yes, my lady, that will be all," said Edward, shutting the door.

Peter had lit some tobacco in the corner but not before he'd docked his clothes into a pile on the floor. And with pipe in mouth, he strode out of the room, bare naked across the garden.

Edward looked over completely stunned; that in such an establishment could Peter still fall short in conduct. *Pirates!* he thought.

Obi took a seat, picking out the old tobacco from the chamber of his own pipe. "It's been a while since I've had a smoke on this thing. I just haven't had the urge, rather, I haven't had the time."

"I don't care for the stuff," said Edward, turning up his nose.

Obi searched his jacket pocket, took out a small silver tin of fresh tobacco and jammed a pinch into the pipe with his thumb. Then, over a candle he dangled it to ignite the rich brown contents. Peter came back inside having used the outhouse's amenities to warm a bucket for a wash. Edward was next to leave and he was eager to, as both his companions were now tooting away at their pipes, filling up the room with plumes of grey smoke, so the whole place looked angrier than a storm cloud.

Edward stood in the garden, peering into the abyss of night that had befallen the town. He gazed deep into the stars, longing for the touch of his wife's skin and the sweet taste of her lips. "I'll see you soon, my darling," he whispered, hoping by some miracle his words would find her.

Peter was now slumped into the rocking chair, swaying to and fro by the window. Edward, having finished in the outhouse, entered the room and sat beside him on the furthest bed. Obi took a stance, bent down to touch his toes, then stretched backwards in a great arch. The room door clicked shut behind him.

"It feels like we've been out here for months," said Edward, his hands rubbing his tired eyes.

"What do you mean?" asked Peter.

"The days just seem longer, that's all. It feels like an eternity since I last sat down in my own chair and talked the night away with Charlotte. I think what I'm saying is ... I wish I could wake up tomorrow and all of this be done with."

Peter blew a plume of smoke against the glass; and there, at the bottom of his breath he slumped into a feeling of depression.

"Not for many years have I welcomed a new day," he said sadly. "Nor do I keep track of them anymore. I don't believe I even remember my own age."

Edward forced a breath through his nose, like half a laugh. "I don't think I've ever met a pirate quite like you, Peter Beaumont."

"That's because you haven't met a pirate quite like me."

"I believe there might be more to you than meets the eye," said Edward, examining Peter and their time together. "I admit to judging you too quickly. I thought you were just another rotten soul. Perhaps I've grown to miss the good in folk. You'll forgive me, I hope?"

Peter put down his pipe; he looked to have filled with sorrow and spoke his next words fighting the lump in his throat.

"I deserved the judgement, Edward. I'm far from a good man. But, for what little it might be worth ... of course I forgive you. As long as you can forgive me?"

"What for?"

"I've not been entirely truthful with you, Edward," said Peter, wiping away a tear. "Well, at least on the one occasion. Do you remember when I told you that I once knew a girl called Elizabeth, who would ride into town with her father and we would play together?"

Edward nodded. "Yes."

"And I told you she went away, never coming back?"

"Yes."

"Well that's not exactly true," said Peter embarrassed. "Her father would no longer let me see her. I went looking for her but she was gone. He thought very little of me and my family, and I never thought I'd ever see her again. Until one day she was standing outside my house in the freezing rain, peering through the window with her bags packed full. I hadn't seen her in over two years. By then, we were maybe eighteen years old. My mother was a wonderful woman and she allowed her to stay with us, but it wasn't long before her father came looking. So, we ran away, far, far away, and we didn't stop until we reached the south sea." Peter smiled. "We lived there for many years, and kept cattle and chickens, making just enough silver to get by. We even came across a gold krül once, ha! I'd spent it before it ever had chance to reach the bottom of my pocket."

Edward squinted, thoroughly engaged. Peter started again.

"We planted seeds and watched them grow. We sold the eggs and milk to our neighbours. Reared lambs, fed from our own hands. All with the sound of the sea crashing around us. We planned to have children someday, Edward. We were so happy."

Then, Peter's head fell.

"But one day ... she fell ill, and no matter how hard they tried, they couldn't do anything to save her. And I lost her ... my Lizzie."

Edward felt unsettled, his eyes stung and his throat tightened.

"How long ago?" he stuttered.

"Seven years now, I think," said Peter, wiping away another tear. "Nothing was the same after that. I only felt a void, a pain. So, I went to Court Marsh and fell deep into a spiral, into a chasm that I couldn't escape from. Before I knew it, I was stealing to get by and yes, I was ashamed of it, and terrified at the same time. Then, I became acquainted with those rotten folks ... but I felt nothing. I was utterly numb from all else but my own grief."

"We've all done regrettable things, Peter," said Edward. "Some perhaps not, but most can say that once in a while, they didn't make the correct choices or follow the right path. Listen, happiness has a currency that can be easily spent. Especially when the thing that makes you the happiest is taken away."

Peter nodded in agreement, and with that the mood lightened a little. He wiped more trickles of tears from his cheeks.

"Whilst I'm being honest, I should say this. Colonel Gürad didn't beat me for what I did to him. He beat me because I was caught stealing an old man's last spinnel. I was far too ashamed to ever admit that, so I just made up some silly and ridiculous tale to try and forget what I'd done."

"I knew there was something different about you," said Edward. "I saw it, after Obi was taken. I've seen many pirates, countless scoundrels, crooks, and believe me, I've turned the key against the liberty of many. I know that pirates care for nothing but themselves and their plunder, but you, Peter, proved me otherwise. Let's be clear ... I will not condone your past; mostly because I know not of your crimes, but from here on out, I will make my own judgements and ignore that of others. You have been a friend to me this far."

"I will never expect forgiveness for the things I've done, Edward," said Peter. "At first, I had no remorse. But once that burning pain began to visit me less, I slept better knowing that in all the terrible things I ever did, *never* did I take a life. That was until I shot that guard. If I was ashamed of my past, there aren't the words to describe how I'm feeling today. Just the thought of seeing my Lizzie again was enough for me to pull that trigger. The diamond is my only hope."

"You think the diamond can bring her back?"

"Well nothing else can," said Peter. "Like I said ... the smallest chance."

"You dream about her, don't you?" asked Edward.

"Yes, always, although I wish I didn't. Because every time I do, I wake up just before I get to hold her."

Edward spent a few seconds thinking deeply about those words. "If there *is* such power in this stone, then *that* will be the first wrong we make right. You have my word," he said.

"Thank you, Edward."

Edward stared through the window. "So ... what did you buy with that gold krül?"

Peter smiled. "It was blue with white lace patterns."

"What was?"

"Her dress, she thought it looked like the waves crashing against the beach. Like the seaside."

Obi came stumbling back in, looking all cheery and bright as Edward and Peter shared a look to end the conversation on a warm note. Perhaps Edward had become fond of the pirate. But deep down, he wondered, truly, what price would Peter pay to see his Lizzie again?

Obi went straight for the sack and brought out the whiskey bottle. "I really should stop drinking so much of this stuff," he said, laughing. "But truth be told, I don't really want to."

"Then pour us all one, Obi," said Peter, shaking off his emotions.

"Right gentlemen," said Edward, taking a glass from Obi's hand. "In a few days we'll arrive at Fort Gaze. Many people come and go through that city gate and if we're extra careful, there shouldn't be any snags. The pirates that sacked the fortress leave the folk there in peace, so the city's old heart still beats. My one concern is getting to Ridikus. Yet, we *do* have a pirate in our company, and should he tell them which clan we belong to, we might find ourselves on board a ship that will take us."

Peter shook his head vehemently. "No! No way!" he snapped. "The captain of that clan wants me dead! I stole the scroll from right under his nose. He sent the *Venturous* to find me, which they did, remember? If the *Baliant* hadn't of defeated it, I'd already be dead. They don't call Captain Bill the Murderous for nothing! He basically governs the whole strait. Any suspicious folks trying to cross to Ridikus will do so on his authority alone. We need a better plan."

"The Murderous, you say? I just *might* have a better plan," said Edward. "I've waited many years to look that man in the eyes."

"I don't know why," said Peter, nervously, "but I'm not sure I like the sound of that."

"This captain you speak of ... where is he likely to be?" asked Edward.

"Aboard the *Dürlarain*," said Peter.

"He wants the scroll, that's certain," said Edward. "Why don't we tell him where he can find it? We'll arrange to meet this man, explain that we're willing to part with the scroll should he grant us safe passage. Then, I'll have him sail his crew away from the strait to wherever it is we've 'supposedly' hidden the scroll. That'll buy us some time."

"I suspect he's going to smell a rat, Edward," said Obi. "Unless the man's a simpleton, I just can't see him allowing us to cross without being assured this isn't simply a scheme."

"You won't be going to Ridikus, old boy," said Edward. "I will not see you in danger. Not again. Fort Gaze is where you agreed to part us. But come to think of it, Peter, you're as good as dead if they see you. I'll go alone."

Peter scowled over. "Edward, I trust you, but you're not going alone; I haven't come so far to not see it through. Again, we need a better plan."

Obi sat sipping his whiskey, when mid swig, his eyes lit up with an idea. "How about you take Peter with you?" he said suddenly. "Take him as your captive. Peter already wears the fresh wounds to partially prove there's been a struggle. Gag and bond him and this pirate fellow might be fooled?"

Edward let it be known he liked the idea with the raising of his brows alone.

"Yes, that might work," he said, smiling.

"Wait a minute!" snapped Peter, shocked, sitting up in his chair, shaking a finger. "Let me make one thing clear. If Edward wanders brazenly into the open jaws of that snake, holding a man who betrayed him as his prisoner, you better believe those teeth will fall and the venom will flow. We wouldn't have time to speak before he had us locked up in chains. Then, he'd beat us until we divulged the precise reason for our intrusion. The plan is folly!"

"Folly, maybe," said Edward. "But not if we had something to bargain with."

"The scroll alone will not be enough, Edward, he'll see us dead the second he knows where to find it," sighed Peter. "I'll wager he'd slit our throats."

"I'm not talking about the scroll."

"Then what?"

Edward stood to his feet, walked over to the sack and reached down into the very bottom. Out he pulled the King's crown, shining gold and glorious. "Will this do?"

Peter froze as a mischievous grin crept slowly across his lips. "I think that perhaps, things just got a little interesting," he said.

"I'll make that rat think I'm crooked!" said Edward, grinning. "Make it seem as though I've every intention of seeing Peter Beaumont face the King's justice, saving him a job. Offer the crown as payment for safe passage to Ridikus and then send him off to find the scroll he so desires. I just have to make certain he believes there's value in keeping me alive. Make him believe he could use an ally like me. And the hope is, he won't return, inevitably scroll-less, before our business on Ridikus is complete."

"You mustn't use your own name," said Obi. "Keep the name Edward Clavell to yourself."

Edward scratched his chin, thinking. "How about, Colonel Eustace Gürad of the Kingsguard?"

Peter sent Edward a look of approval. "I just knew that chunk of gold would prove useful. Ha! Well then, it appears we have a plan, gentlemen?"

There came another knock at the door. Mr Whittle had carried across a tray full of tea from the kitchen. Peter answered.

"A good evening to you gentlemen. May I give you this little treat to warm you through? Would you allow me to stock up the fireplace?" said Mr Whittle. "It's going to be a cold one, I'll tell you. Your garments might not have dried by the morning at this rate, so I'll take them all right away. Doesn't seem to want to rain though. Pardon me, sir, move aside and I'll throw some logs on for you."

Which he did, taking each log of dry timber from a sack he had resting over his shoulder.

"Right!" he said, scooping up all the dirty clothes. "Breakfast will be available in the morning. I'll be in the kitchen not long after dawn. I hope you like bacon and eggs?"

Then, Mr Whittle left, leaving the gathering flames in the hearth behind him.

Chapter 24
The Fourteenth Man

Charlotte was locked in a room at the very top of the Plummet. Not a cell, exactly, but a bleak and dark space bare of any furnishings. After Colonel Gürad had discovered that Charlotte knew all about Edward's fleeing and the reasons behind it, he'd informed Lord Harrington, who had no other choice but to seize her for questioning. She said nothing, to anyone, and remained silent. At first, this was just the escape of a prisoner and a disgraced officer who'd abandoned his principles for the same cause. But after the Kingsguard had been killed on the palace walls, everything changed. Edward's jacket was found in the palace courtyard the day after the priceless crown of the King was snatched. So, in the eyes of Lord Harrington, Charlotte was an accomplice.

She stood quietly by the window, looking out over the brook, listening to the criminals cry out from beneath her. A thick fog of trepidation filled the room, the four walls beginning to feel like one giant shackle.

Amongst the racket, she heard the door behind her creak open. Turning, she locked eyes with Captain Galaway as he stepped in. She looked at what he was carrying. It was a small chair. He sat it down gently and smiled cautiously.

By the time he had shut the door behind him, Charlotte had turned back to the window. She started to run her fingers in a pattern through the dust on the sill, where over the past few days she had created the shapes of many flowers - a product of monotony.

"Charlotte, please listen to me," he said, lifting off his hat. "I shouldn't be telling you this, but this is now a very grave situation and I feel it's best that you know. Edward was captured with the pirate at Guntrick Castle."

Charlotte started to weep into her hands. The drops of tears fell through her fingers onto the sill, tainting the dusty drawings.

"But ... he has escaped," said Galaway. "Colonel Gürad had them both in his clutches, but somehow they broke free."

Charlotte's tears ceased and she wiped her face dry. Galaway walked a little closer to her.

"You know why you're here, my lady," he said. "The colonel told us what he heard. They know he searches for a diamond. But that is all they know. You need to tell me exactly where Edward has gone so I can try to help him. Maybe he'll be pardoned; given a room just like this to live out his days. Anything to escape the fate he's brought upon himself. To Lord Harrington, his actions are nothing short of piracy, aiding the likes of Peter Beaumont and running off in search of some treasure."

Galaway heard himself becoming frustrated and breathed deeply to gain his composure.

"He is one of my oldest friends, my lady, but a man has been killed, and the crown of the King stolen. This matter is now far bigger than our friendship. If I am to do *anything*, I'll need to know more. I need the truth, at once! Please, Charlotte?"

Her gaze left the window.

"My husband would have never taken the life of a Kingsguard," she growled quietly. "Not for *any* cause. It's despicable to even think so. I know his actions may cost him his life, but let me tell you something, Captain, Edward Clavell is for King and country always. And you, along with all the others, Harrington and that filthy colonel, should know one thing; wherever his path has taken him ... it's for the good of the people. I know him, Wallace. I have seen the fire in his eyes, burning with the desire for a world rid of pirates. If you're a noble man, Captain Galaway, you should put aside your own orders and join him in his search for a better world."

Charlotte wiped away more tears, that even through her iron will, still seeped from her eyes.

"I have spent my life searching for a better world, my lady, and with Edward by my side. I'm trying to help him."

Charlotte looked deep into the brown of his eyes, seeing that honest glimmer she knew so well.

"Can I trust you, Wallace?"

"My lady Charlotte; I would give my life for Edward Clavell and his family. And I know good and well that you believe that."

Charlotte turned back toward the window and smeared away all of the dust flowers. "Edward found something aboard the last ship the *Baliant* sacked. A scroll, encased in some kind of silver. The words therein spoke of a jewel that he believes might hold the power to bring peace to Graelind. Its name is the Black Diamond."

Galaway shuddered. "Did you just say … the Black Diamond?"

Charlotte nodded.

Galaway froze, thinking fiercely about what to do next, as haunting memories of pearly eyes began to emerge from the dark pools in his mind in which he'd once drowned them. He stepped back with his head down.

"Perhaps I have not been thinking clearly enough," he said, finally able to comprehend. "I've never known Edward to fail me in all the years I've known him. Never have I been so sharp to judge the actions of others without knowing the entire story. But what choice has he given me? I must help him. Yet I am fearful, for this diamond will only destroy him if he ever touches it. The people who live in the Eastern caves are proof enough of that."

"You know of what he seeks?" asked Charlotte.

"Yes! Why didn't I realise? For what else would he sacrifice so much? I once believed in its power too. I must find him, and stop him, whether his cause is just or otherwise he must *never* find that diamond. My lady, I'll see to it you're removed from this room and sent home immediately. I'm truly sorry. I should have done more."

Galaway donned his hat and left. The guard at the door slammed it shut; the sound of the key grinding in the lock echoed through the room. Charlotte crept slowly towards the chair Galaway had left behind. She sat there and cried bitter tears; her sorrow seemed irremediable.

Galaway left the Plummet with haste; agonising over what might have become of his friend. Fresh images of pearly eyes jarred his vision as he leapt onto his horse. With his heart racing, he dug in his heels and rode into the city, halting at the house of Officer Hackett.

He knocked on the door with heavy beats of his fist.

Hackett opened, concerned to find Galaway looking so terribly troubled, the whites of his captain's eyes covered in spikes of red.

"What is it, Wallace?"

"Rupert, we need to gather the men at once," he said. "All the officers, and it *must* be secret. Meet me at the Drum & Fiddle, not in uniform. I won't be long."

Before Hackett could gather a response, Galaway had already put dust and distance between them.

Each officer was paid the same visit, all obeying their summons with a deeply seeded feeling of curiosity. The last door he came to belonged to a house in the hills. It was his sister's home, and out in the garden, tending to the washing, were his two nephews: James and Johnathon Percy.

The both of them leapt up to greet him, troubled to see the drawn-out look on his face that seemed to have aged him by ten years.

"James, I need you to come with me, right away. No questions."

"What's the emergency, uncle?" asked Johnathon.

"A matter I have no time to discuss, my boy," said Galaway, steadying his horse; the urgency in his voice made Johnathon raise his brows.

James Percy didn't hesitate and went sprinting for his jacket, returning to the outstretched hand of his uncle that helped pull him onto the saddle.

They sped down the road, quickly disappearing over the hillside. Arriving at the Drum & Fiddle, where all the *Baliant's* officers had now gathered. Mr Piggs was startled to find so many folks in his tavern before noon, and quickly sprung up to fill teapots and stack plates with biscuits.

Galaway walked in with James Percy by his side; each officer having a similar expression drawn across their countenance.

"Are we all here, gentlemen? Good!" said Galaway, scanning the room. "This meeting must remain a secret. Lord Harrington must never know. Officers, in the past week, as you all well know, our friend and comrade has fled the city."

This was interrupted by a barrage of shouts.

"He's no friend or comrade of mine!" blazed Officer Billings.

"I'll have order, Officer Billings!" snapped Galaway. "What has happened has truly disgraced our company, I know that, but allow me to finish!"

Officer Billings showed his palm in retreat and shifted backward on his chair, silenced. The captain didn't like being interrupted, nor would he stand for it. The room fell quiet again. The captain could feel the anger in the air and the sheer weight of their questioning gaze laid heavily around him like a rain-soaked winter jacket. "I'm sure you might have already heard the stories," he continued. "But here is the truth, as it was told to me by his own wife. Edward found something aboard the *Venturous* the night we took it. Something that spoke of a diamond. And not just any diamond, but one thought to have been buried away in the Eastern caves years ago. He believes this jewel can be used as a weapon; a weapon to help protect

Graelind. Yet, I am afraid the only power it holds is that of the curse that lies upon it."

"Am I hearing this correctly?" asked Billings, filled with astonishment.

"Yes, Officer, you are. Almost thirty years ago, I was part of an expedition to find the Black Diamond. And find it we did, hidden deep in the abyss. My captain sent the youngest deckhand to retrieve it, and when he touched it …"

Galaway had never before spoken his next words aloud and he feared they would taste as bitter as they felt … "I saw the blue drain from his eyes, his skin turn a mottled grey and the flesh around his knuckles and cheekbones all but disappear before me. Then they came, those eyes, those pearly eyes. Hundreds of them, from out of the dark. We ran for our lives; one crewman after another was snatched as we chased the light.

"For years after, there have been many sightings around Graelind, of men and women with gaunt complexions and eyes as white as duck eggs, bulging from their sunken sockets. It was agreed that the people could never know of this horror and anyone who claimed to have seen such beings, well … were simply threatened with death, so to stop the word spreading. What we saw has been completely and purposefully forgotten. I wish it could have stayed that way. If Edward touches this diamond, he will secure himself the same fate as whatever lives in those caves."

The room was so deathly still you could hear the patter of mice feet under the floorboards … *tap, tap, tap, tap.*

The officers were left utterly awestruck.

"I know just how preposterous this sounds," said Galaway. "But I assure you that every word of it is true."

"Not just a tale told to children then?" said Hackett, scowling lines into his forehead.

The captain shook his head despairingly, taking a seat. "No, my lad. I wish it was."

The tavern was now filled with the most diverse arrangement of expressions one might ever see.

"Are you saying that whatever you saw has been living amongst us?" asked Billings.

"Whatever or whoever lives down in those caves, they're different," said the captain. "They barely resembled a man at all, and in the darkness is where they seemed to have remained. But those who *do* live amongst us, they're almost entirely human – except the eyes, nothing human about that. Why they differ or how is far beyond my knowledge. The people who witnessed them weren't the only ones who were told to keep their lips sealed."

"Then what are we to do, Captain?" asked Hackett, trying to digest things.

"We must go after him, Rupert."

Officer Gildred rose from his chair. "Aren't we forgetting something?" he said angrily as everyone turned to face him. "A Kingsguard is dead!" he bawled, slamming his shaking fist onto a nearby table. "At the hands of one of our own! And you talk about saving him from his perils?"

"Sit down, Gildred!" warned Hackett with a growl. "If you believe Edward Clavell is capable of such a crime then you're a blithering fool. That filthy pirate killed the Kingsguard, that much is a certainty. If only you'd cared to ask the right folks the right questions, you might learn a thing or two. Can I suggest that perhaps it's best you spend less time staring down the neck of the whiskey bottle–"

"Enough!" snarled Galaway.

Hackett continued. "The guard in the tunnel, the one who suffered the crack to the head? Well, he knows Edward's face and confirmed it was *not* him in the palace."

Gildred scowled and sat down. "My apologies, Captain."

A calm, steely voice sounded from the back; one of few that had remained quiet throughout the meeting, until now. The voice of Officer Addley. "When I heard our comrade had fled with that rotten ball of filth, I cursed him until the day grew old. But after hearing what I have, as crazy as it may seem, I can no longer condemn his actions. There is only one man alive who I trust more than Edward Clavell, and that is you, Captain Galaway. If you're certain that his intentions were for the good of this nation, then all I can say ... is count me in."

Hackett laughed at what he was about to say. "I'd be lying if I said the idea of all this doesn't scare the hair off my back ... but, count me in."

Billings let his face fall between his outstretched hands, utterly unable to comprehend what he had just heard. "Captain ... these beings, the ones living on our side of the dirt. What is their fate?" he asked, taking the conversation back a step.

"Well," started Galaway. "Having agreed that it was best the truth never saw the light of day, they simply had to be killed. Believe me when I say, it was merciful. To tell it all, my then captain, a man whom you all know very well, was Augustus Harrington. Even then, he was a very powerful man, and he had his spies placed in every corner of the east. One sighting turned into many, and to this very day, Lord Harrington has soldiers sifting through the lands in search of them."

"How can such things be kept so ... quiet?" asked Hackett.

"Word spread that a peasant man told his entire village of what he'd seen. The trouble there is that the man had been explicitly reminded to never speak of it again. So, when he was sliced from belly to throat the rest of the villagers quickly learnt to keep their mouths shut. There are men still out there hunting. We cannot let our friend become their prey. If Edward touches that diamond, prey is all he will be."

"And those left in the caves?" asked Addley.

Galaway cleared his throat. "Well, the caves are watched day and night, the entrances buried beneath rubble for good measure. When I was down there myself, I got the impression those *things* were guarding something. I believe that to be the diamond we were looking for. That leads me to my next concern; should Officer Clavell know something that we didn't, and he is able to take the diamond *without* suffering the consequences I witnessed, well, may there be mercy when those *things* step out from the deep in order to retrieve it."

"If Edward steps foot in those caves, he's as good as dead. Alternatively, if he is able to retrieve this Black Diamond unscathed ... a pure evil from the abyss might be unleashed on the people of Graelind?" said Billings, finally making it all fit together logically in his mind. "Count me in, Captain."

Galaway curled the fingers of his right fist, turning his knuckles white, smiling and watching as all his men began to rally around him.

Each officer, one by one, took a stance. Gildred still remained seated, when everything about the situation began to make him feel very strange. The chair beneath his rear, that not a minute ago felt so pleasantly comfortable, now did not. The overwhelming feeling of his comrades standing tall around him made him feel small, inferior. The aching pain that snaked from his gut to his throat caused a sweaty film to gather on his face. What was that feeling? Ah! Guilt! He knew it well. Gildred took a stance and placed his clasped fist against his chest. "Count me in."

The others matched the gesture and Galaway's smile grew by double as his officers – no, his brothers – stood united.

"Okay then, it's settled," said the captain. "We'll ride for Guntrick Castle. That is where Edward was last seen and no thanks to Colonel Gürad, he's on the run again. Bastard had him caught once already. Edward will not let that happen again, so this time, I suspect he'll be harder to track. Any more questions? Good! That just leaves us with one little problem … we need a fourteenth man."

James Percy sat alone in the corner, wondering exactly why he was here, just minding his own business. Galaway glared into his eyes. As did all the officers. He looked surprised, or maybe that word didn't cut it, he looked shocked to be hearing this, thinking that perhaps he had fallen asleep midway through the meeting and missed the important parts entirely.

The captain walked over to a table, and upon it, lay a sword in a brown leather sheath. "Officer Percy … you'll be needing this!" said Galaway, throwing the blade towards its new keeper.

James' breath was taken from his chest. The hand that caught the sword's hilt was shaking. He was utterly unprepared and even though he'd played out this day a thousand times in his mind, not one of those times looked anything like this. He sliced out the blade, holding it straight in front of him. It glistened against the morning sunlight that peeped through the window; he was in awe of it.

"Officers!" shouted Galaway. "We will ride out tomorrow at first light. Pack enough provisions for your horse, but nothing you can't carry yourself should our journey take us off the road. Colonel Gürad sent a messenger when Edward escaped. He and the pirate were captured at Guntrick Castle. Maybe there's someone there who can help us. Now be gone with you!"

Galaway called over to his nephew. "This uniform is for you, James," he said, pointing to a pile of garments on the table.

James ran his hand over the grey coat; it was exactly as he imagined. "Thank you, Captain," he stuttered, perhaps not convincingly enough for his uncle's liking.

"Something seems to be troubling you, my boy?" said Galaway. "I know this is a strange situation, but I thought you'd be … happier?"

James had only just promised Adeline he'd stay in Summer's Reach and this unexpected development had left him in a rather confining quandary. Galaway noticed the gentle expressions he showed in his face, expressions that could not so easily be seen by others who knew him less. The captain was wary now; never did he expect James Percy to scream in jubilation over such an honour, but a little more than a simple thanks might have sufficed.

All of a sudden, James became acutely aware of his attitude, straightening his posture. "Forgive me, Captain," he said. "All happened so quickly, that's all. An honour, truly. I'll wear my uniform proudly and serve my country with pride."

Galaway nodded and patted his nephew on the shoulder. "That's my boy."

James smiled, although his eyes didn't mimic his lips. The captain walked towards the tavern door and looked back. "James Percy. Do you remember the words I said to you in this very room?"

"Yes."

"Go on?" said Galaway.

"Take every chance you're given, despite the fear of the consequence ... the clock won't wait."

"Indeed, it will not," said Galaway, with a little wink.

James lifted the grey coat and let it drape over his arm. The material was soft but sturdy, much heavier than he'd imagined. His heart started to beat faster, momentarily distracting him from all the conflicting thoughts circling inside his mind. He didn't immediately try on the coat; he had promised his brother Johnathon he would be the first to see it and he didn't want to break his word.

Grabbing his cap, he left the tavern and headed for home, taking a studying glimpse of his grandfather's watch, inhaling the fresh breeze that smelt of wild garlic and rain.

James Percy placed his new uniform under the bed. Johnathon hadn't seen him arrive home, which helped, because he wasn't ready to tell anyone yet.

He walked idly into the living room and sat down by the hearth his mother was tending. She was warming a silver crock of pottage, stirring as the steamy aromas danced above the bubbling surface of the meat and vegetable concoction. Johnathon nearly broke down the door when he came flying in to investigate what he'd smelt.

James hardly felt like eating. It was the last thing on his mind. He watched as his brother took a spoon to the crock, tasting, and then how his mother slapped his hand away for his bad manners. Johnathon laughed, James didn't.

He must tell Adeline. That's entirely all he could think about. She would be heartbroken. He had promised her.

Jumping from his seat, he unhooked his jacket and cap, and set off down the hill with a purpose. Running into the square, his long, measured strides had him fluttering through the markets like a butterfly, dodging merchants and the odd merryman, as a cold rain began to fall upon Summer's Reach once again.

And then, he came upon it. That house with the blue shutters. Adeline had seen him through the window and came running out to embrace him. With his hands tight around her waist, he lifted her and swirled; the rain gambolling across the cobbles, flowing down her dress like rivers down a golden mountain.

He kissed her cheek and set her down in the street.

"Come inside, James! You're soaking!"

Inside, the fire was roaring. On the table were many of Adeline's books she'd been studying. Books of history, folklore and old scrolls covered with poems. Adeline loved to read, and for that, she was far smarter than most. The poems ignited her imagination, and she often wrote her own with a little quill and ink set her grandmother had given her when she was a child.

James sat at the table and started to flick through some of her workings. They made him feel warm with a sense of admiration for her. He asked himself the question: how was it possible to write so flowingly and draw so gracefully?

Adeline brought out some tea, sitting down with the pot nestled in her lap. She was smiling over nervously. James looked up at her beauty then realised … that's how.

She was seated by the fire, peering over at James as he turned page after page. She could see he was admiring her work which embarrassed her a little, a lot actually. Nobody had ever seen her drawings or poems before and it had given her a nervous ache in her belly. James picked one from the pile, a poem that he thought beautiful. He turned towards her, beginning to read it aloud.

> *One night I woke, to a cry in the air,*
> *it seemed that something was riled.*
> *No longer could I stay, no longer did I dare,*
> *the visions, the noises, the wild.*

> *I stepped on the grass, from the porch at last,*
> *to find nothing but a twittering bird.*
> *It seemed at the time, in this mind of mine,*
> *that something else I had certainly heard.*
> *I looked long and hard, about the trees and bush,*
> *until the bird came fluttering back.*
> *It landed and whispered, a sweet tiny whistler,*
> *and then told me I was on the right track.*
> *On the darkest night, to the lake beyond,*
> *I was guided all the way.*
> *The bird then said, look to the water instead,*
> *at the fireflies ready to play.*
> *The sky lit up, with a glow so divine,*
> *I could hardly believe my eyes.*
> *The whistler flew round with a swing and a sway,*
> *and said ... I'll see you again, someday.*

Adeline could feel her cheeks flush. Part of her wished she'd cleared the table to avoid the embarrassment. Part of her was happy that James had liked them all so much. James found her words to be beautiful, and he rustled through the other papers to find more to read, halting halfway through the turn of a page, realising he hadn't come here to read her poems.

"Adeline, I have news," he said, lifting his gaze from the table. "I've been made an officer."

Adeline took a deep breath and stared deep into the fire. He stood and walked towards her, clasping her hands tight inside his.

"You promised me you would stay," she said softly.

"I mean to leave the navy, I do," said James. "But I must do this one thing. An officer is in peril and my uncle has summoned his men to ride east. I shall go with them as requested, and deal with telling him of my withdrawal when I return."

"But you promised me, James," she said again.

"I have to do this, Adeline," he said, at a loss. "The officer is my friend and there is danger at his every turn. I give you my word, that when I return, it will be forever."

"How can I be sure you'll come back to me?" she said, with a whimpering in her voice.

James took a little box from his pocket and lifted the lid. "Will you marry me, Adeline?" he asked, showing her a ring that was wrapped in purple silk.

Adeline didn't know what to do, for she had lost the words from her own mouth, scrambling within her mind to find them. She looked at James, and deeper into his eyes she fell. "Yes, James Percy. I will marry you."

He was so happy it made his heart beat to the speed of a galloping horse. Then, he took her hands, helping her to stand. He run his hand down the soft skin of her wrists, gently bringing her closer.

Removing the ring from the box, he placed it on her finger. The feelings she felt when he did, tingled throughout her whole body. The flames inside the hearth flickered in the ring's polished reflectiveness, and Adeline, she couldn't help but burst out laughing; that kind of happiness laughter, because there was nothing funny about it. This was just how she felt and having never been so happy in her whole life, she didn't know what to expect, didn't know how she would react. She just laughed. James did too.

That night, Adeline stayed with James at his house in the hills. The sun had set, the fire blazed, the new officer now busy packing his essentials. In fact, it was barely packing at all, more like a limp attempt to fold and stuff; and even that he managed to carry out without the slightest grace. He could barely take his eyes off Adeline the whole time.

She watched him fill a sack with blankets and other provisions. He lifted a fresh loaf off the hearth that had been baked that day and wrapped it in cloth. This was packed too, along with his sword and musket.

Adeline didn't like the look of the weapons; she wondered how many men had been struck down with them. Although, those strange thoughts came and went, almost in a blink. "What will you do, when you return?" she asked.

Folding a fresh linen shirt, James sat down beside her. "I think I'll go fishing," he said, in thought. "Well, whatever it takes to make a few spinnels is precisely what I'll be doing. Maybe Mr Piggs will give me some work in the tavern, or perhaps, I could clear the stables at the palace. As long as I'm home, it matters little to me."

"You were so close to realising your dream," said Adeline. "And you would leave it all for us?"

"When I think long about it," he said, "I'm not sure I would have chosen this path had my uncle not been the captain of a ship. A Kingsguard, is what I might have liked, given the option. But if I was going to be in the navy, I would have never settled for being just a crewman. So, in many ways, it *was* my dream … just not one I feel I should chase anymore. Anyway, after we find Edward, it will all be in the past."

The latter of his words settled her. James left her side and continued about his business.

After the sun had fallen, and the family had eaten, James showed Adeline to his room. He kissed her on the cheek and told her he loved her. Then, closing the door behind him, he made for the living room where he'd sleep beside the fire.

It was early in the morning when he woke, still tired, having barely slept a wink the whole night. He crept up and rubbed his eyes, stretched and yawned his way into the morning. He gathered a bowl and filled it with water before setting it out on the stove. Once it was warm, he carried it to the outhouse and took a wash, and then shaved his face to a clean-cut finish. His mother was already up and warming a pot of milk when he returned to the kitchen. He asked her if she'd be so kind as to wake Adeline while he warmed her a wash bowl of her own. James' mother obliged with a smile, giving the bedroom door three knocks before stepping in and laying the cup of steaming milk on the bedside.

James could hear Adeline's sweet voice say thank you; and even that caused his heart to race. He was so flush with every emotion one could feel for another human being. James adjusted the bowl on the stovetop and nearly dropped the whole thing when he heard Adeline's voice from within the same room.

She wished him a good morning; he stuttered out, "Morning, yes, good," and then laughed. She did too.

They sat beside the fire, sipping quietly at the milk until James suddenly realised the wash bowl had by now gone cold. He leapt up and began to warm it again, dropping spoons and cups on the floor in his urgency. Adeline left for the outhouse beaming nervously.

"I love you, Adi," he said, as she left the room.

"I love you, James Percy." Her voice a distant shimmer. James swallowed hard, suppressing his delirium.

The sun had yet to fully emerge, but from far over the hills it lit up the sky with shades of pink and orange. From the pocket of his waistcoat, James brought out his grandfather's watch and looked over it carefully, as if it had another use other than simply telling the time. Through the bedroom window he could see his brother Johnathon hanging clothes on the line to dry. James quickly put on his uniform and went outside.

"Let me try it on, brother," asked Johnathon, running around James like an excited child. "And can I hold your sword, too?"

"Calm down, brother!" laughed James, removing his coat. "Here, take it."

"My goodness, this is tremendous!" said Johnathon. "Far too tremendous for a roughed-up scallywag like you!"

"You little ..." James chased Johnathon around the lawn, eventually grabbing him by the waist then lifting him onto his shoulder. Johnathon laughed until he choked. James set him down on the garden bench and sat beside him.

Johnathon looked down at the grey coat.

"I'm proud of you, James. And father would be too, wherever he is."

James paused on that thought then shrugged it away. "I'm nervous," he said.

"Why?" asked Johnathon.

"I'm just not sure I'm making the right decision."

"I don't understand?" Johnathon thought hard and then realised. "Oh. I see. Adeline?"

James nodded.

"I take it you have two options? Stay here with her or leave for duty?"

"Indeed. She knows I need to leave for a little while, but in the long run, I can't have both. What do you think I should do?"

"I'd be on the *Baliant*'s next voyage out of here. Because women scare the shit out of me."

James chortled at that. "If not me, who would look out for you? Out there at sea, I mean."

"Ah. I'm sure I'd be in good hands. Our Uncle Wallace being the captain must have its perks?"

"He can't be captain forever," said James seriously.

"Don't base your decision on my becoming a sailor, James. I'm not convinced Uncle thinks I'm up to it anyway. Throw your nerves to the wind and do what you think's right. And if someday I do become a sailor and get myself killed, just remember it will be all your fault." Johnathon put an arm over his brother. "I don't know anyone more deserving of this uniform. Yet if you flip the coin, I know you would make that girl in there very happy. And don't worry, I'll show the rest of them that the Percys haven't gone soft."

"You'll make a good sailor," said James.

"Make sure you keep on to Uncle about that, now you've a bit of clout. Come here you." Johnathon hugged his brother and tapped his cheek to alleviate any uncomfortableness. "Your lady awaits you," he added with another tap.

Back inside, Adeline helped James finish his packing.

"You will be safe, James, won't you?" she asked.

James turned to her. "I am with a company of great men, as I have been in many battles before. I do believe that whatever might challenge us on our journey, we will be ready for."

"I have something for you," said Adeline, stepping closer. It was a rolled-up piece of parchment, tied neatly with a red bow at the middle.

"What is it?" he asked.

She placed it in his hands. "You'll see," she said. "Read it when you miss me the most."

James' eyes lit up brightly; he nestled the parchment into his bag and then kissed her softly on the hand. Bringing her close, he held her body against his. "May my love for you carry me swift and safe to the lands afar, but even more swiftly back to you, my lady Adeline. Goodbye, for now."

By the time James had made it to the city, Captain Galaway was counting his officers through the door of the Drum & Fiddle. He was so proud that on his fourteenth count, his nephew stepped in.

"It's good to have you with us, Officer Percy."

Chapter 25
Fort Gaze

After the best night's sleep in days, the men woke to the sound of Mr Whittle tending his gardens. They were quickly up, having remembered the landlord's promise about the eggs and bacon available for breakfast. The smell of the meat blew over from the kitchen, arriving under Obi's nostrils, forcing some urgency into him. Three knocks on the door and the words of "Breakfast, gentleman," had Peter racing the old man for the kitchen. Edward flung the sack over his back and followed the sound of meat frying in a pan.

Breakfast was had at a rapid pace, as delectable as promised, then, after a few handshakes, they bade Mr Whittle and Rushing's Hall a fond farewell.

Fort Gaze was a three-day march over dreadful terrain, made easier now the clouds had decided to take a break from their crying, and the fresh linens worth every single spinnel they had paid for them.

That day and the next, they marched their way east. Peter was oddly excited; Obi could feel an unwelcome imbalance in the pit of his gut and Edward had a more determined look in his eye.

After two nights of sleeping on the cold ground, they woke that next morning, knowing by the time the next night engulfed the sky, they should have made it to the fortress by the sea.

But what they didn't know, is by that same afternoon, Captain Galaway and his officers had reached Guntrick Castle.

*

Fifteen greycoats upon horseback strolled through the gates, greeted by a guard who bowed his head in welcome. They were asked to state their business to which Captain Galaway obliged, asking for a moment of Lord Billian's time. The officers were ushered into the castle's tower, their horses were tied up safely in the stables and on the yard from which Billian was hanged, is where Jasper came out to greet them.

"Officers! Please, come inside. Take something warm to drink and a meal to fill your bellies. King's men are most welcome here, so they are."

"That won't be necessary, sir," said Galaway, waving his hand. "News came to us that our comrade, Edward Clavell, was last seen here at Guntrick. We only ask if you might help us in our search for him, then we shouldn't trouble you anymore. Pardon me, sir, but may I speak with Lord Billian. Is he here?"

The captain's expression let on he knew something.

Jasper spoke his next words with a cold, calculated vengeance. "Lord Billian is dead," he hissed. "I threw him from the walls, neck in noose."

Galaway took a long look around himself. "I'm not sure that was part of the deal, Jasper," he said in a quiet whisper, returning to a normal volume for his next words. "I've changed my mind, I'll take a warm drink and my men would appreciate the same, I'm sure. Is there somewhere we can talk ... in private?"

"Certainly. As you wish, Captain Galaway," bowed Jasper. "Guards, see our guests to the kitchens."

Galaway tipped off his feathered hat and followed.

"Take a seat there, Captain," said Jasper, pointing to a chair by the table in his chamber.

Galaway sat down. "Lord Harrington promised you Guntrick Castle, Jasper," he said with a sidelong glance. "I take it you've carried out what he asked?"

"Yes. We do believe we've found the last of them," said Jasper, sitting down. "Folks around here called him the *Jackal*. I removed his head myself."

"Then the deal is complete," said Galaway. "Yet, Lord Billian was to be given mercy, no doubt hanging the man will only cause an unwanted stir. Harrington will be displeased, I'm sure."

"Shouldn't Harrington know already?"

"Colonel Gürad of the Kingsguard sent a messenger to the capital. The words written said nothing regarding Lord Billian. The colonel couldn't care less who rules from this tower. Nor does he know anything about the deal."

"Your comrade, Edward," said Jasper. "The colonel took him and his pirate accomplice. Was that not in the message?"

"Yes, Edward escaped," said Galaway.

"I see," said Jasper, secretly pleased.

"Why was Edward here ... at Guntrick?"

"We found them in the trees, a few miles from here. They were being hunted. Had we not arrived just in time ... the Jackal would have nabbed them first."

"That doesn't explain why he was here."

"Edward and his friends agreed to help us in our quest to retake the castle. In return, I gave them my word that should they ever need it, help would always be given."

"If your end of the deal was sealed, then the castle was yours. Why risk your lives, and the life of an officer you seemed to trust?"

"We never intended to take back Guntrick without *some* collateral damage, Captain," said Jasper. "We simply needed reassurance we wouldn't pay with our heads when Billian hung limp from the castle walls. A perfect example of mercy, if you ask me. Had things gone the way I'd envisioned, well ... I'd have delivered his bollocks to the palace on a silver fucking platter."

"Jasper, I care little for Billian's death," said Galaway. "But it isn't me you'll have to answer to, is it? Allow me to state the true meaning of our visit. Edward Clavell is in danger. Is there anything you can tell me that might help us find him?"

"Edward was secretive, you could say," said Jasper. "I respected the fact he didn't wish to divulge the truth of it – or the whole truth, at least. He said they were heading off to Fort Gaze. Edward seemed determined to eradicate all the pirate filth from our lands, starting on Ridikus. Can I ask, what danger?"

There was an almost jovial tone in Jasper's question. A piercing cold shivered through the captain's body. "The Black Diamond, is what he seeks."

Jasper's heart curled and knotted. These words had wiped the smirk clean off his face in an instant. "Are ... y-y-you sure?"

"Certain."

"Then a damn fool I have been!" said Jasper, striking the table.

"All this trouble could have been avoided had Gürad simply done his job!" cursed Galaway, wide-eyed.

Jasper's heart curled even tighter. "It was me."

"What?"

"I helped them escape. If I'd have known I–"

"You helped them escape? Jasper, you could be hanged for this treason! You know as well as any, you cannot meddle with the King's justice."

Jasper's scarred face dropped into his hands. He stood and paced the room as Galaway scowled holes into his skin. "Care to explain why?"

"Because I believed in their cause, Captain!"

"Whether you believed in it or not, is irrelevant! You meddled!" Galaway stood up angrily and walked to the window. "How?"

"How what?" asked Jasper.

"How did they escape?"

"I slid a blade into Edward's sleeve," said Jasper, despairingly. "He must've cut himself free."

Galaway huffed in disbelief. "That filthy pirate bastard killed a Kingsguard! Thanks to you he runs loose!"

"I'm truly sorry, allow me to make this right. I'll do anything!"

"You'll ride out with us," snapped Galaway. "It would be wise to cooperate, Jasper. Lord Harrington will see you over that wall swinging if he *ever* finds out. You're lucky that I'm only here to find my friend. Tell me everything you know and pour me a glass of whatever it is in that bottle over there, to calm my nerves."

Jasper obliged. A glass was filled. "They have a third member of their party. An old man named Obi, so it was. He left the morning after they were captured. He told me that he'd get them to Fort Gaze even if it killed him. The old man is either dead in the woods, or – and this is what I'm hoping – has found his companions. If their road was without trouble, they'll be at Fort Gaze by now."

"Well then, we've no time to lose," said Galaway, throwing back the glass of spirit. "Did Edward mention anything else?"

"He mentioned the captain of the *Dürlarain*. Yet, his true name he does not know."

"The Murderous," sighed Galaway, sinking into his chair. "Sometimes called Bill the Baneful. That rotten soul is the very beating heart of all the evil in this world, and his fleet are the dying black veins that entwine one another down a path of defilement and wrath. He has gained a callous grip on our country, and I wonder, what right has anyone to condemn the man for risking everything trying to loosen it. You're not the only one who believes in Edward's cause, Jasper. We just have to keep him out of the hands of those who don't."

"I'll have my men ready to ride out in two hours."

"Make it one."

Jasper hurried from the tower. Galaway stood staring through the window, deep into the cold of the trees.

"But Edward *does* know his true name," he whispered to himself.

*

By this time, Edward, Peter and Obi had made camp on the hill outside the city walls of Fort Gaze. They stared down upon its formidable cannons that had every nearby wave and rock covered within their deadly aim. And across the water, was Ridikus island, oozing with the poison of many terrible foes.

The fortress walls that stood before them were as thick as five men abreast, its turrets and towers were terrifyingly armed.

Inside the city there stretched a long and wide street running right the way through like a spine, with markets and stalls and taverns down each side. The street ended at an archway that opened onto the harbour where many smaller ships were anchored close by and many bigger ships were anchored out in the deep. This was indeed a pirate city; yet the rotten souls rarely ventured too far into the streets, leaving the city-folk to go about their own business, seldom crossing paths. The pirates used only the walls and the rooms within as their stronghold.

There was no lord at Fort Gaze, and surprisingly it hadn't yet become lawless in the time since it was governed by the Graelind army. The story of its capture, and how it ended up in the hands of such a mob of filthy degenerates, and more importantly the true nature of the event, nobody knows. What is known, is that for years before its capture, the Graelind army hadn't had a presence there of any real size. As long as the cannons remained manned, the fortress would be protected, simply because the fearsome guns were worth a thousand men and were moved so very easily, aimed in any direction, sea to hill - an advancement in weaponry far beyond their time. But one day, the occupying army of small numbers deployed their ranks out west, and it took only the number of men needed to man the guns to take control of the city. No mercy was given to the gunners after the pirates crept through the streets and up the walls, shedding blood in what was a massacre.

The ships in the harbour were destroyed, the navy anchored there, defeated. Any poor souls who came forward in defiance were mercilessly cut down by steel - sharp or ballistic. That day went down in history, as a moment in time that brought the most shame upon the King. And it is said, he still sits in his palace chambers, staring at maps and military notes, trying to devise a plan for its recapture. Yet what boiled his blood the most, was how the city was left unguarded. And more importantly, why? He figured there was a snitch, a man on the inside. But he would never know the whole truth. All he knew for certain was there would be a cell at the Plummet waiting for that traitor - *a cell made up really pretty*, he always said.

The men now rested on the hillside, with no flames to warm them. That's a chance they couldn't take. It wouldn't be wise to entice the pirate guards into their midst. So, until the morning, they sat in the pitch darkness, with the cover of trees keeping away the sea spray that the wind scooped from the shore. They barely slept a wink; huddled into their sleeping furs like three giant, shivering cocoons.

Seagulls, thought Edward, cheerlessly, rolling over from one uncomfortable position to another. *Hu-oh, hu-oh*, they called from above. He hated them. He opened his eyes and tried to rub away the ache from them; the crashing sound of waves fell heavily around his ears. Dawn had arrived, but not as quickly as he would have hoped; not a minute of the cold night did he sleep. Edward stood up, trying not to concern himself with the crick running through his neck. He turned to Peter who had clearly been awake for a good while; he was staring directly through the trees at the fortress, deliberating over a smoke on his pipe.

Edward noticed he had a cold glaze in his eye. A look of a man who seemed to be silently considering what the wicked side of his conscience had to say.

Peter saw him watching and smiled back. The cold glaze in his eye dispersed like sea spray, and he spoke, in stern words but with a subtlety that perfectly matched the fire that poured back into his pupils. "We are going to make this. I have a feeling."

"I hope you're right," said Obi, flicking the twigs that had gotten stuck to his cheek.

Edward sat down heavily. "I believe our journey together ends here, old boy." Edward's voice cracked a little. "We couldn't have done this without you."

"Truly," said Peter, with a sadness he couldn't conceal. "Both be dead a few times over."

Edward took a handful of spinnels from his bag and reached for Obi's hand.

"That won't be necessary, Edward," said Obi, with his brightest smile. "Free will brought me along, not the chance of a few spinnels. Ah! Maybe I'll take just one, see if I can find myself a bartender in this city who'll pour me a nice pint."

Peter ached. Their friend was to leave them. It seemed wrong after all this time, looking back on all they had been through. Edward was right, they truly couldn't have come this far without him. As Peter so aptly put it, the gatekeeper from Bidle's Edge, with the heart of a lion and bow-wielding fingers as light as feathers.

Peter quickly dried his cheek, hoping nobody saw, hiding the pain the only way he knew how. "I've heard the ale here tastes like seagull piss," he quipped.

There was a short, momentary silence that gradually grew into a concoction of laughs and chuckles.

Edward looked upon his two new companions, unable to comprehend how he'd become so fond of a pirate and a gatekeeper.

Obi nearly laughed himself out of his boots. The kind of laughter where your shoulders bounce a little harder than they normally would, the kind of laughter that dams impending tears.

"Well, we best be getting to it," said Edward, straightening his cap. "Before I change my mind and end this whole thing here and now."

The men shared a look. Edward brought Obi under his shoulder. "We'll see you again soon, my friend."

"You better," said Obi with a snap. "Now let's be going. There's a pint waiting for *me* and a diamond waiting for *you*. I'll walk you to the harbour, see if I can find some of that seagull piss."

Peter hung back and cast his eyes out to sea.

"But what if we never see you again, Obi?" he asked grievously.

"In that case, I'll look back on our short friendship very fondly, Peter," said Obi, resting his hand on Peter's shoulder. They embraced. Obi coughed away the pang of sadness he knew was about to fill his chest, then walked on.

Peter nodded to himself in absolute agreement with the virtuous side of his conscience; that Obi was truly a friend he might never find the likes of again.

"Come on," said Obi, gesturing for the men to follow.

The pirate guards at the gate paid them no mind as they strolled through the portcullis, out onto the street of limestone the years had polished like a mirror. There was an alleyway, a quiet one, to the right of the city's main street. "Follow me," said Peter, sensing it would afford them a less obstreperous passage to the harbour. The alleys went off in all directions, the parapets of the castle walls kept them on track as they followed the high line of them. Down, left, then straight ahead along another. Edward had an odd, sickly feeling they were being followed. He spun to take in his surroundings. Peter curiously turned with him. Obi halted in his tracks after hearing footsteps up ahead, his heart jumping as both ends of the alleyway became blocked by five shadowy figures edging closer.

The miscreants advanced towards them, tightening their trap. Edward's mind was spinning with so many conflicting thoughts; was this just a chance encounter with some cruel opportunists, or had they been caught by the very pirates they were meaning to cheat? He had little time to think longer before one of them spoke in a screeching tone that unnerved Obi instantly.

"Well, well," he snarled, gritting his black teeth. "I haven't seen you around here before. I wonder if you've anything valuable in yer pockets, and I wonder if you'll squeal when I cut you up to find out!"

Peter stood to one side and Edward to the other. *Not again!* thought Obi, standing between them.

One of the approaching men pulled a knife from his belt and started to cackle; maniacal shrieks that unearthed a wicked excitement in the other four pirates.

Peter drew his axe. Edward dropped the sack from his back and unsheathed his blade. The assailants surged forward with a fierce slashing of daggers.

Edward cut two of them down, dead. They were no match for an officer of the *Baliant*. Peter parried the attack of another, slipped to the side, and came rushing back with a strike of his own that felled a third. Then, he loosed the axe from his hand and it flew off spinning, coming to a halt in the chest of a fourth.

One remained.

Blood gushed down the alley, the last man standing stood shaking. He was scared, of that there was little doubt. The lids of his dark eyes tightened as he examined Peter's bruised face … thinking, remembering.

"Beaumont?" he said in surprise.

Peter's heart sunk like a stone, crash-landing in a lake of dread and realisation. The pirate knew him. And now he was running.

Peter slid the axe from the dead man's chest and gave chase. Edward turned back to Obi. "You must leave us, old boy. Take this!" he snapped, handing him the sack. "No longer can you bear this burden. You need not die for us! Do you hear me? You must go!"

Obi was in shock. He fell to his knees amongst the running rivers of blood, clutching the sack Edward had given him.

"But what about the plan, Edward?" he whimpered.

"It is too late to strike a bargain, and I'll be dead before I see that crown in the hands of a pirate for nothing in return. That bastard knew Peter. I must help him before it's too late!"

Obi shouldered the sack and scrambled back to his feet. There were no words that could cut through his panic. The whole thing had happened so quickly. It was utter terror. Edward stepped away, giving a quick glancing look of farewell. "Go!" he said, then vanished.

There Obi stood, in the lifeless alley of silence, sack on back, blood flowing beneath his boots. There was nothing he could do to keep from vomiting. Then an urge came. *I need to find help!*

Edward searched the alleys, frantically, one after another. The blade in his hand dripped with blood, dotting a crimson trail behind him.

Nothing.

He couldn't hear any sounds, not an utterance of words; nor could he see a single glimmer of life in any direction. He was now deep into the darker streets. Anxious and pouring in sweat. His stomps were heavy, his eyes cutting along the shadowy distance that stretched out before him. There wasn't a single trace of Peter and Edward's breaths became more and more erratic, his eyes losing focus in the panic.

Then, it all went dark and suffocating. He felt the weight on his feet lift and a crushing pain scream through his arm. Then a crack, as the back of his head popped beneath the weight of something blunt and unforgiving.

He woke in a dark room, gagged and tied; with only a small window of light to pierce the black.

Chapter 26

The Captain of the *Dürlarain*

Peter lay calmly beside the deceased body of the pirate. He'd caught him, and not a second to soon. He stared down at the man's face pressed flat against the stone. Was it guilt he felt churning away inside him? Of course not, he enjoyed this. In the distance, Peter heard voices, cutting short the burning sensation of satisfaction. He slid across the ground, up against the alley wall, and crept an eye around the corner. Edward lay motionless in the suspended grip of four pirates, head covered, his hands bound. Peter thrust his head back against the wall, and there, an anguish consumed him, quenching the feeling of triumph. He slowly stood; the men he'd just killed forgotten within his own sorrow. *This is all my fault*, he couldn't help but think. Thoughts like daggers cutting away inside his mind ... *this* is what guilt felt like. Edging his body around the corner, he took each stride carefully. Very distantly, he could hear the people of the city thronging around the main street, but in his immediate vicinity, it was nearly silent. The windows that were set within the alley walls unnerved him; he kept jumping in fear, thinking he had seen some kind of ghostly presence lurking behind them. But they were clearly deserted and he urged himself to focus and find his courage.

He came to a huge door in the wall. Bolts, black steel and stained wood; the obstruction between him and what he imagined to be an infectious hollow of dread beyond. He must have tried the door twenty times, all to no avail, like he expected the lock to have miraculously clicked open just because he willed it so. In sheer desperation and panic he couldn't think quickly enough about what to do next. "Think!" he kept on whispering to himself. "Think, you fool!" But nothing came to him.

He looked up to the roof of the building behind, wondering if the gap between the roof and the wall's ledge might be jumped. Surely not. His body was tired and hurting, but the only other alternative was to try the locked door again, so he had no other option but to take the leap. After taking a minute to reset, Peter noticed an empty space in the wall; it seemed like there might have been some kind of yard or balcony there, and it looked reachable if only he could make it across that ledge.

Peter began to climb, finding little crevices around the windows of a building he could fit his fingers and boots in. At the very top, he pulled himself onto the precariously sloping slates.

There was a guard above him, yet somehow he went unheard over his heavy gasps and what felt like, to him, drumbeats of his heart. *It's now or never*, he thought, this time unable to recognise which side of his conscience had said it.

He held his breath, measured the gap with his eyes, mustered every ounce of his remaining strength, then jumped towards the lowest part of the ledge.

He landed heavily; his boots scrambling to gain the balance and solid footing he needed. This roused the wits of the lookout who peered down from some fifty feet, squinting curiously. Peter had tucked in tight against the wall where only the toes of his boots could be seen by the long stretching gaze of the man.

The ledge he was on was narrow, and he remained with his back to the stone as he traversed it. After many gruelling steps, the wall veered off behind him, and it did in fact run around the perimeter of a little yard that was set into the structure by about ten feet. At the back of the yard, stood a door. Peter closed his eyes before trying the latch, fearing this to be yet another locked door he didn't have the key to. But it was open. A sigh of relief interrupted by a stench that burned his nostrils.

Edward was nodding in and out of a troubled sleep; woken each time by the throbbing pain in his skull. It was then for the first time on his journey that he felt truly desperate. Locked in a cell of nothing but four dark corners and one spear of sunlight shining in, expecting to never again see Peter Beaumont in any form other than a memory. Edward heard a clicking and a grinding of metal coming from the door to the cell, that slowly began to creep open on its hinges. A dark figure walked in. Edward tensed up, preparing for whatever horror may come. The spear of light revealed the face of a man. It was Peter!

"For the love of the sea, you look absolutely dreadful," he said, taking the axe blade to Edward's bonds.

"How did you find me?" mumbled Edward through his drowsy state.

"By a stroke of luck!"

"And how on earth are we getting out of here?"

"I'm a thief, my friend, and a bloody good one at that. Never been caught yet! Although, in truth, I'm far more accustomed to stealing things I can fit in my pocket. But you are quite the oaf, so I won't be carrying you! Now snap out of it."

Peter lifted Edward's cap from his jacket pocket, dusted it off, and fixed it on his head. "Looks like you've had a crack to the skull, you're all dozy looking."

Peter positioned the cap, bringing back his hand to realise that Edward had indeed been struck to bleeding, recoiling at the sight of the blood on his fingers.

"This is going to hurt, Edward. Bite down on this," said Peter, placing a short length of frayed bonding rope between Edward's teeth.

Peter uncorked his whiskey flask and poured the brown contents into the wound. Edward near on shattered his teeth as he bit down in agony, writhing as it burned fiercely.

"That should stop it going rotten for now. But we'll need to dress it quickly. Come on, stand up! Not a minute longer shall we linger in this shit hole."

Peter took Edward under his arms and helped him up. The officer gained a stance and took a few seconds to breathe away the dizziness.

"I'm fine, Peter. Just get me out of here."

They stepped out onto the desolate corridors of Fort Gaze; the scurrying of rats sparking unwelcome memories of the house of the Jackal. Peter lost hope for a second, having forgotten the way; the fear had drained his wits until his mind was rendered empty of any rational calculation.

"This way," he guessed, trying to keep Edward far away from the knowledge that he hadn't the faintest idea in which direction offered freedom.

"Shh!" whispered Peter. There were voices drawing nearer. The corridor was pitch dark until at the very end it began to light up. Edward and Peter spun on their heels and had started to run when a loud voice hollered a summons and the corridor fell into a dark silence. Peter stopped in his tracks. "It looks like it's safe now. Come on. Follow me."

"You better know which way is out!"

Peter didn't, but he was determined to find it. Edward felt like the world was spinning around him. He reached to feel the wound on his head as he became more and more nauseous.

At last, they came to the door to the outside, revealed by the strips of daylight glowing around its casing. Peter reached down blindly for the latch, finding it and then twisting it. The moment he pushed open the door, Edward burst past him into the alleyway, sucked in a deep breath and then fell into the wall.

Peter urged Edward to keep as quiet as possible, pointing to where the pirate guard was lurking. "Follow me and keep tight to the wall."

The officer gave no response. He just did as he was asked. Peter guided them carefully through the buildings, keeping to the alleys the guards couldn't see.

Edward had blood stains the dash of whiskey had diluted into longer streaks of crimson that now run down his neck. They couldn't simply waltz into the city looking so suspicious. Edward could barely stand up straight.

"Wait here," said Peter, handing Edward his water pouch. "And hide. I won't be long."

Edward gulped at the water before finding a space between the buildings that looked suitable enough to lay low in. He sunk into the ground and curled up in a ball. He was shivering cold, and he could feel the wound on his head begin to bleed again. "This is hopeless," he whispered, swaying slowly from side to side, cupping his palm to stop the flow of blood. Edward's memory seemed to be missing pieces. He couldn't remember what happened or how he got himself caught. All he remembered was ... Obi. "Shit! Please let him be safe ... please."

Edward?" said a familiar voice. "Edward, it's me."

"I'm around here."

Peter came scuttling around the corner with a fist full of silk ribbon, needle and thread. "I'm going to need to stitch that wound, Edward," he said, tearing off strips of silk.

"Forget it. Not by your hand."

"You've no choice! A wound exposed is a wound waiting to fester. Turn your head."

Peter fed a line of thick thread through a needle and began to stitch. Edward's face curled in discomfort as the wound slowly joined with each swoop of Peter's hand.

"How on earth did you find what you needed?" asked Edward wincing.

"I'm a professional. Now be quiet, I'm trying to concentrate."

Peter finished and tied the end. "That should hold, but don't count on it," he said, dousing a strip of silk with whiskey and wiping the stitches.

Next, he folded up another strip into a neat triangle, stretched it tight over Edward's head and tied it at the back. "We need to move," said Peter.

"Thank you," said Edward wholeheartedly, reaching out for a hand up, replacing his cap. "I didn't think I'd see you again."

Obi halted, turning to look back at the parapets of Fort Gaze half a mile in the distance. His memory flashed vivid pictures through his mind that swooped him back to that night they'd made camp with Jasper's men. A night when Obi had eavesdropped on Edward's honest disclosure about the one thing that tormented him the most ... the death of his brother Arthur.

After hearing this, Obi never intended to just walk away once they'd reached Fort Gaze. Edward's story unearthed a torment of his own, and from that point on, he felt as though he'd become inescapably attached to the whole thing, for reasons he finally felt the need to speak of. He just stood there, motionless in the road, *like a coward!* he thought. *Why did you leave, Oliver?* he questioned himself with severe reproach. *Help them, you old fool!*

Obi covered the half mile back to Fort Gaze in what seemed like five colossal strides, unable to feel the movement in his own legs for the anxiety that coursed around them in pulsating tingles. He passed the gate, barged his way through the people, tripped here and there on the polished stone and cursed at himself for leaving it so long before turning back. He couldn't think straight for all the people jostling with one another, and the drunkards stumbling out of taverns from a long night on the ale; not to mention the merchants shouting for custom and the children scampering around everyone's feet. The only spare room in his mind was taken up by the foreboding ache that something terrible might have happened to Edward and Peter. They were nowhere to be seen; and even if there were half as many people in the city, he would still struggle to pick them out of the crowd. This was terrible. He needed space and air. His lungs felt hot. He needed to make it off this street without screaming and he was just about to when from out of a crowd he was nudged through the archway and into the harbour. And that is when he saw them. Edward and Peter were at that precise moment being dragged into a wherry by a gang of pirates.

It was at gunpoint that Edward and Peter were forced into said wherry that lay rotting by the harbour. Each row thereafter taking them closer to the towering black mass of torn sails that was the *Dürlarain*. The pirates' captives could see nothing. The sacks over their heads allowed only little speckles of the daylight through the fibres.

The wherry thumped against the great, black hull as the men were dragged to the edge, tied and hoisted by a pulley, until they emerged, still visionless, on the massive ship's deck. The ship lay eerily quiet, but Edward could sense the presence of many people around him, like ghosts in a darkened world, drifting through his state of semi-conscious confusion. To the brig they were escorted, and it was there they were beaten.

It was pitch dark. Edward woke to the sensation of pain around his nose and lips, and he could taste blood. The lobe of his right ear was stinging as if a wasp had angrily made an enemy of it, vividly reminding him of the blow that caused it. His shirt was torn open, the cold air rushing over his chest, chilling the sweat across his skin. Then all his senses heightened at the same time, feeling a gentle sway beneath him, hearing the squawking gulls in the sky outside. *I'm on a ship*, he remembered, as more blood trickled into his mouth.

His hands were bound behind his back and the pain that afflicted his spine was beginning to increase with a vengeance.

"Peter?" he said quietly.

No answer.

"Peter!"

"Edward ... is that you?"

"Yes! Are you hurt?"

"I've had worse. You?"

"I've had worse. Are you bound?"

"Yes. How long have we been here?" asked Peter, trying to shake the sack from his head.

"I don't know," said Edward, gasping for clarity. "I can barely stay awake. My head! I'm all ... drowsy."

"Me too. Taken one too many beatings, if you ask me. I'm tired of it!"

It was at that moment that Edward all but gave up. The desire he had set out with no longer burned. Now, there was only a lifeless and extinguished flutter of hope in its place.

"All I wanted was peace," he whispered sadly. "A world to live in where the people were safe and where families could grow unhindered by evil.

Where towns and cities could prosper despite all the damage left behind. We live in a time where the rotten respect nothing they don't fear. Nothing that's without consequence. I wanted to be that consequence, Peter. And now it's over."

"So, you're just giving up then?"

"I'm afraid I am, my friend."

"Had you down as more than just a quitter," scoffed Peter. "I'm going to make it off this ship and pity will not hold me back. Be glad I'm bound to this post or I'd slap this despair right out of you! Giving up? Having come so far ... makes me sick to hear it. Let me tell you something, Edward. I'm going to find this diamond, or I'll die trying. Don't leave me now! There's fight in you yet, I know it!"

Edward remained silent. At a loss for anything to say.

It felt like weeks that they had been trapped here, with nothing but the foul air within the sack to breathe in; night and day indistinguishable but for the faint sounds from the harbour.

The afternoon of the second day was when life other than the sound of distant conversation presented itself.

Edward woke to footsteps sounding above him as scatterings of dust fell from the wood slats under heavy boots, landing with gentle patters on his shoulders. A stairway in the distance lit up in an orange hue; and down walked a man, his lantern stretched out to illuminate the room.

Through the fibres, the man looked to glide towards them like a phantom; a dull shape of nothingness poised within the light. The man came to halt in the empty space between Edward and Peter, his foul stench of sweat and whiskey desecrated the already rancid hole in which they were trapped. He dropped a water pouch on the floor, just out of their reach as if to goad them. And in a tone filled with evil, he said, "I'm going to carve out your heart and feed it to the pigs, Peter Beaumont." He took the sack from Peter's head, forcing the burning iron of his lantern but an inch from his captive's nose. "How wise of you to return what is mine. It's a pity I know nothing of the meaning of mercy. Where is it?"

Peter could see the man's eyes clearly in the flickering glow of flames. They were light green like summer grass but the black of his pupils seemed to fall hopelessly into a dark and woeful place of unforgivable wickedness, scarred everlastingly by the horror they had seen.

"Speak, boy!" the man screamed, as streams of his spittle showered from his mouth.

"I will tell you nothing," came a whimpered attempt at words Peter spoke through gritted teeth.

The man recoiled to a stance and began to circle the room, his countenance a seething exclamation of anger. "Dark is the world, boy," he snarled. "Dark is the world, and you misreckon the power of light. Whatever honour you may have discovered since last we met, is worthless. Tell me ... where is the scroll?"

"The scroll is of no use to you," said Peter. "There is no crown. The words written on that parchment aren't worth the ink."

"Don't take me for an imbecile, rat!" said the man. "The golden crown of the King lies hidden beneath the palace, locked away in the armoury. Something tells me, you wouldn't have dared venture so close to peril had you not already found it. My men tell me you seek passage to Ridikus? I wonder what piece of the puzzle lies there?"

"You're wasting your time; the armoury was bare. Like I said ... not worth the ink."

"What is it you seek, Beaumont? What power do you believe this diamond possesses? I'd bet you're hoping it's that of resurrection ... so maybe you can see that dead wife of yours again? Sad isn't it, losing the ones we love. They leave a space in the heart that can never be filled. For what it's worth ... I do hope she suffered terribly."

"You know nothing of love!" snapped Peter, having let the words of the man, however meaningless, hurt him.

"I know your flesh will feed many starving swine, and what's more, is that I will make certain you are still breathing while they fill their bellies. Yet, before we commence the feast, I will ask you again, and this time you are going to tell me ... where is the scroll, and where is the crown?"

"What use is the scroll if the crown is found?" said Peter.

"The words written on the parchment are worth nothing to me. I merely remembered the details that were important. But the pure silver jacket that encompasses those scribblings of ink, well, let's just say ... should you find the right keyhole ..."

"Such an intricate detail ... why tell me?"

"Because you're powerless to act upon it. You'll be lucky to ever see the light of a new day."

"You speak well for a pirate!" called Edward from the darkness.

The man turned sharply in anger, lifting his lantern, scrutinising the captive who had spoken unwelcome words. The pirate drew a long blade from his belt, crouched before Edward and brushed the steel across the starling on his bandolier.

"An officer," he tutted. "I was led to believe that your kind were supposed to stand firm in devotion to our lawful monarch? Taking a pirate accomplice will have landed a rather generous price on your head, I would imagine? A welcome dilemma. Do I force this blade through your flesh, or hand you back, missing your tongue, then leave with a sack full of spinnels for my loyal deed?"

Edward took a breath of composure. "As much as the thought of hanging by the neck compels me to choose such a demise, I'll take the blade. But first, allow me to look upon the face of the man who is to wield it."

The man crept closer, his cold eyes glistening from the warm orange blaze in his hand. He lifted off the sack. A shock of pain hit Edward's chest. He knew the man's face. Vivid memories flashed before him like a lightning storm.

"William Fane?" he eventually muttered.

The pirate was as still as stone having heard his name – and there, the evil subsided if only for half a second. "Edward?" he spoke back in a soft mutter.

Yet Edward remained aghast and in horror, unable to speak.

The pirate's eyes were locked on Edward's as he stood; turning away with a gasp of disbelief before racing up the stairs and slamming the iron door behind him.

In all their anguish, little did they know, that a friend had once again come to their aid. Obi had walked for a full day along the road back to Guntrick, where he met a charging cavalry with a united purpose. He jumped into the trees for cover and watched on as the horses flew past, kicking up the dusty road with every hoof beat. The man at the front wore a long scar down his cheek, an easily recognisable feature that Obi clicked onto in an instant. He rushed out from his cover and bellowed a great call. "Sir Jasper! SIR JASPER!"

The leader of the Soldiers Slain brought his mount to a screaming halt and veered off into the grass by the roadside.

"Obi?" called Jasper, leaping down from his towering black stallion. "What of Edward and Peter?"

"Captured! The pirates have taken them!" said Obi, distressed. "Aboard that great big horror in the strait. I was on my way to bring you this news in the hope that you could help me."

The officers dismounted with an air of intrigue about their approach, forming a circle of greycoats around a frightened Obi.

Jasper was the first to speak, addressing Captain Galaway and his men in the expected formal manner.

"This is Captain Wallace Galaway of the *Baliant*, and these are his officers. They are here to find Edward. You must tell us everything. Your friends are in peril beyond imagining."

"Of course, sir. But first, we must make haste to Fort Gaze. I fear the worst."

Galaway jumped down from his mount. "You'll ride with me, sir," he said, extending a hand. "Hold on to your cap."

And make haste they did, screaming along the roads that weaved through the forests, fighting the wind and the gentle spray of rain that chilled them in the winter cold.

The next morning, the men arrived outside the city limits, around a mile from the front gate. Their horses were ridden near to death, the men were shaking from the wickedness of Mother Nature's ever-changing display of elemental control.

A camp was made nearby with fires and spits, where pots of hot concoctions were brewed and guzzled to tame the bite.

"We cannot enter Fort Gaze bare of a disguise, Captain Galaway," said Jasper, pacing around the campfire, clutching his chest to stay warm. "Almost certain death is what awaits us if we storm in without a sure plan."

Galaway sat puffing his pipe. "I know the power of those cannons, sir, make no mistake. You need only hear the rumble once. That kind of thing will stay with you."

"Then what do you suggest?"

"Bring me the old man," said Galaway, as the feather on his hat wobbled and his tobacco smoke whished around the camp along the breeze. Sheepishly, Obi stepped forward.

"Tell me the plan, my friend," said Galaway, with his eyes locked intently into the distance.

"The plan?"

"Yes. Let's hear it."

"With respect, Captain. What makes you so sure I have one?"

"Edward Clavell would not have set foot near this forsaken place had he not devised something. And if it's good enough for him, it's good enough for me."

Galaway turned to look Obi dead in the eye. "You might well be Edward's only chance of making it out of this mess. So ..." He turned back to his lengthy distant gaze. "... let's be hearing it. And spare none of it ... I know about the Black Diamond."

Obi found himself unprepared, and pursed his lips in deep thought, trying to conceal his oscillating knees.

"Well ... I ... maybe ... oh here goes! Peter Beaumont belonged to the clan of rotten souls captained by the ..." He paused then to think. "... the Murderous, be it his befitting sobriquet. Peter had betrayed his captain and set out to better his life and free himself from the pain he no longer wished to be a part of. He stole the scroll from under his captain's nose in the hope its contents would lead him to the Black Diamond. He believed the jewel could protect him from the consequences and see him safe to a land far away to live out his days in peace. Such was the catalyst that raged his pirate leader.

"When Peter escaped the Plummet, he came to Edward for help, and just as I did, the officer saw the good in him. They acquired my assistance along the way and then our journey led us here, needing safe passage to Ridikus, as it is believed that a man by the name of Leander who resides there, could help us.

"Let it be known ... that when I set out, I had no desire for diamonds or power or any other jewels or riches; I saw two men with a just cause, each for their own reasons, and I wanted to help. So, the question was asked ... what bargain could be struck for said safe passage? Well, it was agreed upon that Edward would lead Peter in bonds, to the captain of the Dürlarain. Warn him the traitor was now a prisoner of the King and assure him that should he turn a blind eye, he would be rewarded with the scroll that was taken and the golden crown of the King. Surely such treasures would be worth more to him than one traitor already condemned to the gallows under another man's justice. Edward hoped to convince the man that he could use a man like him; a man on the inside, if you will. That's where it all went wrong. One of those scum recognised Peter and the rest is history – the plan fell apart before it had even begun."

"Tell me about the scroll, Obi," said Galaway inquisitively.

"Written on the parchment is a riddle, of sorts," said Obi. "The words therein led Edward and Peter to the crown, upon which, was yet another riddle scribed into the gold. After taking the crown they turned to Bidle's Edge for a night's rest, hoping to find someone who held knowledge of the being the riddle spoke of. That someone happened to be me, and that being was the Jackal. I've never seen anything quite like it, that beast! I slung an arrow through his neck but he came back. Edward drove a blade through his heart … but he came back!

"As he laid there on the ground, bleeding and still, his widow wept. She was now free from his callous grip. But what hurt me the most … was that her eyes told you *nothing*. They were only pearly white and desolate, cold and dying – I cannot imagine the life she'd lived under his control. Mustering her courage, she said to look for a man by the name of Leander. And here we are, Captain."

"You say this Jackal came back?"

"Yes, followed us through the woods. Had it not been for Jasper and his men, we'd be dead."

Galaway contemplated the horrors of the story, parts of which he already knew enough about, or at least just enough so the whole thing didn't strike all kinds of fear into his bones. "And all the pieces of the puzzle now lie in the hands of a pirate?" he sighed.

"Not exactly, Captain. Edward made sure of that," said Obi, working free the golden crown from his sack. "Here's to hoping that such treasures are worth more to that pirate than the lives of my friends." And from behind the crown, he revealed the scroll. "I believe we might have enough to bargain with."

The officers stood astounded by the sight of royal gold, never before believed to have truly existed.

"Then how do you suppose we go about this?" asked Officer Addley, stepping forward, admiring the crown in Obi's hand.

"I'll go," said Obi, as sure as the sunset. "I'll make the offer in exchange for their freedom."

"*Their* freedom?" exclaimed Hackett. "Listen, old man! If you believe we're here to bargain for the life of a pirate, you're a fool."

Hackett's words were met with many calls of, *here, here*, making Obi shake a little harder in his boots.

"I'm afraid that Officer Hackett is right, Obi," said Galaway. "If we do this, it's for Edward only. The pirate must fend for himself."

"What if he's already dead, Captain?" called Officer Billings. "We could be chasing a ghost!"

"Who is to attempt this errand?" asked Gildred. "I won't stand by whilst the old man stakes his life against this pirate's mercy."

Jasper stepped further into the crowd. "Captain, I will nominate myself for the task. I shouldn't be recognised and I do not fear death. However, I do not believe that a sure plan has yet been formed. If you step into the lion's den with fresh meat stuffed into your pockets, you're sure to be mauled."

Officer Percy spoke. "Use the crown as bait, have the pirate sail the *Dürlarain* as far from the strait as possible, releasing Officer Clavell on safer lands. That will then leave them vulnerable to attack, and *that's* when we should take our chance, if you ask me."

"Do you not see how many we number?" laughed Billings. "What chance?"

"A chance to sink the bastards!" said Addley.

"Impossible," said Hackett, shaking his head. "We get Edward and get out!"

"Agreed," said Billings. "There's no reason to linger here any longer, Officer Percy. Finding Edward alive is our only priority, not vengeance, not today. The *Dürlarain's* time will come. Captain, what are we to do?"

"Jasper, are you certain this is your wish? Will you go?" asked Galaway.

"Yes, Captain. I feel it's right that I do."

"Very well then. And I think Officer Percy has the right idea. It's about time those scumeths get what's coming to them."

"Forgive me, Captain," said a bewildered Hackett. "But to me, it sounds like you plan to take a fight to the *Dürlarain*. Have you developed a power to repel cannon fire?"

Galaway chuckled in his cloud of smoke, tapped out his pipe on a rock and turned to all his men. "Do you know what it was that brought you all with me on this quest?" he asked, adjusting his coat, striding out into the middle of the camp with an extended ear, waiting for an answer. "The same loyalty you share with the men that have sailed the *Baliant* to meet us."

An enduring silence covered the camp, only to be broken when Hackett came forth with a beaming grin. "Always one step ahead, Captain Galaway."

"Jasper!" said Galaway. "Take my bandolier and have their captain presume you're an officer. Then, offer him the contents Obi carries and steer him into the path of the *Baliant's* cannons in Fithering's Bay. When you and Edward are freed, climb to the hillside and set a signal fire. Then, when the *Dürlarain* sails into sight – we engage to kill."

"I'll do my very best, Captain," said Jasper, taking Galaway's bandolier in his grasp.

"Soldiers!" called Jasper. "Take your orders from Captain Galaway in my absence. Go with the officers and I'll meet you at Fithering's Bay. Wish me luck."

And at that, Jasper left.

"Officers! Soldiers! Saddle up!" bellowed Galaway.

Obi pushed through the crowd and grabbed Jasper by his arm. "Save Peter. I beg you, Jasper. He's a good man."

"Fear not, Obi. I plan to."

Jasper walked through the arch at the end of the long street. The high harbour towers of Fort Gaze stood erect above him. He trembled a little, although this wasn't fear but excitement, for such daring escapades he'd become accustomed to since his castle exile. By the harbour, there stood a group of pirates. Jasper stepped calmly into their midst and puffed out his chest as if he owned the city.

"I wish to be taken to the captain of the *Dürlarain*. I have a proposition for him," he said as eloquently as he could, arranging the bandolier for all the evil eyes to see.

"And who might you be then?" one of the pirates snarled. "A Kingsman by the smell o' ya!"

"I'm a Kingsguard. I bring word from Lord Harrington. Your captain holds a prisoner of his and I exhort you to release him."

"Lord Harrington has no power in Fort Gaze an' neither do you! Run along now, slitherworm, or I'll put a bullet in that thick head of yours."

"I'm sure he'd like to hear what I have for him in return before you do, fool," snapped Jasper.

"How about I cut you into tiny pieces?"

"Yes, do!" said Jasper, smiling. "And then run along like a good boy and tell your captain that you killed the man willing to offer him the golden crown of the King!"

The pirates were lost for words and looked about one another knowing they'd been bettered. Another of them stepped forward, his rotting boots squelching on the harbour deck. "Right this way," he croaked through gritted teeth.

They boarded a tired old wherry that barely looked capable of taking much weight, and before he knew it, Jasper was staring up at the colossal beast long remembered as the greatest ship on the seas. The *Dürlarain*.

He reached for the roped ladders, climbed rung after rung and hauled himself onto the vast deck of smeared black wood. There, beneath black sails, stood many of Fane's men, all as wretched as the next. And they glared at him with a glimmer of malevolence that sliced deep into his nerve, cleaner than a hot knife through butter. He was escorted to the back of the ship by a pirate who had him gripped unrelentingly. They arrived at a huge door of stained glass. The pirate growled and pushed him through. And there, in his darkened cabin, stood William Fane with his back turned to them.

"Captain Bill? Fella claims to be a Kingsguard. He has a proposition for you, he says."

"Leave us, now," said Fane, without the slightest flinch. "You must be a brave man, Kingsguard?"

"Or perhaps foolish? Yet here I stand, bound by duty," said Jasper. "Captain, you hold a prisoner of Lord Harrington's he kindly requests that you return to him."

"You are neither brave nor foolish!" snapped Fane, spinning to confront his guest. "Reckless is what you are! The gall to come aboard my ship and ask me to part with one of my own prisoners. I should see you strapped to a cannon!"

"You think I would come aboard without something to bargain with?" asked Jasper. "Deem it what you will, Captain, but that's hardly reckless, in my eyes. Now will you hear my proposition, pirate, or shall I close my eyes and think of the stars as you put a bullet in my chest? Of course, should I not return, I'd say it's likely Lord Harrington would seek revenge for such an act of treason."

"You're mistaken, guard. I do not fear Augustus Harrington," said

Fane. "His men have been splashing around the seas for years hoping to catch me. Failing, failing, *failing!* And as for treason ... just add it to the list of atrocities I'm wanted for, slitherworm. It makes no difference to me; my neck will meet the noose either way should I ever be caught. Now! Let's make something clear, you are no longer here to bargain for the life of Edward Clavell, but for your own. Tell me what it is you have that I'd be willing to trade for your existence."

Jasper swallowed. "For the release of Edward Clavell and our safe return to land, you shall receive the golden crown of the King."

"I'm listening."

"Upon our release, I will point on a map to where the crown is buried, and beside it you'll find the scroll encased in a pure silver jacket. I'm led to believe that trinket is of some worth to you? Do we have a deal?"

Fane's eyes flung wide open as he digested Jasper's words.

"That is quite an interesting proposition, guard," said Fane, smiling back, his black teeth on show like a row of ancient gravestones. "One that I'm inclined to willingly accept. What a coincidental set of circumstances that you should lead me to the very items that I desire. Had you not been such a hopeless liar, I may have spared your life for such generous terms."

"Liar? I don't follow."

"A Kingsguard, you say?"

Jasper took another great gulp. "Indeed."

"But I can't help but notice your bandolier?"

Jasper looked down and then his heart skipped a beat. What had he done? How could he have been so careless?

"Only an officer's belt is white and embellished with a starling," said Fane, in a tone laced with dread. "We have an imposter. Maybe you were right after all. Reckless, perhaps not, but witless, yes indeed. There's someone I'd like you to meet. Let's see if *he* knows the identity of my mysterious guest."

The door to the cabin flung open. Jasper's heart was thumping like a carnival drum. Heavy footsteps came thudding towards him from behind as the wind blew through, dancing amongst the black flags that hung from the walls.

Jasper turned and saw a man behind a pistol. He stared into the barrel and watched as the man clicked back the hammer.

"Colonel Gürad," said Fane. "Kill the man!"

Chapter 27
Fithering's Bay

A gunshot woke Peter from his drowsy state. Edward was already wide awake, and now even more so after the chilling sound of ballistic fire from above. One single shot that filled the air and one single cold tremor of dread that climbed Edward's spine. Something just didn't feel right in that moment.

The gulls outside had settled and music could be heard from the harbour. *It must be nightfall by now,* Edward thought to himself. Peter was too withered to make any of his own deductions. No food and no water had his lips dryer than stable hay on a summer's afternoon. Hope was beginning to fade in this dark brig far from home. They wouldn't last much longer without a drink.

But then, in the distance, those unmistakable beats could be heard again, like that of an erratic heart. Footsteps moving closer, unpredictably stomping as they quickened along the level above. The door crashed open and five pirates bundled down the stairs - one holding a huge lantern and the other four each with the limb of a dead man in their grasp. The limp body was thrown to the ground with a great thud and came sprawling out in front of Edward and Peter. It was Jasper. His eyes had turned black, his fingers covered in crimson; blood had wept from his ears, down his neck and congealed by his collar.

Fane stood above Jasper's corpse with a sense of pride easily revealed. Then he rushed forward, shining the lantern in Edward's face.

"This man was an imposter, and for that ... he died!" said Fane, in a cold, quiet breath of anger. "He came here trying to help you, Clavell; to bargain for your life thinking I wouldn't suspect a damn thing. He tried to take me for a fool and I WON'T HAVE IT!"

The pirate writhed in a fit of fury until his temper slowly eased. He kneeled before Edward again, taking a deep breath, wiping the spittle from his mouth.

"He offered me the crown and scroll for your life. He must have known how valuable those items are to me. And now I know that he's not alone. One of my many scouts tells me there's a great ship docked over at Fithering's Bay – the *Baliant* – if the identity has not been mistaken. It seems their plan was to lure my ship from the strait, an ambush. But his disguise was flawed and pathetic, and foolishness is a disease that no remedy other than death can cure. Now I know where his friends are hiding and I think it's time we paid them a visit."

Fane withdrew from the brig whilst the rest of the pirates lifted Jasper and carried him away. The door slammed shut. Peter stayed silent as two streams of tears found the wrinkles in his face. Edward tried with all his might to free his hands from the bonds, but he had no energy left inside him. His wrists were now covered in sores from the ropes and the skin began to tear and bleed. He stared into the blank space where Jasper had laid and with a heavy heart he gave in.

Then, they began to feel movement. The *Dürlarain*'s sails had caught a gentle breeze and the sound of the anchor chain rattling against the hull reverberated through the cabins.

Voices called from above, one deeper and fiercer than the rest of them, commanding his men.

"How has this happened, Edward?" said Peter.

"I have no idea. Obi must have found Jasper and asked for help. His plan sounds all too familiar, doesn't it?"

"Indeed. And the *Baliant*?"

"Captain Galaway didn't believe in my cause. How the *Baliant* and her crew have any part to play in this, I do not know. I fear what is to come."

*

Captain Galaway was resting in his own cabin aboard the *Baliant* just waiting. *When might the Dürlarain peer its vicious eyes from around the bay's edge?* he thought. That actuality remained unknown and as time went by, and the night grew older, Galaway began to wander into the past. His mind travelled back to the time when Bill the Baneful's ship belonged to the navy. It was magnificent; the figurehead was a lady, with an emerald flowing dress that seemed to blow in the wind whilst she sailed. When the pirates commandeered the *Dürlarain* the figurehead was destroyed, sawn off and burnt. Nailed in her place was a gargoyle, with eyes as red as death and claws like knives. The hull was painted tar-black and all the ship's old grace became a distant memory. He could not allow himself to believe that the sight of those deathly eyes would not unnerve him a little.

There was a darkness about his mood, with things in such a lamentable state. His reality was falling far short of his expectations, having only in very recent months decided his time as captain might well be up. Before this scandal, he intended to make his next voyage his last, hoping to enjoy it, to celebrate and rejoice at the possibility of a life away from the sea. A life back home with his family. Although he feared such a time, because that wasn't Captain Galaway. The sea was all he knew. Yes, he knew he was no longer as accurate with a musket or as slick with a blade as he once was, but nobody had that fire in their heart quite like him. This just wasn't the way he expected it all to end.

He leaned over the table, reaching for the tin of tobacco Edward had given him the night they'd taken the *Venturous*. He stuffed a pinch into his pipe and began to puff away. It was awful. A few deep inhalations were enough before he set it down on the table, leaving it to burn and gently smoke by itself. The silence was broken.

"Captain, you really need to see this!" said Addley, stepping in through the door. "Inky has spotted something by the harbour over at Fithering's."

The captain boarded a small rowing boat along with a few other officers. They touched the shale of the beach and sprinted up the dunes to where Inky was stood, spyglass fixed in his young hand, pressed against his keen eye.

"Take a look, Captain," said Inkleman, passing it over.

Galaway took a hold and cast a magnified look toward the harbour. What he saw was a man, torched in a blaze of flames, tied to a post. And below, painted in blood upon a stake lashed upright, read ... *Jasper the Imposter.*

Jasper's men were laying low in the trees, waiting patiently for the signal fire. Then confusion, for the orange flickers through the thickets were burning in entirely the wrong place.

In Jasper's absence, a man named Anders Murphy had taken charge of the Soldiers Slain. He ordered his men to investigate the peculiarity, for the flames were not burning upon the hillside as planned. When the soldiers arrived at the harbour their hearts were filled with a dread they could not endure, shining as fiercely as the sun right before their eyes. The crackles like one hundred battling warships spat from the timber below Jasper's suspended body.

Galaway returned to the *Baliant*, beside himself in rage, feeling as though one of his own men had been taken. "Revenge will be had!" he growled. "Mark my words!" His cabin door slammed behind him, shattering a window.

Obi had overheard what had happened and fled to the lower cabins to grieve in his own way. The soldiers doused Jasper's body and lifted him down. They were torn by this atrocity. Long would the grief over their leader's death linger in their hearts. For he had been the guiding force when all seemed bleak. The voice of encouragement when all hope seemed lost.

Anders Murphy was to take the mantle of leader in Jasper's place. He cursed the foul miscreants to blame, vowing to his men that vengeance would be had at any cost, in the face of any peril those responsible could wage against them.

One of the younger soldiers was tasked with returning Jasper to Guntrick Castle. He didn't want to leave behind his comrades, but taking his loyal leader home was as much an honour to him as staying for the fight. They cheered and wept as the soldier rode off into the trees. Jasper Montague – a brave and loyal leader until the very end.

The Soldiers Slain boarded the *Baliant*. Anders Murphy rushed to speak with Captain Galaway. The officers consoled the grieving. Obi had remained firmly where he was after finding a bottle of whiskey he deemed suitable enough to slump into for a little while.

Galaway's lips were now swollen, his grimacing teeth had worn purple marks into the soft flesh. He was bitter, and Jasper's death had twisted him, Although, his own grief felt nothing like the crippled hearts of the Soldiers Slain.

"With or without your help, Captain, we attack the *Dürlarain*, tonight!" said Anders Murphy in a fit of rage.

"We will be torn apart from bow to stern if we enter that strait," said Galaway apologetically. "I'm sorry, Anders, but now is not the time to encourage battle!"

"Then what are we to do?"

The words were interrupted by a tumult outside the cabin, as Hackett came bursting in. "It's the *Dürlarain*, Captain!" he said breathlessly. "Heading straight for us! A mile out at the most."

"The bastards have come to us!" growled Galaway.

Anders Murphy smiled callously.

The captain snatched his spyglass and raced up the *Baliant*'s deck. "Weigh anchor! Turn this ship starboard!" he screamed, at the very top of his lungs. "Officer Gildred! Obi must leave this ship immediately. See to it!"

Gildred took to the stairs and found Obi confused by all the racket. "Obi, you need to follow me, now!" he said sternly.

"What's happening, Officer?"

"This is no place for a fellow like you when battle threatens. By orders of the captain. Now come!"

Gildred helped Obi into a wherry then lowered him down, the black water turning blacker by the second as the *Baliant* sailed deeper.

Galaway leaned far over the edge, sending him a gesture of goodbye. "Be safe, Obi!" he called.

Obi was utterly lost for words, only managing to lift his hand to gently wave back. He grabbed the paddle and began to row, when out of the corner of his eye, enlightened by the moon's white hue, a dark ship in the distance sailed into vision. His boat bumped against the shale beach a few hundred yards from the *Baliant*, and from there, he ran up the dunes to hide, keeping low, finding a tree fit to crawl under. He looked out at the sea, anxiously waiting, coiled in a ball like a frightened pup. The sea was restless, the waves beat the rocks of Fithering's Bay beneath him. And there under the stars, it was time for battle.

The *Dürlarain* closed in on the empty expanse between it and the *Baliant*. Obi held his breath for a few seconds, rendered stiff with perturbation.

Galaway locked eyes with the gargoyle and watched on anxiously as the waves were consumed beneath its hanging claws. The crewmen all scrambled to the cannons. The officers loaded their muskets, taking aim over the sides.

The *Dürlarain* turned sharply over to its portside, as the *Baliant* straightened sail out east away from land. On this path, they would soon meet in the deep for the dreadful inevitable.

The captain studied the enemy through his spy glass, as the host of pirates rushed across the *Dürlarain's* deck into formation. And at the head of which, standing tall on the forecastle, was the Murderous himself, with his sword high in the air, slashing it in their eastern direction.

The two mighty ships were now side by side and the pirates roared like raved lions. There looked to be hundreds of them, all as rotten as the next.

In the midst of the madness, Galaway had missed something. *Edward?* he thought.

"Aim for the gunports and higher!" he called out to the gunners. "Do not fire at the hold, we have a man aboard!"

The cannons were primed then discharged with calamitous force, shaking the sea and the trees on lands afar. Wood was split and fractured. Men on both sides were slaughtered. The noise was truly terrifying. Obi shuddered at every boom. The screaming and the yelling, the cries of pain and suffering from the blistering gunfire were just too much to bear. But the colours were like nothing he had ever seen. Obi thought the flashes of light looked like exploding stars; he wanted nothing more but to look away but he simply couldn't.

The battle raged on. Bill the Baneful was so brutal that the sight of slain men bothered him little – it only inspired his evil. Yet, the *Baliant's* furious firepower was beginning to overcome his men. Countless pirates began to fall, one after another, dropping like squatted flies. The *Dürlarain* was a warrior warship, but not impregnable, and now the deck was awash with crimson.

William Fane gave a call to retreat. He wouldn't risk the *Dürlarain* being sunk – not today. His pride would be shattered indeed, but they would live to fight another day. The *Dürlarain* swung to port and they were off into the night.

Victory had been claimed for the officers and crew of the *Baliant*. The deck rang out in triumphant jubilation; Galaway sprung his spyglass, and within the lens, Bill the Baneful stood poised on the *Dürlarain's* deck, just staring back, gesturing his blade over his own throat.

"We will see you again ... William Fane!" called Galaway.

During the battle, one cannon shot blew through into the hold where Edward and Peter were bonded. They were cowering for their lives as a huge cavity opened up in the hull. And from it, the silver clouds could be seen, as well as the glow of the broadsides that lit the night sky. Something had caught Peter's eye. Lying there on the floor was a long splinter of wood. He reached for it with the very tip of his toes to pull in nearer, feeding it behind him, at last clutching it inside his fingers. Desperately he tried to cut himself free with a series of blind strokes full of relentless determination. The splinter was beginning to lacerate his palm, when eventually the bonds started to fray and come apart. He wriggled from them and crawled towards Edward, taking the splinter to the rope around his companion's wrists. Once Edward was free, they both leapt for the water pouch that Fane had left behind. It was warm and filthy, but it was life giving. They drained the lot.

Then, they ran with their heads covered to where the moonlight peered in, but it was too small a hole from which to escape. With urgency they mustered all the strength they had left, violently striking at the panels with kicks, demanding the gap to widen enough to climb through. As the *Dürlarain* turned in retreat, the panels were broken - Peter jumped first, then Edward. The both of them bloody, exhausted and shaken with fear, now floating in the bitter cold of the eastern sea.

Obi saw two shadows bobbing upon the surface. He had seen men fall from the *Dürlarain* but sink without motion to the depths. Yet, the two shadows he could see now were swimming for the shore, paddling frantically.

He walked over the sandy dunes, inland, keeping his eyes fixed on the two men. Their splashes were clear, faint but true. He shot a look behind toward the *Baliant* that sailed away, broken but victorious. He found himself staring down at Fithering's Bay, at the charred post where Jasper had been tied and burned.

He descended the hill of sand, gingerly stepping out onto the harbour deck, as feelings of grief made their expected arrival in the form of crushing pains to his chest. Jasper had been so kind to him. The day that Colonel Gürad had taken Edward and Peter they had spoken at length, and the food and comfort he'd received as a stranger was nothing short of gratuitous solicitude. His eyes seeped tears of sorrow as he stood unmoving beside the black post, observing the warm ashes that still clung to life.

The harbour was silent and tranquil. Obi had dozed into a sad daydream about this terrible day, and at that moment, all seemed lost. Not a quiver of wind or sound could he hear, save the crunches of Edward and Peter's boots as they came stumbling onto the shale beach. Obi threw himself behind a pile of old fisherman's netting and sat peering through the gaps, not yet aware of the men's identities. Peter came striding along the beach, collapsing by the harbour deck, shivering like the sea had washed away his blood's warmth. Edward followed behind whilst ringing the seawater from his jacket, until the shale cracked beneath his knees as he fell to them.

Obi squinted his eyes to better his vision, the dark of the night immersing the space the moonlight could not reach. *My friends!* he thought, slipping across the deck in haste, waving and calling to them. Edward jumped to his feet. Peter still lay flat out, staring at the stars, all sound muffled by the water in his ears.

"Edward!"

"Obi?"

"You're alive!?"

"By what miracle I do not know!"

"Where's Peter?"

"I'm here!" called a faint voice. "For the love of the sea, get a fire going!"

Obi fell at Edward's feet. "Jasper is dead, and it's all my fault, Edward," he wept. "They burned him alive!"

"Jasper was shot, Obi! None of this is your fault!" said Edward, taking him softly by the arms and then embracing him. "Please, pull yourself together now. If anyone here takes the blame, it's me!"

"But, Edward. I met with them and divulged our plan, there's no denying my part in it! Jasper took it upon himself to confront the pirate and exchange the crown for your freedom. It should have been me! *Me!* And now he's gone."

"Them? The Soldiers?" asked Edward.

"Yes, and Captain Galaway."

"Galaway?"

"They've come for you, Edward, come here to help you. All the way from the capital, with the Soldiers beside them."

There was a murmur, a slight voice, a calling whisper, coming from the trees. Edward spun quickly when the sound caught his ears. The whisper got louder and this time they all heard it. Now on high alert, the men scanned along the line of bushes where a man stood gesturing with his hand for them to follow him. He pressed his finger tight to his lips, again and again, whispering, "Keep quiet and follow me."

The men were suddenly very wary of just how exposed they were. Peter was delirious from the cold and observed the stranger through a film of blur that embraced his irises. Then the man spoke again. "I mean no harm," he grunted, in a deep reverberating tone. "Food and fire … this way."

The men were desperate for the very luxuries this stranger was offering. Obi and Peter gave Edward a confused look of, *what on earth do we do?* To which Edward returned a look of, *I don't have any better ideas.*

Just away from the harbour on its north side, they came to a house, with a gentle plume of smoke rising from the chimney. Peter's eyes lit up like stars. "Fire!" he gasped, as his shoulders sunk low in relief. The man flung open the front door and ushered the men inside, clicking over the bolt after a quick look about the trees, hoping they hadn't been followed.

A great stone hearth stood at the room's centre. The walls were stone too, with paintings of old ships hung about the whole place, covering almost every inch. In the corner, there was an easel holding a large sheet of parchment. Next to it was a stand full of many brushes and a palette smothered in more colours than one could imagine. Edward stood and admired. Peter was now curled by the fire. Obi was thinking deeply; thoughts that had him trembling to the very tips of his toes. The dark circles around his eyes throbbed after each blink and his parched mouth was crying out for something hot to sip at. He looked to Peter, whom by now had absorbed enough of the fire's heat to control his shivering.

Edward hadn't sat down, for something very interesting had caught his eye. He could feel the deep, dark history in these paintings, and at a closer look, the burning wreckage of many ships in bold oranges and reds were clear to see, cast across the strait before the dreaded grey backdrop of Fort Gaze. He was so familiar with this scene he half expected to see himself present within the brush strokes.

Edward looked down; the water was dripping from his jacket to the ground below. He let the garment fall from his arms, hanging it by the fire. Their host came back from the kitchen holding three bowls of pottage he'd balanced in his hands. Peter wasted little time, called a quick, inaudible grunt of a thanks, and began to gulp it all up. Obi's manners were as admirable as always, receiving the bowl with a sincere, "Greatly appreciated, sir."

Whilst reaching out for a bowl, Edward finally got a decent look of the man who had passed him it. The man had shed his dark cloak in exchange for a cook's apron he'd tied roughly around the back.

"Thank you, sir," he said staring. "But why are you helping us?"

"You don't exactly strike me as dangerous folk," said the man, with a hint of force to his answer. "If I thought you were any harm at all you wouldn't be here. I saw the two of you fall from that filthy ship out there and I know the difference between pirates and common lads."

"May I ask your name?"

"Bannermane," said the man, hesitantly if anything.

Edward squinted and carefully slotted the name Bannermane into the neat folds of his memory. The result was that of surprise, for he knew that name – the pieces were beginning to fit. Once again, the man left for the kitchen. The unmistakable smell of goose roasting on the bottle jack by the fire had Peter's undivided attention.

Obi had worked his way down the bowl and the final drops brought a warm glow to his cheeks. Bannermane came back in with a sack full of logs and piled one after another neatly on the burning stack. He freed a knife from his apron and sliced off a huge piece of goose and dropped it into Peter's empty bowl. The golden meat disappeared the moment it touched the pot.

Bannermane began to pace around the living room, rearranging trinkets and chairs, but muttered nothing, almost like he was in the middle of something important. He seemed kind and caring, not at all like what first appearances suggested. His hoarse, grunting voice and abruptly constructed answers could easily be perceived as rude, or perhaps audacious. Yet, after contemplating the man for a short while, Edward thought to himself, *this man likes the company.*

Looking back at the paintings, Edward came to a conclusion. "I know your face, Mr Bannermane," he said, laying down his half empty bowl on a nearby table. "You were once an officer, weren't you?"

A slight pause, followed by, "Yes, I was. How did you–"

"That painting ... you were there that day?"

"How did you figure?"

"I was there too," said Edward. "Such a true representation could have only been depicted by a man that had seen it with his own eyes, wouldn't you say?"

Bannermane stepped up to his own work. "It's even more vivid in my dreams, ya know," he whispered gravely. "You must have sailed aboard the

Baliant? I don't know anyone who survived other than those under Wallace Galaway."

"The *Baliant*, yes. And under which captain did *you* sail?"

"Captain Dillinger of the *Fortuna*."

"*Fortuna*? Then you must have known my brother, Arthur?"

"Arthur Clavell?"

Edward nodded excitedly. "Yes, that's him."

The man took a seat by the fire. "I knew him well. I still think about him some days; he was actually a great friend of mine. And now he's gone, and I still hear the cannon fire whether I'm awake or sleeping." The man paused for a little while, for it had been a long time since he'd spoken of such events. He gripped the arms of the chair tightly and continued. "You might not have known this, but that was to be Arthur's last voyage. He'd seen enough war and battle - well, his last it truly became to be. I'm not saying we underestimated the danger that day, but we had no idea that Fort Gaze was so heavily fortified, did we? We were torn apart - smashed to bloody pieces!"

"We were betrayed that day, Officer Bannermane," said Edward. "Attacking the Fort in the dark of night didn't afford us the expected advantage. I've always wondered why. There's corruption amongst the King's men, I can just feel it in the depths of my heart. That fortress was watched for weeks and it was clear the pirates' complacency rose as the sunlight fell. Had they not known we were coming, we may have succeeded."

"I often wonder what it's like down in the deep," said Bannermane, staring at his feet. "A sunken graveyard, absent of any coffin or headstone under which the dead may rest. This is where I washed up, here on Fithering's Bay, with a splinter stuck through my gut the size of a damn longsword. Sometimes I wish I'd have fallen with them."

The men leaned in to listen more closely. Edward took a seat. Bannermane's grip tightened around the chair's arm. These stories struck nerves.

"Why didn't you come back to the capital?" asked Edward.

"I had my wounds tended to in this very room by a man whom thereafter I owed a great debt. So, I stayed to help him. He was old and fragile so I did what I could; like chopping his firewood and fishing for our suppers. When he died, nobody came by to claim his home, and the people nearby

229

were happy to have me, so long as I did my part for our small community. Ever since that day, I've painted all of my thoughts and memories on that easel over there."

"And when the old man passed away," said Edward, "was it your place in the community that kept you here, or was it the thought of missing the action should the fortress someday fall? I can see vengeance in a man's eyes. Trust me. I've seen it; every time I've looked in the mirror for the past fifteen years. You still believe it's possible, don't you?"

"Call it what you will, Officer Clavell - vengeance, retribution - I lie awake at night thirsting for it. I've stayed here all these years for the front row seat! How did you know?"

Edward smiled. "Because I hurt in the very same way, sir. The man who was burned on the harbour died trying to help us. He was a soldier. A callous man named Bill the Baneful will answer for that and then Fort Gaze shall fall. Those bastards will pay for what they did, and I'll promise you that front row seat. Could you get us to Ridikus? I take it you have a boat?"

"I do indeed, but that's a perilous journey to say the least. I can get you there, but only in the dark and it's almost dawn. Might I ask what business you have on Ridikus island, of all places?"

"There's a man there we must meet," said Edward.

"And when all is in order, how do you intend to topple that impenetrable spit of rock?" said Bannermane.

"I have no idea," said Edward shaking his head. "It is beyond belief how we've made it here alive, so planning too far into the future might well prove to be folly. I cannot tell you the reason we are here, there is too much at stake, but we are clinging to a small hope that may yield the might for everlasting peace in our lands."

"Hope," smiled Bannermane, twiddling the strings on his apron. "The heart's warm anticipation for the things you long for. I cannot say the hope in my heart is anything but ice cold anymore."

"Is that not just revenge taking hope's place?" asked Edward.

Bannermane nodded in sure agreement. "Perhaps it is," he whispered, taking another look at his wall of paintings. "Very well then, gentlemen. I'll take you to Ridikus. By the looks of it, you've risked a lot to get here and I admire what you're trying to achieve. But hear me now, this is no easy task, and I'm afraid whatever troubles you have endured up until now, well, let's just say this ... I can't see it getting any easier! I suspect there's more to this than meets the eye. There better be an ace up your sleeve … otherwise you're just three lunatics."

Peter was the first to chuckle at that. Bannermane meant what he said but he didn't intend for his remark to offend. The broad smile that began to shine across Edward's face clarified the contrary.

The laughing subsided. "Promise me something?" said Bannermane as he took Edward by the arm.

"What is it?"

"I really don't know how any of this is possible. After all, you are but three mortal men. But if by some miracle you succeed here, just promise me, that all our fallen brothers will be honoured in the right way. Our acquaintance will prove to be truly valuable to me; to have met a fellow officer who shares the pain of that fateful day. I often feel like those memories are all mine to bear and it's bloody nice to be reminded I'm not alone. Let me get you gentlemen some things together before we head out."

Chapter 28
The Lost and the Found

James Percy's natural instinct was to find his friend Inky - but there was no sign of him. He searched the deck, checking each row of fallen bodies, one after another turning over the limp masses of bloody flesh.

"Please don't let it be Inky," he kept on repeating, as each lifeless face was revealed to him.

Officer Addley appeared amongst the dead, his right arm was severed and his body splintered head to toe. All this destruction was too much to bear and James' bottom lip began to oscillate as pools of tears formed in his eyes.

"INKY!"

The night was calm, with odd gusts of wind scudding across the sails, helping the *Baliant* along in her southerly direction. James looked around from one knee at all the ruin. When he'd wiped the tears from his eyes, he stood to his feet and walked the deck again, finding Inky, half-covered in a shroud of rope and torn sail - motionless.

He crept over with his arms slumped to his side over the now ripped grey coat he had only recently earned. James removed the debris of ropes and white fabric and run his finger along Inky's neck in the hope of finding a pulse. But there was nothing. Suddenly, he felt the bitter cold gnaw at his skin. All else around him seemed numb, the sound of clambering feet, waves and distressing shouts, all became nothing but a loud meaningless throbbing in his head. In all his young life, he had never felt such despair as he wept at his best friend's side, cradling the back of his head with both hands, just holding him there, carefully.

James closed Inky's eyes, calling away the crewmen as they came by to help lift him. Through his pain, he fought to a stance, with Inky in his arms. Again, he screamed at the men who tried to assist for he didn't need any help; his grief had somehow made him stronger. The crew watched in awe as James carried Ray Inkleman across the entire deck, dropping to his knees at the top of the forecastle steps. Two crewmen rushed to console him, and with great care they took hold of the body, laying him down beside the others. "Don't you hurt him," said James, in a crying whisper.

Officer Hackett had taken a wound to the chest and in the coming hours it would take him. Many more great men passed on that day, taken by the evil doings of other humans; creatures controlled by greed, destined to someday eradicate one another for the sake of wealth, power, control and all the other desirable gains that manifest one's vices.

It was now time to go home. Captain Galaway had set out on a quest to save one of his men, consequently losing many more. With hope all but lost for Edward Clavell, home was truly the only place to be. The men that were lost were to be laid peacefully to rest beneath the trees in the fields of Summer's Reach.

James Percy laid all alone in his hammock. His eyes were stinging from the weeping and his chest tightened with every shallow breath. He was dead still, glaring at the wall between himself and the open sea. Some seek justice for their loss of loved ones and some seek vengeance. James just wanted to go home; to forget about everything, to see Adeline, Johnathon and his mother. He wished he could turn back the clock, but his uncle was quite right in his wisdom that time, being such a continuous and irreversible sequence of existence, truly, wouldn't wait.

He wanted to be the one to tell Inky's mother, feeling that was the only way she should hear it. But above all, he just wanted to walk on to the *Baliant's* deck and see his friend, and kick over his mop bucket for one last time.

The gift Adeline had given him was laid out in his palm. He just stared at it for a while, too sad to untie the red ribbon. He wiped his tears and pinched his fingers around the silk and pulled. The parchment came open.

There were words, swirling, flawless upon the white piece. He remembered the poem she had written about the tiny whistler, and he even managed a smile when he learned that there was more ...

It was summer, sun dancing and prancing that day,
and I was sitting in my old wood chair.
For the chirp of the crickets, from deep in the thickets,
I gave little of a thought or a care.

Then out jumped a stoat, with a scream then a shout,
he had tears in his squinty brown eyes.
He yelled and bawled, come quickly he called,
I must take you to where she now cries.
Where whom I asked, but the stoat was off fast,
so I ran until my heart beat quick.
We came to the trees, in the withering breeze,
where underfoot, gathered leaf and stick.
The stoat, he said, I fear the whistler is dead,
and he leapt through a hole in a tree.
Then out he sprung, and in his arms, he clung,
to the whistler, then passed her to me.
I held her so soft, for her wing was torn,
she had fallen down spinning from the sky.
I rushed her straight back, and in my old chair I sat,
hoping someday she'd be able to fly.
The stoat never left, and wept by the window,
until one day he came inside,
he sat with the whistler, and gently kissed her,
then suddenly she opened an eye.
Up she flew, as if a great wind blew through,
and she landed on the top of my head.
She flew off singing, her tweets long and ringing,
thank you, my lady, she said.
Her wing was now healed, her feathers revealed,
shining bright in the sun's gold ray.
She swung down and whispered, that sweet tiny whistler ...
I just knew I'd see you again, someday.

James rolled up the parchment and tucked it inside his pocket. His hammock rocked as the waves picked up speed in their pursuit for the shoreline, swinging him to and fro in gentle motions that brought him some comfort. His uncle was standing by the door, watching with downcast eyes as James twirled the ribbon between his fingers. The captain knew him well enough to know that right now, he was quite content with his own company. So, he left, parting with an almost silent, "I'm sorry, my boy. I truly am."

James spent that night far from at peace with his own feelings; they were mocking him, and poking him into a wide-eyed trance he couldn't escape from. He hated how he felt, but he was failing to muster even a flicker of vengeance. His grief was … just grief.

*

Back in the strait at Fort Gaze, William Fane was pacing about the *Dürlarain*. His men around him worked tirelessly into the morning to fix the damage and gather the dead. The ship was beaten. The deceased high in number. Fane was beyond enraged and not a soul dared approach him; his cheeks were as red as summer apples and vessels of blood had tainted the white in his eyes.

"Bring me the prisoners!" he growled, barely able to control himself.

A crewman returned; he was frightened and came forward shaking like a leaf in the wind. "The brig is empty, Captain Bill," came a pathetic mumbling.

Fane leapt forward and caught the pirate tight by the throat, gripping with enormous strength until the veins in the man's neck bulged in a deep blue. He pushed him away and unsheathed his rapier.

"You have a son aboard, don't you?" he snapped to the man.

"Yes, Captain."

"Someone bring him to me," said Fane. "If the wretch still breathes."

"Captain? What are you doing?" asked the pirate, helplessly.

There was a perturbed flurry of incoherent deliberation amongst the crew, until the man's son was finally brought forward and thrown to the deck floor. The whole ship then fell silent.

"Stand up, boy," growled Fane.

The boy obeyed his captain. Fane thrust his rapier, straight like an arrow, and almost half the blade buried into the young pirate's chest. The entire crew were shaken with fear. Fane towered up, staring into the boy's eyes as he choked on his last breath. The boy's father fell to his knees and began to wail, until his cries were muted, all thanks to a well-placed bullet from Fane's pistol.

The pirate captain truly lived up to his sobriquets. A veracious example of a baneful murderer, he was.

Sliding his rapier from the corpse, "Toss them both in the pile!" he screamed, spitting and cursing.

He sharply turned and raced around the ship, eyeing every man vehemently – his voice cracking at the height of his cries.

"Should I have news of such incompetency brought to me again, Silas, I will have you watch as I murder your entire bloodline."

These words were screamed but an inch from his chief-mate's nose. "Do not fail me again," he finished in a quiet, blood-curdling snarl.

He whipped his rapier downward to rid the steel of dripping crimson, then took off for his cabin.

Sitting alone at his table he began to write in black ink from the strokes of a goose quill. Repeating the same words ... *Clavell, Clavell.*

There came a light knock at the door. A brave man, surely. His chief-mate had gathered enough courage to approach, yet he half expected to be slain upon his entrance – but duty called. Fane didn't respond with words, only with the ink jar that he hurled at the wall, splashing the black liquid across the window.

The chief-mate peered through the frosted, ink-splattered glass and tried the handle. Fane had turned away to wipe his blade with an already blood-stained rag.

"Have the fleet ready to sail for Summer's Reach," he ordered, as Silas finally stepped through.

"Captain?"

"You have forever been my most loyal, Silas, let's not tarnish that now. Ready the fleet! I will *not* be made a fool of by these slitherworms. Now go!"

The chief-mate nodded and walked outside. He was no more than two paces down the hall before he heard Fane's voice again.

"Dark is the world, Silas ... dark is the world."

*

The morning sun had begun to threaten, yet a dark, dense blanket still covered Fithering's Bay. Bannermane worked away by the harbour deck, readying his wherry. Back inside, Edward stood deliberating over his wet jacket, concluding with the assumption he'd catch his death should he venture out in it. Peter was peeling off morsels of goose breast. Obi had found himself admiring the man's paintings and was running his fingers over the textures of each divinely placed colour.

"Do you remember much of it, Edward? Or like most grief, have you tried hard to forget it?"

Edward walked up beside Obi.

"I remember some parts of it very distinctly, yet others barely," he said. "But I cannot say I've ever tried to forget it."

"Everyone's different, I suppose," said Obi. "Never been too good at dealing with grief myself."

Edward blew out his cheeks and shook his head; a gesture that clearly meant *me neither*. "I never said I was good at it. Perhaps I'm afraid to forget it."

"Afraid?" said Obi, with a look of surprise.

"Yes. I'm afraid if I consciously try to erase all the bad things, maybe I'll lose some of the good, too."

Bannermane stepped in through the door, bringing a cold flush of wind with him.

"It's time to go," he said, as bluntly as they'd now come to expect. "But before we do, I've something I feel I should part with."

On that note, Bannermane scurried off into another room, returning with a sword sheathed in a makeshift leather scabbard and two pistols both strapped to a white bandolier. "What good is an officer without his effects?"

Edward smiled then thanked the man. He'd lost his own weapons when the pirates had stripped him of them. "You've been more than kind to us, Officer Bannermane," he said, taking the gift.

The man shook his head, as if Edward's gratitude was misplaced or rather, unnecessary.

"Folks on Ridikus will kill a man for his boot laces - keep the starling hidden!" he exclaimed. "Now, take this, it'll tame the nerves."

Bannermane passed Peter a green bottle full of liquor. "Now ... don't you drink that all at once, it'll have you half seas over in a blink."

Peter popped the cork and took a long sniff. The potent fumes burned as he inhaled them.

"Let's be getting going, it's almost dawn," said Bannermane, handing Peter and Obi a pistol each.

Edward looked up at the stars from his seat inside the wherry. Peter almost fell in the water, still chewing on more goose that had now left juices around his lips. Obi sat carefully, watching as Bannermane readied the sails.

"Before you say anything," said Obi, scowling at Edward and Peter, pulling on his hat's strings to fix it over his head. "I'm coming with you, and I'll hear no more of it."

Edward inhaled ready to speak. Obi clapped his hands to halt him. "I'll hear no more of it!" he snapped.

"The wind is in a hurry," said Bannermane, leaning over to untie the mooring ropes. "And blowing in our favour!"

Edward kept his mouth shut. Peter smiled happily. The journey was cold, the water was choppy at best; but as they drifted over the waves, the dark outline of Ridikus island grew until it consumed their periphery. Bannermane guided the wherry to the south bank of the island, coming to a stop upon the wet sands of a secluded cove.

"This is it," he said, with a disgusted grimace. "Best of luck, gentlemen."

The men parted ways with a few thanks and three handshakes. Bannermane floated off after Peter gave him the push. "Goodbye!"

They set off north, with a little guess work to find the way, for the island was thick with trees, swamp pools, sinking muddy filth and swarms of flies. They knew well enough that the main town stood around the western harbour, that much one could see from the mainland, in the form of a glow of orange beneath a silhouette of arching half-dead trees.

After a while, the noises of early morning excitement came scurrying through the leafless branches.

"We're close," whispered Edward.

An old, ruined tower stood erect before them, reaching to the height of at least ten men. Its abandonment had allowed Mother Nature to consume it, the grass and vines had conquered its walls like creeping veins. The structure looked to have grown there like an ancient, stone-barked tree, absent of any leaf or needle, hollowed by rot and years of decay. They climbed inside, up a spiral of steep steps and out on to a terrace of uneven moss-covered stones. On its western wall, many other stones had fallen down to the ground, making a window of sorts, providing a great vantage. The men peered out over the wintered terrain, and in the far distance, a harbour could be seen. There seemed to be life there, and as the wind settled around them, more sounds could be heard. There were voices.

"I've entirely lost my appetite for treasure hunting," said Peter, as the severity of the task at hand took a firm grip of his throat.

"It truly is a foul place," said Edward. He could feel the sweat building on his palms. "One might find it hard to believe how anything could ever grow here."

"But we've made it!" said Obi, lightening the mood as he had come to make a habit of. "And all in one piece, save for a few bruises here and there."

Edward smiled; his shoulders jumped to the motion of short laughs. "You're a remarkable man, Obi. We've made it here because of you," he said warmly.

Peter wrapped his arm over Obi's shoulders; he needn't have said anything more. The three of them just fell silent for a few moments.

"My name is Oliver Dillinger," said Obi at last.

Edward's eyes tightened in thought until something struck him. "You flinched when Bannermane mentioned his captain's name," he said. "I wondered why at the time, but I soon thought nothing of it. Who was he to you?"

"My brother," said Obi.

Peter's face curled up in surprise.

"Your brother died at Fort Gaze?"

Obi nodded regrettably, and quickly wiped away a tear that tried to fall down his cheek. Both Edward and Peter were caught way off guard by this previously unknown and rather pivotal reasoning as to why Obi had stuck around for so long. All this time they had thought he was simply helping them out of his own kindness, and his, albeit only little, penchant for adventure. As a matter of fact, Obi's kindness had led him much of the way, but what he'd heard that night in the soldiers' camp, had roused a multitude of feelings - none of which he felt he had any previous power to enact upon.

"I might have a small confession," he said, twisting his mouth as if he knew this wouldn't go down too well. "On the night we met Jasper, after supper had passed, I'd slipped off into the trees for a - ya know. Well, as I walked back into camp, minding my business, I might have overheard you, Edward. Speaking about said battle, your brother and murdering pirates. From then on, I knew we had far more in common than it first seemed."

"Far more, indeed," said Edward, with a smile that was both happy and sad. "This explains a lot, I'll say. I was starting to think you liked the trouble."

Peter didn't know what to say, he just quickly decided to open the bottle that Bannermane had given them. He popped the cork; Obi got the first taste.

"I rarely speak of it," he said, taking a sip. "It pains me too much, to tell you the truth. It shouldn't be like this, and it certainly wasn't when I was a young lad. Before Fort Gaze was defeated, the lands in the east were relatively safe, save for the odd bandit trying his luck. All those brave men that died trying to defend that fortress, and all those who died trying to reclaim it. Perilously. It angers me to my bones! I'm certainly no soldier, but the ability to wield a sword does not define what makes a fighter. I'm here till the end, men."

"There are many cowards who hide behind swords and call themselves brave, Obi," said Edward. "You are the bravest man I've ever met. Indeed, you are no soldier, and yes, soldiers win wars ... but they also lose them. Anyway, tell me of a soldier you know that has felled a beast like the Jackal, to then face him again in the gravest of peril. What about being captured by the Kingsguard and beaten blue for your troubles. Or striking the most unlikely of friendships with a disgraced officer and a pirate. Then sailing to Ridikus to find the one power capable of avenging all the evil this world has had to endure." Edward paused for a few seconds to reflect upon his words. "All for the ones we love the most. You, Obi, are worth much more than any title they could bestow upon you, my friend."

Peter took a gulp from the bottle and it made his eyes leak. "Well, he didn't exactly face the Jackal twice!" he said in jest.

"No ... but the people back home don't need to know that!" said Obi laughing.

They all shared a chortle. Peter extended the bottle of spirit towards Edward who quickly shooed it away. He had seen Peter's grimace and decided against a taste.

"Where do you think this Leander chap is then?" asked Obi.

"I have no idea," said Edward. "But we're about to find out."

They set about the steps and came out on the muddy forest floor. Peter's right boot had begun to loosen at the stitches, each stride drawing in the cold air, chilling his toes. Obi set his own aching feet in motion, hastily past the dank bushes; Edward had started to develop an awful dread in his stomach.

They reached the edge of the town; a mass of hovels that seemed to bear no notable name. Perhaps there weren't any words befitting of such a wretched place, for every block of stone and plank of decomposing wood was as harsh on the eyes as it was on the nose. Nothing but rotten souls trudged the paths here and even the sea itself looked to halt before it reached land in a bid to remain untainted from whatever disease exuded the earth underfoot.

Men were being dragged and beaten. Droves of pigs were hauled up in pens, screeching in all manner of screeches. Pirates lay in the mud, blind drunk and filthy, and the harbour was crowded with ships. The men quietly crept through the town, between the thatched roofed shacks, avoiding the trickling waste that flowed the streets. Obi couldn't quite believe what he was seeing, struggling to keep down the pottage in his belly.

Peter had turned up his jacket collar for fear of being recognised. Obi started wondering whether he'd forfeit his sense of smell if someone offered it to him at that very moment. *Perhaps that would be a small price to pay, to rid one's nose of such a sickly scent,* he thought.

The men continued on, passing countless numbers of seemingly docile folk that emanated strange smells and even stranger expressions. One of them had eyed Obi quite intently – unnerving him justly – but turned away to spit out a viscous ball of tobacco he'd been chewing on, then went calmly about his own business. Further on, a few of the buildings had large hounds chained to the porches; vicious-looking guard dogs that all seemed to spring up at once and growl at the men as they passed by. Peter almost jumped out of his own skin. Edward remained calm, on guard, pointedly flicking his eyes from side to side to keep close scrutinising focus on everything in sight. Obi made for the centre of the road in an attempt to keep as far away from the barking beasts as he possibly could.

After passing the dogs, something caught Edward's attention. Hanging over a wet and muddy yard, there was a sign ... *Leander's Smithy and Cobblers.*

He tapped Peter on the arm, pointing. Obi watched on as a pirate came falling from a low window, or perhaps he was thrown, by the equally unpleasant man he saw rubbing the dust from his hands and spitting down at the whelp laid flat on his rear. At closer observation, Obi noticed the window the man came tumbling from belonged to a lodging house of some description – one can only imagine it was of terrible repute.

Peter grabbed Obi's attention with a sharp nudge to the arm, gesturing his hand to the sign swinging above them.

There was a gate of iron, constructed with spears of black metal, shaped into stars and flowers, that stood at the end of the yard. Edward lifted the latch and stepped in. The men followed. Peter brought up the rear and when the men in front stepped through the open door of the smithy, he quickly glanced behind to see if anyone was creeping, then went inside.

Chapter 29
Leander

The smithy was empty, at first glance, yet the burning embers in the forge were still blazing. Edward stood by the anvil and picked up a cold black hammer and pondered over it. Peter was examining the wall clad in battle steel and lifted off an axe that balanced perfectly in his hand. The cutting edge was razor sharp and the handle was exquisitely formed and oiled. Hundreds of blades of all kinds were hung there; each one an example of a truly skilled blacksmith.

They all walked closer to the forge to feel the warmth of it, when suddenly, an ear-splitting blow of a hammer shocked their wits.

A giant of a man stood behind them, his face blackened in the shadows; their hearts were now pumping vigorously. The man crept forward, his right hand gripped tight to an unkind-looking steel beater. He stared at them threateningly from his speckled brown eyes, sunken into a skull that looked to be perched at least seven feet from the ground. The man was colossal, like a bear on its hind legs, towering over hapless prey. He tucked the hammer into his black leathers and puffed out his chest.

"Who are you?" he growled like a bear too.

"Are you ... Leander?" asked Edward, apprehensively to say the least.

"You didn't answer my question," the man snapped. "Around here, I ask the questions, and you better hope I like your answers."

"I'm Edward Clavell and these are my friends, Peter and Obi. If it's no trouble, we are here to see Leander." Edward shook a little as he spoke, his right hand poised over his pistol.

The man's eyes moved quickly within his head, like that of a lizard. Obi stood waiting for the forked tongue to appear, but it never did.

"Brunt!" called a voice, as an old, grey man slunk out of nowhere, hobbling with a tilting limp. The bear-man turned, having heard his name, then grinned icily at the men.

"Clear off, and leave these men be! Get back to work, you halfwit oaf," said the old man, shaking his walking cane.

Brunt walked off and began to sharpen a long cutlass with a fine stone, unable to remove the conniving grin from his giant face, seeming proud he'd given the men such a fright.

"I'm Leander," said the old man, with a croak. "What business does an officer, a pirate and a gatekeeper have in my smithy? You're in entirely the wrong place to be wandering."

The men were flabbergasted at these words, for no such detailed introduction had yet been given. Edward tried to speak but his mind was full up, trying to recall all the words he'd said since arriving.

Leander was old, you could tell this from his manner alone, without seeing his grey, flowing hair and his heavily wrinkled face. He wore a neat, grey cloak with blue embroidery around the collar and cuff, beneath a black, smith's apron like Brunt's, only *much* smaller.

"Leander," said Edward. "Forgive us for sneaking in uninvited, but I'm afraid it's not one of your fine weapons we'll be needing today. So, I'll be straight to the point."

Brunt pulled a molten blade from the forge and began to shape it noisily in the background. Leander was stood holding the head of his cane in both hands. "Go on?" he muttered.

Keeping to his word, Edward cut to the point. "We believe you can help us find the Black Diamond?" he said.

The hammer blows of Brunt fell silent and Leander's mouth curled as if he was thinking deeply. "The Bla-" Leander froze. "What is it you'll be wanting with such a gem?" he eventually spoke rather sternly.

Peter and Obi found themselves wishing they were anywhere else in the world, for they didn't have any idea what to say or do. It suddenly struck them that, amidst all their troubles, they'd forgotten to develop even the weakest of plans for the precise situation they were now in. Of course Edward had realised this a while back, and simply concluded there wasn't one.

Edward began to think on his feet and entirely avoided Leander's question. He thought it best the pirate didn't know any of the specific details. "So, you're a collector, I hear?"

"I am indeed," said Leander, well aware Edward had swerved the question, yet delighted the talk had turned to such a topic. His eyes themselves could be mistaken for jewels from the manner in which they had lit up at the thought. "How'd you come by this information?" said the old blacksmith. "I don't recall ever seeing you around these parts."

"A friend of ours," answered Edward.

Leander smiled widely. He seemed to have the three of them pinned down already. "Would you like to see my collection?" he asked, as his countenance suddenly brightened into an even bigger smile. Peter and Obi shared a sceptical look. Edward politely urged Leander to lead the way.

The blood-curdling racket of Brunt's hammer returned, only to be quelled by the door Leander shut behind them in the next room. This room was lit with lanterns that burned in tendrils of green and smelled pungent like exotic oil. The men sat round a circular table and the old blacksmith pulled a fourth chair up beside them.

"Strange, isn't it?" he said. "It's the eyes that scare me! Pearl-like, deathly, rather unnerving to behold; misery for all who've ever touched that diamond. But I'd sure like to have it in my collection." Leander ran his hand over the top of his cane curiously. "You've seen those eyes, haven't you? Yes, the Jackal!"

The men were in disbelief. "How could you have known that?" asked Peter.

"I'll make us all some tea," said Leander, jumping up. His limp looked to have disappeared, and he wasn't as reliant on his cane as it first seemed. The door clicked shut behind him, leaving Edward, Peter and Obi with already much to talk about.

"How did he know about the Jackal?" whispered Peter.

"I have no idea," said Edward, rubbing his chin, now bewhiskered from days of neglect.

"I have an oddly unnatural feeling about the man," said Obi.

"Me too," said Peter. "Edward, what exactly are we doing here? It has dawned on me rather abruptly that we have absolutely no plan."

"The man's a pirate, Obi, what exactly did you expect?" said Edward. "As for a plan, Peter, well ... I don't have one."

Edward had realised how ridiculous this was. Why *didn't* they have a plan?

"Listen, the lady gave us his name and that's it. Should we have taken a little more care when barging over here? Yes! Is this man likely to be the one pirate who has even a shred of common decency? I doubt it. But we are here now, and I don't see any other way."

"What about an escape plan if things go to shit?" said Peter.

"Improvise," said Edward, curling his lips.

"That's just great," said Peter.

The door came swinging open with a gnawing creak. Leander burst through holding a steaming jug of tea that smelled of apples. He poured it into four pots and took a seat. To Edward and Obi's surprise, the tea was sweet and delicious and it gently soothed as it trickled into their bellies. Peter rudely refused and turned his nose up at it. "Not for me, thank you," he said, as Edward glared at him disapprovingly.

Obi was looking Leander up and down when he noticed a purple gemstone encrusted upon the head of his cane, hidden under his pale, outstretched fingers. He was undoubtedly impressed by its beauty.

"Your collection?" asked Edward, taking a sip of the apple tea.

Leander leapt up from his chair, as if a rush of youth had possessed him. He brought with him to the table a wooden box, lifting the lid to reveal a collection of precious stones and a looking glass. There were emeralds, rubies, diamonds and sapphires, all deliberately placed within a golden silk lining.

"I've been collecting for many years," said Leander. "Some of these gems I've ripped from the hands of men I've slain myself. There are, of course, many such gems. But the Black Diamond is different. And should remain far out of reach of any man who values his sanity."

"And what's so special about the one on your cane?" asked Obi curiously.

Leander jerked his hand over the purple gem. "It's just a worthless old stone," he snapped in defence. "There are gems that hold power, and there are gems that do not, rather like *my* collection. I consider myself an expert when it comes to these things. The jewel in which you seek, should remain hidden. No good can come of it, believe me. None! It takes a true expert to become involved with such a thing without experiencing terrible consequences. Yet, you asked me a question, and I think it would be rude of me not to answer it, so-"

"Do you know where we can find the diamond, or not, old man?" said Peter impatiently.

Leander was terribly offended by this interruption. Edward could clearly tell, even if it didn't spill from the old man's countenance.

"Mr Leander. I apologise for my friend's discourteous outburst; it has been a testing journey thus far. Forgive us for our lack of patience. We don't mean to outstay our welcome here, and we only ask for your help, so we can leave you in peace."

"Forgive me," said Peter, reluctantly. "I might have lost my manners along the way."

"Manners?" said Leander, waving dismissively. "I'd forgotten the meaning. There are no such niceties here on Ridikus. Apology accepted, Peter."

Leander once again curled his fingers around the purple gemstone. "I'll tell you where to find the Black Diamond," he said. "But let me be very clear. You will *not* return from the depths in which it is hidden. There are creatures that lurk beneath the cold rocks in every cave, and you can be certain they won't let you take it. If by some miracle you survive, don't let it touch your naked skin!"

Leander slammed shut his box of gems, taking them away. The men just sat and waited in the recently developed silence, having expected more to the tale.

"Caves, you say?" asked Obi.

"Yes, Oliver … caves!"

Leander scrambled round the table, pushed open a shutter and then pointed.

"There!" he exclaimed with assurance.

Through the smithy and over the yard, then past the thatched houses and out beyond the harbour, was a black cavernous hole, eating into the sheer rock of Graelind's coast.

"That is where you'll find it!"

"Brilliant," said Peter. "How do we get there then?"

Leander did not appreciate the sarcasm, he just shook his head at Peter and scurried off into the next room, slamming the door.

"I never told him my name was Oliver," said Obi, in a quiet voice. "Something isn't right with the man. He keeps rubbing that gem on his cane all creepily."

Leander suddenly reappeared and went running towards a door at the back of the room. He unlatched a series of iron bolts and slipped a long, bronze key into the keyhole. The rusty door screamed on its hinges as he dragged it open with his cane. Then, after taking a lantern off a nearby hook, he thrust it into the darkness beyond.

"A tunnel?" said Edward, walking towards a gap in the stone floor.

"This will take you right to it," whispered Leander, in the lantern's flicker.

"Might I ask the glaringly obvious question?" said Peter. "Why in the name of Graelind do you have a tunnel under your smithy?"

"You're an intemperate little waif, aren't you, Peter," scowled Leander. "If you must know, I suppose I'll start with this. I'm a collector of jewels, although I use the term 'collector' rather loosely. One might say that I'd obtained all my stones through less than reputable means - I am a pirate after all. But I have an eye for the finest quality, and along the way I have discovered some of the most precious and, more importantly, valuable stones there are to be found in this world. But on Ridikus, well, this hole is full of thieves and snakes. That is why my collection is kept entirely secret. So, in return for my help, I only ask that you would honour that same secret.

"Many years ago, some priceless information fell at my feet. I heard the Black Diamond lie dormant within a chamber, deep down in the Eastern caves. As luck would have it, my smithy is built on top of an abandoned mining tunnel that connects the island to the mainland. It took Brunt years to clear the tunnel, and what better way to mask the sounds of his efforts than with the good old-fashioned clanging of steel beating? All the detritus he removed from down there was either burnt in our forge or ... forged, into weapons.

"Yet, there was a slight bump in the road, one might care to say. When Brunt had made it all the way through, we searched those caves, high and low. Let's just say, there's a reason why the tunnel was abandoned."

The men all looked unequivocally intrigued.

"There's something living down there," said Leander. "Something unkind. But, surely enough, we saw it. The Black Diamond."

"So, it does exist?" smiled Edward, as floods of relief and excitement gushed around his body.

"I can confirm, that indeed it does."

"What do you mean there's something down there?" asked Obi.

"I cannot be certain," said Leander. "But I haven't been down there since, and that's eight years passed. Whatever lingers there, protects the jewel ... I heard them whispering things."

"The second glaringly obvious question," said Peter. "You want this diamond for your collection, there was an empty space in that box? You desire it. And I think you know of its power. So, why tell us all this? Why give away the biggest secret of them all?"

"Because if you fools go down that hole you're never coming back!" snapped Leander; a sinister slip of the man's character. "Anyway, it's not as if you have any idea how to wield it should you make it to the diamond alive, ha, ha."

Edward curled his brows, now very suspicious. "There's quite a lot about us you seem strangely familiar with, Leander? You cannot possibly know if or not we have knowledge of how to wield the Black Diamond's power, if in fact it is powerful."

Leander had realised he'd now said too much and dithered.

"Of course not, what I meant was ..." he said, clawing out of the hole he'd dug for himself. "I'm quite the expert you see, and to *my* knowledge there's no way to tame that diamond. That's all I meant, ha, ha."

Leander slammed shut the door and locked it. He turned to the corner and began to mutter inaudible words to himself, seemingly arguing with thin air. Then, he turned and took a seat. The room was silent, save for Brunt's hammer still cracking steel.

"I think it's time we head off, Leander," said Edward, now acutely aware the man was unstable and altogether odd. "We do appreciate your counsel, but we haven't come this far to back out now. The tunnel it shall have to be."

Edward had a strong feeling the man had indeed told them too much, and based on that, his gut had already decided that the tunnel was their best option. He started to feel uneasy as he watched Leander's eyes squint in disapproval of his words. The old man leaned far across the table to observe the half-drunk teapots, winced, then gripped harder on his cane.

"Don't be hasty now, gentlemen," he said, disappointed they meant to leave so soon. "Finish your tea, by all means stay a while. I'll tell you more ... do you want more?"

Leander seemed to be growing increasingly fidgety by the second.

"Tell us about the woman," said Edward.

"I've no idea what you're talking about," said the old blacksmith.

"But I think you do," said Edward. "You seemed content with not knowing who put us onto your trail, and that seems odd to me, especially with all those secrets. At a guess, you already knew. I'll ask that question again, tell us about the woman – the one who sent us here."

Leander chuckled to himself. "There's no flies on you, Edward," he said with a cold, wry smile. "Very well. When I discovered the diamond, I became utterly consumed by it. I set out to discover anything I could, anything that would help me understand the mystery of it and, of course, the creatures that guard it. I found nothing, nothing at all – aside from the acknowledgment of its existence in various songs and tales. But after many fruitless months, I did hear this one, very interesting detail. The eyes! Rumour spread of strange folks with pearly eyes wandering the lands; the same pearly eyes as those creatures down in the deep."

"Sorry, what … creatures?" asked Obi, his jaw dropping.

The men were aghast with anticipation.

"I went searching through Graelind," said Leander. "Keeping my ears keen to the talk of anything, let's say, unnatural. Turns out, folks with pearl-like eyes tend not to go unnoticed and asking the right questions of the right people led me to a particularly fascinating house in the forest. That is where I met her. I pressed her relentlessly about the diamond, and at first, she wasn't so willing to tell me anything – the talk of it enraged her. I was fascinated by the effects of what I came to realise was some kind of curse; and now I was in the presence of someone who had lived with it. But our time was cut short once that beast returned, and I was lucky to escape with my life. You know all too well what pain this diamond inflicts upon the poor souls who touch it. That is why the three of you intrigue me."

"The lady is dead," said Edward.

"Tragic," said Leander. "News of the Jackal's death travelled quickly, but I didn't know about her."

The old blacksmith began to fidget again. Obi noticed his hand crawl over the gemstone and Leander looked to be deeply engrossed in his thoughts.

"It unnerves me a little," said Leander, thinking. "That after I've told you of all the horror, you're still willing to venture into the danger. I find that strange. It begs the question, what *do* you know about the Black Diamond?" Leander began to tremble very noticeably.

The men were beyond puzzled. Firstly, because they knew very little about it. And secondly, because they couldn't fathom the old man's constant change in mood. When they had arrived, he'd appeared unwelcoming, to then turn once Edward had mentioned his collection, after that becoming quite hospitable – which is most unlike the pirate kind to any degree. But now, he was visibly unsettled and looked to be losing control.

"You seem to know so much about us already," said Edward. "Perhaps you can tell us what we know about the diamond?"

Leander slammed his fist on the table, the teapots jumped and rattled against the saucers. "Tell me what you know, damn it!" he barked and then coughed hysterically.

The bleak possibility that someone other than himself could tame the Black Diamond appeared to be cutting him deep. He couldn't stand for it. "Why can't I see!" he kept saying, gripping his cane again.

"Why can't you see what?" said Obi, confused, as his eyes kept returning to the purple gemstone the old blacksmith continued to caress longingly.

Leander ignored the question outright. Edward's heart filled up with dread as he began to realise that Leander seemed to be buying himself time for some reason.

"You can see things, can't you?" said Obi. "There are gems that hold power and there are gems that do not. Much like your collection. You said that, and I'm beginning to think that statement holds little truth. Don't tell me it's just a coincidence that you rub that gemstone each time you utter previously untold details. There are a slack handful of folks in this world who know me by Oliver and there are three of them in this very room. I only remember telling two, and I'm sure my memory has not abandoned me yet!"

"Ha, ha. It appears you have figured me out, gentlemen," sniggered Leander. "You see, when three strangers walk into my smithy asking about the one jewel I desire the most and the one jewel I could never possess, I'm sure you can understand when I say I was a little excited. Perhaps I have let the excitement get the better of me.

"I began to hope you knew something that I didn't. After all, why on this green earth would you still wish to pursue it, knowing what you now know. A little rub on my amethyst told me everything I needed. Chiefly, that you believed every last word I said. And you were right to, there *are* creatures that lurk down there, for I've seen them. But yet you still insisted. I questioned myself and the power of my amethyst, thinking there's no chance that three men could be so equally foolish, ha, ha. But I was wrong. This gem will tell its keeper a man's secrets, but it appears you have nothing of interest for me. So, seeing as you cannot help me, your options stand at a grand total of two: chance the tunnel and wander down to your inevitable death, or let's see if Brunt would like to try out one of his new toys ... he's quite the forge-master."

"You sick bastard. You never planned to let us leave here either way, did you?" snarled Peter, watching as Brunt came creeping into the frame of the window holding a blunderbuss in each hand.

"Clever boy, Mr Beaumont," cheered Leander, tapping his hand on the table, as if in applause. "I merely wanted to show off my collection."

Chapter 30
The Tunnel

Edward was the first to climb down into the tunnel, helping Obi find a steady footing amongst what detritus was still left down there. Peter had hold of three lanterns that Leander had filled with oil. He passed them down, then dropped into the entrance himself. Edward looked back at Leander who was standing above the dark hole with Brunt, still aiming his two blunderbusses, watching from high over the old blacksmith's shoulder.

"You'll notice we let you keep your weapons, gentlemen," sniggered Leander. "Believe me ... you'll be needing them."

Obi took one last look at the amethyst before that creaking door was slammed shut and the whole place went black. The tunnel was as dark as pitch. Edward lit the first lantern and passed it along, until the three of them had each a green aura of light in their outstretched hands, the exotic oil burning their nostrils as they breathed in the dank air. Behind them they heard the iron bolts on the smithy door slide into place. A sobering sound that seemed to exclaim the gravity of the task before them.

Leander turned to his apprentice, who was filling the entire door to the smithy with his massive frame.

"There's only two ways out of that cave, Brunt," he said. "One by this door, and the other by a deathly drop to the rocks over there. If I have indeed missed any intricate details and those three imbeciles know something my amethyst could not see, then I'm sure they'll once again chance the perils of Leander's smithy - and we'll be waiting."

"The old man is smart," said Brunt coldly.

"Indeed, he is. Had me figured out rather quickly," said Leander, shouldering Brunt aside. "Anyway, I wasn't being entirely inconspicuous. I was just trying to buy myself some time. This amethyst has never forsaken me, but no matter how deeply I thought, there was *nothing* there, they knew no secrets of the diamond, ha, ha. They will never see daylight again, those fools."

"What is it they seek?" asked Brunt, handling his steel beater, ready to begin striking more shaping blows.

"Hmm ... well, two of them seek a world rid of pirates," said Leander, his grey eyes twinkling in the light of the forge.

The tunnel began with a plunge of stone steps that fell deep into the earth. The walls were built of thick, slimy stones, the darkness was heavy and unforgiving.

When they had reached the bottom, the tunnel went off ahead for a seemingly infinite distance of black, beyond the reach of the lantern's green extent. It was numbingly silent. Peter spoke, but his words fell dully against the slime.

"This place makes my skin crawl," he said, rubbing the goosebumps on his arm. "I can't believe I am actually doing this."

"What did Leander mean by ... creatures?" asked Obi, shivering.

Edward squirmed in his silence.

The tunnel was built below sea level and the air was thin. Obi felt lightheaded only a few steps in. Peter's lantern arm was trembling and Edward was feeling around his chest for his pistol, just in case. Guided by nothing other than their desire for the end of it, a mile of the tunnel passed, where it split into three, like the points of a trident. Obi came to a sharp halt having heard something in the distance.

"Did you hear that?" he asked the others, with a quiver in his lip.

"Hear what?" asked Peter, immediately alert.

"I heard voices," whispered Obi.

"Me too," said Edward, now firmly gripping his pistol.

Edward made a gesture for the others to hold back, taking two long strides towards the three openings. His eyes adjusted; the lantern had the slimy stones glowing green and the smell was beyond putrid. Two more slow steps into the abyss ... then the three lanterns blew out.

Trembling in the dark, Edward hurried to rekindle the flame; hearing Obi's calls only hurried him in a more trying manner. His friends' voices began to fade away, prompting Edward to work faster and faster to light the lantern. It was almost futile, for his hands shook with fear and a panic began to take him. Each match that he struck extinguished in the foul air, until at last, one of them caught a roaring orange flame. Finally, he had light, and he drove the lantern up into the air from his knees, his arm shaking. Yet, he found himself alone and helpless, on the blackest of paths, terribly frightened. He called to his friends, yet nothing but a hollow dripping of water returned to his ears.

You need to move, Edward! he thought, beginning to follow the tunnel, near blindly, for his lantern had yet to gain its full flame. It was freezing down there, but somehow, he was sweating. His skin prickled and his eyes stung with each blink. His lips had turned blue and his toes burned like someone had lit a fire in his boots.

Not a glimmer of light in front or behind.

He fell after reaching for the wall, slipping to the ground when the slime yielded him no firm grip. The damp beneath him seeped through his trousers as he sat there, taking a deep, gathering breath. He hadn't yet made it to his feet when he heard something moving behind him. He jerked round, offered the dark his lantern, and stared into the distance.

Out of the shadows, there came a strange creature, stooped low to the ground in a crawl. As it began to move nearer and nearer, Edward's lips tightened to stop the screaming, when a dread set about his body like a wave of shuddering fright.

Edward drew his pistol and pulled back the hammer, yet the creature didn't flinch; it only slowly began to creep towards him, its pearly eyes illuminated, its form rising onto two legs to tower above him.

Then it leapt for him, as it keened like nothing he'd ever heard before. Edward discharged his pistol and spun, the bullet hit the slimy wall and ricocheted into the black.

He sprinted for his life, dropping the pistol, the thudding from the creature's hands and feet galloping on all the walls around him filled the air.

He didn't get a good look at the creature, save for the final glance alight in green, before he turned on his heels to make a break for it. It moved swiftly and sharp within his weary gaze, with the limbs of a man, and bulging pearly eyes.

Edward crashed into more stairs, feeling the bitter stone with his hands for direction. He raced up them, missing steps, cracking his knees so the blood mottled on the fabric of his trousers. He found the top, no longer enclosed in a tunnel ... but still, there was no light but for his own. He welcomed the breeze he felt skip over his skin, and when he looked back, he found the creature had ceased its chase.

The sea? he thought, taking a deep breath of the fresh air. He could hear the shrill of the waves louder than ever, echoing through the caverns. And in that vast chamber he stood, as merely a flicker amongst a backdrop of emptiness.

Green lights like his own, burned away in the distance. He called towards them and they vanished again. Edward clambered across the floor, through rocky pools of water and uneven stones. Then the lights came back, but only faintly flickering. He followed them, falling over again, this time, unsettling rocks that tumbled and then echoed around him. Water had now flood through his boots and a shivering wind creased his core into a huddle. Dusting the dirt from the hand that steadied his fall, he began to feel hopeless. He was wiping a sheet of sweat from his brow, when suddenly his name was spoken, in a voice he did not know. He stood, tripped, and his lantern perished. Blackness.

The smell of the oil was strong, now dripping upon the rocks. It was so dark, it greatly stifled him, feeling the hairs on his arms stand up like sharp pines in a forest. In that moment, Edward thought of home, truly believing he would meet his end in this desolate place. All he could think about was Charlotte, and their little cottage in Harkness.

He drew Bannermane's blade. The cold screech of steel rushed up the cavern walls, returning back to him, times over.

Thud, thud, thud, came the sound of footsteps, closing in. It was unbearable, to feel like the cavern walls were growing, filling the empty spaces in between. But these walls were now alive and he could hear their many deep and heavy breaths like the panting of a huge wolf pack. Their eyes opened, like stars set against a winter sky, hundreds of them, scattered in every direction. He froze, quaking out of his own skin. Silence.

Two pearly eyes came up beside him. It's hot foul breath tingling against his shivering neck, inhaling Edward's scent like a predator. In a rush of fear, he took off. The heart in his chest ready to burst with anxiety.

"Edward!" came a call from out of nowhere. That familiar voice he'd hoped to hear came louder with the lantern light. It was Peter's voice and he screamed back to him, "PETER!"

The dark creatures were tight on Edward's heels as he thrashed his sword left and right to keep them at bay.

Peter had emerged from another tunnel in a frantic manner, and could hear the pursuit and the sounds of clambering feet and heavy breathing.

Edward made for the light, finding the tunnel's entrance. Snatching Peter by the arm, he dragged him away, screaming, "Run!" at the top of his lungs. The creatures followed them into the next narrow void, on a hunt, bearing razor-sharp teeth in their foaming jaws, engulfing the tunnel walls like a swarm of insects.

Edward and Peter's path spread open into another chamber, where a gaping tear in the ceiling hovered above them. They had light! Peter checked behind to see no chasers. Edward grabbed his elbow and yanked him on.

"Where are they? What are they?" shouted Peter, waving his pistol.

"Peter! Where is Obi?" bawled Edward, spinning madly to better observe his surroundings.

"We've lost him," said Peter, holding his head low in despair.

The chamber walls were haunting, with many painted and carved symbols, glyphs and ancient texts, randomly strewn across the rock face from ceiling to floor. Edward's eyes were dripping with tears; the sweat had now transcended his whole body. Peter was stricken with fear, ever watchful of the delves that remained absent of the daylight's reach.

"Look," whispered Edward. "Green lights!"

"Obi?" said Peter, beginning a sprinting run. Edward struggled to keep pace over the jagged rocks. Peter had halted before a towering stone arch carved into the cave wall. Edward caught up; his eyes widened at the soaring structure that was aloft before him. He looked down to find his companion was already many strides in front, growing smaller with each of them. The smell of the lantern oil was burning his nose again, and ahead, Peter's green flame dropped out of sight. Edward was again all alone in the darkness, reaching around to find the way, calling, "Peter! Peter!" over and over again. He was delirious. His mind whirled, and the confusion seemed to come upon him much more powerfully each time he inhaled the fumes that emanated from Leander's lanterns. At this point, all around him seemed demented. Then, he fell down a height of steps that sent him wailing in pain from the impact. For a minute, he laid at the very bottom; wet, freezing cold and disorientated beyond words. When he came to his wits, he saw something in the distance, something shining bright; yet, the light was not green, nor unnatural. He painfully stood, gripping his aching bones, and walked on.

Edward found himself standing beneath another archway, although this time it was much smaller - only two men high and perhaps the same width abreast. He passed through it and entered another room, where he came across a man, crouched to his knees, as still as stone.

"Obi!" he cried out, taking a sure hold of his companion. "Are you hurt? Have you seen Peter?"

Obi began to weep helplessly, looking Edward deep in the eye.

"Get me out of this wretched place," he whispered chillingly.

"Have you seen Peter?" Edward asked again.

"Not since the lanterns went out!" Obi answered. "Please, get me out of here, Edward!"

Edward held him whilst he shook, then helped him to his feet. Obi's lantern was shattered beside him and only thin, silver spears of daylight shone through the ceiling.

"We must carry on!" said Edward. "We cannot linger here. Obi, whatever it is Leander has put in these lanterns is sending us all mad. I'm losing my mind down here."

This room was different. It seemed to have purpose. Its adjacent walls were formed in a perfect, parallel fashion, yet the carvings upon the stone were much the same as they'd already seen. At the end of the room, stood a door, sunken within an array of inscribed formations, like apparitions. They slowly opened it. A rush of warmth blew past them, embracing their cold, bitten faces.

The next room was crackling with fire torches, bolted to the walls, down both sides of a passageway. They lingered here, to feel the heat on their wet skin. To restore the feeling in their fingertips. To ease the pain of their shivering bones.

They stayed close together until the passageway ended, where another door stood hanging on crippled hinges. They prised it open, half expecting a bitter chill to knock them back - but no such chill came.

Edward stepped inside first, and looked out over a bridge that was suspended above a pool of ink black water that rippled as the burrowing sea current swept over its murky surface. Fire torches roared on the walls and scorched the slime on the stones.

And there it was. The Black Diamond, as dark as the night beyond the moon, encrusted into the very centre of a huge pillar; a monolith that was enveloped by hundreds of eyes made of precious gems, like sapphires, emeralds, brown topaz and grey moonstones - each set inside a white crystal.

The diamond itself drew Edward closer across the bridge. It screamed at him, yet made no sound. It flashed like lightning in his mind, yet shone no light. He stared deep into the black sphere; down an endless chasm he could feel himself helplessly falling into. Something startled him then; he was being pulled back by assertive hands, and Edward was sure that it would be Obi that had grabbed a hold of him. But it was not. A dark silhouette of a human stood before him, cloaked and hooded in a cascade of leather. Edward's memory flashed vividly; the visions that were seared into his mind had manifested themselves in every colour imaginable, as clear as a summer sky. That figure he saw outside the Drum & Fiddle, and at the tavern in Court Marsh, and under the trees in the blustering rain upon the fields before Guntrick, was now standing yards away.

"Finally ... we are together again, little brother," said the man.

Edward stared into the gloom beneath the hood. "Arthur?" he whispered.

The man slowly lifted his face to let it catch the light.

"It is really you, my brother?" cried Edward, throwing his arms around him to secure a deep embrace.

Arthur Clavell's heart turned warm from his brother's touch and nothing hurt in that moment. Edward pulled away and held his hands on Arthur's cheeks, as the hue of his blue eyes shone, and heavy tears trickled down from them.

"I've missed you, Edward," said Arthur, wiping his face.

"It cannot be?" said Edward. "I was certain you were dead. How is this even possible?""

"I was carried away along the waves, Edward," said Arthur. "All but sure my wounds would take me. That was until I felt a burst of new life flow through my veins and into my heart. When I woke, I was right here ... yet all the colours of the world were gone."

"It's you that's been watching me, isn't it?" asked Edward, not quite knowing what to say.

His brother smiled, and for a moment, there was a subtle scarlet glow in his pale cheeks. "I have never left you, little brother. I was always there. Always watching, keeping you safe."

"Did you lead me here, Arthur?" asked Edward. "The writings on the scroll, and the crown ... was that you?"

"No, those words came from the hand of Benjamin Blackwood," said Arthur.

"You know about Benjamin Blackwood?" asked Edward.

"I do, yes," said Arthur. "The Black Diamond ruined him and all the goodness in his heart perished. He thought that all should suffer like he did, so he placed the scroll inside that silver jacket hoping whoever found it would go looking. It was all just a game to him, the crown and the Jackal. Thankfully no one ever came so far ... until you. He only wanted to lure more souls into his legions, and simply having the Jackal do his bidding wasn't enough anymore. He wanted to build an army of unfortunate men and women who had touched it, and with the first riddle leading to the King's palace, I fear his intentions were to lure a man of high position into his clutches. To become one of them."

"Wait ... the Jackal ... doing Blackwood's bidding?"

"Blackwood had the Jackal bring them to him. Peasants. Wanderers. Pirates, it really didn't matter. He saw them as payment for his misfortunes. And pay they did, as you have seen for yourself. It drains your soul of all that once made it prosper ... starting with the eyes."

"The creatures!" said Edward, spinning, watching shadows cavort across the walls behind the torchlight.

"You are safe here, for now," said Arthur. "Don't be scared."

Edward was so quickly reassured by his brother's words, he almost felt like a child again.

"Where is Blackwood now?" asked Edward.

"He is dead. When he came to Graelind many years ago, he already possessed the Black Diamond. He ended up here, hidden in the dark, away from the rest of the world. Then, he came across the cave's residents, so to speak. An ancient tribe of people who have lived in the shadows for longer than one can imagine. The diamond consumed them, like it consumes everyone, Edward. Had I not held you back just now, you would have suffered, equally so. The people here saw Blackwood as some kind of king, and the diamond as invaluable treasure, that under no circumstances would they part with. When I myself touched it, I somehow took Blackwood's place in this maelstrom of misery. Ever since that day, I have been able to control them. At least most of the time."

Edward was lost for words, and had to shake his head to try and rid it of all the confusion.

"What about the pillar?" he asked.

"The pillar symbolises the souls taken–"

"–in the colours of their eyes," finished Edward, sadly.

"Indeed," said Arthur; his own eyes like two pits of hurt.

"This is all so ..." Edward had no more words for it. He'd concluded quickly that no words could possibly explain this to him, not from his own tongue at any length.

"The diamond holds great power for good," said Arthur. "And for many years have I searched for the truth of it. Now I have found it, Edward. The power lies within ... it's only the curse that conceals it in black!"

Arthur turned his face in sadness. "The curse to which I have been bound for fifteen years."

"If you knew this, brother, then why not lead us straight here?" said Edward, perplexed. "What about the Jackal? We nearly died at the hands of that beast, Arthur!"

"I know how this looks," said Arthur. "I wish I could have placed the diamond right in the palm of your hand, Edward. But the protectors would have never let me leave this cave alive and all these years of searching would have been for nothing."

"That doesn't nearly answer my question," snapped Edward. "Why couldn't you have led us straight here?"

Arthur stepped round Edward trying to quench the faint bubble of anger he was feeling.

"Do you think I didn't want to, brother?" said Arthur. "The diamond sees my every move and hears my every breath. The second I told you of this pillar, the very beating of my heart would have ceased, no matter how many leagues there were between me and this wretched stone. I know of the power and *it* knows I do. Blackwood knew only of the curse, that became clear to me. In luring those souls, he merely succumbed to the diamond's evil will. Or at least that of the sorceress who bestowed the darkness upon it. To have led you here by my own doing meant I would have died far sooner. But the riddles were already written, the crown was already graved. I only helped you along, do you see?"

"Forgive me, brother, but what I see is you alive and well," said Edward. "You said, the second you told me of this pillar, would have been your last?

Yet here you stand before me."

Arthur let his head fall. "The diamond cannot harm those who have never touched it," he explained. "Nor can it harm those who are already dead."

"I really have no idea what you are trying to-" Edward took a long pause of realisation, as Arthur's words began to make sense to him. "Your eyes ... they're blue?" he said quietly.

Arthur looked back over his shoulder. Edward followed his gaze behind the pillar.

There was a body, lying in the dirt, slumped against the stone. A lump in Edward's throat began to form as he removed the hood from over the man's brow. His eyes were still open - bearing no hue of any kind.

"This is you, brother?" said Edward, wide mouthed, beginning to cry.

Arthur inclined his head with deep regret. "At least what was left of me, yes," he said.

"But how?"

"For so long the diamond was deep in my mind, scratching away, ruling my thoughts. For so long did I succumb to the pain of it, clawing away at me from the inside. But after so many years, the clawing became a little softer and the constant incessant pain became a little weaker. I could feel something different, something bright! It began to take over all the terrible intrusions in my head and it seemed like there was a force fighting back. Less and less of my thoughts I had to share, until finally, I had secrets. There is light in that diamond, but it is deep. It was fighting for me. I am certain *that* is the force I feel and the reason why I stand before you in this form. But the darkness will always find a way to expose those who try to deceive it! Therefore, some secrets are too dangerous, Edward. Simply because of the consequences, should they ever be revealed."

"What is it you revealed?" asked Edward, taking a tired stance.

"The love for my little brother; a secret impossible to keep."

"The diamond killed you when I came here?"

Arthur gave a sorrowful nod.

"I am so sorry, my brother," said Edward.

"Do not mourn for me, Edward. I died fifteen years ago. I only stuck around because there was still something worth fighting for. I thought that if the curse was broken, I might once again live a normal life and fight beside you. I never gave up on myself. But now I have played my part, and for that I am proud."

"How did you know I'd find the scroll?" asked Edward, fighting tears.

"Because I did everything I could to make certain you'd find it."

"How?"

"Through the words of a startled fisherman."

Edward was aghast. "That was you?"

"Like I said, Edward, I've never stopped looking out for you, little brother. I buried that scroll on an island in the north, fifteen years ago, so no unfortunate souls could be lured here by it. The years passed, the scroll hidden and no more had to endure the suffering of the diamond's touch. Benjamin Blackwood's plan failed. I searched these lands, in every book, song, riddle and tale, for a way to destroy the diamond and then, it came to me. But there was nothing I could do until the pirates found the scroll, that is. I knew the Baliant would easily defeat that crew of knaves and that my little brother's curiosities would force him to act."

"You just pointed me in the direction of Blackwood's clues, so to quench any of the diamond's suspicions?"

"Exactly." Arthur placed his hand on Edward's shoulder. "I was the knock on the tavern door-"

"-to warn me of the colonel," said Edward, smiling fraternally.

"And the silent whisper in Obi's ear that urged him to turn back to the house of the Jackal," said Arthur.

Edward looked over to Obi who was rather surprised himself, but bore a wide smile across his cheeks.

"Although, I was a little concerned you might have recognised my voice when I called those pirates away. But you and Peter were a little preoccupied in trying to escape … so I forgive you."

"In the corridor at Fort Gaze?" said Edward, his eyes filling with tears.

"I know you have been questioning yourself and your morality," said Arthur. "That voice in your head, that was telling you to leave the city and pursue this quest, wasn't yours, my brother … it was mine. It didn't take much to persuade Peter to do the same. I figured you'd need a companion with a rebellious streak in him. He's a good man at heart. You should keep him around."

"You knew that to this day, all I ever wanted was peace on our lands, and all this time you have been with me?"

"All this time."

Obi watched with much sadness and found an unspoiled shred of his jacket to wipe his face.

"Peter thinks the diamond can bring back his wife, Lizzie. You didn't make him believe that if it wasn't true, did you?"

"We're running out of time, Edward," snapped Arthur urgently, seeming to ignore Edward's question. "I take it you have the scroll?"

Edward's heart dropped as he searched his pockets. A dread stabbed him in the chest. Obi reached into his own pocket. "It's here," he said, handing it over. "I think stealing the crown might have landed me some jail time. I didn't think they'd miss this old thing, though."

Edward beamed; he was utterly amazed. Arthur grinned happily. "Saving the day again, Oliver, I see?" he said.

Edward looked at Obi and considered him intently. "Will you do the honours, old boy?" he said, his hand proffering the scroll.

Obi stepped forward and grabbed it, although, he was confused about what to do next.

"You must know, little brother," said Arthur, "that if I had dropped a simple trail straight to it, who knows who might have come ashore. I just couldn't take that risk. Now listen to me carefully. When you remove the diamond, they will come for you. Never in your whole life will you have seen vengeance quite like it. Under no circumstances should you look back. Keep a keen eye on the path and run like never before. Do you understand me? Good. Obi, the Pillar of Eyes is not wholly complete without the scroll. Only then will it release the Black Diamond. You must do it right away; I cannot hold off the creatures for much longer."

Understanding the urgency in Arthur's words, Obi approached the Pillar of Eyes. Arthur pointed at an aperture within the stone, inside which, the pure silver jacket fitted perfectly. As Obi locked it in, the Black Diamond clicked up, as if to offer itself. Obi stepped back in fear of it. Edward tore a rag from his shirt to wrap it in - so not to touch it with his naked skin.

"And the curse, Arthur, how do I break it?" asked Edward, gripping the Black Diamond for the first time. The feeling of it was overwhelmingly mystifying.

But there was silence, and no answer came, so Edward turned expectantly to find out why.

Arthur's body had begun to perish, swirling away into nothingness, like white dandelion seeds caught on a summer's breeze. Arthur smiled as the final pieces of his form disappeared. "I love you, little brother," were the last words that he could muster. Then, he was gone.

Edward knew there was so much more to say, and was broken at the thought of losing Arthur all over again. He couldn't turn his legs to move. Feeling as though his heart was fused to where he stood and turning would only tear it from his chest. Edward's words were lost in his anguish as he reached out to grasp what was left of his brother. His fingers passed through thin air as he clenched his hands.

He shot a look towards the dark water as the surface bubbled. Obi screamed in retreat, calling back for Edward to run. The creatures began to rise, crawling like evil shadows from the bleakest of dreams. Edward stuffed the diamond into his jacket and ran. Obi was poised and ready in the doorway, and the second his companion came through he slammed it shut, drawing the bolt.

They found themselves on the passageway, both reaching for a fire torch to take along with them. The harrowing keening from the room behind, shrieking and clanging against the door, shuddered their bones. Edward made light work of the next door with a desperate barge of his shoulder, falling through to the ground as Obi came stumbling in behind. There was Peter, lost in the room of spearing light, still gripping his green flaming lantern, shaking from head to toe. "What *are* those things!?" he cried. Seeing Peter alive had injected a little hope into Edward and Obi's hearts. Obi stood looking back, intently listening as a great numbness came over him, his gut feeling as though it had unravelled within him. "Leave me here!" he called. "You won't make it out unless I draw them off."

"No!" cried Peter, feeling Edward take his elbow and pull.

"What are you saying, Obi?" snapped Edward. "No! You're coming with us! Together ... until the end."

Obi pleaded with them. "My part in this is now over, men," he said in earnest. "You need to finish what you started, and this is the only way. Peter, give me the lantern."

The end of the passageway sounded like a carnival drum being beaten to the rhythm of trampling horse hooves. The creatures were almost upon them, having broken their way through at various points across the timber.

Obi smiled as tears trickled onto his jacket. Peter had a flash in his mind of the moment the three of them had met at Bidle's Edge. His heart pounded so hard, for he was unable to reason with the idea he might lose a friend whom he'd had so little time to cherish.

"I will stay, Obi," said Peter, sternly. "I'll take these bastards one by one should it see you safely out of here."

Obi stepped back toward the passageway, ignoring Peter's words. "Avenge my brother," he said imploringly. "And wherever it is I'm going ... I'll save you a glass of the good stuff, my friends."

A grey hand of cadaver-like fingers appeared through the door as the wood continued to shard under the pressure. Peter was beside himself, and set off towards Obi, unable to just watch on as he was inevitably torn to pieces.

Edward had a sudden moment of comprehension, grabbing Peter's jacket sleeve at the last second. It was *one* of them, or *three*. Edward knew that, and for a split second he thought of drawing the creatures off himself – but it was too late. Eyes peered through the broken door, before it flung from its rusty hinges with a crash. Edward yanked Peter by the arm, dragging him through the other door. Obi slammed it shut, and then dropped the crossbar, locking himself inside. Then he threw the lantern towards the creatures as they came bundling in. The oil within the chamber ignited and then it went bang!

Could they remember the way out of this dark pit of misery? With the thoughts of losing Obi, surely not. Edward led the way, quickly along the paths plucked from his memory. Peter couldn't hold his emotion, scarcely able to see for the tears that gushed from his eyes, his chest now burning with pain.

In seconds they were up the steps to where the sunlight poured through the crack. The natural light lit the walls and the way could be seen in the distance, as a black hole set into the rock face. Peter slipped and landed heavily, feeling a crack in the arm that took the weight of his fall. He rushed to his feet and shook the pain away. He wanted so badly to turn back but his instincts said no, and forced him back into a sprint again.

Edward feared the next cavern; the dark one. He feared seeing those eyes and feeling its hot breath again. The hair on his back pricked up as they entered. Everything looked so different in the natural flames of his fire torch. They could hear nothing over their own panting and clunking footfall. The scent of the oil that was splashed upon the rocks tingled Edward's senses – a stark reminder of when he'd last stood in this same spot, the smell of its breath and the eerie glow in its eyes came back to him.

He felt dizzy.

Edward stretched out his torch and went on. Peter dared not scream in anger, but he wanted to. Leaving Obi was haunting him and he found himself wishing the creatures would take him as well and have done with it. He hated himself in that moment. *Obi shouldn't have died for us!* he thought angrily. With great angst, Peter carried on, his feet quickening over the dark ground. Edward was out in front by a good ten paces, when out in front of him, the cave floor fell off down some steps – the tunnel lying beneath their descent.

Descend they did, as the walls gradually changed from cold rock to slimy, wet stone, the air thickening like a musky fog. The tunnel stretched out before them and they began to sprint madly down it, hurrying their strides with every shred of energy they had left.

A presence emerged from behind; they could almost sense it. The creatures let out their screams and fell into the tunnel, infesting it like parasites in a vein.

Gasping for breath, they ran, with each determined stride of a leg burning with pain. It seemed like hours until the next tower of steps came upon them. Edward climbed first, Peter right behind him.

The final passage, the final stretch of miserable tunnel passed them by as Edward tossed the fire torch into the hole and leapt upwards. His reach was enough to catch the ledge, and with his remaining strength he pulled himself up. He dropped his hand for Peter who sprung into his grip; with great effort, they were no longer beneath the earth.

They rapped hard on the smithy door with sheer, reckless abandon, shooting glances back toward the hole, knowing the creatures would soon meet them to see to their end. "LEANDER!!"

The door came open with a swing and the men tumbled onto the cold floor of the smithy. Leander slammed it shut, bringing down a huge crossbar, fitting bolts and latches and locks.

Then came the heavy beating of timber, that shuddered with each attempt to break through. Edward and Peter lay flat on their backs, and from there they could see the frenzy of shadows under the foot of the door.

Chapter 31
A New Discovery

Leander had a twinkle in his eye, made from a mixture of fear and delight as if the goings-on were exciting him. "Make certain this door holds!" he called to Brunt, who clambered around the anvil with haste. "Nails, bolts, whatever we have; or whatever you can fashion!"

The door continued to shudder. Peter looked upon it in shock, hoping with all his heart that it would withstand the onslaught that besieged it. Edward had drawn his remaining pistol, but knew good and well such a weapon was no use should the smithy door actually fall. He wedged it back in his shoulder belt and made for the wall, clad in sharp steel. He picked an axe, turning with it gripped in his hand, halting as the steel of a bayonet flickered before his eyes.

"Drop the axe and sit down, now!" snarled Leander, pointing a musket.

Peter leapt to his feet in defence. "Stay put, boy," warned the old blacksmith. "Do not chance reaching me faster than I can pull this trigger."

Brunt had indeed fashioned a makeshift lock made of iron chain, and had driven two huge nails through the links to secure the door a little more strongly. Although, there was little point to it, for the door never looked like giving way, and perhaps for a second, in all this madness, Leander and Brunt had forgotten just how strong they'd built it.

The creatures fell silent, and from beneath the door their steps could be heard, skulking off down the tunnel, into the darkness.

Brunt, his face tensed and wrinkled like sun-scorched leather, turned towards Peter with his hammer raised, as if ready to strike.

It wasn't Leander who Edward feared. It was Brunt. Should the halfwit have been absent, he could have easily disarmed the old blacksmith and made him regret the day he turned a weapon on a Kingsman. But the fear ached his heart, knowing that if Brunt lost what little composure he seemed to have, it might spell the end for both of them.

"The diamond?" said Leander sharply. "I know you have it. Lay it down on the anvil, or join your old friend in the abyss!"

Peter gathered in beside Edward, holding himself as still as his shakes would allow, suddenly feeling the pain of their loss again. Peter seemed hardly moved by their current plight; he just stared coldly into Leander's grey eyes, imagining the sound of his bones snapping, should a stroke of luck offer him a chance to ring the old blacksmith's scrawny little neck. All he wanted to do was succumb to his grief and cry a little.

Edward laid down the axe, glowering reluctantly whilst Brunt removed the pistol from his shoulder belt. The huge man grimaced, baring his teeth like a wild dog about to pounce. "Hand it over," he snarled, with evil in his eyes.

"I'd do as he says," said Leander. "Brunt only asks nicely once."

"So it would seem," said Edward, watching as Brunt's temper bubbled like a teapot near to whistling.

Hesitating at first, Edward drew out the diamond and placed it on the anvil with careful precision, unwrapping the cloth to reveal it.

"At long last, have my old, weary eyes been delivered what they have forever wished to see," said Leander in amazement. "The one Black Diamond, secure within the four walls of my smithy!"

There was cruelty within his gaze as he curled his fingers over the amethyst.

"Ah! The power lies within!" he said, his eyes unmoved from the diamond's luring charm. "I believe we have your dead brother to thank for confirming my suspicions, Edward? Must have been quite the reunion? Brunt? Break it!"

Brunt took up a war hammer so big, only a man of his own ilk could have possibly wielded it. He went bounding over to the anvil and lifted the weapon clear above his head, swinging it down with such brute force that it screamed through the air as it fell. The hammer crashed into the diamond, sending a shock through Brunt that launched him from his feet and into the yard.

There he lay, still gripping the hammer firmly, as if the clouds had sundered and a bolt of lightning had hurtled down and struck him stiff.

Leander froze; his sharp whiskered jaw hanging low in shock. He began to slide over to the window to take a look outside; the barrel of his musket still aimed as he flittered his glance back and forth between Brunt's body and the two men he had held up.

The old blacksmith turned towards them. Edward turned to Peter who had a nervous yet daring look in his eye. Edward felt a sudden surge of foreboding, when as if in slow motion, Peter sunk to the ground, lunging himself behind a suit of armour that stood gleaming on its stand.

Leander fired a shot aimlessly; the bullet went whistling over Peter's head as he hunched down behind the steel. Before Leander could make his next move, Edward came charging through the gun smoke and sent the old blacksmith sprawling with a barge, knocking the musket from his hands and the air from his lungs.

Peter had vengeance in his heart and reached for the first weapon he could find. He would have killed him right there had Edward not intervened. Peter stuck a knife into his belt buckle with an angry shake of his head. "It's no better than he deserves, Edward," he said coldly.

Leander rose to his feet, cradling his injured ribs.

"Sit down!" snarled Edward. "I only ask nicely once!"

Peter dragged over a carven rocking chair. Edward held a blade by Leander's throat until he slowly sat down in it.

"So, the lives of your companions are worth so little?" asked Edward. "That doesn't bode too well for us does it, Peter?" including him in the interrogation. "You can bet your boots he'll put a bullet in us, should he get another chance. You knew good and well what would happen didn't you? Poor old Brunt, didn't see that coming, did he? You wanted the man dead, didn't you? Brunt was too dangerous to keep alive with such a valuable asset lying around. You knew how easily he could take it, should he have betrayed you."

Leander didn't defend himself. His silence spoke so loud.

Peter handed Edward his pistol, then came up beside the now frightened old man. "Your cane ... hand it over!" he snapped. "I think you know quite enough about us."

Leander recoiled in defence; he wouldn't part with it. "No! No!"

"Hand it over!" cried Peter. "Or I'll prise it from your fingers and beat you all around this smithy with it!"

"Not yet, Peter," said Edward, but not with any sympathy. "You're going to help us, old man."

"And if you don't," snarled Peter, "I'm going to try my hand at a bit of smith work, to see if I can fashion something to gut you with. Believe me, it won't be sharp!"

"What is it you idiots will have me do?" said Leander, having finally caught his breath. "Seeing as my shallow well of options has run thoroughly dry."

"That stone on your cane? Tell me more about it," said Edward, pondering over the purple gemstone.

Leander cleared his throat. "It will tell me anything I wish to know about a man. You already know that."

"What about ... anything you wish to know about a diamond?" asked Edward.

"Don't be a fool. That's surely impossible," scoffed Leander.

"Pardon me but I thought you were an expert?" said Edward. "No? Well, isn't that convenient, Peter? Not a few hours ago, this was a man in the know. You listen to me, Leander. You're going to look into that diamond whether you like it or not."

"Or I'll get this forge burning hot!" said Peter angrily.

Leander feared what might come, quickly observing the room for a quick exit or a slip in his adversaries' defences. After all, he'd just watched on as Brunt was reduced to a pile of limp flesh, and he didn't fancy meeting his end in a similar fashion.

There was no option that wouldn't chance death. Edward would overpower him easily should he lunge for the officer's blade, that idea was folly. But at least the Kingsman had a sense of self mastery. The pirate on the other hand, was showing little restraint, sharpening his newly acquired knife, just staring coldly at him.

"What if the diamond defends itself?" said the old blacksmith.

"Consider yourself warned," said Edward. "A pleasure your dead accomplice was not afforded."

"And if I don't, what then?" asked Leander bravely.

Edward leaned in towards him. "You'll be joining Brunt in the dirt!" he said, smiling.

"And you'll be gutless!" added Peter, throwing coal onto the forge hearth.

Leander stood with a grimace; his ribs still throbbing from his fall. He walked over to the anvil, grasped the amethyst begrudgingly and stared deep into the dark of the Black Diamond. A vision came to him. Of great trees upon grassy hilltops; of seas as clear as crystal, splashing against coves; of a thick morning dew, settling on the petals of harebells across a vast green field.

He smiled to himself. Edward and Peter shared a look of surprise, wondering exactly what the old man had seen to justify his expression. But then, Leander's arm began to shake. His feet looked to be frozen to the ground, and the anvil upon which the diamond was placed, began to shine – as if a sheet of ice had engulfed its iron surface.

The grip in both of his hands was lost and the old blacksmith crashed to the ground; the amethyst was knocked from the cane's head and went tumbling across the stones with a *clink, clink, clink, clink.*

"Is he dead?" wondered Peter with narrowing eyes.

Edward crept over to the old man and checked his neck for a pulse, which surprisingly was still faintly ticking. Leander gasped for a breath and woke in terror at what he'd seen. He scrambled to the chair, finding his cane to aid him and then sat there as if in fear of everything in the room. Peter very quietly took up the amethyst and slid it into his breast pocket.

"Tell us what you saw, and tell it true!" bawled Edward.

"I need water ... w-w-water! My throat!" coughed Leander in distorted words.

Peter handed him his own pouch. The old man drooped into the chair as the cool water relieved his parched mouth. He let his head fall; a single tear fell on to his cloak.

"Beautiful blue skies," he said happily as he came to his wits. "The spray of the sea on my cheeks. Trees taller than all the towers in Graelind, and flowers brighter than any I have ever seen. Then I was lifted from the grass and taken away. I couldn't breathe, and all I could see were the passing clouds above growing darker. In no words known to mankind could I truly explain what I saw ... not in a thousand years of trying."

Leander couldn't stand to look at the diamond just lying there unwrapped on the anvil. "Please ... I beg of you, would you cover it?" he croaked in agony. "I cannot go on unless my eyes are free of it!"

Edward laid the cloth on the diamond, urging the old blacksmith to continue.

"A sorceress, veiled in crimson," said Leander finally. "Bearing an evil that will forever haunt me to my bones. I saw her wickedness. It is she who cursed it! And only she who could break it!"

"And where do we find her?" asked Peter.

"I do not know. But she's not here in Graelind, of that I'm certain."

Edward walked outside; his shoulders had fallen low in despair. He pondered over the muddy yard where Brunt lay flat on his back.

Peter gripped Leander. "You're lying, old man!" he screamed.

"No!" cried Leander, shaking from the sting in Peter's voice. "I'm not lying, you fool!"

Edward came rushing in, after an idea had entered his mind.

"That amethyst of yours, let's put its power to the test, shall we?" he said.

Leander snatched away his cane, but was left sick to discover the stone was missing from beneath his fingers. He jumped to the floor, crawling around in search of it, only to lift his head to see Peter kneeling beside him with the stone in his grasp. "Give it back!" squealed the old blacksmith. "Give it back!"

Peter tossed the stone at Edward who was sharp to catch it. The officer grabbed Leander by the leather strings of his apron, yanking him back to the chair, firmly fixing him, rear on wood.

The amethyst disappeared into Edward's hand as he locked eyes with the now petrified collector of gems.

Leander's memories were clear to him. Edward's mind felt full up then; but it didn't seem overcrowded. The old blacksmith's thoughts were very neatly on display, like books sitting on library shelves; all he needed to do was choose the appropriate one and open the pages.

And there it was. Edward could see the grassy hilltops, trees and the crashing waves against the coves. But then, the clouds turned black and the sky rumbled with thunder as spears of lightning cracked upon the once sun-scorched stones of the forts by the sea. The rain poured and the waves bulged, clattering the beaches, scarring the sands. Deeper into the storm this vision fell, through the now lifeless leaves in the thickets and over towns dying of decay and disease. The vision flew along shuddering winds to a house; a manor whose parapets towered above the frosty, smoked haze of a cold day. There she was, high in a tower, veiled in crimson, with eyes as black as the sky above her.

In a melody of harrowing notes and calls she sang her songs from the heights, as the world beneath her lived in fear, scarcely human from the entrapment of dark spells and the manner in which she so harmoniously afflicted them.

Edward wiped the blur from his eyes and found himself pressed against the cold floor by the smithy wall.

"What is it? What did you see?" asked Peter, sharp and curious.

Edward let the amethyst fall from his hand, almost in fear of its power. Power he never imagined he would possess. "The old man's not lying," he said, feeling a frost crawl over his bones at just how empty his mind now felt without the amethyst in his grasp.

"About what, Edward?" said Peter, noticing Edward was utterly stupefied. "For the love of the sea, about what?"

"She isn't here," said Edward. "I've sailed every mile of Graelind's coast, and what I saw does not belong to it."

Edward stepped out for air. Peter followed in search of the answer.

"You know where she is don't you?" said Peter.

"Yes, something tells me I do."

All of a sudden, Leander reached for the forge and pulled a half-molten blade from the flames. He leapt with a cold malice shrieking in his eyes and thrust the iron straight towards Edward's back.

Peter was quicker, and grabbed the old man around the neck, dragging him down.

Edward spun round to see Leander swinging the searing blade in slashing motions, trying desperately to catch Peter with its burning bite. But the old man was far too frail to endure the grip around his throat and as Peter squeezed with everything he had, Leander perished on the smithy floor, his fighting legs shaking through his last moments.

The old blacksmith lay there still, with the skin of his palm smoking from the heat of the steel.

"He would have killed you if I hadn't, Edward," said Peter, releasing him from his grip. Edward thanked his luck and took a huge gulp.

"Don't try to explain, Peter. The lives of pirates have little value to me, never mind one who's tried to kill me more than once. He had it coming. We've got what we came for."

Peter lifted the axe from the wall; the axe he'd grown immediately fond of when they arrived here. "How are we to get off this island?" he said, stroking the cutting edge of it.

"I hadn't thought that far ahead, Peter, in all honesty," answered Edward, consciously beginning to notice how little Leander's death had affected him.

In all his years aboard the *Baliant*, death was never easy to watch – perhaps he had changed.

Peter walked outside and sat down on a barrel in the yard.

"I can't believe we let him die, Edward," he said. "He didn't deserve that. I'm nothing, if not the most cowardly bastard that ever stood in shoe leather. Obi has paid the ultimate price. For me … a no-good pirate."

Edward joined his companion in the yard.

"Do you think Obi would have sacrificed himself for a no-good pirate?" he said, sitting beside him. "Listen, Peter. We're playing with fire here. I know that, you know that and Obi knew that. How foolish must we have been to think the diamond would be so easily attainable? Yes, it sits on that anvil, almost within touching distance. But here we are, with yet another obstacle to leap. In truth, I'm beginning to wonder if any of us will make it through this. Whatever lurks behind that door might only be the start of the horror. A sorceress? And you saw what it did to that mountain of a man," he added, pointing at Brunt. "We are way out of our depth here and the fault lies with me. I should have never left Summer's Reach. Obi would still be alive if I hadn't gone chasing this doomed fantasy. You are not a coward, my friend. Certainly not to me, and certainly not to Obi."

"If we fail … then he died for nothing. I can't let that happen, Edward. If you're telling me you're backing out now, then draw that pistol and put a bullet in my head. Because I can't do this on my own, and without the hope this diamond gives me, I have nothing left to live for. Truly."

"I never said I was backing out."

The tunnel door began to rattle, as bangs and shouts came bellowing from behind it. Yet these were no shouts of any creature, but of a man, soft-voiced and trembling. Peter rushed over after hearing a grave call of, "LEANDER! HELP! HELP!"

The men knew that voice.

Edward jumped over Leander's body and started on the bolts. Peter flung his hands on the door's crossbar and tossed it aside, taking up his newly acquired axe to slice through the chain that Brunt had nailed to the door frame. A man fell at their feet, flat on his back, and slid backwards on his haunches as fast as he could manage.

Edward slammed shut the door and slid the crossbar back in place. Obi leapt to his feet in panic, pointing his pistol in every direction, screaming, "Stay back! Stay back!"

He scoured the room to find no sign of Leander or his hideous apprentice; only his two friends, who were standing with their mouths agape, riddled with shock.

"Thank goodness, it's you!" sighed Obi. "I swear, if that crazy old man tries to read my mind one more time, I'll shoot him–" Obi saw Leander lying flat on his back. "–oh!"

"It cannot be!" said Peter, in a low gasp of disbelief.

"You're alive, old boy?" smiled Edward, using the anvil to aid his tiresome bones, as the relief of seeing Obi alive seemed to weaken them. "But … how?"

Peter dropped the axe and fell to his knees. Obi was kneeling by the forge, the heat soothing the cold skin of his cheeks. "It's good to see you, my friends," he managed to say. "Oh, I have seen some things, let me tell you. I just need to lie here for a minute, though; my heart feels like it might explode."

"I have never been happier to see anybody in my whole life!" cried Peter, his hands clutched to his chest. Searching his pocket, he lifted Bannermane's gifted bottle and gulped down a mouthful.

Obi helped himself up, his old knees creaking from the chill in them. Edward watched intently as he came closer and laid a glistening green emerald on the anvil.

"Do I have a story for you, men," he said, as the world around him began to spin a little less.

"What is that?" asked Edward.

"That, is an emerald."

"Yes, I can see that, old boy, but what's the significance?"

"Arthur gave it to me, Edward. By the Pillar. It will take you anywhere! I used it to fend off those creatures so you could escape. He truly did have your back all this time."

From Edward's confused expression, Obi continued.

"He called to me. I don't know how, but he called to me. I've always known folks to move their lips when they speak, but not this time. I didn't stop to ask any questions; I only did what he asked. This jewel was in Arthur's pocket. Yes, things keep getting stranger and stranger, don't they?"

"This must have been how he got around all this time," said Edward, beyond shocked. "How did you–"

"When the creatures smashed through the door, I thought I was a goner. But Arthur was right. I closed my eyes and then vanished! I'm so happy to see that it worked. My disappearing must have confused the creatures enough to buy you some time."

"I haven't the faintest idea what's going on here," said Peter. "Any of you care to apprise me?"

Edward readied himself for the tale to be told with a calming sigh.

"It was my brother," he said. "He had been helping us all along, I just didn't know it."

"But your brother's … dead?" said Peter.

"He is now," said Edward, letting his head fall. "Arthur Clavell was cursed by the Black Diamond. He searched all these years for a way to destroy it and his search was not fruitless. But when we took the diamond, he perished before he could tell us the way. All we know, is the diamond's true power lies within, and only its curse conceals it in black."

"I take it this sorceress has yet a part to play in our journey?" said Peter.

"Sorceress?" jumped Obi. "Did I hear it correctly? I was hoping I'd misheard Arthur when he said that."

"You heard it correctly, old boy. Had the Black Diamond spared my brother for just a little longer, I believe that's what he was about to tell us," said Edward. "The visions I could see through the power of the amethyst only double that theory. The old blacksmith spoke the words, 'it is she who cursed it, and only she who could break it.' Seems we have no other choice but to find her."

"My goodness!" gasped Obi.

"And where do we find her?" asked Peter.

"Sherringtree," said Edward. "If my memory serves me correctly."

"I've heard that name before," said Peter curiously.

"A journey, many leagues across the sea," said Edward. "Far past the bounds within which our ships are permitted to sail under legal circumstances."

"Then, how can you be sure you have the right place, if you've never actually been there?" said Peter.

"In this instance, myself and Obi hold an advantage, having seen many more winters than yourself, Peter," said Edward. "You see, not for forty years have our markets and stalls here in Graelind been blessed with the sweet-tasting sap from the Sherringtree. Tell me, in what form does the bark of the Sherringtree grow, old boy?"

"It spirals right up the trunk, root to branches," said Obi, lifting his whiskey flask from his pocket. "That sweet sap is the reason why *this* tastes so good."

"Indeed," said Edward. "And there is only one rock on the map that grows Sherringtrees. That's how the island got its name."

"You saw that in your vision?" asked Peter.

"Yes; as clear as the harebells," said Edward. "Now, I'm sure you will both agree when I say I think it's time we moved. Somehow the idea of a sorceress scares me less than what lurks behind that door. Let's go."

"Edward ... you must take this," said Obi, picking up the emerald. "Only one might use its power. So here, take it. Do as you must; Peter and I will follow, if we can make it off this rock."

Edward hesitated. His hunger for vengeance had his hand reaching out for the emerald. But he couldn't leave his friends on Ridikus, not after all they had fought through.

"I will not go alone," said Edward, defiantly. "We have come so far as one and I implore you to keep it so!"

"Edward, just listen to me," said Obi. "Do you want to know the first place I disappeared to when I held this stone? The tower in the trees where I told you about my brother. The time when you realised, we were far more alike than what you first imagined. I lost my brother, just as you did. The only difference is I only lost mine once. Edward, you cannot avenge the dead by joining them. The Black Diamond mustn't remain hidden, buried in some cave, or in the hands of a filthy pirate."

"But Obi-"

"Edward! From that tower, I saw something. The pirates had left the strait! They were heading south. Before I knew it, I was aboard the *Dürlarain*, tucked away secretly in Bill the Baneful's cabin. They mean to attack Summer's Reach! Lord Harrington must be warned."

Obi flicked the emerald into the air. Edward caught it in both hands.

"With the strait scarcely manned, we might make it across," said Obi. "Maybe we'll find a little luck and join you in a few days for the fight."

Edward looked at Peter, who was now smiling widely. "Go, my friend," he said approvingly. "Obi's right. This is our doing. Bill's fleet must not reach the capital before the city's defences are readied. I've enough blood on my hands for ten lifetimes."

Edward lifted the Black Diamond off the anvil and carefully wrapped it in the cloth. Then, he slid it into this jacket pocket.

"Just close your eyes," said Obi. "Think of where it is you wish to go, and then open them. It's that simple."

"You better make it back in one piece!" said Edward, as if in demand. "I'll see you again soon?"

"You can count on it," said Peter.

With a nervous nod to his friends, Edward closed his eyes, and every inch of his body went limp. He felt like he was flying. Never had he experienced such indescribable ecstasy. The hairs on his neck stood to attention. The tips of his fingers tingled. Then, without him willing them to, his eyes shot open; the dark, soot-filled smithy had vanished, and had made way to a blue sky that squinted his eyes and a sea breeze that stroked his face. The waves crashed around him; his legs working hard to steady his swaying frame over each hump of sparkling water.

He was on the *Baliant*'s quarterdeck, stiffened by the purist breath of air he'd ever taken. For in that moment, he felt euphoric and invincible, the instant hit of sea spray and the perfectly clean air was almost too much to bear.

His knees weakened as he turned to find Captain Galaway standing beside the ship's wheel. "Wallace?" he whispered, still entranced.

Galaway was utterly blown away to find Edward Clavell standing before him, and his jaw fell over his neck in complete surprise. "Edward! How can it be?" said Galaway, looking all around him in a state of complete confusion.

"You ... where did ... just how in the name of Graelind are you here?"

"Wallace, there is much to tell you," said Edward. "But firstly, I am so sorry. I beg for your forgiveness. I *never* meant for any harm to come to our men."

"Should I remind you of how you deserted our men, Edward?" snapped the captain, pointing at the rows of dead on the deck. "There are consequences."

Edward felt sick to his stomach at the sight of it.

"Wallace. You must have known there was good reason for me to leave? Or you never would have come!" said Edward. "I know you better."

Having seen what was unfolding, the crew, one by one, began to jostle their way onto the quarterdeck, all trading equally confused glances.

Officer Percy and Officer Gildred were among them. Raven had climbed into the rigging for a better look, whilst Officer Billings pushed through the crowd for his own vantage; the rest scrambling for a good spot, peering through the sea of huddled bodies and craning their necks as shouts of "What's going on, 'ere?" rung out.

Galaway had reasoned with Edward – in his absence – but couldn't help vex at the sight of him in the flesh. He had paused for a long while until words came forth with an air of understanding about them.

"Charlotte told me about the Black Diamond. Only me. They imprisoned her, Edward. They figured she must have known something."

"Tell me she was not harmed, Wallace?" said Edward furiously.

"No, no. She is with her sister. I made certain her pardon letters were written up before I left. I'll deal with Harrington on that matter when I return."

"Thank you, Captain. Now please, let me explain–"

"–no, let *me* explain!" said Galaway. "You fled the city with a pirate, Edward. Once Charlotte gave word of it, I rallied these men to your aid. The men you abandoned for a wasteful, treasonous quest. We lost officers and crew fighting the wretched *Dürlarain*. All for a worthless stone!"

"If this is what you truly believe, then why did you come here?" said Edward. "I left the city, running on hope alone. More than anything did I wish to tell you the–"

"You are an officer of the *Baliant* serving the King of Graelind! You should have come to *me*, Edward!" bawled Galaway.

"You wouldn't have listened to me, Captain!" said Edward. "Lord Harrington would have seen me locked away and Gürad, well, he'd have me killed. So why did you come?"

"Because I trusted you, Edward!" snapped Galaway, saddened. "I've never known you to be disloyal, not in twenty years. Edward, we tried to protect you, and for our part we failed. How you are still alive is beyond reckoning."

"That doesn't explain it," said Edward. "I broke my oath to serve the King. Why did you come?"

"I thought very long and hard about it," said Galaway, after a moment of reflection. "Until Charlotte's words made me realise something I already knew. You would never betray our men, or your country. But that changes little; I am furious that you would abandon your principles in such a way."

Galaway paced round madly, uttering words under his breath in anger. "How did you make it on board?" he asked. "Hiding in the brig all this time?"

"I have much to explain," said Edward.

"You're damn right you do," snapped Officer Percy.

"I set out to find this," said Edward, revealing the dark cursed sphere from his pocket. "This is what our men have died for, if for nothing else."

Officer Billings stepped forward curiously. The rest of the men took a single step back in fear of it.

"If this is in fact the jewel you spoke of, Captain," said Billings, with an angry glint in his eye, "it should be tossed overboard immediately. Clavell too, if he does not wish to part with it."

"Stand down, Officer Billings," said Edward. "That's an order."

"You have no authority here, Edward Clavell," said Billings.

A young man walked forward, with anger bursting in his cheeks.

"You must have us for bloody fools, Clavell!" barked Officer Percy, wriggling free of a crewman who'd gripped his shoulder. "Hackett. Addley. *Inky!* They're all fucking dead because of you!"

The captain watched on as James passed by. He almost reached for his arm to halt him but quickly withdrew his outstretched hand to let his nephew go on. Edward stepped towards the young officer's anger, braced in anticipation, for James looked as though he was readying a strike.

"I never meant for any of this, James," said Edward. "Hear these words and you will understand."

Percy grimaced hard until all the kindness in his face crumpled into darkness.

"Speak! You owe it to each and every man on this ship," he said, coldly.

"Clearly, you all know more about the Black Diamond than I realised," said Edward. "And you might be wondering how I can hold it without consequence. Only when the diamond touches one's naked skin can the curse be passed on. My entire quest has been one of discovery, of realisation. I set out to find the one Black Diamond; yet along the way, many more wonders of this world did I acquire. Now I know the way to break the curse and free the power within; about that I will explain when the time is right. This could mean peace in our lands forever! A better future for our children, unhindered by rotten souls. The world outside Summer's Reach is bleak. Yes, we see the horrors of the open sea and the cruelty of pirates, but for us it always ends at the foot of our hearths, with a full belly and all the coin one could ever need. Now, I see our last battle in the distance, my friends. For the people of Graelind."

The officers and crew were deathly silent. Only the breeze rushing past the sails made any sound.

"If my words are not enough, allow me to show you?" said Edward. "I was aboard the *Dürlarain* when the *Baliant* attacked. I was able to escape through a gap one of our cannons ripped into the hull. Do you think I swam all the way here, James?"

Percy lowered his head to see what Edward had offered him. "Take this in your hand," said Edward, proffering the emerald. James accepted it without hesitation.

"Now, listen to me," said Edward. "Close your eyes and think of anywhere in the world you'd like to be."

"Is this some kind of joke, Edward?"

"James, if you'd rather let someone else demonstrate?"

Percy gripped the emerald and then closed his eyes, vanishing in an instant, as if a hurricane had swept him clear off the deck. The gusts of wind left behind shuddered every man on board, kicking over buckets and blowing the sails to and fro. The crew awed at such a spectacle and gasped to catch their breath, searching the ship like excited children.

After a few addled moments, James Percy returned. Tears trickled down his cheeks and a great big smile now stretched across his lips. A few crewmen rushed over to help him up.

James pushed his way to the ship's edge after feeling that watery-mouthed sensation behind his teeth. He threw up over the side.

"I'm not a fool who abandoned his principles on false hope," said Edward, cupping his hand as James Percy returned the emerald. "There are more just like this! I know of at least one and I've held it in my own hand. Imagine what power lies within the Black Diamond's core. Why else would it be cursed?"

Now he had the attention of all.

"For now, I have news that is far more pressing!" called Edward, using his palm to project words. "The captain of the *Dürlarain* sails his fleet to Summer's Reach, as we speak. Not half a day behind."

The deck broke out with angry chatter and Captain Galaway grimaced like a bulldog.

"Then it appears his beating hasn't settled on him too kindly," he said, as if welcoming the challenge again. "I half expected it in truth. Man the sails! See us home boys, faster than the wind!"

Galaway grabbed Edward's arm. "I cannot guarantee your freedom back in Summer's Reach, my lad," he whispered. "Nor can I be sure they won't hang me beside you. Are you certain about what you have discovered?"

"After what I've seen, you'd be certain too, Captain."

"I need a stiff drink and a smoke … then you can tell me all about it."

Chapter 32
A City to Defend

Edward took a seat in the captain's cabin. Galaway knocked the old dust from his pipe and replaced it with some fresh, rich tobacco from a golden tin, then reached across the table to pour a whiskey as steadily as the *Baliant's* gentle sway would allow.

"You're not going to believe me when I tell you this, Captain," said Edward, before a great long pause. He was about to divulge the information about his brother, Arthur, but he changed his mind at the very last second. For now, he realised, he'd rather hold that memory to himself.

"What is it, my lad? Speak up!" urged the captain, blowing smoky clouds around the room.

"Never mind. I've seen many strange things on my journey, some of them I might have imagined."

"Show me the diamond," said Galaway, pushing a full glass toward his subordinate.

Edward unravelled the Black Diamond and watched as his captain shivered at the mere sight of it.

"The power lies in its core," said Edward. "It is cursed in its current form and doom befalls all those who touch it."

"Like the Jackal?" said Galaway.

"Indeed," said Edward, with a curious squint. "How did you know?"

"Ever since Jasper Montague's castle exile and miraculous return, he and his men have been working closely with Lord Harrington," said Galaway. "He was tasked with ridding the lands of all those poor folk doomed to live out their lives bereft of a soul. Harrington decided that was the least they deserved. The Jackal was the last of them, if all accounts are true."

Galaway sucked another deep breath of smoke and pondered over the white plume as it left his lips.

"Perhaps I *should* have come to you, Captain," said Edward, in battle with his own thoughts.

"There's no doubt about that, my lad," said Galaway. "But how were you to know. I told no one of my knowledge of it. Some secrets are best kept locked away in one's heart."

"Harrington would have sent an army to the Eastern caves had he known the things I do," said Edward. "I set out with only the words of a forgetful old man for guidance. Yet I return with the proof. There can be no doubt of its power. I know that for sure."

"So, this 'curse'. How can it be broken?" said Galaway, shaking his head in short bursts, letting go of quiet, uncomfortable laughs here and there. "I can't believe I'm saying these words."

"There is a reason why this stone is like it is, Captain. What better object is there to curse, than a stone that half the world would go searching for if they thought that it was attainable? What better way to ensnare all those ill-fated opportunists?"

"And what kind of evil had such wicked intentions?" asked Galaway.

"A man named Benjamin Blackwood," answered Edward.

"And this Blackwood is the fella who cursed it?"

"Thankfully not," said Edward. "Because the man's dead. He only used the diamond to fulfil his need to inflict pain on others. Probably a pirate before the diamond took him. It's a long story. I'll tell it true when there's not a fleet of pirates on our tail."

"What's it matter if he's dead?" said Galaway coldly, returning to the subject.

"I learned that the only way to break the curse is to find the one who cursed it," said Edward.

"I see. I'm guessing you're going to tell me where to find him? Spit it out then, my lad," said Galaway, who'd actually found himself intrigued.

"I'm going to tell you where to find *her*."

"Pahh! If a woman has had a hand in this, we're all doomed!" said Galaway, starting to chuckle. "They are far more resilient than any one of us gives them credit for. This ship would be full of them, if only they could swing a sword as fiercely as those blockheads out there."

"Well, that may be true," said Edward. "It's just, I don't believe you've ever met a woman like this before, Wallace."

"And where do we find her?"

"The island of Sherringtree," said Edward, expecting his captain to spit back a harsh word or two.

"Then that is where our part in this tale ends, my lad. Folks with half a sound mind don't venture to Sherringtree, not for all the wealth or love in this world. Anyway, such lands are far beyond our navy's legal boundary. Wouldn't want to go pissing off the neighbours now."

"Perhaps not," said Edward, thinking. "But we're searching for something far more valuable than gold and silver."

Galaway stood from his chair and perched on the table. "Ask yourself this, my friend. Is the power that lingers inside this jewel worth more to you than the soft touch of your wife's skin? Or the feeling of a warm hearth as the flames dance across your cheeks? I fear nothing good would come of sailing away into the distance. I'm baffled you feel the need to go on, having seen first-hand what this diamond is capable of. If you want my advice, lock the diamond in the armoury. But it's Lord Harrington you'll be answering to, not me."

Galaway leaned over the table and finished the glass of whiskey that Edward had failed to drink. "There are two more pressing matters which we must speak on," he said gravely, wiping his lips. "I take it you became acquainted with Bill the Baneful?"

"William Fane," said Edward. "Yes, I did."

"For more years than I can remember, I have shielded you from the truth. Yet you have crossed paths when I could do so little about it. I knew that someday the *Baliant* would meet the *Dürlarain* in battle. I could never risk your feelings towards our greatest enemy becoming any less vengeful. I hope you can find it in your heart to forgive me, Edward. William was a decent man. It's a shame he chose the path he did."

"I understand," said Edward, very quietly.

"Secondly. Jasper Montague is dead."

"That I know," said Edward, sadly. "William Fane tossed his corpse into the brig where myself and Peter were bonded. He was an honourable man. Believe my words, Captain, the William Fane I once knew is long dead. Our chance for revenge is upon us ... and it cannot come soon enough."

"It's really good to see you, Edward," said Galaway, patting his friend on the shoulder. "Perhaps you should put that emerald to good use. Harrington must be warned what's coming. I must take my leave. My nephew needs a familiar hand on *his* shoulder, I feel."

"Give this to James," said Edward, showing Galaway the emerald.

"You and I both know that what he seeks lies far beyond the bounds of the *Baliant's* deck. I can see it in his eyes. He can warn Harrington. I'd go myself, but somehow I feel there's a greater chance I'll escape the noose if I enter the city beside you, Captain."

"I wouldn't bet your boots on it," said Galaway. "Harrington's a merciless old toad ... yet a curious one the more I think about it. Drop that diamond at his feet and who knows what might happen. You've accomplished something he couldn't. I'll tell it true when there's not a fleet of pirates on our tail."

Edward smiled on one side of his face as he passed Galaway the emerald.

"Don't you go disappearing on us, Captain," he said in jest.

"There's no place I'd rather be," said Galaway.

Edward watched on as the captain left, muttering inaudible words under his breath, handling the emerald in his fingers. In that moment, Edward suddenly felt lighter, as if he could jump ten feet in the air and float down to the ground like a feather coasting the breeze. He realised the Black Diamond was no longer as close to him, rather it was wedged between a loose cluster of parchment rolls that were lined neatly on the table. He couldn't remember putting it there, and the rag of cloak it was wrapped in was partiality unravelled, revealing a slither of black. He lifted it from the table, peeling away the cloth to see it.

Grabbing the lantern beside him, he opened the latch in its metal structure and carefully placed the diamond inside. The lantern's flame fell dully against its surface - it reflected nothing.

Galaway was standing by the door to James' cabin for quite some time before his nephew had realised. Years as a crewman, sleeping stacked beside the other smelly, ill-mannered fellows on board, had given the lad a profound caring for his newly acquired, and not to mention, very comfortable hammock. He was twiddling Adeline's poem in his hand when he heard his uncle speak.

"So, where was it you went off to?" asked Galaway, dropping the emerald onto James' lap.

"To Adeline," said James, shyly. "But only for a second. Had I stayed any longer, I would not have returned."

"If there's something you'd like to tell me, James Percy, now is the time," said Galaway, taking a seat in the cabin's corner.

James felt a rush of shame come upon him, momentarily forgetting Galaway was his mother's brother, seeing only the hard, bitten lines on the captain's weathered face as he stared back at him.

"There is something I must tell you," said James, standing to dust down his coat. "At the conclusion of this quest I wish to relinquish my position. I know that you will think far less of me, and yes, this news will disgrace our family. But please, I hope you can understand."

Galaway smiled widely. "You only ever turned in for duty aboard the *Baliant* at your own free will, James," he said. "The prisoners of this ship lay in the brig, not in her hammocks. You are a fine young man and I am proud. I will not fight against your wishes."

These words took James by surprise. Although he didn't really know what to expect.

"I cannot thank you enough," he said, quite lost for words and overcome with emotion.

"But I think you can," said Galaway, without thinking. "You must warn Lord Harrington of what is coming. Tell him, that sooner than he would like, a fleet of pirates will storm Summer's Reach, ready for battle. You must go right away, as I feel haste is on your side."

Haste was not on James Percy's side, but in the palm of his hand. The young officer grinned contentedly, gripping the emerald hard in his fist.

"Take your mother to safety," said Galaway. "Head for the hills."

James did exactly as he was asked, catching a rather vexed Lord Harrington, mid-supper, very much by surprise. Harrington's jaw dropped as the juices of his evening's fare trickled off his naked chin.

"Summon Lord-Colonel Denton, this instant!" Harrington called to the guard who'd shown Percy to the door. He wiped his chin clean and looked the young officer directly in the eye.

"How can you be so sure, boy?" he said, with a subtle pulse of anxiety in his stomach.

"Captain Galaway, my lord," said James. "He sent me here to warn you. It's the one they call the Murderous, my lord."

"So, I was right to suspect this quest of his would provoke our enemy," said Harrington bitterly, biting off another slither of fat from a bacon slice. "I'll see to it he's hanged for this treason, boy. Now get out."

That night, the capital was readied for battle. Lord Harrington had entrusted the task of securing the city to the most senior member of the Graelind army – Lord-Colonel Conrad Denton.

Soldiers were placed around the harbour, the palace cannons were manned two-fold and the people of the city were ushered away into the hills, taking with them their loved ones, too young or too old to fight.

Wagons full of munitions were carted in by great white horses, and all able-bodied men took up arms beside the greycoats, as clusters of Kingsguards settled by each of the palace's entrances.

The sky had turned pink as the sun fell, the once bustling square creeping slowly into darkness. James Percy was wandering by the harbour, glancing around at the preparations, feeling the cold bite on his skin that came whizzing off the water. After a time, he found himself stood outside Adeline's cottage, in Harkness.

"James?" came a soft, quiet voice, after a few moments of cold silence.

James beamed as Adeline's face came alight under the street lantern across the cobbles.

"The news reached you?" he asked, readying himself for the impact of her embrace.

"Half the city's now abandoned, James," said Adeline, swinging around him in circles, again feeling weightless from his strength. "Everything's gone mad, what is happening?"

"Pirates, Adi. They are coming," said James. "Hurry your mother. She can follow us to the hills. I'll collect my family along the way."

"Are you coming with us?" asked Adeline, with a deep sense of hope written plainly across her face.

"I am, my lady, I am."

James Percy had helped gather Adeline's remaining essentials, kept minimal for the urgent need to move quickly. Evelyn left her home with utter reluctance. She was extremely stubborn, more so in the years after her husband's passing, unwilling to let herself rely on any other, ever again.

Adeline loved her mother dearly, she was fierce and strong, and together they had flourished – today was going to be no different, Evelyn had said.

Many of the people had gathered in an old, abandoned castle about three miles northwest of Summer's Reach; a tiresome trek into the hills through the black of night.

Cooking fires were lit and makeshift tents were erected, that hung from the walls as families huddled beneath them, awaiting news from the city. Scouts were placed high on the castle's remaining parapets, watching and waiting, whilst the people below delivered them food and hot whiskey. They would be safe here for the night, in either eventuality, yet, should the grey flags of victory fail to rise – well, that didn't bear thinking about for the people of Summer's Reach.

James had drawn a blanket over Adeline's shoulders, nestling in beside her, resting his chin on the crown of her honey-like hair. He stared around at the camp, feeling the pain of the others just as strongly as his own. Adeline was humming a song, almost inaudibly under her breath. Johnathon Percy was pacing around the camp, leaning into rings of huddled families, offering his help should anybody have needed it. James' eyes followed his little brother as he went here and there, and he was proud – this wasn't the boy he once knew, but a man taking matters into his own hands, for his people. *He'll make a good officer someday,* thought James. Yet something irked him, and although there was impending, inevitable destruction on the horizon, he couldn't help worry about telling Johnathon that he'd relinquished his position so soon after their uncle had honoured him. Johnathon would have given anything for what his brother had.

Adeline spoke and James lost his stare.

"We need more weapons, James," she said suddenly. "We are vulnerable."

Johnathon came closer, having heard what Adeline had said.

"She's right, brother," he whispered. "Are we to sit here like grouse, waiting to be killed?"

"What do you suppose we do, brother?" asked James.

"I'll take a horse to the city," said Johnathon. "I'll grab as much as I can."

"They won't let you take weapons," said James abruptly.

"Perhaps not, but they'll let you!" said Johnathon enthusiastically. "Should the city fall–"

"The city will not fall," snapped James. "Men with nothing to lose are easily beaten. Those who stand to lose it all, are formidable."

"Then tell me, why do we cower in the hills like sheep hiding from wolves?" snapped Johnathon.

James considered his words carefully, feeling Adeline's gaze from down by his shoulder. "We should be ready if the time comes," said Adeline.

"Very well. I will go," said James. "Johnathon, you stay here, keep everyone safe. I'll bring back everything we'll need."

Adeline flinched when James moved away, suddenly feeling all cold and bare. He pecked her on the cheek, straightened his jacket and walked away.

Johnathon watched as his brother stood whispering convincing words into a man's ear, quite obviously asking the fellow if he'd be so kind as to part with his filly for a little while. The man had not a hint of hesitation in his decision to say yes. One of the perks of being a Kingsman was that people truly respected them.

James took hold of the filly's rein and with the flick of his hand he waved a goodbye to his family, mounting the saddle in one swift leap. Adeline came running to him, strongly taking his hand, to pull him down towards her. "I love you!" she said, assuredly.

"I love you too, my lady Adeline," he smiled, whipping the rein to urge the filly into movement. Their hands parted, and he was away.

The city was a sombre, hazy reflection of what it once was. Now, the market was barren and bleak, the stalls a naked shell of nihility against the dark night. James Percy came cantering into the square, to find the munitions wagons empty. He pulled up his filly beside one of the wagons and peered in, finding only one last musket and a bag of shots. It was hardly the trove of weapons he had hoped to see.

He dismounted and checked the others, halting when he heard the hoarse voice of Lord Harrington, who was tucked into a long coat of furs, scowling in the moonlight.

"You'll report to Lord-Colonel Denton, right away, boy," snarled Harrington. "He'll turn you into shape, sharply enough."

"But-"

"I needn't tell you again."

James Percy had no other choice but to obey.

"Certainly, my lord," he said. It was by the virtue of his early return that Lord Harrington had been so demanding of him. Someone had to take the heat for such an unauthorised and treasonous quest, and Captain Galaway wasn't here. This was the least Lord Harrington thought was necessary, until the captain returned to face his punishment. He saw a weakness in James Percy, and had concluded that the boy mustn't have had the stomach for it, and perhaps, running Galaway's errands might have been all he was good for.

Through the rest of that night, James worked tirelessly under the command of Lord-Colonel Denton. More than once did it cross his mind to make a break for the hills, but he'd rather not die at the gallows.

When the next morning had arrived, the strategically positioned battalions stood waiting. Errand runners came to and from the palace, as well as the odd remaining grocer, delivering bread, vegetables and honey tea to each man who raised a hand.

James had dozed into a restless sleep, his mind flickering detailed images of those he'd left behind. He woke suddenly with a twisted sense of dread pulsing through his veins. Surely his family knew he wouldn't have abandoned them. Surely, they would suspect he'd been called to duty. He believed in the latter, but the whole thing still burdened him.

Lord Harrington was present again. James was staring deep caverns into the back of his head, cursing quietly from under the peak of his cap.

"You said they'd be upon us by now, boy?" called Harrington from amongst the crowd.

James stepped forward, a tickle of anger bubbling from inside. "I'd prefer to be addressed by my rank, Lord Harrington," he said firmly, yet controlled. "A courtesy I have never failed to extend to you."

Just as James finished his words, the *Baliant's* figurehead crept out from the mouth of the Green Hollow River.

Edward was standing on the forecastle watching as the parapets of the King's palace came into view, glowing wonderfully in the rising sun. The shadow the *Baliant* cast stretched far behind her, out over the black of the lake, dancing upon the ripples.

Harrington appeared to be a little shaken from the tone James had taken with him, although rather impressed to find the boy possessed more courage than it first seemed.

The *Baliant* docked. The crew were under orders to return within the hour, so the ship could be prepared. Although a few crewmen stayed behind to form a head start, many came flying down the ropes in search of any family that might have remained. Some headed for the markets of Bardrain's Square, finding nothing but lifeless sheets of fabric, blowing briskly in the wind.

Lord Harrington and James Percy walked to meet Captain Galaway by the harbour. The old lord had been crossed and he meant every last ounce of the ferocity he spat forth. "I really ought to have you hanged, Galaway!" he raged. "You would defy orders from *me*?"

"Spare me, Lord Harrington," said Galaway, feeling an irritable, tiredness creep in. "I did what was necessary. So, hang me if you must, but I along with Edward Clavell deserve a fair trial. And I think you ought to hear what Edward has to say."

Edward pushed his way through the crowds, fully expecting to be detained by the Kingsguard who were dotted within every turn of his gaze.

"B-b-bond this traitor!" stuttered Lord Harrington, pointing in excitement. "Seize him!"

"My Lord Harrington," said Edward, beginning to be handled. "I see these people ready for war. Allow me to fight beside them. Then you must hear what I have to say, and if it suits you ill, I will not struggle up the steps to the gallows. You have my word, that what I set out to accomplish was for the good of my people. I swear to it!"

"As do I, my lord," said Galaway sternly.

"He is a man of honour, my lord," added Officer Gildred. "He fights for his people, yet how could you know? Must be hard to keep track, sat on your arse, all warm in your chambers?"

"You'll mind your tongue," snapped Harrington. "Or I'll have a guard loosen it, Gildred."

"If this man is guilty," said Officer Billings, "then I too have broken my oath to the King. You'll have to hang me with him!"

Cheers erupted from the crewmen.

"Hang me up, tight!" called one.

"Looks like it's the noose for me!" called another.

"SILENCE!" screamed Harrington, who's advisor, upon hearing the crew's unwavering spirit, leaned in close to speak with him.

"With respect, my lord," he said, in a quiet yet forceful whisper, "we can't go hanging an entire crew. Perhaps we listen to the man? Avoid the dark shadow such lasting justice would cast."

Lord Harrington gritted his teeth. Colonel Gürad had stayed relatively unseen in the background, yet Edward's eyes found him and they shared a blinkless stare that Gürad was the first to turn away from.

"The both of you, to the palace, now!" snapped Harrington.

Edward writhed, wriggling free from the Kingsguard's grip, straightening his jacket. James Percy came towards him. The young officer slipped the emerald into Edward's pocket and then nodded.

Galaway didn't budge. "Lord Harrington!" he called. "William Fane and his fleet of scumeths will have made it to the river by now. My men will spend the rest of the day preparing, and I'll be with them."

Harrington slowly walked over to him. "Wallace. I will not be made to look a fool amongst the people," he snapped fiercely. "It's the palace or the Plummet! Your choice."

Galaway begrudgingly backed down, knowing better than to test the limit of Harrington's patience. "As you wish, my lord," he sighed, turning to his men. "Officer Billings. You'll take charge in my absence."

Lord Harrington gave the gesture and the two of them were seized by their arms and bonded.

"Walk, now!" bawled Harrington, his cold eyes then turning to the crowds of people. "Don't you have a city to defend?"

His shouts filled Bardrain's Square, upon which many scurrying feet were set in motion.

Edward felt the firm grip of the Kingsguard shoving him down into a chair. Galaway was shuffling away uncomfortably next to him. Harrington stormed through the door of his counsel chamber and spun to face them, red in rage.

"Are my actions truly worthy of these bonds?" asked Galaway.

"Cut them free!" snapped Harrington, twisting his hands behind his back, standing menacingly tall, in his familiar posture.

"Perhaps not," he said, curtly. "But I'll be under the fucking dirt before I allow the people of this city to believe my grip has weakened in the matter of justice!"

Edward was utterly relieved when the Kingsguard cut his bonds. The ropes were tied firmly around his already damaged wrists, and blood had once again begun to spill down his fingers.

"Officer Clavell. I see no other option here," said Harrington, who had calmed somewhat. "I hereby strip you of your rank. You will no longer hold a place amongst the officers of the great *Baliant*. Effective, immediately. You shall meet Judge Farley when the opportunity arises."

"My lord, I beg for you to reconsider this action!" said Galaway.

"Silence, Galaway! Tell me something, when did rank begin to matter so little?" said Harrington as he shrunk into his chair, proceeding to lay words on a sheet of parchment, ink from quill.

Edward jumped to his feet and slammed his hand onto the table, defiling the parchment with a splash of crimson that burst from his blood-soaked fingers.

Harrington jerked in shock. Galaway was wide-eyed. The Black Diamond was revealed when Edward withdrew the rag of cloak, leaving the table dripping in the fluid of his wounds. Harrington flung back in his chair, so fast, he scarcely kept his rear in the seat. The drops of blood had splattered his white waistcoat and the fury now poured from his unyielding eyes.

"What in the name of the King is *this*? I ought to have you–"

There, Harrington fell silent. He shook as the darkness of the diamond took a firm grip of him. He reached out for it, but Edward anticipated the move and slapped away his hand. Harrington fell deeper into his chair.

"Is there something cheating my eyes, boy, or is that the Black Diamond?"

"Indeed it is, and you've seen it before, haven't you?" said Edward, knowing that much was true from Harrington's reaction alone.

"We saw it together, Edward," said Galaway. "Many years ago. You were but a boy back then."

"Why would you bring such evil to peaceful lands?" said Harrington.

"This stone is the *defeater* of evil!" snapped Edward. "When it is freed from the darkness, no army of men will hold the might to defeat us!"

Galaway stood to his feet. "I stand by what he says, my lord."

"This is our way to an everlasting victory. But that out there!" said Edward, pointing to the lake. "That is a battle that can only be won by the strength of the people. And they need every sword and every strong arm to swing them. Strip me of my rank, condemn my actions, hang me if you must, but first, allow me to fight for my city."

Harrington gripped the chair arms until his hands bulged purple.

"It's almost thirty years ago," he said, loosening his grip, appearing to drift. "I remember the King's words, so very clearly. 'You'd better find that diamond, Captain Harrington.' He had no idea what he'd sent us in to. We lost ten good men that day. Chased through the darkness by who knows what!"

Harrington gingerly left his chair, went to stand by the nearest window and looked out upon the courtyard. "Tell me how you can be so sure of the stone's power?"

"My words would be wasteful, my lord," said Edward. "I'll do better than tell you. I'll show you. In the meantime, the pirates breathe down our necks and their threat could well exceed that of which we are capable of defending. When I can, you have my word, I will explain all of this."

Harrington shook his head and scoffed in disbelief. "How one man and his filthy pirate accomplice braved the depths of the world and fought past those creatures, making it out alive, *with* the diamond, I will never know."

Edward suddenly remembered what James Percy had handed back to him. And there it was, green and glistening in his breast pocket.

"I've asked myself the same thing, my lord," he said. "But sometimes you just run into the unexpected."

There was a flurry of wind that came ripping through the room; the blood-spattered parchment on the table blew up into the air. The frame of the window came swinging open and smashed into the wall near where Harrington was standing.

Edward had vanished. Harrington had been knocked to the ground, finding himself sitting flat on his rear in utter astonishment, searching the room with sharp, speedy glances that revealed none of the answers to his questions.

Galaway smirked. "Well ... it appears I believe in magic," he said.

Harrington scrambled hopelessly for his chair. "I have never seen anything quite like it in all my life," he choked, loosening his collar. "Just what on earth is going on here?" he snapped. "Are you playing some kind of trick on me? I'll have you for this, Wallace, that's a promise!"

Captain Galaway stood, placing his clasped fist close to his chest. "If you don't mind, my lord," he said. "There's a ship out on that lake in need of a captain."

"GUARD!" screamed Harrington. "Find Edward Clavell!"

"But, my lord ..." stuttered the guard as he entered. "I never let him leave."

"Well, now he's gone, and my patience is beginning to run dangerously thin!" said Harrington, lividly. "Find him! And as for you, Galaway. Get the hell out of my sight. I'll deal with you later."

"At once, my lord," said Galaway, appearing to smile a little.

By now, Edward had made it home, and had found himself sitting lifelessly by the warm hearth, brimming with logs. His arm crept into motion, only to slowly raise a whiskey bottle to his lips. He contemplated his life, and what had become of it. *What have I brought upon my people?* he thought, taking a huge gulp of the gold liquid. He set another log on the fire that kindled a flare of red flames. He stayed by the hearth, poured some whiskey into the kettle on the hook and waited until the steam plumed out from the spout. He warmed his belly with a hot glass, then made for the bedroom.

With a candle in hand, Edward parted the doors to his wardrobe, where in a neat row, hung all his uniforms. He slid his hands between the garments and pulled out a grey coat and pondered over it, contemplating its significance. The world he once knew was gone and somehow, the sight of this garment reminded him of that. It was once a well-deserved symbol of merit, but now it was merely a keepsake. Hanging it neatly in the wardrobe, he settled for a plain jacket. And from the hook beside it, he lifted a white bandolier, fit with three pistols and a short blade.

He set down the candlestick on the bedside table, and emptied a drawer of fresh linens he then changed into. He slung the jacket over his shoulders, then the bandolier over his head, brushing his hands over his torso to smarten the material.

His gaze shifted to the darkest corner of the room. On the way by, he took up the candlestick and thrust it down to light the kink in the floorboard, just big enough to lift with a finger. There, beneath the wood, lay his officers sword. He lifted it from its bed of dust then gently rested the Black Diamond and the emerald in its place.

The sword was tied to his belt, and the floorboard was returned to its piece in the puzzle. He closed the wardrobe doors and pushed the bedside drawers to a stop.

He left the bedroom, and after quenching the hearth with a bucket brought from the well, he stepped out into the streets of Harkness.

It was now midday, the winter sun was beaming over the city, yet the cold still lingered, forcing Edward to close his jacket tightly around himself. The palace shone in the far distance, and he wondered just how different the city might look come nightfall. Would those formidable palace walls still stand so mightily and untouched? Edward knew that Summer's Reach was almost impregnable, simply because of the cannon power that sat atop its turrets; yet, each precious brick that made the city so special now seemed hopelessly exposed, to his eyes.

When he arrived at Bardrain's Square, Galaway was ordering the addition of supplies aboard the *Baliant*. Crewmen scrambled to load the great ship with ammunition, the officers aiding in the organisation. James Percy had only just finished tying up his wherry when Edward came by.

"Officer Percy?" he said. "I'm sorry about Inky. He was a good man."

"I'm not an officer anymore, Edward," said James. "And please, spare your sympathy for the families of the men that will die tonight."

A sadness fell upon Edward. "Look, James, I didn't strike this conversation to settle our differences," he said. "I only wanted to apologise for the part I've played in all this."

"The part you played?" said James, perplexed. "This is *all* your doing!"

James Percy had every right to be angry. Edward respected that and placed a clasped fist against his chest. "Indeed, it is," he said. "But I'll make it right, I promise."

"Perhaps, Edward, you should measure your ability to make things right once we've counted our dead," said James angrily.

"Do you condemn the intention of my actions, James?" asked Edward.

"No, I don't," answered James, beginning to pack the last of the supplies into his wherry. "I just don't think you understand what it's like to lose someone for someone else's cause."

Edward didn't want to speak; he knew his words would only whimper from his lips. So, he turned away and left.

Galaway was standing nearby and had heard the altercation.

"You'll stand to gain, should you take the time to learn a little more about the man, James Percy," he said, walking away.

Galaway joined Edward on the harbour.

"You might well have sent Lord Harrington to an early grave, Edward!" he laughed, stepping down into a wherry. "Come, join me."

"I imagine I'm going to regret that," said Edward, perching beside him.

"Pay no mind, my lad. The spiteful old bastard will have to come round to it at some point," said Galaway. "Remember, Lord Harrington loves power more than his own offspring."

Edward took a moment to look back upon the harbour.

"Don't take any notice of my nephew," said Galaway. "The boy doesn't know about Arthur; he only sees through his own grieving eyes, for now. You knew that anyway, didn't you? Otherwise, he might have found himself red-faced. Sometimes the truth can wait, ey?"

Edward smiled. "He's a good man. Let him grieve."

"Agreed, my lad."

Edward looked at his captain, questioningly. "How do you know so much about the diamond, Wallace?"

"When word of an infinite power reaches the ears of a King," said Galaway, "you can bet your boots he will go searching for it. We were simply ordered to retrieve it."

"That didn't go so well, it seems?" asked Edward.

"To say the least," said Galaway. "After what happened, the King denied any such expedition ever took place, and any talk of the Black Diamond, or simply the acknowledgement of its existence, was forbidden. That didn't sit well with any of us. Lord Harrington thought this to be a stain on our honour, yet he did as he was bid. That's what might save you from the gallows, my lad."

"How so?" asked Edward, as the wherry bumped against the *Baliant's* hull.

"To prove there is power in that diamond, would mean our men didn't die for nothing," said Galaway, taking the rope. "It appears we have company," he added, nodding towards land as a host of Kingsguards filled the harbour.

"Would you lend me your spyglass, Captain?"

Galaway obliged. Edward squinted a lengthy look across the black mirror of water, to see James Percy clearly steering away the attention of the prowling guards. Edward silently thanked the boy and reached for the rungs that would lead him to the *Baliant's* deck.

The smell of roasting pork came billowing up from the galley. Officer Billings called across the deck to ask Edward if he would like to join them; he obliged, with a warm sense of belonging in his heart. The *Baliant's* dining quarters were alive. Many tales were told, and one of the crewmen even broke out into a song, which many of the others hummed and clapped along to. Edward smiled as he gorged on the sliced pig that Raven had fried up for him.

But his thoughts quickly turned to Peter and Obi. He had no idea if they were still alive and that hurt him, deeply. He laid down his fork; his stomach had set a blockade between it and his throat. He had quite lost his appetite. If there were any respite from his anguish, it was that gained from knowing Charlotte was safe in Bidle's Edge. The woman he loved. The woman who had stood by him through thick and thin; at least until now. He wondered if he would ever see her again.

At that moment, Edward felt a sickness bubble in his stomach. The officers jumped as he leapt to his feet and sprinted up to the deck. The fresh air hit him. He lunged his head over the *Baliant's* edge and then threw up.

"What have I done?" he whimpered. "What have I done?"

There were crewmen all around. Edward felt as though millions of eyes were staring deep into the very fibres of his soul. He felt no authority over these men anymore. He had no authority. Red-faced, Edward set off below deck, a film of tears swimming in his eyes. Finding his old cabin, he stepped inside, hanging his keys on the porthole latch before trying to sleep.

The *Baliant* erupted into action. The thumping steps on the deck above woke Edward from what could scarcely be described as sleeping. He wiped the blur from his eyes and jumped when the anchor was weighed. Grabbing his keys, he sprung into life.

The ship began to glide starboard so the cannons faced the mouth of the river. The broadsides were primed with lead. The crew hurried around, clearing the deck; handing out muskets and swords and it was manic. Yet it was anything but what one might consider disorganised.

Edward had to take a deep breath when he stepped above board, and he was a little startled when a crewman called to him to lend a hand, chiefly because of the way that he had said it.

"Officer, help us, would ya?"

Edward put a little pace into his step and took a hold of one end of a barrel. He and the crewman lifted it to where it needed to be; Edward couldn't help but feel a pang of pride at being addressed by his old rank, and for a moment, it felt like before.

"Good work, sailor!" he said assertively.

The crewman went quickly about his business after stoically replying, "Sir!"

Realising he still had Galaway's spyglass in his jacket, Edward leaned over the edge to survey the harbour, where row on row of musketeers had lined up; all the way from the waterside through Bardrain's Square.

Deeper into the lake, two more ships were anchored in waiting. The last time Edward had seen such an assemblage of military personnel, it was fifteen years ago at Fort Gaze. The suspense was hellacious. Darkness now upon them, yet the bleak, shadowy shapes of clouds were still visible, and hung low amongst the fells; it was spooky just how much today reminded him of that battle in the strait of Ridikus.

"I hope Lord Harrington doesn't take William Fane for a fool, Captain?" he said, as Galaway joined him. "You and I both know he will not sail his entire fleet down that river."

"No, he will not," said Galaway. "Yet, if he sends his men into the city on foot, he will be run down in equal measure."

"And the first ship to appear from the river mouth will be sunk, blocking the way," said Edward, handing Galaway back his spyglass. "Leaving the rest of his fleet lined up in a row like sitting ducks. That's one chance he won't take."

"Agreed," said Galaway. "Then there's the palace turrets, they see for miles, any movement out beyond and the soldiers will light them up – be sure of that."

"Almost sounds like a death trap to me," said Edward suspiciously.

"Indeed," said Galaway. "If William Fane has the bollocks to attack this city, then he knows something we don't. And I have a hunch what it might be."

"Do tell?"

"William Fane came looking for Peter Beaumont not long after you left the city. His ships made it safely past the sentries at Byhollow. I think someone is sabotaging Graelind's defences. It sounds familiar, doesn't it?"

"Fort Gaze," said Edward, understanding.

Edward was thinking deeply whilst gazing off into the distance, scouring the surrounding fells and forests.

"I'm so sorry, Wallace. This is all my fault," he said, his head dropping.

"William Fane only sails to Summer's Reach because his pride is shattered, nothing else, my lad," said Galaway. "You might have drowned in the eastern sea for all he knows. Remember, that sometimes a man's pride is his weakness – the very weakness that will see him defeated."

Galaway pulled on his gloves and turned up his collar. "It's good to have you back, my old friend."

At that moment, an errand runner came aboard and cut the sentiment short.

"Captain Galaway, the scouts report that only one ship sails the river, not ten miles east. No sign of any fleet." The scout took off his cap. "And I have more grave news ... Byhollow is in flames."

Galaway turned fiercely. "To arms!" he called to his men. "Seems my hunch was correct, ey?"

The crewmen swarmed on the three cannon decks. Galaway's piercing stare stretched down to the mouth of the river. All posts were manned. The *Baliant*'s hull creaked to the gentle flow of the water as rumblings of growling thunder cracked the sky, shaking the clouds to release falls of rain that drenched the deck.

And there they waited.

Chapter 33

The Battle of Summer's Reach

Every man and woman left in the city stood waiting with fearful anticipation. Edward turned a sideways glance towards Galaway.

"I think we're about to find out what Fane's got hidden up his sleeve, my lad," said the captain.

The rain fell harder, thudding against the sails above them, while the crew waited and waited, until one of them finally spoke. "There's hope beyond the rain, I hope you can see it?" he said, clutching a pendant that hung around his neck. "If I was a bird, my wings would be stained, I can feel it. Our musketeers will march and with my drenched wings I shall rise beside them to pierce our enemies' hearts. There's hope beyond the rain … just believe it."

Gunshots sounded from within the palace. The crewmen swapped confused glances as some of the officers climbed the steps to the quarterdeck for a better view. Captain Galaway came running up frantically, drawing out his spyglass for a look.

He wouldn't have believed it, had he not seen it with his own eyes - the guards atop the palace walls began to fall.

Edward grasped the rigging and stretched out over the edge as far as he could reach. The firing of distant muskets filled the air and flickers of sparks lit the palace parapets.

"Enemies … in the courtyard?" said Edward to himself.

Bedlam had broken out inside the city. The soldiers appeared to be trying to breach the palace gate yet it wouldn't budge. It had been barred shut from the inside, and many of the Kingsguard trapped within were being slaughtered.

The crewmen of the *Baliant* looked to their captain for the answer, but he was lost in shock - the city was imploding.

"How could this have happened, Captain?" asked Edward. "We need to do something!"

Galaway tried to speak, but his words trickled out like a gentle breeze; a quiet utterance lost within the noise. There was little time to think before the sound of a cannon went boom, fired from the palace walls. The iron ripped through the ship beside them; the *Baliant's* crew jumped for cover.

"Our city has been compromised," said Galaway softly, watching as more cannons were discharged toward the lake.

James Percy lay flat on his back; a painful ringing burned inside his head. He looked out from his cover to see the palace gate still unbreached, as soldier after soldier fought madly to try and break it down. Flaming projectiles came raining from the walls, engulfing the soldiers and burning up carts that exploded when the black powder within them caught a spark.

Lord-Colonel Denton of the Graelind army stepped into the light of the flames. He was clad in his grey coat and gold bandolier, finished with a shining silver gorget by his throat.

The impressive man took a great, deep breath and bellowed an order to turn a cannon upon the palace gate. Many soldiers rushed to obey, heaving one of the huge masses of iron into aim. Another resounding boom rung out over the lake – the palace gate was destroyed. Soldiers stormed the courtyard and James Percy fell in behind their ranks, discharging his musket on the first enemy to catch his eye. Pirates bawled like wild animals and came diving from the walls. Swelling plumes of gun smoke filled the air; the palace cannons continued to be discharged towards their own men.

The musketeers formed a series of lines, far enough away from the palace so the heads of the rotten souls atop the parapets peeped into view. The soldiers then began to unload volley after volley of shots in that direction.

Galaway watched in disbelief as a cannon ball connected with the *Baliant*. He found himself staring up at the stars from down on the deck, and for a moment, he couldn't see any of the chaos.

"Make for the river!" he screamed, feeling every year of his age as he dragged himself to his feet.

Edward joined him on the quarterdeck, his hands clasped over his head to block the falling debris.

"Who's the sitting ducks now?" cried Galaway, taking a hold of the *Baliant's* wheel, screaming orders. "I won't have my entire crew slaughtered on this lake, damn it!"

More cannon blows clattered the *Baliant*. Crewmen were thrown off into the lake. Splinters of timber flew everywhere. Masts fell across the deck, thumping into the men not fast enough to dodge them.

The *Baliant* set sail. Waves tainted with fallen bodies began to break behind her, yet the palace cannons continued to hit their mark.

A crewman below discharged a single cannon that struck the palace wall with devastating force, tearing a gash into the stone, destroying one of its turrets.

"CEASE FIRE!" cried Galaway. "Billings! Bring me the reckless swine who fired that shot!"

Officer Billings leapt over the quarterdeck's balustrade, landing with a thud on the deck below. He disappeared down the hatch, only to return a minute later with the frightened crewman in tow. The boy was thrown to the ground.

"Officer Billings! Keep this impetuous wazzock away from those cannons!" snarled Galaway. "Next time, you'll fire on *my* orders, boy!"

A rallying chorus of evil cries sounded from the forest, just west of the city, where as many as seven hundred pirates fell upon Bardrain's Square, armed to the nines. With blackened teeth and shrieking screams, they came with pikes, swords, pistols, muskets, sabres - all wielded with the cruellest intentions.

They swarmed the city, meeting the soldiers head-on, who stood tall and mightily in a formation of grey, that looked impenetrable. The clashing sounds of hundreds of swords danced off the palace walls, as the two forces fought to the death beneath the night sky.

In the moonlight, the soldiers' rapiers twinkled with every swing; their silver gorgets sparkling beneath gritted teeth. Blood washed over the ground, pirates and soldiers lay dying amongst the deathly red rivers that now flowed through the streets of Summer's Reach; the wind carrying the stench of it on its back.

"What are we doing now, Captain?" asked Gildred, as the *Baliant* closed in on the river mouth.

"Fane has taken the upper hand!" said Galaway. "How those scumeths made it into the palace, I have no idea. But his plan is simple; once the ships on the lake have been taken care of, it'll leave the *Dürlarain* an opening ... to sail in and unleash the fury. That palace must be returned to us at all costs;

we need those cannons back!"

"Yes, but what about us?" shouted Billings, who was in earshot.

"We're going to set up a blockade!" called Galaway, turning the ship's wheel into line.

The officers gasped, for they knew the *Baliant* had just become sacrificial.

"But then we'd be powerless, Captain," said Gildred, wide-eyed and startled.

"Indeed, we would," said Galaway. "But not nearly as powerless as when the *Dürlarain* makes it out onto the lake. We'll make for the city, and fight with the others!"

Unbeknown to Captain Galaway and his men, control had been won over in the courtyard and the cannon fire had concluded. Rotten souls lay broken and bleeding beneath the walls. Kingsguards littered the ground, dead or dying and many soldiers had perished too.

Muskets were reloaded with haste and a single munitions wagon was heaved in front of the gate, while other defenders set their aims. A host of pirates came flushing through the blockade, tossing the wagon on its side as they climbed over the rest of the obstacles that hindered their path. They were gunned down without mercy, like vengeful, caged animals let loose - their bodies beginning to pile by the gate.

James Percy rushed up the steps of the palace wall and gazed upon the lake. The *Baliant* was nowhere to be seen. The other two warships had been sunk to a sandy bottom, leaving only their torn sails afloat on the surface.

The *Baliant* had slipped out of view into the river behind the forest. She was heavily damaged, but still, she pressed on.

Galaway guided the ship starboard, viciously swinging the huge vessel into the shale on the riverbank. He called his men together. "My brothers!" he said, with his arms outstretched. "Defending this ship is no longer your duty ... now, we march for the city!"

Ropes were thrown over the edge, the crew descended into the shallow water, armed and ready.

Edward leapt onto the quarterdeck, taking three steps per stride. He hadn't heard the captain's plans and was confused as to why they had grounded her.

"Are we to leave the *Baliant* unguarded, Captain ... truly?" he said, in shock.

Galaway gripped the ship's wheel tight, admiring the perfectly carved timber; his eyes began to fill up with tears and his lip wobbled.

"The *Baliant* will defend this city, Edward ... even if it's not with cannon fire."

The captain called to the remaining crewmen. "Loose as many broadsides as we can. See us afloat again!"

Edward's expression noticeably tightened. "Captain, what are you doing?"

"Get off the ship, Edward. Go!"

Galaway gave another order for the sails to be repositioned.

"Wallace?" said Edward, bewildered. "I can't make any sense of this?"

"The *Dürlarain* must not make it to the lake, Edward!" said Galaway. "I'm making it a certainty that it doesn't."

Edward peered down the river at the cliff that jutted out over the water's edge.

"You're going to block their path?" he said, after realising.

"That I am, my lad!" said Galaway, feeling the weight of the ship lift. "Have a rope ready for me on that rock over there."

The crew pushed cannon after cannon overboard, and the *Baliant's* keel lifted from the shale, gently creeping into the deeper waters.

Edward climbed down; landing waist high in the bitter cold. The rest of the crew splashed around him as they landed.

From the riverbank they watched as the mighty vessel floated away along the current. Captain Galaway made a hard turn left, then a sweeping right, sending the *Baliant* crashing into the cliff edge. The Golden Lady's huge, splintered stern blocked the way – and now, a vessel the size of the *Dürlarain* would only run aground attempting to manoeuvre it.

A rope was dropped, the captain rushed upon the damaged forecastle where his lifeline swung in the breeze. He climbed over the sharp rock, with the help of his men – and then, the moment he turned, the red eyes of the *Dürlarain* met the blue of his.

Galaway's crew made a sprint for the trees, whilst aimlessly dodging shots fired by the enemies atop the *Dürlarain's* deck. William Fane looked angrily down his spyglass, enraged to find the *Baliant* blocking his path into the city. He had half expected this outcome, yet his plan had been scuppered and the blood within him began to boil, settling in red blotches around his cheeks. He lifted his spyglass again, catching sight of a group of greycoats, sprinting from the *Baliant*. He locked onto them with his magnified aim.

"SILAS!" he screamed.

"Aye, Captain!"

"Fetch me the woman, Silas," said Fane, coldly. "I think I've just seen a ghost. The rest of you ... KILL THEM ALL!"

Fane's loyal knaves began to chant his name, swinging down from the ship's edges, rushing through the shallow waters onto the riverbank.

Silas Slint silently disappeared, creeping off into the night.

At the harbour, the battle still raged on; the palace was now secure, yet soldiers, Kingsguards and pirates alike still fell to the cruel bite of steel. James Percy was splattered in crimson, the blood was dripping from his sword as he walked the square, cutting down Fane's men one after another.

Body after body in grey coats James passed, lying motionless on the ground. He felt helpless and scared, but his sword arm still swung with a purpose and he had taken many lives. As he pulled his sword from a dying pirate, he heard something – the galloping of horses coming closer.

He whirled to see twenty men on huge stallions, cantering into the city. The Soldiers Slain had returned and came blazing through the battleground like a wave of wrath, slaying men left and right. And amongst the Soldiers, was Peter Beaumont, swinging his axe, knocking countless enemies to the ground.

James Percy stood in awe as their fortunes began to turn. His fear had gone, his heart palpitating in all his excitement, as more pirates perished at the hands of the brave and valiant Graelinders.

Galaway, Edward and the rest of the *Baliant's* men came screaming from the trees. They crashed into the battle with might, firing their muskets and slicing down the now hapless enemy.

James smiled as if wonderstruck; he looked around at the welcome sight of a sea of grey in every direction, standing firmly in defiance.

The crew of the *Dürlarain* fell upon them from out of the dark. James made a break for it, hurtling up the palace steps to set a plan of his own in motion.

"FIRE AT THE TREES!" he screamed, taking a hold of a cannon, gesturing for more soldiers to help him manoeuvre it.

It was devastating; the cannons peppered the forest like nothing he had ever seen, and the pirates bringing up the rear of their host were decimated.

The pirate presence slowly began to capitulate. The Soldiers Slain circled the harbour, and the Kingsguard set a perimeter of muskets around the palace.

Peter Beaumont came down from his mount, watching the treeline as he did so. One single, helpless pirate limped out into the open, clutching his bleeding body; his visions nothing but a dark haze of defeat. Peter gave chase, but the pirate moved surprisingly swiftly for a man with such wounds. The dark of the trees concealed the pirate for a quarter mile. Peter could only follow the distant sounds of his footfall, dodging branches and clusters of bushes – when finally, he reached him.

Peter leapt from his feet, catching a grip of the rotten soul's neck, tearing him to the cold ground. There was a short struggle, but Peter was far stronger and unhurt. The pirate exhaled when Peter's axe split his chest, again and again.

Peter fell on his back; wiping a layer of sweat from his face. Another kill he had enjoyed more than he should have.

His mind throbbed wildly. The eerie popping sound of the muskets coming from the city ricocheted through the forest. Kneeling to catch a breath, he could hear faintly spoken voices. He moved slowly towards them, carefully avoiding the fallen twigs that would reveal his presence.

In the distance, he saw two men angrily deliberating in the midst of a lantern flame. One of them was wearing a grey coat, yet in the darkness, his face was a shadow beneath a brown cap. The second was unmistakably a pirate, who looked to have the Kingsguard gripped by the throat.

Peter couldn't distinguish any of their words, but he dared not get too close and chance being seen.

The pirate slunk off into the distance. The Kingsguard spun about in fury, and came marching straight towards Peter, whose heart was now thumping heavily as the man passed. Why was he speaking with a pirate? Why were his garments free from the stains of battle?

"Colonel Gürad?" said Peter, stepping out from behind the branches, pistol aimed.

"Beaumont," said the colonel, squinting in the lantern light, a little shaken to find he wasn't alone.

"So, tell me how has that pretty coat of yours managed to remain so grey?" smirked Peter.

"I'm not sure what you're trying to insinuate, boy."

"You're right, how wrong of me to assume that you're a coward. Let's have the truth of it, shall we?" said Peter, removing the amethyst from his pocket, beginning to think deeply.

Colonel Gürad's eyes squinted as he tried to stay calm – he was fraught with rage. He clenched his rapier so tightly his knuckles turned an almost snow-white.

"I think it's time I killed you, boy," snarled Gürad. "Drop the pistol and we'll duel like Kingsmen."

Peter took a few seconds to think. "Kill *me* ... like you killed Jasper?" he said sadly. A sadness that bloomed ferociously into anger.

Gürad was aghast. How could Peter have known? It was impossible.

"There is no truth in such an accusation," snapped Gürad. "You are nothing but a deceitful little worm, Peter Beaumont. Now draw your sword and let me see you bleed."

"Perhaps I should kill you for what you've done," said Peter, deep in a maze of contemplation. "Yet it would be a dreadful pity to silence you now. I think the men of honour you've betrayed deserve to hear it for themselves, from the traitor himself. Hm, come to think of it, a man who conspires against his own people, makes allegiance with pirate lords, and sneaks an army of knaves into the very city he swore an oath to protect ... perhaps it's best I make it swift for him."

"How did you know?" asked Gürad, his lip beginning to quiver.

"Men like you reek of treachery," said Peter, imagining Gürad die, over and over in his mind.

He smiled at the power of the amethyst.

"Harrington won't hear it, not from a filthy pirate!" snapped Gürad. "It's your worthless word against mine, a colonel of the Kingsguard! Don't be foolish now, Peter, lay down your weapons, and you will be offered mercy."

"I've already earned my place at the gallows, Colonel," said Peter. "Mercy cannot save me now."

"Then you choose to die, boy?"

"Come at me you treacherous bastard! Let's see whose blood is spilt first!" snapped Peter, drawing a blade, tossing his pistol into the dirt.

Gürad rushed in maniacally, lifting the rapier over his shoulder before it came screaming down – Peter parried the blow. A second strike came but Peter was quick to slide beneath it, returning a strike of his own. Steel hit steel. Gürad stepped back then launched forward with a thrust that missed by a fraction. His eyes filled with rage, and his next attack came heavier, knocking Peter's sword to the forest floor. Gürad opened his mouth and growled, then threw what he thought would be the killing blow. Peter slipped to his right, lifted another knife from his belt and pierced it through the Colonel's arm. The rapier fell from Gürad's hand as he wailed in pain. Peter twisted the blade, slid it from the wound and pressed it hard against Gürad's neck.

"For Jasper," he whispered, cutting his throat.

The battle of Summer's Reach had been won. The pirates that remained alive had fled in every direction. Each man and woman in the city who was still able helped lift the others who could be saved into wagons. The Soldiers Slain still prowled Bardrain's Square; the taste of revenge a bitter sting in their mouths. Lord-Colonel Denton was kneeling, thinking, digesting what had happened, sickened by the count of the dead.

Edward loaded his musket and pistols.

"The battle is won, my lad," said Galaway, confused. "What–"

"Yet William Fane still breathes," Edward reminded him in anger. "I cannot linger here in victory whilst he goes free."

Murphy dismounted his horse. "Edward. We owe it to Jasper to come with you," he said; red streaks of blood an abundant presence on his jacket. "I seem to remember a promise he made you."

"Thank you, Anders! Anyone else?"

"I will fight!" a voice called from the trees.

Edward swung around, his eyes fixing on the man who'd called out.

"I thought I'd never see you again, Peter!" said Edward, embracing his friend. "How did you make it back here? Where's the old boy, is he safe?"

There was a fearful urgency in his last question.

"Obi is home, where he should be," reassured Peter. "As for how we made it off that dreadful rock, well … we have our friend Bannermane to thank for that."

Edward smiled. "He stayed behind?"

"Yes. He sailed us ashore then saddled us two horses for the ride home. We caught the Soldiers Slain on the road back to Guntrick. When they heard of the threat that was heading for the capital, they rode alongside us for the fight. We saw Obi safely to Bidle's Edge on the way. He was not happy about us leaving him."

"I'm glad you are both safe, my friend," said Edward in relief. "It's good to have you fighting with us. Fane cannot escape the city; we must go now."

Edward shouldered his musket and sheathed his sword.

"Are you with us, Captain?" he asked.

"Always, my lad," said Galaway. "But as for this lot, I'm-"

Galaway went quiet; the officers of the *Baliant* had already begun to follow.

"Let's go," said Billings, on his way by.

Edward's smile beamed as he sprung into a sprint. Peter followed closely behind with the officers of the *Baliant*, the Soldiers Slain right beside them.

They reached the edge of the forest, and in the distance, the *Dürlarain's* black sails towered up to the sky. Edward halted the men, Galaway came over and crouched beside him – and from there, they observed.

The *Dürlarain* looked barren and empty, leaning up against the shale, like an empty carcass of shadow. They moved into the field; the wind rustling the long, wet grass around them. The pale green blades reached to their chests, and the dew left dark streaks on their coats as they crept through.

Galaway began to feel a strange sense of unease like they were being watched. His head jerked from side to side, scanning the thickets for any movement. They were close; so close they could hear the creaking joints of the *Dürlarain*, rocking in the breeze.

There was a cracking sound, then a rush of wind, the grass blew from side to side and in the distance, Edward caught a glimpse of something.

He halted the men again, when not a second later, a host of pirates leapt from behind the grass, opening fire.

Murphy tumbled to the ground, fatally wounded. The ship's deck lit up with musket sparks as shots ripped through the men stood wide open in the grass. Ten men were shot down, disappearing below the blanket of green, as the rest dispersed for cover.

They returned fire when they could: from the bushes, the trees, the rocks – anywhere they could find to escape the onslaught of bullets.

Edward had taken cover by the bushes near the riverbank. The wind blew the pleasant smell of black powder into his nostrils as he forced a shot down his musket barrel. He clicked the hammer into place, twisted his body to take aim, then fired. The shot caught a pirate clean through the heart and sent him flailing from the deck, landing with a splash in the shallow cut. The pirate's blood flowed endlessly down the river.

Fane's men began to perish, one after another, for what was left of them were outnumbered and pinned down within the ship. The sound of shots ceased, and those who were dying breathed their last breaths; the *Dürlarain* fell utterly quiet. Then, the rotten souls aboard gave the call of surrender.

Their weapons were tossed into the river and one by one they climbed down. William Fane was not amongst them.

The pirates were lined up in the grass and dealt with in a manner appropriate to their crimes against the King. Edward and a few other officers boarded the *Dürlarain* and searched it high and low for the one man they'd come to find. There was no sign of him.

Edward felt a cold chill move to the tip of his spine. The deck was bestrewn with blood. He stepped over countless corpses and kicked open the door to the captain's cabin. It was empty, but for a smell so foul and thick, it almost had a taste to it.

Paintings still hung about the walls, of valiant depictions of the *Dürlarain* in all its glory. Edward found himself drawn to them. He loved paintings and the colours that made them, and although the room was an eerie, dark mess, void of any charm, these vibrant, artistic memories somehow made the place look finished.

Officer Gildred walked in behind him, beginning to inspect the room and all its furnishings. He scowled at his debased surroundings aboard this brutally commandeered vessel once considered to be the very pinnacle of naval power. He was truly sick to see what had become of it.

Gildred was rummaging through the contents of the table at the centre of the cabin and the splashes of ink that soiled it. Beside a quill, there was a piece of parchment with words written upon it. *Clavell, Clavell, Clavell.* He grimaced and spoke. "Officer, you should see this."

He handed Edward the parchment who then studied it closely.

Gildred continued to look about, his hand halting over a startlingly beautiful ruby stone, fastened to a necklace of golden strands.

"Well, my goodness," he said. "The bastard must have left in a hurry to leave such a precious thing behind."

Edward glanced at what Gildred was holding; the golden strands draped over his outstretched fingers. In that moment, Edward stumbled hopelessly upon a harrowing realisation. The necklace Gildred was holding was Charlotte's.

His feet froze to their place amongst the floorboards, he just couldn't move. Gildred noticed the red glow drain from his cheeks and the helpless stare in his eyes grow darker.

"What is it, Edward?" asked Gildred.

"That is my wife's necklace, Henry."

"How can you be so sure?" asked Gildred, at a loss for anything else to say, handing it over.

"I have never been more certain of anything in my whole life," said Edward. "I gave her it myself."

Gildred shook his head, mystified. "What does this mean?" he asked.

Edward looked down at the parchment in his hand and turned it over. "He's taken her," he said, showing Gildred the words on the back of it.

Come alone, or I will show her no mercy.

wf

"We must inform Captain Galaway, at once!" snapped Gildred. "He'll have us dispatched to retrieve her."

"No!" snapped Edward. "William Fane intends for me to go alone, and that I shall. Galaway mustn't know, Henry, please; the Captain will send the entire crew and it'll spook him. Charlotte is in enough danger. Do I have your word, Officer?"

"You have my word, Edward," said Gildred. "I swear it. But I strongly advise against this, let it be known."

"There is no other way that doesn't endanger my wife."

"Very well. My lips are sealed."

Both officers brought clenched fists to their chests. Galaway's call to attention bellowed from the field below. Edward fell to his knees when Gildred had left, his mouth watering with sickness as he held back the vomit.

The officers and crew had assembled; Edward climbed down clutching the necklace, his body absent of any feeling. The Soldiers Slain carried Murphy back to the city. The *Baliant's* crew carrying nine of their own. The dead were laid beside the others to be honoured. The fallen pirates were piled up and then torched.

The people of Summer's Reach flooded the streets to tend the wounded and bury their dead. The square once again glowed with lanterns and the city came alive with an undivided purpose, to disguise the scars that were now so deeply carved into the city's history.

Edward had rushed home, and sitting beside the fire he'd begun to ink some words onto a piece of parchment. Once he'd finished, he folded the letter in half and sealed it in an envelope. On the front, he wrote the name, *Peter Beaumont.*

Back in Bardrain's Square, Lord Harrington had ordered his men to seize Peter Beaumont; he was to finally answer for his own crimes against the King.

Captain Galaway had borne witness to this man taking up arms beside them, fighting against the very clan of miscreants his people had seen fit to convict him of belonging to. In his own little way, Galaway didn't wish to see this man face the gallows, after all.

The Kingsguard who bound Peter, spoke the stern words.

"Peter Beaumont, I hereby detain you, by the order of Lord Harrington. The series of crimes of which it is believed you are responsible, are as follows: the murder of a Kingsguard: the thievery of the King's crown: and last but not least, the participation in the unlawful acts of piracy."

Peter was taken to the Plummet without resistance. The clothes from his back were stripped and the Kingsguard threw him violently to the ground; his naked flesh tearing on the cell floor.

"Let's see you escape this time, pirate," the guard laughed, slamming the cell door.

Peter curled into the corner. The cell was bare and cold, and the wind blew through the bars, chilling his bones. The rats that scuttered around made him shudder.

Perhaps they had come for the Jackal's revenge? he thought, kicking one of them away.

Chapter 34
An Old Friend

Edward walked out through his front door to find Officer Gildred with his hand raised, ready to knock.

"Lord Harrington gave the order to arrest the pirate," said Gildred. "A Kingsguard recognised him. Peter didn't resist, thanks to the pistol shoved in his back."

Edward hurt inside but he'd expected this news. He'd heard the Kingsguard muttering to each other about it on their way back into the city.

"Will you help me, Henry?" he asked, locking the door.

"What do you need?"

"Would you see that Peter receives this letter?" said Edward, holding out an envelope sealed with a grey, wax starling.

"That's all you need?"

Edward nodded. "Yes."

It seemed like only a matter of seconds before Edward was staring up at the *Dürlarain* - a dark lonely mass in the moonlight.

He crept onto the deck. It was so quiet. He could hear the river trickling along beneath him and the gentle thumps of a wherry, bouncing in the water, hitting the hull.

He clutched the necklace tight in his hand and walked into William Fane's cabin.

"So, you came?" a voice whispered from within.

"Where is she, William?"

"Let's not get ahead of ourselves now, old friend," said Fane. "Where is the diamond? I know you have it, tell me where you're keeping it and she lives. Do *not* force my hand."

"Even if there was a shred of honour in your word," said Edward, "the diamond cannot make it into the hands of a man like you. I've seen what you're capable of."

"Pity … such a pretty woman, your wife," said Fane. "Would be a shame for her to meet her end in such a way, for the sake of a stone. I *will* give the order, Edward. Do not think our history changes anything."

"You were there the day I gave Charlotte this necklace," said Edward. "You were my friend, William; our fathers were friends. What happened to the boy I once knew?"

"That boy you once knew was never given the chance he deserved!" snapped Fane fiercely. "Not bold enough, or brave enough; didn't have the heart for it, someone once told me. Lord Harrington saw me as lowly scum and would have renounced his rank before seeing *me* in a grey coat. He sailed with my father and their friendship turned, let's say, sour, in the end. The old fool didn't even remember my face when last we met. I was denied the very thing I was born to be!

"So, I left this wretched city, and promised myself that never again would I bend the knee to any man. I forgot the meaning of honour when I was robbed of the rank I had earned!"

Fane crept out from the darkness and into the moonlight that broke through the cabin window. "My father used to tell me tales of the Black Diamond," he began again. "I was fascinated by it and I dreamt that someday I might find it. Now, you stand in my way, Edward. Do not chance the life of your beloved hoping there is any compassion left in my heart."

"How did you know I was alive?" asked Edward. "And how did you know I had the diamond?"

"A mutual friend of ours," said Fane. "You see, every man has a price, my old friend. Find that price and you shall have his allegiance; double it and you shall have him dancing on strings like a puppet. Even men in grey can be bought."

Edward had a lump in his throat he couldn't swallow.

"There's a traitor amongst the King's men?"

"I take it you were informed that Charlotte Clavell was safe with her sister?" said Fane, cockily. "Not exactly the case. You see, our mutual friend thought she would prove useful. She was taken somewhere secret."

Edward gripped the hilt of his sword.

"I wouldn't," snapped Fane. "A little pull on the strings is all it takes."

"So, the traitor is here?" asked Edward, excitedly, hoping he'd walk out so he could cut him down.

"He is indeed," said Fane, proudly. "Perhaps it is time you were acquainted, then I'm sure he'd reap as much pleasure from taking *your* life as he did that of Jasper Montague."

Edward's heart almost stopped.

"Colonel Gürad, would you kindly join us?" called Fane towards the deck – but not a pinch of sound returned.

Fane was left mortified by each passing second of silence. Edward sunk into his own thoughts, cursing this traitor who so brazenly operated under his nose. He never truly trusted Eustace Gürad, but to side with the Murderous – well, that was beyond betrayal.

As for Jasper Montague, the honourable and great man whose life was taken by a treacherous snake – revenge must be had.

Still no sound.

"It appears the strings of the puppet have been severed?" smiled Edward. "That coward saw your knaves safely into the palace, didn't he?"

Edward became angry, the whole thing starting to make sense.

"Tell me, William, what is it you offered him in return for this treachery?" he asked. "Taking his absence into account, not enough? Men who are so easily bought and rarely loyal; a man with such little honour should have known that. It's over now, William. Where is my wife?"

William Fane couldn't bear to have lost the upper hand and, in that moment, he lashed out with much venom in his words. "Tell me where you've hidden the diamond or I will watch her burn from over your bleeding corpse!"

"WHERE IS SHE?" screamed Edward.

Fane rushed over swinging his rapier. Edward unsheathed his sword at the last second and parried the blow. Huge, crushing strikes were traded until Fane recoiled, drew out his pistol and fired a shot.

But Edward had acted fast and had rolled into cover. He now had precious few seconds to make his next move. Fane lifted a second pistol. Edward rushed to the door and dived headlong out onto the deck. Fane pulled the trigger. The bullet clipped Edward on the thigh.

Fane burst onto the deck. Edward found his footing, turned and blocked the strike from the pirate's rapier. Then a duel ensued. The men equally matched in combat, trading heavy strikes like two warriors – the *Dürlarain* their arena.

Fane took the upper hand as Edward stepped too far into a shot, his boot slipping on the wet deck. Fane unleashed a kick that landed flush on

Edward's chest and he went tumbling over the edge, into the water. The shallow depths broke his fall but he still twisted his knee badly as he landed. It was agony. The thigh wound now burned like a million nettle stings. Edward spat a mouthful of water and crawled gingerly onto dry land.

He looked back at the *Dürlarain*, breathing in short bursts from the cold that shrouded him, and there was his sword, standing upright in the water, sticking out from the shale.

He crawled to it, gripped his bleeding fingers around it, when Fane landed in the water beside him.

"This is your last chance, Edward," snarled the pirate, raising another pistol. "Give me the diamond and I'll tell you where she is."

Edward loosened a pistol from his shoulder belt as quickly as he could; the black powder in the chamber was sodden, the hammer clicked, yet nothing.

Fane fired a shot that pierced Edward's shoulder. "I tried to make this easy, old friend," he said, drawing his blade, extending it to the point of Edward's chin. "Now, I'll see to it you're alive long enough to watch her die!"

The pirate worked Edward's pistols free and cast them into the river. The pain seared through Edward's shoulder as he turned to watch his enemy walk the field to where the *Baliant* lay idle.

The pirate captain leapt down from the sharp stones above the forecastle, then oiled and ignited a fire torch that twinkled orange in Edward's teary eyes. Eyes that turned black with fury as he stood, his face curling with rage. His left arm was hanging limp, his knee was numb and throbbing, but he walked on, through the pale, wet blades of grass.

Dozens of lanterns now lit the *Baliant* as Edward limped toward the rock above the forecastle. He climbed down and landed with a crash. The deck was soaked in oil.

And there was Charlotte; bonded to the masts like a frightened animal.

Fane stretched out the torch, ready to ignite the oil that drenched her.

"Please, William," said Edward, as tears streamed down his cheeks. "You can have it. Here, take it."

Fane recoiled the fire torch with a callous grin. "Finally, you've seen sense, Edward," he said, watching as his old friend walked towards him and revealed the Black Diamond.

Edward limped to where Fane was standing, the lanterns glowed all around them in burning hues of flickering orange.

Charlotte wriggled in her bonds and screamed from behind the cloth that gagged her. Edward looked deep into her eyes. "I am so sorry, Charlotte," he whispered, reaching out to pass Fane the diamond before deliberately letting it slip from his fingers.

Fane lost all control, dropping the fire torch to dive for the stone. He went rolling across the deck, and at full stretch, the very tip of his finger connected with it.

The deck was now alight with fire. Edward cut Charlotte's bonds and dragged her away from the flaming forks of burning oil that rushed to meet the sky – the *Baliant's* white sails ignited like kindling.

Edward threw Charlotte from the deck. She crashed into the river beneath – it was the only choice he had.

Fane rose from the ground, his eyes bulging into two great pearls set inside a face of melting skin. He pocketed the diamond and drew his rapier. The *Baliant* was engulfed, yet Edward found himself standing as still as a statue, watching his enemy.

Fane was spitting from his mouth in a clamour of fury and began to slash his blade left and right until steel met steel with a blood-curdling crack. One strike after another missed its mark, thrown with decades of hate behind them.

The blaze roared uncontrollably as sail and timber turned to ash. Charlotte could only watch in horror whilst the two shadows atop the deck fought for their lives.

Edward struggled with all his remaining strength to dodge Fane's frenzied attacks, only to lose balance and go tumbling down the steps into the brig. He crawled; his wounds hurt terribly as he turned towards the steps.

Fane stepped out into the brig. The walls were burning red; the pirate's eyes stood out like two dying, white dahlias in a poppy field.

Fane lifted his rapier and drove it down. Edward rolled; the blade pierced the ground. The officer kicked out with all his force, connecting with Fane's knee, sending him crashing to the side.

Edward leapt up in agony; the heat was now unbearable on his skin. Fane scrambled for his blade, gripped it tight, then stood. He looked up; Edward was already in motion, charging towards him in sheer desperation and fury. The impact snapped the pirate's head back and forth and sent him crashing through the iron bars of a cell.

Edward took out his ring of keys, grabbed a hold of the iron bars and jerked the cell door shut, quickly slipping the right key into the mechanism to secure it - too many times had he locked this exact cell to pick the wrong one.

"Edward?" pleaded Fane, from his knees. "Please! Don't you leave me here! DON'T LEAVE ME HERE!"

Edward froze - if only for a second - before bursting out from the brig onto the deck. Flames leapt in every direction as the masts began to fall, crashing all around him.

There was nowhere to turn. Nowhere but *through*. He went for it, burning and choking, diving over the edge as great tendrils of fire immersed his body. He crashed into the river; his burning jacket hissing as it was quenched.

Charlotte waded in to retrieve him, taking a grip under his shoulders, trying to paddle back desperately.

A mountain of flames spat and cracked throughout the *Baliant* until she was entirely enveloped.

William Fane's screams were spine-chilling; screams that fell silent as he perished within.

Edward and Charlotte sat huddled in the grass, the breeze carried the flames' heat from the *Baliant*, warming their wet skin. Finally she was safe in his arms and Fane the Murderous had received his long-awaited retribution.

Summer's Reach was now a hollow city of broken spirits with this victory or not. If anything, this was an awakening, a sign, that Graelind was in far deeper peril than the people ever knew. Countless lives had been lost in their bid to defend it. All that would remain certain, were the scars left behind.

James Percy came galloping into the old, abandoned castle where his mother now cradled her youngest son through the last moments of his life.

"JOHN!" cried James, dismounting.

Adeline rushed to him. "The pirates, James," she wept, in floods of tears. "A few of them made it up here. Johnathon saw them all off - he saved us."

James knelt beside his mother. Johnathon was smiling in her arms as his older brother's face came into view.

"James?" whispered Johnathon. "I'm going to be an officer someday ... just like you."

"I know you are, my brother," said James, tears spilling down his cheeks. "In fact, that's exactly what Uncle Wallace has just told me."

In Harkness, Captain Galaway had received word of William Fane's death and the part that Edward and the *Baliant* had played. He slumped deep into his chair, broken hearted, his wife and children by his side.

"My Golden Lady," he whispered, taking a sip of his whiskey. Although the pain of losing his ship paled to that of losing his nephew. The sorrow in his heart was beyond anything he thought possible. He doubted things would ever be the same again.

Officer Gildred found himself sliding the letter that Edward had entrusted him to deliver between the bars of Peter's cell. The officer said nothing, swiftly leaving as if he was never there.

Peter opened the envelope and inside it read ...

Peter.

I'm sorry I couldn't have been there when the Kingsguard arrested you. I must face William Fane alone and leaving the city quickly and in secret is the only way.

I have made many mistakes along our journey, yet trusting you was not one of them. I thank you for your friendship and I will treasure it dearly.

The gallows are no place for a man who brings so much light into a strange and dark world. That's why I've placed the emerald stone at the bottom of this envelope.

Take your freedom, my friend - the whole world now lies in the palm of your hand. Although I think I know exactly where it is you'll end up.

By the seaside.

I hope to see you again soon, and remember ... we owe our friend Obi a glass of the good stuff.

Edward Clavell.

The ships that remained at Fort Gaze lay restfully in the strait; the morning light breaking through as heavy waves fell against the shores of Ridikus island. The people that dwelt there went unknowing of the evil that would soon befall them.

The door to Leander's smithy burst off its hinges under the might of many dark shadows. Their pearly eyes riddled with vengeance as they stepped into the frost-bitten morning – and then, the silent killings began. The people of Ridikus never even had the chance to scream for help.

In the darkest depths of the forest, a host of surviving pirates had made camp in a clearing, a few miles out from Summer's Reach. The men were wounded, many beyond the limits of help.

A fire roared in the middle of them, blazing amongst the rocks of the valley that now shielded them.

One pirate stood; his gaze locked on to the trees as he began to slowly walk towards them. He slipped past the branches, when eventually he came to a narrow spring that wound almost unseen around the trunks. He could hear singing ...

> *Burning, oh mercy, I'm yearning,*
> *in tides that are turning,*
> *will you bring me the world?*
> *My sorrow, as I long for tomorrow,*
> *your power I'll borrow,*
> *will you bring me the world?*
> *In secret, you lie hidden in shadow,*
> *out of reach of the winds blow,*
> *will you bring me the world?*
> *A diamond, with strength beyond measure,*
> *a power to treasure,*
> *in the deep of the world.*

"Captain?" said the pirate, watching as a man standing by the water turned his head, his eyes whiter than two full moons.

"Dark is the world, Silas," said the man. "Dark is the world."

Author's Word

Let's start with the man himself, Edward Clavell. The idea of a turnkey taking centre stage as the main protagonist of my story, seemingly sprung upon me like a flash of lightning, and those details have never changed. I intended from the outset to write a character who strayed from his dutiful bonds, who abandoned his principles, a man willing to throw his honour in the dirt for what he believed in - with vengeance the ultimate goal.

That leads me on to Peter Beaumont, and his and Edward's unlikely friendship, the true backbone of this tale. The troubled, grieving pirate; a man as misunderstood as he is uncouth, destined to fail, desperate for the touch of his lost love. In many ways, Peter was my favourite character to write. If not, he was a close second behind Obi, the kind-hearted old fellow based on every good human being I've ever met.

I'm sure there'll be a few questions about the history of characters such as Leander the blacksmith; his bear-like apprentice Brunt; and of course, Benjamin Blackwood, and I fully intend to explain more about them in the next book.

Now, it's the fourteen officers of the *Baliant* I'd like to touch upon. You'll have noticed I only used the names of five of them - six including James Percy. This was always my intention, as I never wanted to clutter my story with too many characters, partly because I didn't feel that my style of writing lent itself well to that approach, and partly because I set out to keep the book around its current word count. Many more of the officers will feature as we continue our journey along Edward's path of retribution.

I'd like to extend a huge thank you to anyone whose support I received throughout writing this story. I came to learn that the curiosity of another can truly inspire you. I hope that I was able to capture the magic of Graelind, the characters, and the story, the way I'd always imagined it, and that the reader will seek to learn more about Edward and his companions in any forthcoming tales.

To those who were curious, this is for you.

Liam.